The Reading Cafe

'Nalini Singh continues to show her gift at compelling world-building and characterization' *Romance Junkies*

'[A] re   Top Pick)

By Nalini Singh from Gollancz:

Guild Hunter Series

Angels' Blood
Archangel's Kiss
Archangel's Consort
Archangel's Blade
Archangel's Storm
Archangel's Legion
Archangel's Shadows
Archangel's Enigma
Archangel's Heart
Archangel's Viper
Archangel's Prophecy
Archangel's War
Archangel's Sun
Angels' Flight (short story
collection)

Psy-Changeling Series

Slave to Sensation
Visions of Heat
Caressed by Ice
Mine to Possess
Hostage to Pleasure
Branded by Fire

Blaze of Memory
Bonds of Justice
Play of Passion
Kiss of Snow
Tangle of Need
Heart of Obsidian
Shield of Winter
Shards of Hope
Allegiance of Honour
Wild Invitation (short story
collection)
Wild Embrace (novellas
collection)

Psy-Changeling Trinity Series

Silver Silence
Ocean Light
Wolf Rain
Alpha Night

Thrillers

A Madness of Sunshine

Archangel's
Sun

NALINI SINGH

First published in Great Britain in 2020 by Gollancz
an imprint of the Orion Publishing Group Ltd
Carmelite House, 50 Victoria Embankment
London EC4Y 0DZ

An Hachette UK Company

1 3 5 7 9 10 8 6 4 2

ISBN (Mass Market Paperback) 978 1 473 23143 6
ISBN (eBook) 978 1 473 23144 3

Printed and bound in Great Britain by Clays Ltd, Elcograf S.p.A.

www.nalinisingh.com
www.orionbooks.co.uk

1

So long ago it is a lost memory . . .

Angels aren't meant to die.

The words echoed over and over in Sharine's mind as she stood at the burial site of her beloved Raan. She hadn't known what he would've wanted because no one in angel-kind prepared for death, and so she'd chosen his resting place according to all that she'd learned of him in their five decades together.

Such a short time.

She'd thought that he, older and wiser and gentle, would be by her side for an eternity. Her mentor in the art that was liquid flame in her blood had become her lover with an ease that seemed written in the stars, both of them more than content with their life together. She and Raan, they'd spent hours in the sunlight, alone with their canvases and their thoughts and their paints, yet together at the same time.

Angels aren't meant to die.

Her fingers trembled, chilled and bloodless, as she brushed them over the small sculpture Raan had loved so much that he'd never parted with it; the favored piece now marked the location on this windswept part of the Refuge mountains where her Raan lay in eternal rest.

At first, when she'd woken next to him on that morning that still seemed a nightmare mirage, she'd thought that he had decided to go into Sleep, that deep rest of immortals who no longer wished to be part of the world. It was a thing done with intent, and her first response had been a razor-sharp stab of hurt.

She'd asked him so many times never to do that. She'd worried that because he was so much older than her, he'd want to Sleep and she'd want to stay awake and he would just leave her. But Raan had laughed his warm, calming laugh, and told her not to worry.

"Little bird," he'd said, "why would I Sleep now when I've finally found you?"

So she'd been hurt and angry at the apparent broken promise. Then she'd touched his hand because even angry with him, she still loved him. His hand, gifted and strong, had been ice cold.

Her breath broken stalactites in her lungs, her blood crushed frost.

No angel in Sleep was ever that cold. Sharine knew that firsthand—she'd been a half-grown fledgling of eighty-five when she'd sat sentry at her parents' sides as they chose to slip into Sleep. She'd watched the rise and fall of their chests to the final point of stasis, hoping they would change their minds and not leave her all alone, but they hadn't.

"You'll be fine, Sharine." Her mother's voice firm but her eyes tired. "You are an adult now."

"We'll see you when we next wake," her father had added with a pat of her hand, but she could tell he was already gone, thinking of the rest he'd craved for endless years.

But long after they'd sunk deep into Sleep, they had been warm. Fifty years later, when she'd gone to their secret underground shelter to ensure no one had disturbed their rest, they'd *still* been warm. So she'd known that angels in Sleep didn't go cold, didn't have blood chill and blue.

She hadn't needed the healers' shocked gasps to confirm the truth.

Her kind and talented lover was gone.

Dead in the night, as he lay beside Sharine.

A thing so rare among angelkind that none of the healers in attendance had ever experienced the like. They'd had to consult dusty tomes, talk to older angels and archangels, until at last they found someone who remembered another case two millennia ago. Angels were immortal . . . but sometimes, the incidents *so* infrequent that they were forgotten between one lifetime and the next, an angel simply . . . stopped.

As if a long clock had finally run out.

The healers had told her all that and still she didn't comprehend the way of it. Raan had been old, but nowhere close to the oldest of them. Many angels double or even triple his age walked the earth. But it was Raan who had stopped. Stopped as he lay in bed next to her, his life slipping away while she slept unconcerned at his side.

Had he choked for breath? Had he looked to her for help?

The questions tortured her as snow dusted her cheeks, stung her skin. She watched it settle gently over the sculpture. And she wondered if, in the centuries to come, he would be remembered by anyone but her. He had been a great sculptor and painter, but a reclusive one, not a man to have many friends. So perhaps it was his art that would be remembered and she thought he would've liked for that to be his legacy.

A sob rocking through her, she fell to her knees on the stony ground. "Angels aren't meant to die," she whispered, but there was no one to hear her.

The wind ripped the words straight from her mouth and smashed them against the mountaintop. Her wings—wings

Raan had called a gift of indigo light—spread out on the snow and the stone, grew cold and numb, and her knees froze into position, but still she didn't rise. Part of her kept on hoping that he would wake and tell her it had all been a terrible mistake.

She was only one hundred and sixty years old and the love of her life lay cold and dead. At that instant, the winds howling around her, she couldn't imagine a more terrible pain.

Alone in the falling snow, she mourned.

Angels aren't meant to die.

2

Three thousand five hundred years ago . . .

Sire, I have borne a son, strong and with such a voice to him that he keeps the entire Refuge awake! He will not flinch from anyone, this child of mine.

My eldest says that he has my eyes and my temper. The twins already believe he will follow their warrior ways, while Euphenia is the only one who can get him to sleep when he is determined to stay awake and roar out his battle cry.

His father is in astonishment at having helped create such a child. I tell him it will pass, and he will be a good father. He has a patience I lack—but this boy of mine will not be afeared of even his mother, this I know.

I will name him Titus.

—Letter from First General Avelina to Archangel Alexander

3

One month ago . . .

He couldn't remember his name.

His lungs fought to suck in air, his vision blurred . . . and his wings lay heavy and useless on his back. Still he crawled forward, dragging himself out of hell and toward the sunlight.

His eyes fell on the back of his hand, on his formerly ice white skin. Skin he'd pampered and protected and examined with care in the mirror each day. Skin that had highlighted the intense topaz shade of his eyes. Skin that was now mottled with green.

He had to get out.

He had to find a healer.

But he was so weak. How would he . . .

Snatching out a skeletal hand with reptilian speed, he gripped the small creature that had scuttled across his path, had his teeth sunk into its small furred body before his conscious mind could process the decision. The creature's furless tail whipped in panic, but it had little blood and died soon.

Throwing the creature aside, he wiped the back of his hand over his mouth . . . and felt a spurt of energy. So, was he a vampire now? No, that couldn't be. Vampire-angel hybrids existed only in tales spun by mortals. Immortals understood the fundamental truth that vampires and angels weren't biologically compatible . . . but that he'd gained energy from the creature's blood was indisputable.

His head jerked toward the small corpse.

Again, he snatched it up without thought. This time when he bit in, it was to eat the raw flesh, spitting out only the bristled fur. A tiny part of his mind, a mind that had once been of an urbane courtier in an archangel's court, screamed and gibbered, but it was a distant, faded sound. It couldn't stand against the rush of energy hitting his bloodstream.

Now he knew how to fly again.

How to stop the crawl of green beneath his skin, foul and debilitating.

How to clear his mind so he could think.

As for the coughs wracking his frame and the green-black sputum he couldn't stop from spitting out, it would all heal. He just needed enough fuel. Enough flesh plump and red and dripping with life.

Hawking out the chewy, indigestible tail on another cough, he crawled on, his clawed nails creating furrows on the tile and the flesh sloughing off his legs to leave a liquid trail. Caught within that sludge were feathers lovely and unique, a deep brown threaded with filaments of topaz.

4

Sharine stood on the railingless and flat roof of her new home in the sands of Morocco, and looked out at the buildings gilded by the rays of the setting sun. The light had an almost molten quality, a perfect kind of richness to it that appeared only at sunset. As if the star itself had been melted and was being poured over the landscape by a benevolent painter.

The vampires and mortals who walked in the streets below were busy with their business, setting up for the evening market, or heading home after a day's work, but every now and then, one of the townspeople would think to look up and they would see her. It was a thing of pride for her that the children would smile and raise a hand in excited greeting. The older ones would bow with respect.

These same people had scuttled afraid and wary when she'd first come to this place. Damaged by the oversight of an angel who'd cared more for power and cruelty than the valued responsibility he'd been given—to look after angelkind's most precious treasures. Yet Lumia, the repository of angelic art and treasures, would be a cold and lonely place without the thriving life of this adjacent settlement. To Sharine, that made the town and its people treasures as rare and beautiful as those protected in the walls of Lumia.

Spreading out her wings, she held the luxuriant stretch for a full minute before pulling them slowly back into alignment against her spine. She took care to ensure precision muscle control. It was a strengthening exercise she'd long ignored, the discipline lost in the fractured kaleidoscope that had been her self.

Large parts of the last half millennium—give or take a few decades—were shattered and confused images in the landscape of her mind, viewed through a filter that was broken and cracked. She would never get back those years. She would never get back the time during which her mischievous, laughing son had grown into a courageous and powerful man.

The hot flame of anger in her gut flared anew, searing her blood.

"Lady Sharine."

She turned her head to meet Trace's gaze. With his pretty eyes of midnight green and his moonlight skin, his languid voice that of a poet's and his hair a silky black, the slender vampire reminded her of her son. Not the coloring, that was unique to each of them. But, like Trace, her playful boy had caused more than one heart palpitation in those susceptible to such charms in her court.

Many, many had proved susceptible.

"What is it you have for me, youngling?" she asked him with an affectionate smile.

Trace shook his head, his angular features creating shadows against his cheeks; no soft beauty was Trace's, but beauty it was nonetheless. "I've told you, my lady," he said, "I'm a fully mature man, not a boy." Stern words, but his gaze held equal affection.

"And as I have said," she replied, "when you are as old as dirt and the stars combined, everyone is a youngling." Even Raphael, the archangel who'd once been an energetic little boy she'd taken to her studio so he could exhaust himself throwing paint at canvases, his little hands becoming tiny, sticky stamps—even he had accepted that he'd always be a child in her eyes.

She wondered what had become of his exuberant paintings; she was sure she must've stored them away in the Refuge, but those memories were hidden beyond the tangled mental pathways of the splintered madwoman she'd become after Aegaeon's premeditated and inexplicable cruelty.

There was unkindness, and then there was what Aegaeon had done.

Sighing, Trace held out an envelope. Made of thick creamy paper and sealed with the wax stamp of the Cadre, it held a sense of the portentous, as if the news within had been imbued with the power of the archangels who ruled the world.

"A courier dropped this off a moment ago," Trace said in a voice that had seduced many a maiden. "A vampire," he elaborated, before she could ask why the courier hadn't landed on the rooftop next to her.

Taking it, she said, "How did your rounds go?" Trace had come to her only a month past, sent by Raphael after several of her court had to return to their home bases—angels and vampires, junior and senior, they'd gone to help their people cope with the devastation caused by Lijuan's attempt to become the ruler of the world.

The war had ended a month earlier, but no one had time to rest, to heal.

It wasn't just the awful damage to cities and towns and villages, nor the shambling hordes of reborn. Over the past two weeks, a far larger than average number of vampires had begun to surrender to murderous bloodlust.

Trace had been clear in his judgment of those vampires. "No attempt to teach themselves discipline," he'd said, his voice cold and without pity. "The blood hunger lives in all of us—it whispers and cajoles in the twilight hours, seeking to gorge—but I learned to strangle those whispers long ago."

Many vampires had done nothing of the kind, and now with so many powerful angels wounded or dead, and the survivors distracted in the aftermath of war, the urge to feed was overwhelming their sense of reason or conscience. City streets threatened to run red with blood, the air wet iron.

Raphael's territory was in no better position than any other when it came to the surge of murderous vampires— and it was far worse off if you took the destruction of war into account. New York had been pummeled in the cataclysmic battle of archangels, its sky-touching towers broken and battered. He couldn't afford to lose any of his highly trained senior people, but still he'd sent Trace. Because Raphael was as much Sharine's son as Illium.

"All is well," Trace told her, suave as always in his tailored black shirt and black pants, his shoes polished and improbably free of sand or dust. "The foundations you put in place are good and strong."

That was the biggest compliment he could've given her— and she knew that despite all his playful and sophisticated ways, he spoke the absolute truth. There was no flirtation in his eyes, no attempt to flatter. At this moment, Trace was a soldier giving a report to his liege.

When she inclined her head, he bowed and left.

Envelope in hand, she released a quiet breath as she looked out at the setting sun once more. Would she ever get used to this deference from those around her? Not that it was anything unexpected. She was, as she'd just made a point of telling Trace, old in the grand scheme of things, an Ancient in many ways. But inside . . .

No, that was foolishness. The girl she'd been was long gone, and the girl who'd once been Raan's little bird, the woman called Sharine by her friends, had become the Hummingbird. At least she'd begun to reclaim her name, so that no one in her small and happy court called her anything but Lady Sharine.

Sliding a finger under the wax seal, she broke it. Inside the envelope was a letter from the Cadre. She frowned as she read words penned in a strong hand she recognized. Raphael had written this, but he'd not done so as the boy she'd once babysat, or the man she thought of with maternal love. No, he had written this as the Archangel of New York.

After reading to the very end, she dropped her hand to the side, letter and envelope held in one hand, and stared unseeing at the dazzling orange red of the sky. This, she hadn't expected. But, as she thought it over under the sun's dying light, it did make a desperate kind of sense.

So much of the world was in chaos after the combined horror of Lijuan and Charisemnon. Millions were dead, more than one archangel lost or in healing Sleep so deep that no one knew when or if they would return. Most of the rest of even angelkind didn't know what had happened to Michaela and Astaad and the others, but Raphael had told Sharine anything she wished to know.

He understood that she'd never betray him.

All those years when she'd been lost in the twisted pathways of the kaleidoscope, it was Raphael who'd looked after her son—and the other boy who had always been a part of her life. Illium and Aodhan, twin flames of her heart. One, the blood son, the other a son of art. She'd taught him as Raan had once taught her.

Sadness bloomed in her heart at the reminder of that beloved face, those gifted hands, but it was a sadness faded to monochrome by eons . . . though she'd kept vigil over Raan's grave since her mind shattered, her heart aching for the past in which she'd been safe and cherished and full of dreams.

The memories had given her a safe place in which to hide.

But Sharine was done with hiding, done with living in her mind. It was time to face the truth. And the first truth was that while she would mourn Raan till the day she died, she could no longer remember the piercing, beautiful pain that had been her youthful love for him. Had they grown older together, it would've been different . . . But there was no use living in what-ifs.

No use living anywhere but in the present.

She squared her jaw, angry again, this time at herself. Caliane, she knew, would be furious at the direction of her thoughts; her friend was firm in the belief that Sharine wasn't to blame herself.

"Aegaeon knew *exactly* what he was doing," Caliane had said soon after Aegaeon woke from his Sleep, her tone as unbending as her spine. "He knew what you'd been through, the scars those experiences left behind, and still he did something so insufferably cruel that I will never forgive him for it. He took your greatest nightmare and made it come to life."

A grim darkness to her face, she'd shaken her head. "No, Sharine. Don't *ever* blame yourself for the fractures that created in your psyche."

But Sharine did. She blamed herself for not being strong enough. Blamed herself for her blinding grief after Raan . . . and for the mental screams that had echoed within her for years after she walked into her parents' place of Sleep and found their bodies shriveled and dead, their blood dry in their veins. Gone while they Slept.

A bare four decades after strong, talented Raan.

Though angels weren't meant to die except in battle.

Sharine alone, of all her kind, had buried three people

who'd closed their eyes to rest . . . and never again woken. Lover, mother, father, all lay cold and long-decayed in their graves, their voices lost from the world.

It's you, a small, vicious part of her had begun to whisper in the dead of night, when all else was quiet. *Everyone you love dies. No one can stand you. No one wants to be alive in a world where you exist.*

That ugly voice had taunted her and taunted her, until she'd lived in terror after falling for Aegaeon. That terror had grown by magnitudes on the birth of her son. She'd been like a glass bauble spiderwebbed with cracks no one could see. And in the end, she'd shattered, thought and reason splinters at her feet.

Yes, she blamed herself.

It was the greatest of gifts that after all that, her son loved her still.

Thinking of him, she glanced down at the letter again. He'd be proud of her if she did this, proud of her for having the strength and the courage. And so she would. She'd let him down for far too long. It was time Illium had reason to call her his mother with pride.

The last of the sun's rays caressing her wings, she crossed the rooftop to enter the building. She then made her way to the well-appointed room shiny with technology she didn't fully comprehend. However, she'd learned the usefulness of such things in the time since she'd stepped fully out of the kaleidoscope. Now she asked one of her loyal people to put through a call to Raphael.

She took that call in the privacy of the office suite that was her own. An aged white desk with curved legs, soft fabrics on her furnishings, fresh flowers, paintings on the walls, this was a far gentler room than the one that appeared on the wall screen in front of her.

Raphael's office leaned more toward glass and steel, akin to his city. She could see none of Manhattan's glittering lights in view around him, but what she did see were the shelves that held unique treasures—including a feather of purest blue that struck a pang of need in her heart.

"Lady Sharine."

"You look tired, Raphael." Lines of strain, knotted shoulder muscles, faint shadows under the striking blue of his eyes. So many times she'd painted that blue—first in an attempt to capture the eyes of the archangel who was her closest friend, then the eyes of Caliane's son—always it took her an eternity to get the color just right. Crushed sapphires, molten cobalt, the mountain sky at noon, all this and more lived in Raphael's and in Caliane's eyes.

As an artist, the color was one of her greatest challenges and greatest joys.

He thrust a hand through his hair. "It'll be a long journey for all of us before we can rest."

Sharine felt the urge to mother him; she wasn't certain that urge would ever pass. He'd been but a youth when Caliane walked the path of madness, and though Sharine was a fragile creature even then, the spiderweb cracks growing year by year, she'd been *there*. After finding his broken body on a field far from civilization, she'd covered him in the shade of her wings and she'd brushed his tangled hair back from his face, and she'd held him.

Such a determined youth he'd been, but so very wounded inside.

To see him now, strong and vibrant and loved fiercely by a woman who was everything Sharine could've ever wanted for him had she the imagination to consider that someone like Raphael's consort could exist, it made her heart bloom, made her believe in happiness and in changing your destiny.

Caliane had never told her son, but at Raphael's birth, some of the bitter old ones had whispered that this was a child bound for lunacy and decay, that his mother was an Ancient far too long in the tooth. So strange, that such a prejudice could exist in a race of immortals, but there were always those who looked for the darkness in everything.

Those same ones had whispered that Sharine was the harbinger of death.

Caliane's boy had quieted them all. He was a shining embodiment of the best of them, a critical reason why the world wasn't today drowning in blood and death. Not the only reason, however. "Where is Elena?" Her fingers curled into her palm at the memory of the knives she'd held under Elena's tutelage.

"In the park with her best friend, Sara, and Sara's child," Raphael said, his face lighting up in a way it never did for anyone else. "We decided that we could all do with an hour away from the grim task of getting the city to rights. It shatters the spirit, to see our home in ruins."

Sharine could not imagine the devastation of seeing a cherished city broken and burned, but one thing she knew— Raphael's city was a place with a brave heart. It would rise again, gleaming towers of metal and glass that touched the sky, its rivers clean of the debris and gore of battle, and the scorched land rejuvenated.

"What will you do with your hour, my boy?" she said, itching to push a wayward strand of hair away from his eye.

A sudden, dazzling smile. "I'm going flying with Illium. We plan to meet Jason as he flies home."

"I'm surprised that you even know he is in the vicinity. Your spymaster is wont to slip in and out of cities like smoke." She knew very well that Jason had been near Lumia in the months prior to the war, but she'd only discovered that after the fact.

The Cadre trusted her, but that didn't mean she wasn't under watch. A decision with which she had no argument. No one had watched the one before her, and evil had thrived. Simply because she had no intention of doing the same didn't mean the next person to have this responsibility would be as trustworthy.

Raphael laughed, making her smile, it reminded her so of his gleeful childhood laughter as he all but bathed in paints. "I'm of the opinion that Jason allowed himself to be seen. He knows we worry about him when he is beyond our help—and so, sometimes, he throws us a bone."

Shaking her head at these games of the young, Sharine said, "I've received your letter."

Astonishing blue eyes holding her own, laughter yet lingering in them. But his words when they came were of an archangel. "What do you say to our request, Lady Sharine?"

"You're certain that it's me you want for this task? I am far from a warrior."

Expression wry, Raphael said, "Titus requires certain handling." A tug of his lips. "He's a warrior and an archangel I respect beyond many others, but he does like to get his own way."

Sharine interpreted that to mean certain immortals were threatening to quit the service of the Archangel of Africa. "Are you saying I'm to be the go-between?" She raised an eyebrow. "Archangel Titus has run a successful court these many years."

Sharine had never had anything to do with him, their paths simply not crossing over the years. He was millennia younger than her, for one, and her life was art, while his was the path of a warrior. But those of Lumia's forces who'd served under him spoke of the archangel in the highest terms.

"I'm afraid it's gone beyond that," Raphael admitted. "His people are blood loyal, but a number of warriors seconded to him from other territories have quit." His jaw was granite now. "Those who don't know Titus see his current short temper as an insult—and have not the sense to understand he needs every body we can muster."

Oh, now she understood. Some of the old and powerful ones expected sweet ways and delicate words even in exigent circumstances. "I'm surprised that you believe I can deal with him." Angelkind had long handled her with kid gloves. *As you would a delicate and cracked vase.*

"I mean no insult, Lady Sharine, but we have no other option." Grim words. "I did a weeklong stint in Africa half a month past, and it's from Titus's territory that Jason even now returns. Venom is also on his way home from Africa."

Venom, Sharine recalled, was the young but powerful vampire with the eyes of a viper. "You have upheld the bonds of friendship."

"It was beyond that. It was a duty of the Cadre—Africa would've been overrun elsewise." Hands on his hips, his wings held with rigid control. "Alexander crossed the border to assist at the same time. We believed three archangels working together might eliminate enough of the reborn that Titus and his people could then clean up the rest, but the situation is catastrophic."

"I've had news the infection is spreading rapidly." Lumia was isolated, but it wasn't cut off from the external world. More so with the arrival of Trace—the vampire was extremely good at maintaining lines of information.

"Yes—and the strain in Africa appears to be stronger and more virulent than in the rest of the world. Charisemnon must've been collaborating with Lijuan to create a more noxious enemy. It's a small mercy that strain remains confined to Africa, but it leaves Titus in an unenviable position."

Flaring out his wings, he snapped them back in. "If I could, I'd relocate to Africa until we'd erased the danger, but my territory is badly damaged—far worse than we initially believed. And then there are the vampires who've given in to murderous bloodlust. I must stay home and I need my strongest people here. The other territories are in much the same position."

None of which answered the question of why the Cadre believed Sharine could deal with the short-tempered archangel. There were many who'd say that she'd break under such pressure. Sharine knew she wouldn't—she was too angry to break, fury a forge that was tempering her cracks into hardened scars.

Caliane had another theory. "I believe your time in what you call the kaleidoscope was a desperate attempt by your mind to give you the space to heal wounds that never quite healed the first time around. The ugly ones who taunted you in the aftermath of your parents' deaths, they caused catastrophic damage inside you at a time when you were already a bleeding, wounded creature."

Vivid blue eyes rampant with rage. "Aegaeon's sudden reappearance merely sped up your return to reality—but not by much. You were already partway home; you couldn't have run Lumia otherwise."

Sharine was starting to believe Caliane was correct in this. She *couldn't* have run Lumia had she remained in the fractured landscape of her mind—her memories alone bore that out. She could detail each and every day of the past year. A few blurred edges at the start, but nothing forgotten or lost.

None of that explained why she was being asked to join Titus. "I don't have the powers of your Seven, far less the power to take on an archangel."

Raphael looked at her in a careful way. "My mother once told me to look at Illium with care if I wanted to see the root of his power—I didn't understand then, but now I ask myself from whom he inherited his fidelity, his hair, his heart . . . and his speed."

A stirring in the back of her mind, the creaking of long-buried memories. "That is why Raan called me a hummingbird." It was a murmur more to herself than to Raphael, aged memories sighing to wakefulness.

So fast you are, my little bird. Sunshine in your eyes, color streaked across your skin, light of feet—and the speed of a hummingbird. I could not ever catch you should you seek to fly away.

She had forgotten the genesis of her other name until this very instant, forgotten that it had been a loving caress from Raan. Forgotten that he'd done a painting of her in flight, her wings and body creating streaks of color in the sky just like the small, jeweled bird.

"Lady Sharine?" Raphael's voice, interrupting her thoughts, reminding her again of the now, of the here—but without impatience.

The blue-eyed boy's mother was an Ancient; he understood that memories took time to unfurl within the minds of the very old. Tangled skeins with knots and, in Sharine's case, many a cut thread, that was the repository of immortal memory.

"I accept the task," she said with a sense of taking a step into the future. "I will make ready to join Titus."

5

Titus roared to the starless sky as he dispatched another ravenous monster born of those putrid boils on the history of the world, Lijuan and Charisemnon, turning his head at the last moment so that the fetid blood didn't hit his face. He'd had more than enough of that—but he could do nothing about the repulsive smell of the blood.

The reborn down, he picked up his conversation with his troop trainer, Tanae. "The rest of the Cadre are sending me the Hummingbird!" It came out a disbelieving shout.

"So you have said. *Four* times." Dark red strands of hair stuck to her cheeks by a combination of blood and sweat, Tanae dispatched another reborn, then wiped her blade on the already wet dark of her pants.

Her wings were a horror of blood and brain matter from a half hour past when she'd turned into a spinning dervish to eliminate a nest of reborn. "You are one of the Cadre, sire. You don't have to accept anything you do not want."

He glared at her. "The *Humming Bird*," he said, deliberately spacing out the two words that made up the name of the greatest living artist in angelkind. "Do you wish me to make enemies of our entire people?"

Everyone loved the Hummingbird. Even Titus loved her—in a distant kind of way. He didn't know her as a person. He knew *of* her. That she was a gift to angelkind, that her kindness was legendary, that she had never had an enemy in her life. And of course, that she had given birth to Illium, a young angel Titus greatly liked.

Tanae, who had little relationship with her own son and was not a woman of large emotions, rolled eyes of a pale gray. "She isn't a warrior and we're in the midst of an infestation of reborn. No one will be surprised if you—respectfully— reject the offer."

Titus had to turn and take care of another three rotting reborn before he could respond. "No one else will come," he grumbled. "I scared all those who might've been free to join us, and now no warriors are left."

"I told you not to yell at the last one," Tanae said in a steady tone after chopping off a reborn head that featured a crushed eyeball hanging out of its socket. "He was competent."

"He was lily-livered!" Titus roared. "What warrior runs from a good strong yell? *You* don't run."

"That's because I'm deaf after all these years at your side." Glancing around the field and seeing only dissolving bodies, she slid her sword into a thigh sheath.

The dissolving was a new thing that the reborn had begun to do after Lijuan's death. The resulting gelatinous mess had so disgusting a stench that Titus's second, Tzadiq, had rounded up a civilian crew whose sole job it was to dig deep holes using large earthmoving machines, then scrape all those dissolving bodies inside.

It was a luxury given all else that was going on, but it was a luxury for which his people thanked him, else their homes would be filled with the odor of decomposing flesh and no one could eat.

And food was a pleasure Titus treasured.

As for whether the gelatinous goo would poison the earth, Titus had plans to one by one cleanse the graves using archangelic power—but he couldn't do that and fight the reborn at the same time. It'd have to be done at the end. In the interim, the holes were lined with a material created to keep contaminants from escaping into the soil, with his scientists monitoring the situation.

"You show me no respect," he said to Tanae. "I should banish you."

"I have a standing offer from three other courts."

If he didn't like her so much, he *would* banish her, he thought with an inward grumble. But if there was one thing Titus knew, it was that having bowing and scraping syco-phants around an archangel did nothing but lead to rot. Look at Lijuan—all those fawning courtiers and a once compe-tent leader had turned into a woman who thought death was life.

Tanae might have an edge to her tongue and no time for massaging anyone's ego, but she was also loyal to the bone. Though he did sometimes wonder how her mate, Tzadiq, dealt with her. A man liked a little softness in his lover.

Not that Titus was getting any of that at present. While he well appreciated pleasures of the flesh, he had no time or inclination to soothe and gentle the pretty and fragile creatures with whom he usually kept company.

"I'll have to clean up, *entertain* her." It came out a groan unbecoming of an archangel but dear glory, the idea of it!

"Perhaps she'll be more helpful than we believe," Tanae said with her customary practicality. "She has, by all ac-counts, done a stellar job in her oversight of Lumia. You cannot argue that your household is in chaos and could do with a firm hand at the helm."

"That's because anyone who can lift a sword is out battling reborn, the others are digging holes to bury the resulting goo, and I've sent the vulnerable to safe havens." Those
safe havens were mostly islands off the coast of Africa.
"She'll have nothing to do but sit around and take insult at
not being pampered like a lady."

Titus had not expected this of Raphael—after his brutal
and exhausting sojourn assisting in Africa, the pup knew
very well what Titus needed. He categorically did *not* need
a fragile artist renowned for her existence on a higher plane
far from crawling reborn and war and blood.

There was no higher plane here. Just death and decay
and devastation.

"Perhaps the others had no choice," he admitted with a
loud sigh. "We've lost too many good people." Thousands
of warriors had died in the battles, and though Titus now
had control over what remained of Charisemnon's forces,
he couldn't trust them.

Knowing a resentful fighter could do far more harm than
good, he'd offered those troops the choice to leave for another territory if they so wished. Only a minuscule number
had taken him up on it and departed Africa: all people
who'd been high up in Charisemnon's court.

Good riddance.

The rot in his enemy's lands ran deep and it had come
from the top.

Those who'd stayed had likely done so because they'd
face the same lack of welcome outside Africa. Angelkind
knew that fighters lower down in the pecking order had no
control over the actions of their archangel, and so no one
would outwardly shun those fighters, but the simple fact of
the matter was that every angel had a choice.

These angels—and vampires—had made the choice to
follow orders even when those orders were unforgiveable.
That decision would stain them for centuries to come—

how they responded to it, how they acted now, that would be their legacy. At present, however, Titus had command of too many sullen warriors he didn't want anywhere near his people.

Some, he'd left in command of various northern cities—it was pointless to send his own people to do the task when Charisemnon's commanders were already experienced in the job and had intimate knowledge of those cities.

It wasn't as if even the most sullen and hostile would dare foment rebellion against an archangel. No one but the suicidal would listen to them. The worst they could do was deliberately fail in their duties as city commanders, and Titus's spymaster had enough operatives scattered through the cities to ensure they'd soon hear of any such.

As for any overflow of warriors, he'd asked Tzadiq to situate them in the more isolated sections of the territory. They could be useful and clear up the reborn infection in that area, while keeping the poison of their hate safely away from his court.

"That's good," Tanae said in response to his acknowledgment of the Cadre's lack of options. "You're being positive. Is that not what your sisters suggested?"

Titus wanted to stop and bang his head against the nearest hard surface. It was not enough that he had to deal with the vicious seeds left by a bringer of disease. No, he also had to have four elder sisters, all of whom chose to be awake in the world, and all of whom considered it their business to give him advice. Really, a *much* younger brother had to grow a big voice to stand up for himself.

Was it any wonder his voice was now so big it scared and insulted others? That was another thing. "If I'm so terrifying, why is it my sisters show no fear?"

Tanae came as close to a smile as she ever did. "Titus, I know you'd chop off my head in battle should I come against you, but were I someone you thought of as a woman first and everything else second, you wouldn't lift a finger to lay so much as a bruise on my skin. Every woman in the world knows this."

Titus snarled at her, but he had no rebuttal. He didn't believe in harming those who didn't put themselves forward in battle. That applied, regardless of gender, but yes, he had a special soft spot for women. But the instant a woman picked up a sword, she went from woman to warrior. A warrior was fair game. A woman was to be protected.

Yet even though two of his sisters *were* warriors, he didn't meet Zuri and Nala on that field. He met them as brother to sisters. Thus, much as they aggravated him, he wouldn't ever do them harm. Even when they constantly sent him suggestions for battle strategy against the reborn. As if he wasn't in his fourth millennium! As if he wasn't an archangel who'd just defeated another archangel!

The last time around, he'd threatened to tell Alexander they were being lax in their duties if they continued to hound him. *Surely,* he'd written, *you would not have so much time on your hands if you were actually doing your assigned tasks.*

The twins had gone silent. That would last about five minutes.

His sisters didn't know the meaning of defeat.

"Come," he said to Tanae, "we must clear the next field so that the barriers can be put up." That was how they were doing this—section by section, with teams of mortals and young vampires in charge of moving each barrier outward as more land was cleansed of the reborn infection.

It worked, but progress was slow. It would've been glacial if not for Raphael's and Alexander's assistance. The two had helped Titus completely clear the area directly around the thriving hub of commerce and trade that was the city of Narja. That it'd become his battle citadel was an accident of location—Charisemnon had been a friendly neighbor when Titus first took over as Archangel of Southern Africa, and Narja had been born naturally, a result of the trade between the two sides of Africa.

The battles had come long afterward, and by then, the people of Narja were of a mind to hunker down in support of the citadel that sat on a rise at the center of the city. It helped that the city wasn't actually right on the border and thus protected from the worst of the fighting.

Nothing could've protected it from the plague of reborn, however. Charisemnon, that bastard son of a diseased ass, had—while acting the ally—quietly set his ground troops to shepherding the infectious creatures over the border. The reborn had rampaged through Titus's people, a putrid wave of death and horrific resurrection.

Even with Titus, Raphael, and Alexander all in play, they'd had to fight with brutal intensity to erase the threat from Narja. Whatever Charisemnon and/or his megalomaniacal partner had done to the reborn, the strain in Africa was even more vicious and virulent than in the rest of the world.

These new reborn hunted in packs, and seemed to have a rudimentary intelligence that harked back to the very first reborn Lijuan had created; many of the creatures had learned to dig dens in which to hide during the bright hours of daylight, crawling out only at dusk to begin their attacks.

And unlike the transmission rate in other parts of the world, here, as long as the victim's head hadn't been ripped off, it appeared to be one hundred percent. To die by reborn hands was to return reborn. That was nowhere near the worst of it—for a vampire or a mortal to be scratched or bitten by a reborn led to an ugly infection that had a fifty percent fatality rate.

The Archangel of Death and the Archangel of Disease had created a horrific hybrid. But the ugliest "improvement" was why all of the dead in Titus's territory were now being cremated—these reborn had the ability to pass on the infection to the dead who yet had a shred of flesh on their bones. The creatures dug up graves, hauled out corpses, fed on them, but if any flesh remained afterward, the dead would be re-born.

An entire village had been butchered by their just-buried war dead in the hours after Titus left the continent to fight Lijuan. Now, people across this land spent daylight hours digging up their dead as tears streaked their faces and their hearts broke; each body was treated with respect, but there was no choice—their dead had to go into the cleansing cauldron of fire.

"Charisemnon and Lijuan must've had a plan to spread this new strain," Tzadiq had said to him after they first became aware of the horror they faced, his second's clean-shaven head gleaming in the reprieve of the dawn sun. "Why do you think that plan stalled in Africa?"

"We'll never know for certain," Titus had answered, his back drenched with sweat after yet another night fighting the reborn, "but if I had to lay bets, I'd say that whatever Charisemnon did to blend his disease with her death, it cost him." Disease was a "gift" that cut both ways. "He likely couldn't maintain the projected pace."

But the archangel formed of pestilence and vanity had done plenty.

It was all more than enough to deal with—yet a nagging worry haunted Titus. When he'd entered Charisemnon's inner border court after his return from New York, it was to find a number of badly decomposed bodies. No one had been inside the court buildings in the interim, both his and Charisemnon's former forces caught in a desperate battle against the reborn.

The creatures had gone berserk upon the death of their master.

Only later, after questioning several senior members of the enemy court, had he learned that Charisemnon had shut off the inner court to everyone but a favored few. The other courtiers had worried they'd fallen in their archangel's favor. Turned out, from what Titus had discovered, that the favored few had actually been the unlucky few.

For the vampires, Titus believed that their liege had either accidentally infected them with a disease or he'd used them as guinea pigs. It was possible the angels had been thrown to the vampires as sacrificial food, but it was equally possible the decomposition hid what might've been indications of disease. It was the latter prospect that haunted Titus—because angels weren't supposed to be vulnerable to disease.

It was a law written into stone.

As immutable as the wind and the sky.

Or it had been before Charisemnon.

Then Tzadiq had discovered the worst thing: a slimy black-green trail along the hallway that led out of the room of the rotting dead . . . in a shape that couldn't be of anything but an angel. No other being in the world could've made that particular pattern. Only an angel whose wings were dragging along the stone as they clawed and crawled their way down the hall.

Needless to say, Titus was handling serious and deadly problems.

The Hummingbird had exactly zero useful skills when it came to the grim tasks that lay ahead.

He wanted to groan all over again. Did he even have anyone left on his staff who could pretty up a room for her?

This was going to be an unmitigated disaster.

6

Sharine's first action was to consider the well-being of Lumia and its connected township. To that end, she called together those of her current team who wore the mantle of leadership: Trace, Tanicia, and Farah.

The most senior of the three, Tanicia, her black hair delicately braided around the front but a halo at the back, said, "We won't flinch at maintaining the rules you've set down, Lady Sharine." Her voice was husky, her gaze resolute, and her wings a deep autumnal orange-red against skin of darkest brown. "We will allow no stain to fall on your honor."

She should not have favorites, Sharine thought, but Tanicia was one of hers. A warrior through and through, but one with heart. Sharine had seen her slipping sweets into the hands of the younglings who ran after her in the streets, wanting to touch her wings but too well-taught by their parents to dare.

"I have every faith in you," she reassured all three, lest they believe she was questioning their loyalty or commitment. "But we are short in number—and now you'll lose me for a time. We must have contingencies in place should the vampires in the area begin to act out." As Raphael had reminded her, bloodlust was always a threat, especially in the absence of archangelic oversight.

With Elijah, the Archangel of South America, as well as Caliane in the healing sleep of *anshara*, the Cadre was only seven right now, one of them Suyin, newly ascended and finding her feet. Add in the fact that Neha, the Archangel of India, had awakened from *anshara* a bare week ago, and the Cadre was stretched to the limit.

As a result, powerful angels who could maintain the leash of fear were needed far more so than in the normal order of things. Sharine wasn't deadly or an enforcer. But in the time since taking up her position here, she'd learned that she had the ability to bring out the best in others, including warrior squadrons.

Those squadrons held the leash for her.

"We've spoken of that," Tanicia said, her glance taking in Trace and Farah. "A number of vampires from this region were called to fight in Archangel Charisemnon's army."

"Yes." Sorrow wove through her blood for all the people, vampiric and angelic and mortal, who would never again return, their bodies obliterated in war. Those assigned to Lumia at the time had come to her before their departure, making sure she knew she was about to lose them from Lumia's complement and why.

Sharine had begrudged none of them. The war hadn't reached this isolated area—Charisemnon had aimed himself at the southern half of the continent, with the fighting mostly taking place at the north/south border.

"The archangel didn't only recall his soldiers, he drafted in civilians who were technically his people, though they lived inside our borders," Tanicia reminded Sharine. "Sad as it is to say, that means we currently have a very small population of civilian vampires. We should be able to maintain the peace for weeks or longer—you've built a solid foundation on which we can stand."

"The idiots know to behave," Trace drawled. "Everyone else will otherwise haul them into line—and not be gentle about it. No one, mortal or immortal wishes to lose you as Guardian, and to that end, they will ensure the Cadre has no reason to question your leadership."

Oh, she did like him. She liked all of her people. Farah, so quiet and sage in her advice. Trace, erudite and silkily dangerous. Battle-worn Tanicia, who'd been at Sharine's side from the start, when Sharine wasn't sure what she was doing here. The only reason she'd even accepted the position was because Illium had taken her hands and said, "These people are hurt, Mother. You understand pain, and you understand how to be kind. That's what they need."

He could be so wise sometimes, her blue-winged boy who was becoming more powerful each time she turned around. Yet she would always remember him as the ungainly babe who'd wobbled the first time he took off from their kitchen doorway, straight down into the breathtakingly steep drop-off outside.

She'd had her heart in her throat every painful second, but she hadn't gone after him. His father had been watching from below . . . and well, Aegaeon had still been a good father then, even if he'd already lost interest in her as a woman. He'd have caught their small and delighted boy if he'd tangled his wings and fallen.

But he hadn't. Their baby had flown.

And he'd given Sharine wings when she was at her most broken, bringing her to this place where she was considered someone to come to, a person to trust. "I have confidence in your ability to handle anything that arises in my absence," she told her three senior people, and saw their spines lengthen, their faces gain light from within.

"I will prepare tonight and fly on the wing to Titus's court come morning." She held up a hand when Tanicia's eyes flared, her lips parting. "Raphael offered to arrange a ride in one of those flying metal contraptions, but I'm not that modern." The idea of being trapped inside a tube of metal was not her idea of flight. "I also wish to make a survey of the landscape."

Tanicia frowned, and Farah stepped from foot to foot. Surprisingly, it was Trace who inclined his head in defeat. "I wish you good journey, Lady Sharine."

Dawn came on a caress of pink and light yellow across twilight gray skies.

Sharine's maidens had argued for sending her things overland, but Sharine had no intention of risking her people for vanity. She'd borne their distraught silence as she made it clear she'd carry what she needed in a small pack that fit neatly between her wings. "No one is to send anything else after me."

Such long faces they'd had, such bowed shoulders, but they had accepted her word. Now, she double-checked the pack she'd filled the previous night. She'd had such a pack as a young woman, but this one had been a gift from Aodhan. And Aodhan being Aodhan, while the pack was a golden brown suitable for the heat of Morocco, when examined more closely, it proved to be patterned with a design in the same color. Even in the simplest of things, her protégé couldn't stop making art.

She'd taken time to think about what she might need and what she could borrow. Titus was a man who had many female warriors and staff, and while she was at the smaller end, she wasn't so small as to make borrowing clothing or shoes difficult. In the end, the pack had ended up a weight she could easily carry for her entire journey.

As for her clothing for this journey . . . She'd always worn gowns of various kinds—simple patterns without embellishment, as well as more intricate pieces. Even with the latter, however, she was no fan of heavy enhancement, preferring beautiful fabrics and cuts. Still, since taking up her position in Lumia, she'd come to appreciate the versatility offered by the clothing worn by her warriors.

Now, she pulled on brown pants that hugged her legs, and a mid-thigh-length tunic in gray-blue with three-quarter-length sleeves. The tunic bore silver edging on both the sleeves and the bottom edges.

A gift from the Archangel of India when Sharine accepted the post in Lumia, the fabric of both the pants and the tunic included subtle shimmering threads. As well, the embroidery was imperfect—the kind of imperfect that spoke to an artisan's personalized touch. It all sang to Sharine's love of color, of art.

After dressing, she went to the mirror and considered the fall of her hair. She'd become used to wearing the gold-tipped black of it out for the most part, but today she picked up a hairbrush and ran it through the strands, then wove her hair into a braid that she tied off with a plain black tie.

She laughed at the face that looked back at her—with her hair thus, and dressed with simple practicality, she looked young and hopeful.

Immortality left its mark, but not always in the face or the body.

Sharine's marks were all internal. Her face was that of the young woman she'd once been. A woman who'd been scared and anxious much of the time, a girl she wished she could go back and reassure.

Hair done, she went to sit on a stool near the doors that led out to her balcony, and pulled on socks, then boots. Her preference was to remain in sandals that she tied with strings up to her calf, but Titus was currently having to deal with hordes of reborn. Sharine needed footwear that wasn't going to make her a liability should she end up in a fight.

Dawn sunlight fell on her wings as she sat lacing up the boots, and she looked across, imagining how she'd capture that tracery of light on a canvas. Falling into the strokes, into the shades of paint and how she would mix each to precise perfection.

The main part of her feathers would be easy enough—the intense indigo was familiar and a color she'd painted often back when Raan had her practicing portraiture by doing her own, but with that champagne-like shade dusted all over the filaments, it was so filled with light as to be almost impossible to capture. As well, the texture of the sun was further altering the—

"Sharine," she muttered, deliberately breaking her gaze and turning her attention back to her boots. This was a truth she hadn't shared with anyone, not even Caliane. The broken shards of her self hadn't fully healed—every so often, her mind tried to spiral back into that shattered landscape where everything was soft and hazy and she didn't have to think about pain.

It had been so easy to live inside its embrace, to do her art and not confront a life that had left scars so deep they could never be buffed out or erased. She'd been a coward and it was time she admitted that. Caliane might not see it that way, but Caliane didn't have a son who'd had to parent his own mother.

Heart aching, she couldn't help herself from picking up the device Illium had given her last time he visited Lumia. No, it hadn't been the last time, it had been the time prior. He'd come alone then, and he'd nagged her until she sat down with him to learn how to use this device.

"It's called a phone," he'd told her. "A small version of the screen you use to talk to Raphael and Archangel Caliane."

Sharine had never much bothered with technology—even the technology of the time in which she'd been born. She'd been far more interested in working out how to capture all the hues of the world. But, wishing to indulge her son and content to just be with him, she'd sat and listened.

Today, she dug back through her memories in an effort to remember what he'd attempted to teach her. She hadn't paid enough attention at the time, still partially lost in the kaleidoscope, so her retention wasn't as sharp as usual.

But Sharine was through with giving up.

Jaw set, she touched different parts of the screen, activating things until the device began to look familiar at last. Even faded and hazy, her memory was one of her greatest advantages, the reason she could paint so true to life.

Teeth biting down on her lower lip, she created a message: *my son, are you awake? i would speak to you*. It didn't look pretty, but it would do. She sent it. She didn't know what time it was in his city, and she didn't know what duties lay on his shoulders, but she knew he must be very busy.

Yet the phone began to buzz in her hand a moment later, a still portrait of Illium coming onscreen. She glanced frantically at the available options, not knowing which part to touch. Thinking that red was almost universally the color of warning, she decided to touch the green. And her boy's living face appeared on the screen.

He was sweaty, the blue-tipped black of his hair damp against a background of darkness lit up by the lights in the windows of a building behind him, and he had the most enormous smile on his face. "Mother, did you do that yourself?"

Squaring her shoulders, she said, "Of course. You shouldn't doubt your mother."

His laughter made her lips curve, everything inside her suddenly warm and happy. He was so beautiful, her boy. With his golden eyes and his skin kissed by sunshine, and his wings of astonishing silver-blue. But the most beautiful thing about Illium was his heart. He loved so fiercely, her son. And he mourned so deeply that it was pure devastation.

"I am going to Titus's territory," she told him. "Will I be able to use this device there?"

He nodded. "I've set it up so you can use it anywhere. If you want, I can give your contact number to Raphael and Elena and anyone else you want to stay in touch with."

"Yes, I'd like that." No longer would she isolate herself in ways big and small. "Teach me how to retrieve the number and I will give it to my people, too." It was certain that she'd have access to all of Titus's technology while in his court, but Sharine was discovering that she wasn't happy being reliant on others.

Illium taught her how to navigate the phone, then reminded her that she must charge it with electrical energy, as she'd been doing every few days since he first gave her the device. Afterward, she took in his face, the angles of it thinner than usual. "Tell me of your city."

"People say we were lucky." He thrust a hand through his hair. "It's true we don't have to worry about a reborn scourge like so many other territories—but that's only because of how much of the city was destroyed. The earth itself is so badly scorched in places . . ."

A lowering of his head, his voice tight when he next spoke. "There were so many dead, Mother." Golden eyes shiny-wet, he looked away for a second before meeting her gaze again. "So many biers to fly to the Refuge, so many graves to dig, so many friends to mourn whose bodies had to be incinerated after what Lijuan did to them."

His shoulder muscles bunched, his jaw working. "We had to effectively sanitize the entire city before the vulnerable could be permitted to move back in. Aside from a small respite offered by the glittering rain that fell during Suyin's ascension, the smell from the rotting corpses of Lijuan's black-eyed army wouldn't leave. For a while even Raphael worried we'd have to burn the entire city to the ground and start again."

Sharine wanted to reach out and hold him, but all she could do was listen.

"Too many of our own are gone, including the Legion,"

he told her. "It's too silent in the city. It feels strange to say that when the Legion barely spoke, but they were always around—sitting on tops of buildings like gargoyles or flying in small groups, or just gathering on balconies. I miss them. We all miss them."

Sharine didn't truly understand who and what the Legion had been, but she understood the loss of friends. War was not kind, and war did not discriminate. "From what I've heard, your friends gave of their energy so that a great evil could be defeated. They went with honor." Such a thing would make no difference to her should her son have died in the war, but she knew it mattered.

Illium nodded. From the arc of his wings above his shoulders, she could tell that he was holding them with his usual muscle control even though his feathers remained soft and downy. As they'd been when he'd first grown his feathers. A smudged sky blue those baby feathers had been, so delicate and airy that she'd worried about damaging them each time she gave him a bath.

"How are your wings?" He'd lost both during the war, but was growing them back at a pace that terrified her for what it meant for his power levels.

Her sweet boy's father was an archangel. An Ancient. Not every child who had an archangelic parent ended up being Cadre themselves, but that was looking like a certainty with Illium. He was only just over five hundred years old, and already, there were those in the world who thought he should have control of a territory.

She knew he'd been offered many positions, but he stayed with Raphael both out of a deep sense of loyalty and love—and because he was intelligent enough to know that he wasn't ready. But sometimes, power didn't give its wielders a choice. If Illium ascended . . .

No, she wouldn't think about that. Her son would be torn apart by the forces of ascension should he rise too young. She could still remember how difficult it had been for

Raphael—and he'd been a thousand years of age. She'd been terrified Caliane's beloved boy would die, simply fragment into a million pieces from the power surging through his veins.

When he landed, his eyes had been blue fire, his skin crackling with lightning—and his wings ablaze in a way that had reminded her of Nadiel's fiery fall. She'd been distant from the site of the battle where Caliane had executed her true love, but she'd seen Nadiel's beautiful wings crumple, seen fire devour him as he fell—a star that had burned too bright and consumed itself.

7

On the small screen of the phone, her son spread his wings so she could see the progress of his healing. "Getting there," he said. "In the meantime, I'm working on the ground. It keeps my muscles conditioned, and it also helps with wing strength because I'm constantly shifting those muscles when I lift or bend or turn."

They spoke of other things in the time that followed, such things as might be spoken of between a mother and her son. At one point, she said, "How is Aodhan?" Illium's best friend had been so often in their house as a child that she felt entitled to maternal worry.

Illium scowled. "Fine."

Sharine, once out of the last vestiges of the fog in which she'd lived for so long, had sensed a visceral change in the relationship between her boy and his friend; she wondered if she should say something.

Friendships so deep were rare in an angel's lifetime and should be cherished. Anger and bitterness could destroy that which was most precious. But, she remembered, even as they fought, they looked out for each other. The two had too many years of friendship and loyalty between them to allow it to shatter—but she would keep an eye on both, ensure stubbornness didn't get the better of them.

"Give him greetings from me and tell him of this number. I would speak to him, too."

"I will," Illium promised, though he was still scowling. "You'll be careful, Mother." It was an order, a quiet one but an order nonetheless.

She allowed it, for she knew it was reflex after so many centuries of having to care for her, of having to be the parent. There was so much she'd missed of her son's life, so much of his pain that she didn't understand. Never again would she let him down.

"I promise to take every care," she told him, her heart an ache. "I realize I'm going to be dealing with dangerous creatures in Titus's territory." The last thing already worn warriors needed was distraction in the form of watching out for a senseless angel. "You will use this device again to speak with me?"

"I'll call." He grinned, a glint in his eye. "I wonder how Titus will deal with you."

"He is an archangel and I am an old and experienced angel who can assist him. We'll work well together."

Her son's laugh held a glee that had her narrowing her eyes, but she allowed him his mischief, deeply content to see joy fill him to the brim once more.

Sharine saw nothing much of note in the first hour that she flew beyond Lumia. That wasn't surprising—though Lumia's lands stopped well before the hour mark, her troops flew that far regularly to stay in fighting shape and maintain their endurance.

In the ordinary scheme of things, they knew never to

interfere with Charisemnon's people, but Sharine had made the decision to breach that rule when the reborn began to spread across Africa—she'd ordered her warriors to quietly eliminate any reborn threats they saw. The shambling creatures who'd reached this far north had been small in number and soon dispatched.

Charisemnon had been too focused on his battle with Titus to pay attention.

The true scars appeared a half hour or so beyond that perimeter. A small village lay half in ruins, a large central area burned to blackened beams and collapsed roofs. Wanting to understand what had taken place there, she did a careful circle above the dead silence to ensure she wasn't dropping down into danger.

Only when she was certain she saw no movement, no indication of anything living below, did she come down in the center of the long, wide road that seemed to be the heart of the village. Her position gave her an excellent view in all directions; she'd rapidly spot any reborn who might be scuttling toward her.

However, the only things moving in the charred landscape were pieces of fabric that might've once been curtains, tiny flags in the light wind. Perhaps this village had fallen prey to the battle between the two archangels. But no, that could not be. The fighting had taken place far from here, near what had been the north/south border.

Then she saw the red can tumbled on the ground, recognized it as the same type of can she'd seen the people of her town use to carry fuel. Once she began to search, she saw the other cans. Many had rolled away from whatever had been their original position, likely pushed or blown out by the storm of fire, but there was no hiding their widespread nature.

The fuel had been carefully dispersed to burn this place down.

A chill in her blood, she headed toward a large, blackened building that might've once functioned as a school or community hall. She took extreme care; she had no wish to make herself a victim of the reborn. She might be old and thus difficult to kill, but she wouldn't survive decapitation—and, according to Tanicia, recent updates from the border had the creatures hunting in packs.

Again, however, she heard only a silence piercing in its intensity.

She didn't know what she'd expected when she looked through the narrow gap created by the shattered and half-fallen wall of the large building . . . but it wasn't bones. So many bones. Horror struck her at the thought of all who had died within; wondering if she should attempt to find a way to get deeper inside, unearth more answers, she looked down.

Just inside, shadowed by the way the wall had fallen, lay a hand that had somehow become mummified by the inferno, the skin a shiny and unnatural hue and the flesh long melted away. Like a piece of meat smoked too long. Its fingers bore sharp clawlike nails blackened from the smoke. She frowned. Perhaps it was simply her perspective, but the claws appeared oddly elongated.

But no, it wasn't perspective because even when she twisted into the gap to look as closely as possible from her awkward position, the sense of odd dimensions remained. This individual's finger and hand bones were . . . stretched. Spidery.

This wasn't a vampire's hand. As far as she was aware, the reborn, too, didn't look like this. They had the correct proportions of the mortals from whom they were created. Thankfully, Africa hadn't had to deal with the black-eyed dead Lijuan had made of her people. Those black-eyed ones had died with their liege in any case. However, it *was* possible the reborn had begun to mutate. If all within the hall were like this one, then perhaps the burning had been an act of self-protection.

Remembering something Illium had said to her, she stepped back out of the gap, then retrieved the device he'd given her. The phone. He'd told her it could record images. Given the desultory attention she'd paid at the time, it took her five long minutes to work out how, but then she took a careful set of images and recordings to show Titus.

It could be that he'd seen similar corpses many times by now, but that was no reason for her not to be vigilant. Putting the phone safely back into a zippered pocket of the backpack, she walked around the building to see if she could get inside without stepping on bones and finally found a path.

Most of the bones she saw near that area were brittle and disarticulated—no clawed fingers like the earlier one. And there was no way she could get to the original body without having to break walls. She made the decision to leave it. This place was desolate and forgotten. No one would disturb it in the interim.

The eerie silence of the village whispered after her as she made her way to an empty area, then spread her wings and took off. The wind created by her wings disturbed the dust on the ground and for a moment she was almost certain she saw movement. But when she looked again, it was to see a crumpled bit of discarded paper coming to a rolling stop.

No, there.

A striped hyena, thin and light of feet, prowled in the shadows.

Concern heavy in her blood, and unwilling to abandon any survivors to starvation or attack by emboldened natural predators, she did another sweep over the village, going low enough to spot any hint of life. Nothing. No breaths in the air. No hands reaching for help. At last, she flew on, accompanied by a solitary black-winged kite that broke off its flight when it sighted prey on passing grasslands. She saw more damage as she continued on, more abandoned settlements, but nothing like that first one.

Then she began to see the places where people still lived—the cities were too quiet, with tense groups of winged and ground-based guards at the borders, many holding bulky weapons she didn't recognize. Too few people moved in the streets and fire damage was black streaks in the landscape around each city.

As if its people had protected their home with a fortress of fire.

More than one guard spotted her along the way, but it was at the second city she overflew that a battle-hardened warrior with what appeared to be a badly broken arm flew up to talk to her. "Lady Hummingbird," he said on reaching her, the dark skin of his face marked by patches of pink where his skin had either been burned, or shredded by reborn claws. "The landscape is not safe."

Raphael's Elena would no doubt be irritated at being spoken to with such protective care, but Elena was a warrior through and through and had earned her stripes. To this angelic commander, Sharine remained the broken Hummingbird. He had the right to question if she brought more problems to his city, whether he'd have to now offer her an escort.

"I am aware," she said with conscious gentleness, having caught the lines of pain around his eyes. Simply because angels healed quicker than mortals didn't mean the healing didn't hurt. "I fly to Titus, and I'm taking care not to land anywhere except on empty stretches of land that offer total visibility."

An easing of the tension across his shoulders. "Do not land after dark unless it's in a city or a town with plans of protection. That's when the creatures are most active—though please don't let that make you complacent in the sunlight. When they're hungry enough, they do not care about being caught in the light."

"I thank you for the information." She took in his city

again. "You are few in number." A sense of emptiness permeated the landscape.

"We lost many in the war." Flat, tired words. "Others fell to the reborn."

Sharine knew without asking that this warrior would never disparage his former archangel, but she heard the anger in his tone. "Do you wish me to take any news to Titus?"

When he hesitated, she said, "He is your archangel now. Past enmities do not matter, for such enmities are for the Cadre alone."

He searched her face. "Even for the soldiers and people of an enemy archangel who sought to annihilate his land?"

"When titans fight, they pay no attention to the minnows." A simple, brutal fact of life.

"Yes." A bow of his head before he gave her a report that she promised to pass on.

Then, after assuring him she had no need of an escort, she flew past the scorched edge of the city and beyond. If the cities had caused her concern, the isolated rural settlements devastated.

Entire houses were piles of blackened rubble and farm fields lay barren.

Vultures scavenged on the remains of dead domestic animals, while leopards prowled deadly close to a populace become weak and incapable of defending itself. The hunting cat would wait for the night hours to strike, but that it was so far outside its normal wild territory told her the reborn—with their urge to tear apart all living creatures—had done significant damage to the ecosystem.

In one village, the mortals and those few vampires who hadn't been called up to battle looked up with tired eyes that widened when she changed her path and came in to land. Bedraggled, lines of exhaustion carved into their thin faces, the people bowed deeply to her. "Lady," they said. "We are honored."

She didn't know if they said that because they felt it, or

simply because it was expected. It didn't matter to her. She wasn't here to be praised or feted. "Does Titus know of your state?" she asked, spotting the bones pushing against the dark gold skin of a child who was hiding behind his mother.

The villager who'd spoken first, an old woman who seemed to be the elder, swallowed hard. "We wouldn't concern the archangel with our small problems. Not when the eaters of the living roam the landscape."

Sharine could understand her reticence, but as with the angelic warrior, she had the feeling there was more to this. These people had belonged to another archangel their entire lives, and likely also believed that Titus would begrudge them their earlier loyalty.

Such a thing was not possible—and it had nothing to do with Titus himself.

In truth, humans rarely featured in the thoughts of archangels. One of the Cadre would no more blame humans for their archangel's behavior than they would blame a pet cat. A harsh thought but that was the way of so many of the most powerful of her kind.

Raphael was different, but only because he had a consort who'd once been human—a consort who refused to forget her humanity even as she walked in the world of immortals. Without Elena, Sharine didn't believe even Raphael would see mortals and young vampires as anything other than expendable pieces on a chessboard.

Sharine had been the same . . . and always different. Same in that she didn't pay much mind to mortals, her life lived on the immortal plane and among their places. But different in that when she *had* come across mortals, she'd treated them as simply a short-lived species, no more or less worthy than angelkind.

Her beliefs had changed in the time since she'd taken oversight of Lumia. Now she knew humans as individuals. Now she looked forward to the shy, lopsided smile of Kareem, the stall owner who always offered her fresh mint tea. Now she had a favorite among the innocent, mischievous children who followed her in the streets. Now she began to understand why her son had mourned so when he lost his human lover.

Those memories were tangled in her mind, but she remembered his sadness. Sadness so deep and true that it had penetrated her madness with the efficacy of a sharpened blade. Her boy was not naturally a being of sorrow, his laughter the soundtrack of his childhood for her. So she had noticed when he stopped laughing, when he stopped getting that glint in his eye that meant mischief and play. It had returned eventually, but altered in a subtle way.

His loss had left a scar that would live forever in his heart.

She thought she had held him then, rocked him in her arms as she'd done when he was a babe. She hoped that was a true memory and not a figment of her broken mind. She liked to think that she'd been there for him not only then, but at the other dark events in his life.

His small heart had first broken when his father left them. Though Sharine's mind had fractured at the moment of Aegaeon's calculated cruelty—not because he'd left, but because of *how*—she still retained fragments of memory from that time. One of the strongest was of squeezing her little boy close and murmuring to him that it would be all right.

But it hadn't been all right. She hadn't been strong enough. That her boy loved her still was the greatest gift of her life. Often, children strove to be like their parents, but Sharine would strive to be like her son: an honorable, kind angel who saw mortals and did not ever think them lesser.

"I will speak to Titus," she promised the villagers. "He isn't an archangel who would have his people starve. In the interim, I'll ask my people to bring you food." Lumia and the township had their own growing fields and internal storage areas, and those had escaped all harm.

She'd ask Farah to lead the mercy drops, to distribute as much as was safe without putting the township at risk. Immortals could survive a long time without food, but mortals had far less leeway. "Do not despair. Our land has undergone a devastating war, but it'll rise stronger and grow into a beautiful jewel once more."

Eyes bright, the people bowed low and deep, saying, "Thank you, Lady."

It disturbed her, the shining hope in those eyes. They didn't know to whom they bowed. They had no knowledge of the fractures inside her. And they didn't hear the fear that whispered constantly in her ear: *You are broken. You are mad. You will fail. And you will fall.*

8

Avelina, your son does you proud. Barely half-grown, yet he has no fear of an archangel. Did you know he challenged me to a duel?

I stake my claim now—he will come to my court after he is of age. I'll ensure your Titus is taught by the best of the best as he grows into his warrior spirit, as I did for the twins. And if I do my task right, he'll wish to stay with me in the years to come. I would be lucky indeed to have both you and your children by my side in battle.

—Letter from Archangel Alexander to
First General Avelina

9

Titus had just come in from the field, the dawn sun rising in a glory of orange-red, when one of his sentries sent back the message that Lady Sharine had—at long last—been sighted at the city border.

Groaning, he looked down at his blood-and-grime-splattered clothing, thought of his swords that needed to be cleaned, and just threw up his hands. There really was no point in trying to tidy himself up—it'd be more of an insult if he didn't turn up to welcome her when he was at the citadel and not out fighting reborn.

Striding out the huge doors that flowed from his personal living area—doors he mostly kept open—he stepped onto his balcony, then took off. In the massive courtyard below, his people toiled, exhausted but devoted. Some were coming in, some going out, while another section dealt with the animals.

Still another group was sorting the weapons that had been brought in damaged or broken by the teams out in the field. Beside them worked the mechanics whose task it was to keep the vampiric troops' heavy-duty vehicles maintained and ready to take hit after hit from the reborn.

The rotting creatures had yesterday succeeded in acting together to tip over one of the vehicles, but the vampire fighters within had survived because the vehicle was built like a tank. It also helped that they'd had flamethrowers on hand to fry any reborn who tried to crawl through the cracked glass of the windscreen.

The other glass, all of it toughened, had held.

The dull murmur of voices, the clang of weapons and the noise of the engines, the snuffing of the horses, it was familiar music that meant home. But he couldn't rest this morn, couldn't share a mug of ale with his people or just sit in the courtyard and clean weapons to wind down from a night of battle against the reborn. Groaning again at what awaited, he angled his wings and headed out beyond the bustle of his city and toward the northern border.

The sky blazed around him, red and pink and dazzling shades of orange. He loved this landscape and he loved the colors of the sky. He'd been Archangel of Southern Africa some thousand six hundred years and he would swear that each and every sunrise and sunset was different, was unique.

Yet despite the show of glory, he still saw the glint of a far different color in the distance, the indigo of the Hummingbird's distinctive wings caressed by light—as if the sun itself was in love with her ethereal beauty.

Wings beating hard because there was no breeze today, no thermal to ride, he quickly closed the distance between them. The sooner he got to her, the sooner he could do away with the formalities, and have the bath he craved. But his forced smile of welcome turned into a black scowl as he brought himself to a polite hover a short distance away.

She wasn't wearing her customary gown, and her hair was not only covered with dust, but in a braid that dropped over one shoulder. She was, in fact, in black pants and a light brown tunic not so different from his own garb—though he'd long done away with the tunic.

And while the straps that crisscrossed his chest were part of his sword harness, one hilt visible over his left shoulder, the other over his right, it looked like her straps attached to some type of pack.

The Hummingbird was wearing pants and carrying a pack.

He blinked.

Had he not known better, he'd have thought her a young angel out for the day. Perhaps even a warrior, though she was a little too slender to pull that off, no real muscle to her. Like most of the pretty beings in what the people within it chose to call the "gentle court," and he saw as the tender heart of his warrior stronghold.

"Lady Hummingbird!" he boomed, then winced, because he'd *told* himself not to use his proper voice. The last thing he needed was for her to get the vapors and fall out of the sky. That would be wonderful. Then Raphael would be angry with him because he'd managed to insult and pain the mother of one of Raphael's cherished Seven, and no doubt the rest of angelkind would think him an ogre.

But the Hummingbird didn't drop from the sky like a small, startled bird. Instead, she came to hover across from him, a soft smile curving her lips. It struck him at that instant that she was beautiful, stunningly so. Shrugging off that errant thought because this was the Hummingbird and not a woman, he bowed slightly.

Yes, he was an archangel, but the Hummingbird existed outside the hierarchy of angelkind as far as he was concerned. He'd seen her work, been absorbed by it to the extent that he'd hunted down a piece for his own rooms. The person who created such transcendence, the person who had within them such grace, was to be treated with utmost respect.

"Archangel Titus," she said with a bow of her own. "I see I have come at a bad time."

He winced inwardly, wondering at the level of insult she'd taken. "I've just come in from battle," he said. "The reborn have taken strong hold in this landscape. Charisemnon, that pestilent piece of . . . er, rotted meat," he substituted instead of "excrement," "worked with Lijuan to create a stronger, more intelligent strain before he died."

"Yes, I have heard many such reports on my journey here," she said in a voice so rich with texture it felt like a tactile caress. Titus had a weakness for music and art and she was the embodiment of both. Too bad she was also the Hummingbird and the entire angelic world would be insulted beyond repair should he invite her to share his blankets.

He was insulted beyond repair on her behalf at his own base thoughts. The Hummingbird had long risen above all that, and he was—what was the word one of his sisters had used a few centuries ago?—yes, he was a cad for even thinking of her in such a carnal way.

"I saw much during my flight," she said. "I would share that information with you. I think you and your people haven't had a chance to fully survey the rural edges of Charisemnon's territory."

Titus gave a small nod. "I'd be grateful for any new information." He didn't expect much in terms of martial details, for the Hummingbird had probably focused on the artistic merit of various things, but still, perhaps she'd picked up a relevant piece or two of information by accident. "I welcome you to my court, Lady Hummingbird."

A tightness to her face, but her voice remained pure velvet as she said, "It will become tiresome if we are both constantly formal with one another. Please call me Sharine, and if you do not disagree, I shall call you Titus."

Titus almost scowled before he caught himself, his shoulders bunching. It didn't feel right to call her anything but Lady Hummingbird, but he'd make the attempt since that was her preference. As for himself, she could call him whatever she liked. The Hummingbird had such rights.

"As you prefer, La—Sharine." He shook out the tension in his shoulders. "If you'll follow me, I'll lead you to my citadel. We'll sit and have a meal together, though I'm afraid you'll have to wait until after I bathe." He wanted to slap himself—what did he think he was doing, talking about *bathing* to a woman so genteel and refined?

"That is as well," she murmured as they fell into flight side by side. "I'm dusty from my long journey and will need to clean up, too."

Exhaling because that had worked out better than he'd expected, he said, "We expected you two days ago." He'd been concerned enough when she hadn't arrived some days after leaving Lumia that he'd contacted Raphael to ask if Illium had heard from his mother. "Your son assured me that you were safe and on the way else I would've dispatched my people to look for you."

"I should've sent word." A gracious apology in her tone. "I decided to take several detours to check on the status of settlements on either side of my main route. I saw some disturbing things and didn't wish to rush here when I could bring you useful information instead."

Grooves forming in his forehead, Titus glanced sideways at the Hummingbird before quickly looking away. He didn't want her to catch him staring at her, but this woman was *not* behaving at all like the Hummingbird of whom he'd heard. Everyone in angelkind knew the great and gifted artist spent more time in a world of her own making than she did the real one.

The woman currently speaking to him, however, sounded more like one of his intelligence agents. Cool. Calm. Collected. The only significant difference was the richness of her voice, the tones filled with a depth of emotion. But, strange behavior or not, it could not be an imposter.

There was only one individual in all of angelkind who possessed wings of indigo brushed with light and eyes of a shade so pale and golden that they were like captured pieces of the first rays of dawn. This was most assuredly the Hummingbird.

"I haven't seen so much activity my entire flight here," she said as they flew closer to the citadel.

Narja bustled around that fortress of stone and light, his people choosing to live close to their archangel. It was a source of pride for Titus, that the people he ruled came toward him instead of going outward. Even the ones based in other parts of the territory tended to cluster around the senior angels in the area. It was quite different from the way his dead enemy's land was laid out—Charisemnon's people had not hugged close to their leadership.

"Anyone not able-bodied enough to help with the reborn scourge is assisting with the rebuild," Titus said with considerable pride. "Whether that means holding a paintbrush in the hour they're permitted out of the infirmary, or acting as teachers of craft even if their own limbs are shattered.

"My city took considerable damage in the war, close as it is to the border." Scarlet fire burned his blood at the memory of how he'd permitted Charisemnon too close. His snake of an enemy had worn the mask of an ally, choosing cunning over honor. Death was too good for him, but it was all the satisfaction Titus would ever get.

"I didn't realize your city had so much glass and steel. It reminds me of my son's home but for the lack of towers that scrape the sky."

"Narja stands up against any of New York's temptations," he said, chest puffing up. "We boast far more green spaces for one, and as for the towers—that's a consequence of being a border city. The higher the building, the bigger the target." As a result, the city's buildings were constructed to not provide easy sightlines to the enemy, as the roads were designed to be confusing to the eye from above.

Noticing the Hummingbird's wing muscles had begun to droop, he subtly lowered his speed. "My only regret is that you do not see my city in its full glory." He had physically helped build the citadel that was the center of it, had even dug a garden or two that would normally be brilliant with color.

"It's a place with heart, that I can tell regardless." Angling her body to take in another part of his city, she said, "Are you aware that your ability to move the earth has created massive cracks in the earth that continue to creep farther inward? At one village, I was told that the gorge approaching them has advanced by half a foot per day—such a speed has them scrambling to relocate."

He scowled, for he didn't like to think of mortals afraid and alone because of the outcome of an immortal war. It was brutal reality when archangels fought, but he'd never been at peace with such a consequence; his mother had taught him that the strong protected the weak.

"My scholars have been studying the advance and they tell me it should stop soon, as the energy in the earth runs out." His Cascade power to cause earth tremors had helped him defeat his enemy, but as with all archangelic gifts to be born out of that unpredictable confluence of time and power, it had more than one facet.

He'd been uncertain that he retained the ability when the Cascade ended with a sudden finality, taking with it much of what it bestowed. In the end, it turned out that he could still affect the earth, but at a tenth of the capacity he'd possessed during the height of the Cascade. Given what he was hearing about the others in the Cadre and the powers with which they'd emerged from the Cascade, it was a fair enough trade-off. They'd all lost something and retained something.

"That is good news," the Hummingbird said. "I'm glad you continue to give your scholars room to work. It must've been tempting to haul them into the battle against the reborn."

He decided not to take insult, for there was a grain of truth in her supposition. "I have been Cadre long enough to have learned to think for the future. Well I know that my scholars' greatest weapon is their collective brain and not their sword arms.

"All but for one—Ozias is a warrior-scholar and she is my spymaster, her task to gather intelligence about the state of the territory. But she is only one angel doing a mammoth task. I thank you for the information you've brought me." Unexpected though it was from a woman known for her penchant of living in a dreamworld.

"You fight a difficult battle, Titus. I offer what assistance I can."

Spotting the increasing dip in her wings, he chose against giving her an overview of the citadel. "We'll land on the balcony outside your suite," he said. "It's near mine so you can access me at any time should you have any need." That wasn't quite true. He'd be out in the field more often than not. But it seemed like the sort of thing an archangel should at least *say* when the Hummingbird stayed in his home.

It wasn't anything he'd ever before had to consider. With the entire gentle court sent to safety prior to the beginning of the war, he had no one soft and sweet left on his staff to handle such things. Elia, six-hundred-year-old vampire and foster mother—by choice—of the orphaned children who lived in Titus's court, would've no doubt managed it all with smiling joy, Titus none the wiser of the work involved.

He wasn't a complete dullard in such things, however— there was a reason he'd offered Elia a position as senior courtier. She might be kind of heart and prone to dressing in frothy fashions while putting enormous amounts of cosmetic colors on her face, but she also gave his steward a run for his money when it came to dealing with problematic or touchy guests.

However, his steward was currently using his sword arm against the reborn, and Elia was on an offshore island with her charges; he'd had to pull people from other duties to ready things for his guest.

The only positive?

Members of his household staff were so honored by the Hummingbird's visit that they hadn't minded pulling double shifts to pretty up a suite for her while not falling away from their usual duties—whether that be repairing weapons or feeding the troops or a million other critical tasks.

After landing on the balcony and ensuring the clearly exhausted Hummingbird got down safely, he pushed aside the gauzy curtains of the open doors—to see soft, curving feminine furniture and vases full of fresh flowers. Thanks be to the ingenuity of his people; he had absolutely no idea where they'd found those blooms.

"I hope this will suit," he said modestly after they'd both stepped inside—but the modesty was for show; he was very conscious his people had done well and deserved all the praise she would bestow.

Expression tight, she looked around. "I didn't expect you to go to this trouble." A tone to her voice that, on any other woman, he would've described as an edge. But this was the Hummingbird. Perhaps she was displeased about some small element of the room.

Having known more than enough contrary women over his lifetime, beginning with his mother and sisters, Titus decided to leave well enough alone and didn't ask her what was wrong. "My staff is honored by your presence and wished to make you welcome."

Features softening, she inclined her head. "I'm deeply grateful for their care."

"I'll be sure to pass that on." Titus wasn't a man to steal praise that wasn't his to take. "I made sure to remind them to set up an art studio for you," he said with justifiable pride, and pointed upward. "You'll find stairs just beyond the half wall to the right—at the end of the climb is a room full of light set up with an easel and art supplies." He had no idea where his people had sourced any of those things, either.

When the Hummingbird said nothing in response to his

magnanimous gesture, he decided to take his leave. Could be this was one of those moments where she existed out of time. Though . . . for an ethereal being, her jaw appeared unnaturally rigid and he could swear that her shoulders were bunched.

No, he had to be imagining it; the Hummingbird was beyond such things. Beyond anger, beyond petty grievances. The Hummingbird was a being special and gentle, a being who needed care and was to be handled as you would a fragile, broken bird.

10

Sharine glared at the wide sweep of Titus's back as he strode out of the room, shutting the door behind himself. It was as well that he'd left because she might've otherwise given in to the urge to pick up the small vase on the table next to her and throw it at his head. And what exactly would that have achieved? *Nothing.*

Titus—a warrior tired from constant battle—had done nothing but be kind and treat her as he no doubt believed she expected to be treated. As a fragile artist who needed beauty and softness around her and could not be expected to cope with harsh reality.

Well, was that not who you were for centuries?

It was a slap hard and stinging from a part of her that had woken when *she'd* woken, a part that was brutally honest and had no time for self-pity—or for misdirected anger.

Sharine winced.

How could she expect Titus to treat her as anything but

a delicate, breakable butterfly when that was all she'd ever shown the world?

She and the Archangel of Africa hadn't known each other when she was still herself—and even then, she'd been slightly out of time, a wounded bird who'd never quite found her wings. This Sharine, the one she was now, a mature woman shaped by loss and hurt and pain and anger and a fierce love for her son, she was someone Sharine herself was still getting to know. She couldn't expect Titus to divine her new state of being.

Still, she scowled at the curvy velvet sofa, the lush bouquets of flowers, and—when she opened the wardrobe—the floaty and superbly impractical gowns within. Not only had a member of his overworked staff wasted time in getting all this together, it was clear that no one—from the archangel down to his most junior member of staff—expected her to dirty her hands.

Titus's people were ready to take on another burden at a time when they needed every bit of help they could get. Making a sound low in her throat that startled her with its feral nature, she kicked the door of the wardrobe and was satisfied by the loud sound. Then she took off her backpack and removed the clothing items within.

Luckily, she'd stopped near a stream the previous night. She'd needed time alone, and so had stayed away from any settlement, but she hadn't been foolish. She'd chosen an area with a wide-open landscape where nothing and no one could sneak up on her. While there, she hadn't slept, for she'd done so the previous night and an angel of her age didn't need as much sleep as the young. Instead, she'd simply rested her wings and done a few small chores. Including washing out her second set of clothing.

It had reminded her of when she'd first left her familial home. Most fledglings were nudged out of the nest at a hundred years of age. In mortal terms, angels were about eighteen in maturity and growth by then, ready to take up training or further studies or to go exploring.

Sharine's parents had asked her to spread her wings when she was eighty years of age. "We're old, child," they'd said to her. "We want to make sure you are settled in the world before we surrender to the Sleep that whispers to us nightly."

Back then, Sharine had been scared—and also ashamed of her need for them to stay awake. Today, she felt a hot burst of anger. She was older than they'd ever been, and she would *never*, in a million years, walk into Sleep while her son was of an age where he needed her.

Is that not what you did when you walked into the kaleidoscope?

Flinching at the cutting words from the same part of her psyche that had delivered the earlier slap, she shrugged off the wave of shame that threatened. All that would do was cripple her, make her useless. No, the time of shame was past; she had to stride into the future—and make people see her. See *Sharine*, and not the Hummingbird.

After stripping off her dirty clothing, she walked into the bathing chamber. It was as luxuriant as everything else in the suite, complete with scented soaps, plush towels, and other extravagances. She'd heard that Titus had a liking for art and soft, beautiful things—women included. From the look of him now, however, he wasn't bothering with any of that. He looked exactly what he was—a warrior who had little time for fripperies while his territory was overrun with vicious reborn.

Teeth gritted, she bathed quickly then was annoyed at herself for automatically picking up the bottle of lotion afterward. But that was a habit too ingrained to shun and since his people had made the effort to provide for her with such care, she slathered her body in the silky cream scented softly with a flower she couldn't name, before heading out into the bedroom and pulling on her blue-gray tunic and dark brown pants.

Having washed her hair the previous night, she simply brushed it out, then pulled it back into a tight tail at the back of her head. Again, when she looked in the mirror, she saw a fresh-faced young woman looking back at her. Only her eyes gave her away. They were *old*, telling of the life she'd lived . . . and not lived.

Gut tight, she turned away, her hand going to her right wrist, where she wore a bracelet that Illium had sent her from New York. It was made of platinum metal, each of the links slender but strong; the heart that hung from one end bore not her name but his. It had made her laugh, because of course her mischievous boy would do this. She wore the gift with pride, her son's name, her son's love.

She deliberately didn't go up into the art room. It was an act of willpower on her part. Perhaps Titus had done her a favor there after all—he'd placed her drug of choice within reach and now she'd have to resist temptation each time she was in this suite, thus building her strength of will.

She'd spoken to Keir, an angelic healer, not long before she'd come to Lumia, right when she'd begun to find her way out of the kaleidoscope. It was Caliane who'd urged her to do so. "If I were badly wounded in battle," her friend had said, "I'd seek a healer and feel no disquiet in doing so. A wound of the mind is no different."

Keir had made time to spend near to an entire week with her. For some reason, she'd found herself telling the calm-eyed and slender healer all of it, digging right down to the heart of what Caliane had termed her wound.

"Aegaeon's actions impacted on brutal past trauma," Keir had said in his gentle way, this man who was one of the few in angelkind not very much taller than her own diminutive height. "Each event in our life leaves a mark—in your case, two critical events left deep fractures in the same part of your psyche. Those fractures compounded into a break when Aegaeon chose to take an action that I, as a man, as a healer, as a lover, cannot comprehend."

Keir wasn't one to exhibit intense emotion—at least to his patients. He tended to be a haven of calm. But his brown eyes had held a wealth of darkness when he'd said, "You retreated into what you knew best in order to heal. You can't blame yourself for that instinctive action."

Sharine accepted that Aegaeon had acted with unwarranted vindictiveness. To this day, she didn't know why—as vulnerable as she'd been then, to charm of a kind she'd never experienced in her mostly solitary and quiet existence. Aegaeon had overwhelmed her; she'd wanted desperately to cling to him—and that was on her and the ghosts that haunted her—but in actual fact, she *hadn't*.

He'd kept his harem, kept his life away from her and Illium in the Refuge.

Sharine hadn't attempted to clip his wings, hadn't sought to alter the core of his nature, content with the scraps of affection he threw her way.

How foolish she'd been, how hungry for connection.

But it all added up to a single conclusion: he'd had no reason to strike out. Not only at her but at her son. *Their* son. Forget what he'd done to her, it would've cost him nothing to have gone to Illium and hugged him good-bye. It would've taken but a sliver of his time to tell their boy that his father was going to Sleep for a period, but that he loved him and would return.

Such things mattered to a child, mattered deeply.

For breaking their bright, beautiful boy's small heart, Sharine would never forgive him. *Never.* Even if she lived to the end of time and beyond.

No one hurt her child.

Hand fisting at her side, her nails digging into her skin, she opened the door of the suite and stepped out into the hallway. That hallway was wide and fell away onto a massive central core. Walking to the railingless edge, she looked down and realized that she was about three stories up in a huge citadel built of gray stone that was both martial and hard—and lovely.

Fine veins of minerals wove through the stone "bricks" and each piece of stone had gradations of color that caught her eye and had her running a hand over the nearest support pillar. It was warmer than she'd expected, the stone smooth from all the time it had stood here, all the warriors and others who had placed their hands against it.

It could've been a cold place, but the stone had a glowing heart, and against the walls of the central core hung tapestries lush with the life of this land. Huge works of art that she could stand in front of for hours, taking in detail by detail. But that was just the start. Above her curved a gently sloping ceiling on which had been painted a night sky sparkling with the stars she'd see if she looked up after darkfall.

Each star, she realized suddenly, was a dazzling gemstone turned tiny by the distance.

Below her, meanwhile, was a buzz of constant movement.

Titus's people walked this way and that and crisscrossed over what looked to be a massive carpet in the colors of sunset that could've come from Morocco. Perhaps during a time prior to the warlike tension between Titus and Charisemnon. Most of those she saw wore weathered and bloodied warrior gear, including more than one angel in full, lightweight armor that wouldn't impede them in the sky.

But she also spotted one angel and two vampires who looked to be in the livery of household staff, the colors rich gold and deepest brown. Titus's colors. They were rushing, their faces hot and sweat dampening their hair.

Sharine had the terrible feeling it was because of her.

"You are ready!" The heavy boom of sound didn't startle her; she'd heard Titus's door open and close.

Annoyed at his tone and in no mood to hide it, she said, "You sound surprised."

He looked taken aback, all big shoulders and heavy muscle under a pair of brown pants that hugged his thighs, and a white shirt with a rounded collar and an opening that came to partway down his breastbone, the swirling golden tattoo she'd glimpsed earlier now concealed.

He'd folded back the sleeves of his shirt to reveal heavily muscled forearms, his skin a dark, *dark* brown with a richness of depth. Wings of golden honey and cream arched over his shoulders, his control a master class in warrior discipline.

Droplets of water glinted in his closely cut black curls.

He was a beautiful man. But Sharine had no time for beautiful men. One of them had ruined her life. Yes, she had a beautiful man for a son and an equally beautiful man for a protégé, but that was beside the point. Aodhan and Illium— and yes, Raphael, too—occupied a different sphere in her mind. She'd seen them as babies, kissed their skinned knees, smiled under their exuberant affection.

Every other beautiful man in the world could go jump in the molten heart of a volcano and she wouldn't care. That applied especially to the beautiful archangel who thought Sharine was an ornament, breakable and useless in his territory's desperate battle for survival.

"I know the ladies of my court often take their time," Titus ventured at last, his voice moderated to a lower volume that irritated her—did he think her so weak she couldn't even take his *voice*?

That was when his words penetrated: . . . *the ladies of my court* . . .

She hadn't heard that he kept a harem, but it wouldn't surprise her to be wrong. "Where are your ladies?"

"On a safe island." He sighed. "The entire gentle court

begs to come home but it isn't safe—and those of the gentle court wouldn't be happy here."

Bristling at the idea of the women being banished as if they were children, she said, "I've heard that the women of Astaad's harem are helping their people in the aftermath of war. Can not your 'gentle court' assist in the same way?"

Throwing back his head, Titus laughed, the sound echoing around the space, it was such a huge and joyous one. She found herself transfixed by him for a long moment. Forcefully shaking her head the instant she became aware of what she was doing, she looked once more at the floor below. People were smiling now, their cheeks creased and their steps lighter.

As if his warmth and happiness was contagious.

"The gentle court isn't only made up of women—and none bar one within it are warriors or administrators," Titus said when he finally stopped chuckling, then ruined what good he'd achieved by adding, "Elia is a woman of brilliance but her duty is to the court's children. The rest of her brethren are pampered creatures who'd faint at the sight of blood—and expire at a torn hem."

Sharine barely stopped herself from rolling her eyes. "Oh," she said gently.

His eyebrows drew together, the onyx of his eyes getting even darker. *"Oh?"* It came out a deep grumble, his wings flaring out then snapping shut.

She smiled, a heat in her blood that pushed at her to push him. "Where are we to eat? I'm hungry after my long journey."

Titus's wings . . . quivered. That was the only word she could use to describe the tiny motion that rippled through his tightly held wings. "Of course, Lady Sharine," he said in an obnoxiously formal tone, his voice modulated into a lower range.

Eyes narrowed, Sharine nonetheless kept her silence as

he stepped off the edge of the hallway, using his wings to initiate a controlled descent to the ground level. When she followed, she found herself the recipient of many smiles and bows, did her best to return them all.

None of these people had to suffer her bad temper simply because their archangel was a . . . what had one of the young ones in her court muttered recently? Ah yes, a blockhead. Sharine wasn't certain of the definition of that word, but if it meant what it sounded like it meant, then it was the perfect choice of word to describe her host.

"If you will accompany me." Titus's scent was clean and fresh next to her as he led her through a large and ornate hallway decorated with ancient artefacts and weapons, and into a spacious room awash with the morning sun as a result of the huge doors currently open to the outside air.

"I will close those if you wish," Titus said in that same—grating—formal tone. "I find I enjoy the sounds from the courtyard, but they might be overwhelming to someone used to quieter climes."

She felt like telling him she had a knife. It had been a gift from Raphael's Elena, one she'd found on her bedside table after Elena left Lumia prior to the war. With it had been a note: *I'd be honored if you'd accept this gift as a memory of the fun we had stabbing those targets. Also, you should keep up the stabbing practice—you have a rare natural balance when you throw the blade.*

Sharine had been delighted by the gift and the missive—and she *had* kept up the practice. Even Tanicia had remarked on her accuracy. She was no warrior, but she was accurate enough to teach a certain archangel a lesson about assuming anything when it came to Sharine. "This is fine," she said, leaving the knife strapped to her thigh, where she'd discovered she liked wearing it.

Walking to the central doors, she stepped out onto the edge of the central courtyard and into the warmth of morning. It had been cool inside the citadel, likely because of the stone with which it had been built, heavy and solid. Outside, the colors were shades of sun-gold and working brown, along with a pop of lush green from the fresh produce on a large cart.

A small specialized vehicle being operated by a young woman was in the process of ferrying the loaded cart toward what Sharine assumed were the kitchens. She'd seen such vehicles in New York, too, lifting pallets out of trucks, but couldn't recall their name just now.

Most of the courtyard was open space, to be used by Titus's warriors and other staff, and likely as the central location for the legendary parties Tanicia had mentioned Titus was known to throw in better times. But one corner housed the stables, and there were also a number of trees planted to the left, creating a shady haven where tired people sat down to rest and sleek cats prowled up for pets.

Motion was constant, angelic warriors landing or taking off while vampire—and possibly mortal—warriors drove in and out in rugged vehicles such as used by some of her own people. Each and every one of the fighters going out into the field bristled with weapons, from swords to unidentifiable modern devices.

The last time she'd been in a place this active, it had been Raphael's Tower.

Conscious of Titus's muscled bulk beside her, she went to ask him of the progress of the reborn eradication, when a female angel with dark red hair and two-toned wings—dark gray atop and white underneath—landed to Titus's right. "Sire," she said with a bow. "Lady Hummingbird."

"This is my troop-trainer, Tanae," Titus said, but his attention was obviously on the warrior. "What has occurred?"

"I received a report of a nest we might've missed inside the perimeter and went to check—the creatures were hiding in an abandoned grain cellar."

Titus hissed out a breath. "How many?"

"Ten. I took a squadron with me and we were able to clear the cellar. But, sire, the creatures appeared to have sent one of their kind out as bait. I believe they wanted us to spot it, their intent to launch a deadly ambush."

11

I didn't know the reborn were so intelligent," Sharine said, stunned at the idea the flesh-eating beings were able to think and plan to such a high degree.

"Only in Africa," Titus ground out. "Lijuan and Charisemnon were in the process of creating a new, more vicious strain. A feral intelligence is part of it—and it appears some groups of reborn may possess more than others."

His next words were directed at his troop trainer. "Do I need to go out there and sear the landscape?" Titus asked the woman whose features struck Sharine as oddly familiar.

Had Sharine painted her? She couldn't recall. But the flame of hair, the shape of the eyes, the dual-colored wings, she'd seen those before. It was on the tip of her tongue.

"No, the sludge was contained in the cellar, so we used fire to destroy it."

"Then take this time to rest." Titus slapped the woman on the shoulder. "I've just had a report from Ozias that she's seeing more daylight movement from the reborn. We might soon be fighting every hour of the day."

A bow of her head before Tanae took off . . . and it was then, in the flash of wings gray and white, that Sharine found her answer. "Galen," she murmured, her eyes filling with the image of an angelic warrior with choppily cut red hair and eyes of peridot green, his wings gray with white striations visible only in flight.

"Tanae and my second Tzadiq's son," Titus told her. "Galen was a commander in my forces before that pup Raphael stole him away." No humor in those words, but his grim expression had nothing to do with Galen's defection.

"This is what we're facing," he said almost to himself. "An endless surge of infection, mutation, and death. Charisemnon and Lijuan released something monstrous into our world."

In that moment, he was Titus, Archangel of Africa and member of the Cadre, responsibility a weight on his wide shoulders. "If the creatures are becoming more intelligent—"

A hard shake of his head. "You think we could communicate with them?" Deep lines bracketing his mouth, he said, "We tried. I have no desire to exterminate people if they simply have the bad luck to be infected with a disease." His muscles bunched taut under his skin as he folded his arms. "But the reborn's intelligence isn't even that of a hunting leopard. The leopard lies in wait for prey, pouncing and taking down its meal."

As if aware its larger feline brethren were under discussion, a cat with a dark yellow-orange coat and black spots, its ears pointed, padded over to rub its head against Titus's boot. Hunkering down, his pants stretching over his thighs, he scratched the cat behind the ears.

"But the leopard hunts to eat," he continued, "and to protect its territory. The reborn? Their sole purpose is to spread death—in no world can the reborn exist with any other species; the creatures maul and murder any living being that crosses their path, including animals." He looked up, his onyx eyes holding her prisoner. "The reborn are filled with the murderous desire of their original creator."

Lijuan, Archangel of the Dead . . . and a woman who'd sought to subjugate the entire world.

Rising to his feet in a flowing movement, Titus said, "Let's eat so I can get back to my duties." His voice was of an archangel giving an order.

Sharine had been in sympathy with him until then, but now her fingers twitched once more for her blade. Surely she began to understand why New York Tower's internal walls had holes that could only be explained by knives slamming into them. It must be most satisfying for Elena to throw such blades at Raphael's head when he acted the fool.

But Raphael would never dare speak to Elena so preemptively—he respected her as a fellow warrior. Titus, meanwhile, considered Sharine a broken bird he had to babysit. "I wouldn't want to keep you," she said in a voice that dripped with honey. "Please, take what you need and feel free to fly."

The look he gave her was a scowl mixed with pure befuddlement. An extraordinary expression to witness on the rough-hewn handsomeness of his face, but it quickly gave way to a calming smile. "You must be tired by the journey." Soothing words, the natural volume of his voice irritatingly modulated. "Come, a little food will be exactly what you need."

He was treating her like a fractious horse. She'd give him calm in a minute.

Spine taut, she waved off his offers of help and seated herself at the table, her wings falling gracefully to either side of the specially designed chairback. The table in front of them was set with sumptuous dishes—far too complicated a meal for a citadel that was fighting a deadly battle—and it just lit a fire under her already simmering temper.

Then Titus spoke. "I fear my cook was so excited by the

prospect of a formal meal after weeks of simply feeding everyone as fast as possible that it appears he let it go to his head." Loud, warm laughter, flowing over her like water. "Ah well, we shall eat richly this morn and so will anyone else in the citadel who manages to grab a plateful of this feast."

Temper dying under the warmth of the comment, Sharine held out her plate when he lifted a spoon as if to serve her from a dish. He put a huge portion on her plate. "I'm not an elephant," she muttered, and was suddenly acutely aware of her obvious irritation—it really wasn't like her to be so ungracious, but something about Titus kept setting her off.

"Fine." He picked up his plate. "We'll exchange plates. I'd have staff here for they are eager to serve you, but I thought we should talk in private this morn. I can remedy that with a single shout."

Glaring at him, she took his plate while handing him hers. Then she rose to her feet and lifted the lid off a vegetable dish. "As neither of us has lost both arms, I think we're capable of serving ourselves and each other." She placed a serving on his plate as well as her own. "Illium told me you were wounded in the battle against Charisemnon. You've healed?"

"Of course I have," he grumbled, but allowed her to put more food on his plate. "I'm an archangel."

Sharine's plate was more than full enough, but since Titus was over twice her size and was expending enormous amounts of energy on a daily basis, she dished him out more before taking her seat. They began to eat in silence, though she was aware of Titus sending her wary looks.

It pleased her.

No one was ever wary of the Hummingbird. She was meant to be lightness and gentleness and kindness and no threat at all. All that was part of her nature, it was true. But *Sharine* was part of the Hummingbird, too, and a long time ago, Sharine had been far more than an artist with her head in the clouds.

It had been so very long ago, eons before Titus had existed even as a mote in the universe, but the memories had begun to awaken with her return to the real world. She remembered things others had long forgotten or never known . . . except for Caliane.

"Do you remember Akhia-Solay?" Caliane had asked her in one of their final conversations before her friend left to fight Lijuan. "I wonder if he'll wake this Cascade."

Sharine hadn't had any personal memories of the Sleeping Ancient then, the veil yet fading, but it had come to her as she flew across the African landscape, the long flight nudging loose memories of other such flights.

Once, after Raan and long, long before Aegaeon—so long that Akhia-Solay was a myth to even most angels—Sharine had flown with a general as his army's battle historian, the artist who made frantic sketches to add to angelkind's histories. She'd also—she glanced down at her hand, caught in the fragments of memory. At some point, she'd faced an enemy combatant . . . and she'd . . .

"You're displeased with the meal?" Titus's big voice snapped her back to the present, the past fading back where it belonged but for the echoes of knowledge it left behind.

"What?" Looking down at her plate, she saw that she'd stopped eating. "No, not at all. It's all delicious. I must compliment your chef."

"Cook," Titus corrected. "He is adamant that he will quit on the spot if anyone dares call him a chef."

"I'll take care not to anger him." She paid attention to what she was eating, savoring the tastes and textures and scents. Food was another thing she'd allowed to fade from her life in her time in the fog. She'd eaten, but had tasted none of it, her mind distanced.

Only after she'd cleared her plate did she look at Titus again. He was smiling at her. That smile was . . . devastating.

No wonder many of her warriors sighed when talking about him. Though he seemed to take only women as lovers, that didn't stop all and sundry from pining after him. Truly, the adulation went some way toward explaining his high opinion of himself.

"Here." He held out a dish she'd particularly enjoyed.

She hadn't realized he'd been paying close attention. "Thank you," she said, a touch of heat under her skin. "I'm full for now."

Putting down the dish, Titus leaned back in his chair and ran both hands over his head. He seemed about to say something, when a warrior with dust-covered wings that might've been white when clean dropped down outside the doors and yelled, "Sire! Massive reborn nest sighted just beyond the new barriers! They're awake and climbing!"

Titus moved so fast she'd have thought it impossible for such a big man if she hadn't seen it happen. He was outside and taking off before she'd even gotten out of her chair. Heart thunder, she raced after him to see multiple squadrons take to the sky, all of them arrowing southward. Heavy-duty vehicles painted in camouflage colors screeched out of the courtyard at the same time.

When a young and slender warrior dropped next to her, his skin ebony, his eyes a pale brown, his hair twined into falling locs decorated with wooden beads, and his wings a spread of black dusted with green, she said, "You're not with the squadrons?"

"I'm to be your guide here, my Lady Hummingbird," he said with a deep bow, and though he attempted to hide his misery, he was too young—barely beyond a hundred if she was any judge—to succeed. "I am Obren, the newest member of the sire's forces."

And so he'd been given the unenviable task of babysitting Sharine. "Call me Lady Sharine," she said first of all; she'd prefer Sharine alone, but knew the child would expire on the spot should she suggest it.

He already appeared a touch green around the gills at having to say her actual name. "Lady Sharine," he croaked out at last.

"Is there any danger in my flying behind the squadrons?" She had no wish to be a distraction, but while she was tired, she wasn't so tired that she couldn't spend some time in the air getting a firsthand look at what was occurring. She hadn't flown all this way to sit back and do nothing, and the first thing she needed was information.

Only then could she know what she might do to assist.

The boy's head jerked up, his mouth falling open before he snapped it shut. "My lady, the sire was very firm in his order that you're to remain within the bounds of the citadel."

Deciding she truly would kick Titus at the first opportunity, Sharine smiled . . . and was rather delighted to see Obren blink. It appeared the steel growing inside her had shown on her face. "Titus is not my sire," she pointed out with conscious gentleness, for it wasn't this youngling's fault that his archangel was a numbskull. "You can come with me or I'm happy to go alone." They both knew he'd never attempt to physically detain her.

Gulping, he shifted on his feet. "If—if you stay in the air at a height beyond the reach of the reborn, then I can't see the risk." Another swallow. "The creatures have torn angels apart when those angels have been wounded and landed into a nest. The new variant work in packs and swarm so fast that if an angel is alone when they fall . . ."

Sharine touched the boy's shoulder, overcome by maternal affection. "I'll be careful. I have no desire to either distract the fighters or suffer such torture at reborn hands."

Face pinched, but clearly knowing he had no choice, the boy said, "I will lead you to the right location."

"I'll tell Titus this was my decision," Sharine assured him.

A glum look. "Oh, the archangel won't blame me. He thinks I'm an infant yet, still wobbly on my legs."

Hiding her smile, she said, "Let us fly."

They took off together, and Sharine saw at once that she didn't need a guide. Dust flew up into the air some distance beyond the city limits as Titus's forces engaged with the reborn. As she flew closer, she also understood why there was so much dust—large swaths of grasses, trees, and other plants had been destroyed by angelic fire.

Today, the winged fighters were mostly staying above, firing down at the reborn using inborn angelic power—or weapons that spouted fire. Ah, those were the very weapons she'd seen in the cities on her way here. The vampiric fighters hadn't yet reached the site, but she glimpsed several pairs of angelic wings on the ground.

Including Titus's honey-gold and cream.

Heart thundering, she didn't understand why he'd land into danger until she saw him throw a bolt of energy into a hole in a small hillside—a bare bump in the landscape. The power exploded the hillside, throwing out stomach-churning pieces of reborn flesh along the way. That was when she realized the use of the word nest was deliberate and specific. These creatures were clumping together under the earth.

"Tunnels!" Obren shouted, pointing down at a ripple of power traveling back along the way Sharine had flown. As if through a burrow.

Roaring, Titus lifted fisted hands.

The ground bucked, then cracked, exposing a long hollow stuffed with reborn. Some were dead, but too many were yet alive, their eyes red and their claws ripping into each other as they scrambled to escape.

Blood cold, Sharine turned to Obren. "How far do these tunnels go?"

Her young guide's voice was shaky as he said, "This, we haven't seen before, Lady Sharine. They make nests but they have never before created burrows. These could go underneath the barriers we've built to protect the cleared zones, all the way back into the city."

Understanding his terror, Sharine thought quickly. "Titus

and the squadrons are busy dealing with the reborn here."
This nest appeared to be massive. "Let us fly back toward
the city and see if we can spot possible danger. We can also
alert the vampiric teams as well as the guards left at the
barriers."

Obren fell in with her, a young soldier used to orders
from a senior.

Sharine was no scout, but she had an artist's eye and that
eye caught on the slightly misaligned barrier to the northeast. Flying there on heavy wings, she met a nonplussed
angelic warrior in the sky. "My lady," the other woman
began, "is there anything I—"

"The reborn are burrowing under the earth." Sharine
pointed down. "And this barrier is no longer flush to the
ground."

The warrior, to her credit, went on immediate alert. "I'll
have to request assistance and move the guard line back
until it arrives." Lines flaring out from her eyes, her lips
pressed tight. "We have no one at the border who can bore
into the earth with their power and I don't think the weapons at hand will do so."

Do you remember Akhia-Solay?

Memory whispered, Sharine's fingers curling inward.
Power, grown old and potent and stiff from disuse, heated
in her veins. Her palm glowed champagne-pale.

"Tell your ground troops to move away from the barrier."

Mouth falling open, the warrior angel stared at Sharine's
hand—then quickly snapped into action, yelling at her
people to evacuate the danger zone. Sharine waited until
they were just far enough, then released the power.

The resulting hole was only a fraction of the size of Titus's
but it was enough to reveal the tunnel beneath. The border
guard and her people arrowed back at the reborn within, all
of them shooting the weapons that spouted flame.

Sharine, meanwhile, stared at her hand.

Obren was doing the same. "I didn't know you could do

that." It came out a whisper. "I was told the Hummingbird was an artist."

"I'd forgotten," she murmured, her mind using the unraveling skeins of memory to travel right back to the genesis of Sharine.

12

Eons Past

Papa! Papa! Look what I can do." Light shot from Sharine's small fingers to crack one of the stones that littered the wildflower-strewn mountainside. "See!"

Black eyebrows drawing together over his eyes, her father crouched down to touch the rock. He drew back his finger with a hiss, the pad of it red. Face falling, Sharine pressed her lips gently to it. "I kiss it better," she said, having learned that from the mother of her friend who lived the next mountain over.

Her father didn't smile, just took her hands in his and stared at her palms. But there was nothing there now, no hint of the pretty fire. "It's inside me," she told him, bouncing on her feet. "All fizzy and hot."

Her father wasn't like her friend's father, who laughed and took her for rides on his back. Sharine's father was old in a way that made her bones ache. She was too young to know how to put that into words, but she felt the weight of his age like a looming black cloud on the horizon. She knew he loved her—she felt that, too—but it wasn't the same as how other fathers loved their children.

"We need to fly home to your mother," he said in his deep voice, his eyes the same sunlight shade as her own but with streaks of brown.

Sharine wanted to play longer on this mountainside, with the sun shining so bright that the wildflowers appeared to glow, but she knew there was no point in arguing or dragging her feet. The last time she'd tried, her father had left her alone until she "came to her senses" and flew home. It might be fun to play alone here, but then she'd miss him and mama and go home and they'd be disappointed with her behavior.

Sighing, she flew up. She couldn't fly as smooth or as straight as her papa, but she could stay in the air the whole way home now. Before, she'd used to fall, or have to rest. But her wings had become stronger over the past year, though she was still puffed, with her heart going boom-boom, when she landed in the stone courtyard of their home.

"Mama!" she cried as she ran inside, excited to share her new trick.

"Sharine, sweetheart, how often have I told you not to run?" Mama's words were mild, the smile she sent Sharine's way kind . . . and tired. Sharine's mother was always tired. It was just the way she was—Sharine had no memory of a time when her mother wasn't on the edge of exhaustion.

"Sorry," she said with a smile and slowed down. "I showed Papa my fire. Can I have some food?"

Her mother's sky-blue gaze went to her father, her golden hair rippling and the light purple of her wings restless, but they didn't speak until after Sharine'd had her snack and was outside. But she was bad and she tiptoed back to near the window so she could listen. She knew she shouldn't, that it was bad to listen in on other people, but no one *ever* had interesting conversations around her and she wasn't a baby anymore.

"Her fire?" Mama murmured in her husky-soft voice.

"Yes." Papa's deeper tones. "She's showing signs of an offensive ability. It may be that our daughter is destined to be a warrior."

"I can't believe it, not with how she loses herself in her art." Sharine's mother sounded as if she was smiling, and that was nice. "It's apt to be a remnant from my mother. She served Qin until she decided to Sleep."

"But so young?" Papa murmured, the sound of his wings moving as he opened and closed them familiar and comforting. "Offensive abilities don't appear in children for a reason. She could hurt a friend or playmate without intent."

A pause before her mother said, "Yes, you're right in that. We shall have to teach her to never use her abilities. At least until she's older." Endless tiredness in every word. "I don't know if I'll make it, my love. I ached for a child when I was young and full of life, only for fate to bless me when I see nothing of interest in the world any longer but for you and our daughter."

Sharine deliberately stepped away from the window, and walked over to her mother's flower garden to begin pulling weeds. "They shouldn't talk that way." Eyes wet and hot, she ripped out a weed. "I hate it. I do."

She was old enough to understand they were talking about Sleep. Not normal sleep. Sleep that went on for ages and ages and ages. It scared her. Angels weren't like the mortal children she'd been told about but had never met—angels took a long time to grow up. What if Mama and Papa left her while she was still only half a grown-up? What would she do then? She'd be all alone.

Maybe if she listened and minded better, they'd stay longer.

"I won't use the fire," she promised the flowers in a wet, quavering whisper. "I'll be good. I'll be the best little girl."

13

Titus was worried enough about where the burrows might lead that he left his weapons-master Orios in charge of the main section of the nest and flew back to expose other hidden routes. The first suspicious area, however, proved to have already been unearthed.

Fire boiled inside the tunnels, the reborn surely incinerated.

"Who did this?" he asked on a stab of joy, wondering if one of his older angels had come into a new power.

Sweat streaking her face from the heat of the flamethrower, Marifa turned to him and said, "The Hummingbird."

The two of them stared at each other for a long second before the other angel said, "On my honor, sire. It was her. She looked as surprised as I felt, but she blew open the hole for us."

Deciding that particular mystery could wait, Titus left the squadron captain to it and went in the opposite direction to where he could see wings of indigo light. It appeared the

Cadre had sent him far more help than he'd believed. That, or a doppelganger *had* taken over the Hummingbird's body.

It took hours for them to clear out the entire interconnected burrow, but the work wasn't yet done. He and his people—and the powerful imposter with drooping wings who looked like the Hummingbird—had to go backward through every other cleared section to ensure they hadn't missed a burrow that might spout reborn in a nightmare eruption.

It wasn't as if he could simply crack open the earth—an entire city sat on that earth.

"We will have to be vigilant," he said to his people as they gathered on the ramparts of the citadel, sweaty and dirty and with more than one streak of putrid reborn flesh or blood on their clothing and bodies.

He'd been lucky today, hadn't lost any of them, mortal, vampire, or angel, to the vicious creatures. "Alert the populace to the danger and tell them to hail a warrior should they hear *anything* beneath their homes—reassure them we won't be angry at false alarms, no matter how many."

"We could position ground-sensors around the citadel and the city," said a two-hundred-year old vampire who had an intense interest in the technologies of this time.

"Go, speak to Tzadiq, get it under way."

The Hummingbird had returned to the citadel with them, but she stayed on the edge of the group and remained silent until it had disbanded. Only then did she approach Titus, her wings having dropped until the tips dragged on the ground.

"I haven't yet spoken to you of all I saw on my journey." No tiredness in her voice, but he saw it in those wings and in the strain on her face. "Who should I consult regarding the settlements that desperately need assistance?"

"Tzadiq will take care of it," Titus said, not happy to know so many people were suffering. "But right now, I wish to talk about your power."

She waved it off, as if he wasn't an archangel and she could defy him with impunity. "I have something far more interesting for you—I thought the reborn must've begun to mutate, but now I've seen the ones here, I begin to question my conclusion."

While he was still agog at her complete disregard for his authority, she pulled out a phone device from her pocket and touched the screen. "Here, look at the moving pictures I took."

Caught between the urge to snarl at her to respect his authority and a fascination that was rooted in befuddlement, Titus found his attention caught by the images on the screen. The recording showed the hand of what he thought must be a reborn. It was severely burned, but the hand was elongated in a way that turned the stomach, it was so alien . . . and *there*.

He grabbed her wrist without thought, faintly noting the unexpected tensile strength of her bones. "Can you show me again?"

"I believe so, but I need both hands."

Heat burned his skin. "My apologies." Titus wasn't in the habit of grabbing women without permission.

"It is no matter," she murmured, her focus on tapping at the device.

Once again treating him like an errant pup who'd made a misstep, rather than the archangel of an entire *continent*.

Chest rumbling, he went to point out that he was no pup and never would be, but she smiled without warning—and the searing beauty of the light in her expression knocked him flat.

"I have it," she said with open pride, and held out the phone again.

Titus had to force himself to pay attention. "Watch with me, focus on the fingers." He needed to know if she saw it, too.

A second in, she sucked in a hard breath. "It *moved*." Horror in every syllable. "That should be impossible. The bodies were so badly burned that nothing could've survived it—and reborn are susceptible to fire."

"It's possible this reborn was a vampire before being turned, and managed to survive for a considerable period of time." Those were always the nastiest ones to kill. "But it should still not be showing signs of life, given the intensity of the fire." The rest of the recording offered evidence of a violent blaze. "How far is this settlement?" He couldn't ignore the sign of an even more robust strain.

When she told him the location, he did rapid calculations in his head. He couldn't send a proxy for this—he had to see her discovery himself, but he also couldn't leave his people low on manpower. Still, if he flew at archangelic speed . . . "Can you give me exact coordinates to the village?"

Her face dropped, smile fading. "I don't know how to give you such coordinates."

"Your device may have noted it." He reached out mentally to Obren, aware the youth was an aficionado of technology. "Obren joins us soon to check."

But the boy shook his head after checking the device, his locs tied back at his nape with a thin piece of twine. "I'm sorry, sire, it appears that operation has been turned off."

"I may have done it while I was working out how to use the device." The Hummingbird's tone was apologetic. "I'm sorry."

Titus ordered Obren to return to his duties. "In that case," he began.

But the Hummingbird was already speaking. "I can lead you directly to it."

"You'll slow me down," Titus said bluntly, and braced himself for a fit of feminine anger. "I can't lose time, not now."

"Yes," the Hummingbird agreed in a quiet tone. "But I

think even an archangel shouldn't go into such danger alone. And as I am not yet assigned to a specific task, taking me along will leave no hole in your defenses."

Titus didn't believe he was invincible because he was an archangel. Even archangels could be hurt. Right now, an enemy didn't need to kill him to do catastrophic damage to his territory. If they shot a missile at him, blowing his body to pieces, they took out a massive part of his offensive forces for however long it took for his body to knit together.

He didn't believe any of the Cadre currently had the time or energy to launch such an assault, but some of Charisemnon's flunkies might yet act out of stupid loyalty. And, as she'd proved today, the Hummingbird had some power. Enough to scare off anyone who thought they were coming at a tired and worn Titus.

"A good strategic point," he said. "Can you be ready to fly in four hours?" That would give him time to organize his forces—and for her to get a few hours' rest. Her wings had dropped even further.

A nod from the Hummingbird. "I should tell you, my endurance is not yours."

"I'll carry you from the point you get tired, if you'll permit it." It came out stilted. "I mean no insult."

"I take none." Her eyes were intense, and yet somehow . . . lost. No, that wasn't right. When he'd seen her in the distance through the years, he'd thought her a lovely ghost, a woman with so many fractures in her psyche that she only survived by disassociating from the world.

This was different; she hadn't retreated from the world. Rather, it was as if she was looking inward, searching for something she'd forgotten. Such wasn't the least bit unusual in older angels. Even Titus found himself doing it on occasion, and he was only three thousand five hundred years old in comparison to—

It was then that he realized he had no idea of the Hummingbird's age. What knowledge he had said she was a contemporary of Caliane's—and Raphael's mother was an acknowledged Ancient. Yet when he looked at the Hummingbird, he felt no sense of age, no sense of history pressing down on his bones.

Her presence was radiant, full of an unexpected light.

"Is all well?" He tried to temper his voice out of its usual booming register.

Lines furrowing her forehead, she seemed to snap back to reality. "What's wrong with your voice? Are you falling ill?"

Titus wanted to throw back his head and just roar at the sky. Why were women the bane of his existence? He loved them, that much was true. But they also drove him to distraction. "My voice is fine," he grumbled. "I was attempting a tone that wouldn't blow out your eardrums. According to all those borrowed warriors who quit my service, I yell too much."

She tilted her head a fraction to the side. "I don't recall making that complaint." Arch words, no indication of anything but a woman confident and strong.

"My people seem to find my voice just fine, too, but others are weak and lily-livered." It was a gauntlet he'd just thrown down, pushed to the edge by her . . . He didn't know what it was about the Hummingbird that aggravated him, and that just turned the aggravation up another notch.

The edge of her mouth lifted slightly, her extraordinary eyes filling with an effervescence he could've sworn was laughter. "I agree with you," she said in that mellifluous voice rich with tonal layers. "You're an archangel fighting a deadly scourge. Those who expect you to waste time pandering to their needs should be ashamed to call themselves warriors."

He glared at her, not sure if she was making fun of him or not. Regardless, there was nothing he could do about it. She was the Hummingbird. Angelkind would disown him should he lay a finger on her. Not that he would. But it was the principle of the thing. "I am an archangel," he boomed. "I am the law in this territory."

She bowed deep and precise. "Of course."

He felt like he'd just been petted on the head, much as an indulgent mother might do to a small child who was puffing himself up. Growling in his chest, he decided to do as advised by a long-ago trainer, and take a step back.

The adversary he faced wasn't a simple one; to win this war he'd have to be cunning and stealthy. Neither of which was exactly his strong suit, but if he changed cunning to strategy . . . yes, that made more sense. "Please take this opportunity to rest your wings. We fly when the sun is high in the sky."

It was the longest break he could give her. He'd use the time to brief Tzadiq, Orios, Tanae, and the others of his senior court—including Ozias; his spymaster was on her way back to Narja, close enough now that he could reach her with his mind. The short of it was that Titus's people had to push on with the eradication process. They couldn't stop for a single day. Not with the rapid-fire spread of infection.

Even with his many soldiers spread out across the territory, they couldn't protect every village and every town and every city. People were dying. People were being taken by the reborn and changed into a rotting abomination of life. Fathers were having to kill mothers before a mauled loved one became a creature of nightmare. Children were becoming orphans all over his territory . . . if the little ones survived at all.

This war was more heartbreaking than any he'd ever before fought.

14

Sire, I fly to join your court in the spring, a season out from my hundredth birthday. You do me a great honor in accepting me into your army.

I know that part of it is because of your respect for my mother, but I will prove myself to you in the years to come, until you do not think of me as your first general's son, but only as Titus.

—*Letter from Titus to Archangel Alexander*

15

Sharine rested first and foremost; her just over three hours of sleep rejuvenated her a considerable amount. Afterward, she put together the items she'd need for this journey. It wouldn't be much. This was about speed and about what she needed to keep up with Titus.

The latter was why she stopped a harried member of staff and asked them to show her to the kitchens.

Eyes wide, the individual with smooth skin the hue of rich cream, a shaved head, and the barest impression of breasts against the court's brown and gold livery, said, "My lady. I can bring you anything—"

"It'll be faster if I can talk to the cook myself," she said. "But I thank you for your care."

A couple of hard swallows, but the staff member nonetheless didn't protest any longer and led her to a huge kitchen filled with heat and light, and the energetic bustle of those who worked to prepare enough food to fuel this massive army.

Spotting her before his minions, the clear king of this space—a man of medium height blocky with muscle—rushed over. "My lady." He bowed over her hand, his black hair tightly braided in neat rows against his scalp and his skin a light shade of brown. "You do me a great honor."

"You are a fellow artist and I would speak to you of your divine dishes," she said, because it was true. "Today, however, I come to ask you for something simpler." She told him what she needed. "If it'll take too much of your time, I can adapt."

His face lit up, his rich brown eyes shining buttons in a face that was naturally plump and would probably stay that way all his life, regardless of the ongoing effects of vampirism. Some mortals seemed to have a presence so strong, it held sway no matter what. Raphael's second, Dmitri, fell in that camp.

"No, it isn't difficult at all," the cook said. "We keep a store of prepared bars for our warriors who can't stop for a full meal." Rushing into what looked like a cool storage room, he returned with his hands full of bars that contained high levels of energy. "How many do you need?"

"This is more than enough." Accepting the handfuls, she took a moment to look around the kitchen. "You must be tired, for this has been a continuous effort." Even the most powerful angels needed constant replenishment when they were expending so much energy on a daily basis—including in healing wounds.

"What does it matter to be a little tired if what I do helps us fight the ugliness of the scourge?" His fangs flashed as he spoke, his shoulders square with justifiable pride.

Sharine didn't ask how a vampire, a being whose system couldn't process anything but small quantities of food, had ended up cook to an archangel, just smiled at him. "Yes, you and your people provide the fuel for this great engine."

He was beaming when she left.

Once back in her room, she put the bars in her little

pack, then stood there for a second and for the first time, thought of what she'd done with the burrow, how she'd exposed it with her power. Her hand tingled. Looking down, she saw a shadow of the champagne energy that had erupted from her.

It stirred deep within her, so potent that it stole her breath, but still only half-awake. An energy left unused so very long that it had grown darker and denser with each passing century.

Of what was she capable? It had been an eon since she'd allowed herself free rein. First, she'd throttled her power in a vain effort to hold on to her parents, then it had fallen by the wayside of her art but for the few occasions she'd been forced to use it, as on that long-ago battlefield. Then she'd . . . forgotten it.

A youngling like Obren wouldn't understand how a person could forget a central element of their nature, but while angelic memory was in many ways infinite, that didn't mean you could always *access* what had been stored away so very long ago. An angel as old as Sharine, especially one whose mind had carried fractures for so long, could've forgotten many lives, many pieces of her existence.

The realization haunted her even as she stepped out to meet Titus for their journey to the abandoned settlement.

Responsibility lay a heavy cloak over his shoulders.

He didn't speak as they took off, and neither did she, her mind busy with myriad flashes of memory as she attempted to pinpoint the moment when she'd forgotten the power that lived in her veins.

The knowledge had been lost long before she bore Illium, her babe who'd grown into a dangerously powerful man. And she'd never known it with Aegaeon, either. But the time between her childhood and before that critical point in her life was an eternity that spilled out to the horizon.

Head aching from the futility of it, she finally stopped tugging at the memory threads. That could wait. Right now, she had to watch Titus's back, ensure he didn't get taken unawares by anything. He was flying to her left and slightly ahead, his wings powerful, while she rode the draft created in his wake.

Oh.

He was doing it on purpose. The man might be a blockhead who thought she'd collapse at a loud voice, but he was also an honorable and clever warrior. That was one of the few facts she knew about him. All her information on Titus came from comments made by those who served at Lumia, and a few passing words from Illium.

He was beloved of his people.

He was beloved of women.

He was a man of honor and truth.

He was a warrior who showed no mercy against evil.

He wasn't a scholar and his court wasn't a scholarly one— but Sharine no longer took that particular tidbit as fact. Not after hearing him speak of warrior-scholars, and, on her return from the kitchens, glimpsing a number of people working in a great library.

Brows furrowed and shoulders bowed, the scholars had looked as tired as the warriors and household staff. No doubt, they'd been set to the task of seeing if there was another, faster way to stop the reborn.

Last but not least was the information that though Titus enjoyed women—tall and short, slender and voluptuous, pale-skinned or dark—he'd never come close to taking a consort.

The latter seemed to be a point of pride among his people, as if Titus gadding about like a fly laying its eggs on every possible surface was the epitome of masculinity. Sharine snorted to herself. Her mother would've been horrified at the inelegant sound but her mother was long-gone, turned to dust.

Aegaeon's people, too, had been proud of their archangel's virility and inability to commit his heart. Looking back, she saw not virility but weakness. It didn't take any great skill to go about taking lover after lover if one was an archangel. Power alone was an aphrodisiac.

Oh, Archangel Titus's charm is just . . . Sigh.

She'd overheard similar words more than once from those who'd passed through Lumia. Each smitten woman had placed her hands on her heart and spoken of how easy it was to melt into his arms, how gorgeous he was when he smiled, and how attentive he was as a lover. Sharine hadn't thought she was paying attention at the time but, thanks to her accursed selective memory, she now remembered every morsel.

From what she'd seen, however, Titus's charm consisted of being an archangel. She'd spotted no sign of any other talent in how he dealt with women. He was a blunt hammer and everyone seemed ready to fall for it.

Really.

If that was all one needed to be considered charming, she had a castle on a cloud she could sell them.

She snorted again.

Titus glanced to the right and slightly back. He could've sworn the Hummingbird had just snorted, but surely not. She was too refined and delicate a creature to snort.

Though she *was* also examining him as if he were an insect under a slide. There was a reason he didn't spend too much time with the scholars of his court—he respected them as he respected all who had skills he didn't possess—but half the time, he felt as if their greatest wish was to take him apart in order to work out how he functioned.

It was enough to raise the hairs on an archangel's nape.

Deciding not to ask her if anything was the matter, because he'd long ago learned that lesson about women and poking hornets' nests, he focused on his surroundings. His heart broke at seeing the devastation in the areas close to the border, the fallow fields and burned-out villages farther out.

They hadn't yet hit the first major city on the northern side.

Most of the border damage would've come about during his battle with Charisemnon, but as they flew on, he saw that the situation had worsened significantly since his quick scouting run after he first took over his enemy's territory. It also aligned with the updated report Ozias had given him, his spymaster having reached Narja right before he flew out.

The north exists in terror, sire. Starvation is a hovering threat. It's not only the reborn who are responsible for the latter—the plagues of locusts during the Cascade did far worse damage there than in the south.

As far as I've been able to discover, it's because Charisemnon had already drafted large numbers of young and strong mortals into his forces. The farms had little manpower to protect their crops or to replant. Having to fight off reborn was the final straw—city or rural, the people are close to broken.

It didn't sit well with Titus. These were his people now and this was his land to caretake.

"How could he do this?" he found himself saying out loud. "How could he cause such destruction to his own people and not care?" The reborn had been of Lijuan and so, aside from herding them toward the south, Charisemnon'd had no control over them; even had he lived, a number would've escaped and ravaged the north.

An abandoned farm lay below, its fields lonely and forgotten, the windows of the main house smashed. He knew the reborn had gone through it in a horde—he could spot the marks left in the dirt where the creatures had dragged away bodies, knew that no one had survived.

"Some do not think of their people." The Hummingbird's beautiful voice, a lush caress. "Power is all that matters. Humans, to them, are nothing but disposable pieces on the chessboard of immortal politics."

Titus clenched his jaw, thinking of all whose voices had disappeared from this landscape. Even the sight of a herd of gazelles with fine curving horns and red-brown coats grazing peacefully on a field green with grass couldn't temper his anger; he'd never forgive Charisemnon for what he'd done, the noxious poison he'd helped release with no care for the consequence.

"I wish I hadn't killed him so quickly. I had to do so, so that I could join the battle against Lijuan, but I wish I had him here so I could rip him apart and leave him a limbless torso that I could then torture for an answer to this poison." Titus wasn't a man who believed in torture—better to fight your enemies face-to-face, honor to honor, but Charisemnon had no honor. You couldn't reason with one such as him.

The Hummingbird didn't recoil at his brutal words. "What do the scientists and scholars say?" she asked. "My focus during the war was to uphold my duties to Lumia and protect the repository of angelic art. As a result, I haven't been part of any wider conversations on the aftereffects of the war—all I know, I've heard from others."

Titus assumed that included from Raphael, and of course, from Illium. "There is little word of a vaccine to what they are calling the reborn infection—and that relates only to the original reborn created by Lijuan. We have even less knowledge of the variant altered by Charisemnon."

His shoulders tightened as he overflew another abandoned town, its buildings scorched by fire and its gardens left untended. "My enemy was an archangel, for all his faults. And he was an archangel supercharged by the Cascade.

"Whatever it is that he created, it can't be simply understood. It is a thing of power—the scientists say the cells of

Africa's reborn run with a kind of viscous energy that hungers. When they test the cells with droplets of blood, the cells are voracious, never fulfilled—and they are more infectious than anything else on this planet."

A chill shivered its way across his skin as it had the first time he'd heard the report. "With the 'ordinary' reborn, mortals are doomed no matter the intervention, but we now have data to say many strong vampires have recovered after a non-lethal attack. Here, even vampires who chop off an arm or a leg that has been clawed by one of the reborn . . ."

Titus shook his head, his throat dry. "I've lost too many of my people. That's why I've ordered my vampiric troops, as well as the Guild Hunters, and mortal mercenaries, to fight from inside their vehicles, with distance weapons." Any close-contact fighting was to be done by an angel.

"Your people have incredible courage."

Titus had no need for those words—he knew that truth to his bones. But it was nice to hear the acknowledgment. "Raphael told me something when he came to help me." The pup had kept his word, given Titus so much of his time. Titus knew Raphael would return when he was able. "A truth he learned from the Legion fighters who lived in his home territory for so long."

Those fighters had given up their lives so that the Cadre could defeat Lijuan, and for that, Titus honored them.

"Well?" A crisp demand. "Do you plan to tell me?"

Scowling, he glanced at her. "What is wrong with you?" It came out a boom of sound. "You're not acting like the sweet and kind Hummingbird!"

Her response was a glare that would've stripped his skin from his bones were he not the son of First General Avelina, and the brother of Euphenia, Zuri, Nala, and Charo. "I have told you," she enunciated through gritted teeth, "my *name* is Sharine. I would be most pleased if you should deign to use it."

Perhaps she was suffering from the trauma of the war. She was an ephemeral creature. Having so much devastation on her doorstep had no doubt caused damage that was emerging as this strange, antagonistic behavior.

"Sharine," he said with his most charming smile.

Her response was a baring of teeth that had him glad he wasn't within arm's reach. "What did Raphael tell you?" she snapped.

Affronted, he swept away from her for long wingbeats. Until he'd calmed down enough to return to fly at her side and just ahead enough to ease her journey. She didn't look the least bit abashed at having driven him away.

Instead, she raised an eyebrow when he looked at her, and said, "Feeling better?"

Titus's chest rumbled. If she were not the Hummingbird . . . "According to the Legion, there was another great war in our history."

The information had come as no surprise to Titus. A race of immortals, many of them powerful, could not always live in peace. "During that war, an archangel released a poison that infected all of angelkind. Our people went to Sleep for an eon in the hope that our immortal bodies would find an answer to the poison while we Slept, but the poison was still part of our flesh when we woke."

The horror of the story would've made Titus disbelieve it were he not living through Charisemnon's plague. "In the interim, a whole new people were born—the mortals. According to the Legion, angelkind somehow discovered that by purging our poison into mortals, we could retain our health and sanity."

"You're speaking of the birth of vampires?" the Hummingbird said. No, *not* the Hummingbird. The Hummingbird was a creature gentle and vague and sweet. This was Sharine. Sharp-tongued, clear-eyed, and armed with a gaze like acid.

He shouldn't be so fascinated with her. It was probably bad for his health.

"Yes, that's what the Legion intimated." The toxin that built up in angelic bodies over time, initiating a slow descent into horrific murderous madness, was his race's greatest secret. It was their one weakness and it made mortals far more important to angelkind than mortals could ever know.

"I'll ask Raphael more about this."

"Do you think I lie to you?" he roared, his wings aglow with power.

16

She actually rolled her eyes at him. *Rolled her eyes* at the Archangel of Africa. "No," she said. "I'd simply like to make sure we have all the details, so we can see if there's something to be learned from it."

Titus went to grumble back a response, when a herd of buffalo below caught his eye. The large and aggressive creatures with dark coats were moving in erratic ways, slamming their heads against each other and pawing at the earth. More than one set of wickedly thick horns glinted red with blood.

He flew lower. "Don't get close enough for them to make contact!" he yelled back to the Hummingbird; he didn't believe the creatures were in any way sentient, but there was a feral energy to them.

Hovering a few feet above, out of reach of their lunges, he found himself looking down into reddened eyes and slavering mouths. That was when he saw torn-out throats, disemboweled stomachs, and missing limbs that caused some of the animals to drag themselves into the fight.

Cold infiltrated his bones. "They're reborn," he said to Sharine when she came to hover next to him.

Nothing and no one but the reborn had that particular vicious look in the eye—a kind of rapacious voraciousness that nothing could assuage. A hunger that was endless and even worse than the bloodlust that had taken hold in vampires across many territories. Titus's theory on why Africa had been spared that scourge was that even the vampires were terrified of the reborn.

That, and any vampire who got out of fucking line was soon terminated by his fellows. No one sane wanted to foster or create a distraction from the battle taking place on the continent.

Sharine sucked in a breath. "I didn't know it could be transmitted to animals."

"Neither did I," he said, his power alive in his hand. "No one else has reported anything of the like." He had no proof as yet, but he knew this was Charisemnon's doing; whatever poison he'd created, however he'd hybridized the reborn with his disease, it meant the horror could now jump between species.

"Sweet mercy." Sharine's lovely voice was as cold as his blood. "Lijuan and Charisemnon would've turned our entire world into a mockery of life."

"I must end these buffalo, but I'll need to take a sample back for my scholars and scientists." He frowned. "I don't have anything in which to preserve and carry a sample."

"Create a hole in the earth," Sharine suggested. "Dump some feed within. As long as the hole isn't shallow, the creature won't be able to clamber out."

It was a smart idea. There was just one problem. "They're no longer grazing on grass." He pointed out the hunks of flesh that one buffalo had ripped out from the flank of another.

"Such horrors." Sharine's expression was open, her renowned kindness and heart at the forefront—yet there remained nothing fragile about her. "You'll have to leave a dead animal in there with the reborn one, for your scientists need a live sample to study—if the infection melts the flesh of the reborn, you may otherwise end up with no sample at all."

The reborn tended to be drawn to living flesh, but Titus wasn't going to trap two maddened creatures together so one could eat the other. There were some lines he wouldn't cross. "A living creature should survive if I create the hole under shade. I'll send word back to my people as soon as I see a scout."

Titus could speak mind-to-mind with his senior people from some distance away, but they'd flown beyond his maximum range. Mental speech had never been one of his stronger skills regardless, and was perhaps a reason he'd retained so much of his Cascade-born abilities. To even out the spread of power in the Cadre.

"Wait." Sharine's voice was breathy . . . flustered? "I'm foolish. We can use the phone—I have a number within it that connects to your court."

"I don't deal with such." Titus examined the creatures below to see which he could most easily cut from the herd and corral.

"Careful, Titus," she said, "lest you morph into a monument of yourself—one stuck in stone and in the past."

As he watched her touch her fingers to the screen of the device, he chewed over her words, heat in his blood. He was who he was and he had no argument with himself.

Tito! Stop being so stubborn.

His eldest sister's voice, an echo from childhood—or possibly from last year. Phenie still scolded him from time to time. She also went to great lengths to bring him his favorite fruit from the Refuge, and, when he'd been a child, had never begrudged the fledgling who tottered after her, eager to poke his nose into her business.

Come, Tito, we'll go visit Master Carvari. It's possible you have untapped musical abilities.

To Phenie's great horror, Titus's only interest in instruments was how to use them as weapons should he need to. Yet she'd never stopped him from being underfoot, not even when he spent an entire year with her while their mother led Alexander's troops in battle.

Titus had long forgotten what that battle might've been or against whom, but he remembered sitting on the stone wall outside Phenie's house, listening to her play the harp—and waiting in happy anticipation for when she'd inevitably call his name.

It's time for a snack, Tito! Hurry home or I shall eat it all!

The memory made his lips curve. Perhaps, in Phenie's honor, he'd concede that Sharine was right in her reproof. The device in her hand would ensure his scientists could get under way at speed.

Not that he'd tell Sharine he agreed with her—she struck him as the kind of woman who'd say "I told you so" and he'd heard quite enough of that in his childhood, thank you very much.

Especially from Charo. The youngest of his sisters was an inveterate gloater.

"Here." Sharine handed over the device that felt flimsy and breakable in his hand. "I've touched the button that should connect you to your court."

It was his steward who answered the call. "Yash," Titus boomed. "I need you to fetch either Tzadiq, Tanae, Orios, or Ozias." Yash was brilliant at running the household, but it'd be better to give this particular information to someone who'd ensure the scholars and scientists didn't get themselves eaten by a deranged buffalo.

"Sire." A stunned response, but the man recovered fast. "I'll fetch Orios at once; I saw the weapons-master just now."

Glancing down, Titus saw that three of the creatures had managed to take down a fourth, were now feasting on his yet-pink flesh. That meant the infection was recent. Unable to stand by and watch any being writhe in agony, Titus sent down a bolt of power that erased all four from existence. The rest of the herd screamed in a way that was eerily unnatural—buffalo didn't make that sound—but they didn't scatter.

Rather, they turned and looked up at him, trying to jump in a way that was impossible for their ungainly bodies.

Orios came on the line. "Sire, when Yash told me it was you on the line, I thought for certain he'd taken a blow to the head!" The weapons-master's voice was as deep and resonant as Titus's. "What calamity has befallen us now?"

Of all the people in his court, Orios was the one with whom Titus was the closest. Perhaps because Orios had been with him from the very beginning; the only reason he wasn't Titus's second was because he preferred the duties of a weapons-master.

I have no patience for the politics that come with being second, he'd said when Titus brought up the question soon after his ascension. *You need a second with a bit more cunning and charm to him, one who'll soften your blunt edges when it comes to dealing with the seconds of others in the Cadre. You should promote Tzadiq—he's an excellent general, but he will be a brilliant second.*

Orios had been right in his advice, and now Titus had an intelligent and urbane second he trusted to uphold Titus's honor—while not insulting everyone in the vicinity. "It has reached the animals, my friend," he told Orios, then laid out the details.

"I'll send out a science team with an escort," Orios told him, his tone grim. "The scholars have become more practical since the war, but I don't trust them outside without protection."

Neither did Titus; immortal scholars could sometimes live on their own planet. "I leave it in your capable hands." After ending the conversation, he passed the phone back to Sharine, then went about creating the earthen prison for the chosen buffalo.

That done, he erased the rest of the infected animals from existence, his power leaving another scar in the landscape of his territory. It bruised his heart to see that, but it had to be done.

They saw no other unnatural creatures in the hours that passed, but while the cities appeared well enough—if quiet and on edge—the damage to the passing villages and farms was becoming increasingly worse. "Lumia?"

Though he hadn't spoken for the past two hours, Sharine understood what he was asking. "We were safe—the reborn never reached that far." She indicated below. "From what I saw on my previous journey, this is the worst-hit section on this side of the border."

Titus took in the damage. "Charisemnon was playing with fire thinking he could control the reborn." Only Lijuan'd had that ability.

"He also left his people helpless against them," Sharine said, her tone full of cut glass, bright and bloody. "I was informed that he drafted not only angels and vampires, but strong mortals into his troops—including people from farmsteads and villages."

"My spymaster has confirmed this." Titus still had difficulty understanding the why of it. "Farmers and field workers?" None would've stood a chance in a battle between immortals. It wasn't the same as when Guild Hunters or mercenaries joined in—they were highly trained and made the decision of their own free will.

The African Guild had all defected to Titus's side as soon as Charisemnon's perfidy and evil became clear, and they'd fought with courage and heart and skill. The Guild *had* taken losses, but at about the same percentage as the rest of Titus's forces. No one would ever consider a hunter easy prey.

Quite unlike the poor scared mortals called up by Charisemnon.

"I understand now why so many villagers burned their homes to the ground—they would've had no chance one-on-one. It was a smart choice to lead or drive the monsters inside a house, then turn it into a funeral pyre."

"The only choice, I think." Sharine's eyes were soft with sadness. "Even if it left them without a home."

"These people showed more courage than the hind end of an ass who called himself their archangel."

It was at the next battered but still living village, flaming torches marking out its boundaries, that he made a decision. "I will land. These people need to understand that I am now their liege and I *will* send help." Such had always been in his plans—but he hadn't realized the sheer depth of the devastation in this area.

Titus had been a fool; he'd believed that his enemy would've protected his own people, not crippled them. With so much available prey, a few reborn would've quickly turned into many. "I assumed that leaking bag of pus would've at least placed a rear guard whose task it was to eliminate any reborn who scuttled north."

"Assumptions are the enemy of coherence," Sharine said.

In other words, *You're an idiot*.

"I would've never attacked my own people!" It came out thunder in the air that caused startled villagers to jerk their heads upward.

Sharine looked at him for long moments before inclining her head. "I accept that. Your honor made you expect too much from someone who had no honor. Remember that, Titus." A fierce intensity to her. "Remember that there are those in this world who will cross every line and feel no guilt in doing so."

He'd witnessed that ugliness with Lijuan. The Archangel of Death had used *children* to her own ends. Such was not to be borne. And yet, he'd made this mistake, left the north too long untended. Yes, Sharine was right to castigate him. He'd been foolish and these people had paid for it.

Landing in the center of the village, dust swirling around him as he folded back his wings, he waited until she was down, too, before he took in the villagers. He would not have anyone say that he hadn't watched over the Hummingbird while she was in his care—not that she seemed to want or even need his concern.

No one had warned him she was so contrary.

Had all of angelkind *lied* to him for an eon? Surely that was impossible.

"Well," she murmured, for in the time since their landing, every single raggedly dressed villager within sight had gone down flat to the earth, their faces pressed to the dirt and their hands palm-to-palm in front in a pose of supplication that disturbed him on the deepest level.

He ruled with a firm hand, but he'd never sought to unman or humiliate anyone, for these people were mothers and fathers, elders and healers with their own pride and honor. But the people in front of him weren't like his own . . . though they belonged to him now.

Charisemnon, he reminded himself, had somehow convinced his populace that for him to take their young daughters to his bed was an honor and not a perversion. The memory caused a crawling sensation across his skin and his voice was harsh when he said, "Rise! I wish to talk to your faces, not your asses!"

Whimpers whispered into the air, but several trembling citizens got to their feet. At least a few of them had some backbone. Beside him, Sharine might as well have been formed of iron, so stiff was she. No doubt she'd have sharp words for him when they were alone, but this was beyond ridiculous. "Why do you have so many burned buildings in your village?" he asked, wanting to confirm his theory.

It was a man old and shriveled, his beard unexpectedly lush, who answered, his hand shaky on his cane and his bones all but clattering. Yet he spoke, and for that, Titus looked at him with respect. "The rotting ones came," the old man said in his whispery voice. "They took some of our own and we knew that none could be saved."

His Adam's apple bobbed. "The last one to be mauled, he saw what had happened to his neighbors and friends, and before his mind was gone, he used himself as bait to lead them into one of the houses." Water spilled from his eyes. "We were able to lock the door and burn down the house, saving the untainted. And so we learned how to kill the rotting ones."

Titus thought he'd seen and heard of every horror, but this . . . "Did one of your people always act as a lure from then on?"

The speaker's jerky nod was followed by a muffled sob from the crowd, one quickly quieted. A being broken-hearted at the loss of a loved one.

"The old do it," the speaker rasped. "I am next."

Yet he stood here, spine bowed but courage undaunted. Indeed, he was a man to respect, as were all those who'd gone before him. "How many people did you lose?" he asked, already calculating how he could redeploy troops to assist on this side of the former border. "Both to the rotting ones and in the war draft."

The answer shook him; if he was right in his calculations, the village had lost at least half its people. The survivors had a glazed kind of resignation on their faces, their bodies brittle and emaciated.

And . . . he saw no children.

That was an impossibility. In every village in which he had ever before landed, he'd seen the curious face of a child or two peeking at him from behind a door, or from on top of the stoop. They were inevitably inquisitive, smiles carving their faces and energy bouncing through their bodies. A bold heart would approach him once in a while and then Titus would tell the child to come join his stronghold when they were grown.

No small hearts beat in his vicinity today, the lack of their high voices and bright eyes a sharp pain. "Did the reborn take your children?"

From the fear that carved the old man's face, he suddenly realized this was something else altogether. And he wondered what else his enemy had taken from his own people. Had he demanded their young? For what purpose?

His stomach churned. Was it possible Charisemnon had somehow been able to do what Lijuan had and turned the most vulnerable members of their society into a horrific melding of vampire and reborn? If so, *where were they?*

17

"I am your archangel," Titus said from the deepest depth of his chest, so his tone would vibrate in their bones. "You do not need to hide your children from me." It came out far harsher than he'd intended, but he needed to know if the villagers were hiding infected children.

Ugly as it was to consider, those children were already dead, their only aim to infect more and still more until no one truly alive was left in the world.

The old man's bones appeared ready to rattle down to his feet.

"Be quiet," Sharine muttered to him, far too low for anyone else to hear. "I'll handle this."

He was so astonished at her gall that he was struck dumb. She stepped forward. "We are on a long journey," she said in her voice so lush and rich with texture. "We want nothing from you but water and a place to rest for a moment or two. You know well that you cannot hide anything from an archangel. It's better that you are honest."

Fresh tears rolled down the old man's face as he mumbled words to one of the women close at hand. She was crying, too, but she went to a nearby door and opened it, reaching out a hand. A small hand clasped hers and then out came a little boy with his own hand clasping that of another girl—and so on until a string of five little ones stood in front of Titus.

Unlike most children who came face-to-face with an angel, these babes showed no wonder, only a terrible fear that destroyed him. He didn't know what to do, looked to Sharine for an answer. Smiling, she went down on her knees, her wings spread out on the dirt behind.

"My son looked just like you when he was younger," she murmured to one particular boy. "Always with dirt on his knees and scrapes on his cheeks. He was off on one adventure after another."

Though the child didn't respond, Sharine kept on talking in her gentle voice warm with love until that small face twitched at last into a smile. As Titus watched, Sharine ended up seated on the ground with a circle of little ones in front of her, all enraptured by her stories.

When she reached into her backpack and removed the energy bars she'd brought for herself, handing them out to the children, they reached for the food with grateful little hands. Soon, the smallest one of them all, a girl of perhaps two with a thin face and huge shining eyes, was sitting in her lap.

Awestruck by her magic, Titus thought about how he might do the same with the adults. But he wasn't like Sharine. And so he did what came naturally to him. "I would speak to you," he said to the elder who'd spoken first. "You are, I think, the headman of this village."

Two younger males started to step forward, protective fear bunching their muscles, but the elder shook his head. "I will come, my lord Archangel." Breathless words, his skin losing blood. "Until I am gone, this duty and any punishment we must take is mine."

Titus saw it was all going wrong; he looked to Sharine once more. Her mind touched his—he hadn't known she could do that, but as he was coming to learn, there was a lot he didn't know about Sharine. She was an old, old being and simply because she preferred to live in a world of art had no bearing on her levels of power.

The world—and Titus—should've paid attention to the biggest clue out there: Illium. Sharine's son was already being talked off as a future archangel though he was barely past five hundred years of age. Why had they all assumed such power had come from his father's blood alone? Even Raphael, the son of *two* archangels, hadn't been that violently powerful at such a young age.

Why had no one ever considered what gifts Sharine had bequeathed her son?

Ask for tea, she said into his mind.

I don't drink tea, he said, after taking a moment to cope with the song of her voice; it was even more luxuriant on the mental level. *They will think me deranged if I ask for tea.*

A narrowing of her eyes. *Then ask for ale, your archangelic lordship.* The last words couldn't have been more sarcastic had she tried.

But since she seemed to know what she was doing, he looked at the scared and angry young men who'd tried to step up, and said, "Bring us ale!" Then he turned his attention to the old man. "You and I need to discuss the future of this village now that I am your archangel."

Terror smashed into the villagers, locking muscle onto bone and transforming their blood to ice.

Wanting to groan, he glanced helplessly at Sharine. This never happened with his own people—*they* trusted him. He'd have to stop forgetting that Charisemnon had taught his people fear instead of trust.

Sharine emitted a mental sigh. *People keep telling me you are charming. CHARM.*

Glaring at her sounded like a wonderful idea except that he'd been told his visage could appear fearsome when he was in a bad mood, and such would probably cause the terrified villagers to expire on the spot. He decided to break out a smile. "I should warn you that I killed that festering boil, that dog's excrement, that insult to the Cadre who was your previous archangel."

THAT'S your idea of charm?

Ignoring the incredulous comment, he continued on, "I don't know what he told you of me; hear the truth from my own lips—I despised him and all he represented. The only people who have to fear reprisal from me are his toadies and enforcers."

Those ones, Titus would not forgive, no matter what. Unlike these villagers, the others' had been powerful enough to have a choice—even if that choice was to die with honor, or defect to another archangel's territory. He'd been right there at the border and he'd protected previous defectors. No, he'd never trusted those defectors, but he hadn't harmed them.

"All others," he added, ensuring his voice carried, "especially mortals he treated as prey, are safe from my wrath."

Wrath? You had to use the word wrath?

It took effort to keep his smile pinned on his face. *We need to have a conversation about your respect for archangels.*

I had a son with one, was the quelling response. *That waste of immortal cells puts on his pants the same way as any other man.*

Thankfully, the headman gave Titus a shaky smile at that instant and Titus had an excuse to turn his mind to other matters. "You are willing to speak?" he asked, to be certain the man wouldn't quiver throughout—he didn't have the time to coax words, needed information quickly.

"Yes." A firm—and loud—agreement. "If you don't mind me to say, my lord Archangel, I'm glad you have a strong voice. I can barely hear everyone else—they just whisper and murmur and what good comes of that?"

"Exactly!" Titus went to clap him on the back, only at the last minute realizing he'd probably break him; he still did it, just held back most of his power.

Meanwhile, two villagers had set up a table a way down from the children, now placed a pair of seats there. Neither was suitable for an angel's wings, so Titus simply flipped one the wrong way around and straddled it.

The headman settled across from him and waited until one of the youths had poured their ale before saying, "My son."

"You are justifiably proud," Titus said, though he knew nothing of the youth. *See,* he said to his own personal haunt. *I can be polite and charming.*

Her mental snort was even louder this time.

Deciding to ignore her—let her see what she was missing—he turned his attention fully on the headman. "Tell me what I need to know." Then, for some reason he didn't understand, he opened a mental link with Sharine so she could listen in on the conversation.

Being able to so invite others to hear what he did wasn't a skill possessed by many, and he'd only gained the capacity in the second half of his reign, but it was useful when utilized. Stopped having to repeat information.

Sharine didn't protest the link.

"I need to come up to speed with my new territory." Titus had no actual desire to rule Northern Africa; unlike some, he didn't hunger for huge swaths of territory. He'd been quite content with his half of the continent—it was enough space to accommodate his power as an archangel and it allowed him to take care of his people as he wished.

But if he had to have the entire continent under his wing for the time being, then he'd do a good job of it. "You seem like the kind of person who would know all there is to know about this village and the surrounding ones."

"I keep my eyes open—even if I can't hear so well." The

old man's chuckle seemed to take the last of the tension out of the villagers. The group finally began to dissipate—sending awed looks at their archangel as they did so.

Titus allowed his wings to spread, allowed the mortals to admire his feathers.

Not obvious at all.

He asked himself why he'd opened the channel—but didn't close it. *I see tiny mortal hands on your wings,* he grumbled back. *Angels don't permit just anyone to touch their wings.*

They aren't just anyone—they're babies, was the sharp reply.

For some bizarre reason, he was tempted to smile; perhaps he'd unknowingly eaten mushrooms that were playing havoc with his mind. "Tell me what you have seen," he said to the headman.

"Dark things." Sadness washed through the seams of his weathered face. "We were not a wealthy village before it all began, but we were more than able to take care of ourselves and to send our smart young ones to the city for studies. So I suppose we were wealthy in a way. Plenty of food, enough to tithe to the archangel and still—"

"Tithe?" Titus knew such things happened, but most archangels had more than enough wealth and power not to bother—or even if they did, perhaps because they preferred to support their people in other ways, it was a minor amount. With so many people in each territory, a tiny bushelful of anything added up to thousands of pounds.

Titus was no farmer and so his court just bought supplies from those who were; it kept his people thriving for their harvests bought good value to their home regions, and it meant his court could focus on other matters. Even now, reborn threat or not, he was paying for supplies—with his people under strict instructions to buy only the excess, never what the farmer needed for his own family, or the settlement needed for itself.

The rest, Yash was having shipped in from territories that weren't dealing with a scourge of reborn. He wondered if Sharine knew that Yash had recently bought out the excess olives produced by Lumia's town. But that wasn't a matter for today.

"Half our harvest." The elder swallowed and seemed to build himself up. "We are sorry, my lord Archangel. Most of our harvest was destroyed by the reborn. We can give you what—"

Titus waved off the coming question. "I do not ask for a tithe—though I do ask that all those with fertile land continue to plant when they can. We can't always rely on offshore sources." It wasn't a thing of pride but practicality. "The supply chain isn't always guaranteed."

"Yes, yes. Of course that is the way." The headman smiled at Titus, once more in good humor. "So we were all eating well enough and living our lives. Then the evil came. The rotting ones."

"The reborn?"

"Yes, that's what the younger ones call them. But to me, they are the darkness." He coughed, the sound rough and hard, a rattle in his chest. "We had a little warning of their arrival for we'd placed scouts in the trees and they screamed out that the darkness was coming."

A wet sheen in his eyes. "But we'd miscalculated the creatures' speed. They came so very *fast*." His shoulders fell. "We lost the scouts. Our fastest young men ran home with bloodied throats and began to change in front of our eyes . . ."

A long moment where he swallowed repeatedly. "You know the rest, my lord Archangel. After the burning began, we cried for our lost ones as the flames licked the night sky. One was my firstborn grandson. I lost my eldest daughter-in-law in the next attack."

Titus couldn't imagine the depth of this man's pain. Those who saw mortals as weak and without courage had never spoken to one who'd experienced loss such as this, a loss rare among angelkind.

"Then the goats began to get sick, their flesh turning green-black," the elder said after a sip of ale, though his voice remained rough. "We lost half of them. All of us too scared to eat the meat, so it went to waste." He hacked a cough. "The rest appear healthy but we're keeping them penned up under constant watch."

"When was this?" Titus asked. "The animals turning?"

"About three days ago?" The headman scratched his head, then turned to yell out the question to his son.

"Three days ago," the male replied.

"Yes, that sounds right." The headman turned back to Titus. "It feels an endless time, but it has been only days."

"How does it begin?" He had to be sure it wasn't in the air.

"A bite," was the response. "We suspect one of the goats panicked and ran into the rotting ones and that was when it was infected. It then savaged a few others before we realized what was happening."

Titus held back an exhale. *Containable,* he said to Sharine. *If we eliminate the reborn, we eliminate the risk to animals at the same time.*

Ask him if he noticed if the birds were affected. They have domestic fowl here, so he wouldn't have had to look skyward.

The import of her question was an arrow deep in his heart. Angels were unlike any other living creatures on this planet—but birds came the closest. Not in their genetics, but in the simple fact that they lived so long in the sky.

"Were any of your animals untouched by the disease?" he asked instead of specifically speaking about birds. *We can't allow humans to see us as weak or vulnerable,* he reminded Sharine, who wasn't an archangel and couldn't be expected to immediately consider such things.

Every member of the Cadre knew that should humans

begin to see angels as vulnerable, they might get it into their heads to rebel against immortal rule, and that could have only one end: annihilation of mortals.

Angels needed mortals, but they didn't need *a lot* of mortals.

Certain groups of angels had even been known to mutter that mortalkind needed to either be culled or have their population strictly controlled: *They are insects, pests but for their one use. Pen them up in a corner of the globe, and ship out cargo loads as necessary. Mortals do not need to infest the whole planet.*

18

Thankfully most of angelkind didn't live on the fringe with the genocidal. But the reason behind the forbearance wasn't always a thing of kindness. One old angel had put it bluntly to Titus: "Humans are born and die at such a rapid pace, regular outbreaks of disease devastating large swaths of their population, or bloodlust-driven vampires killing entire villages, that their growth isn't really an issue."

At first, Titus had believed that the zealots who argued for partial genocide hadn't considered that the fewer the humans, the fewer the vampires. And many of the same old ones relied on vampires for almost everything in terms of the running of their households, and any necessary grunt work. But it turned out they *had* considered it.

It was Uram who'd told Titus that fact some five years before his death. "The hidebound ones talk of human farms to feed and maintain the vampires in the world, with only a limited number of new vampires created each year—to replace any who are lost. Mortals farmed for blood would have their brains intentionally stunted so they become true cattle, while any extra angelic toxin would be pumped into said cattle who'd then be executed before the transition was complete."

The green-eyed archangel had laughed. "Who do they think will clean up after their cattle, feed and bathe them? Or perhaps they are to be in huge farms with their bodies permanently hooked up to blood-harvesting machines. That's if the toxin transfer even works with all the changes—our kind has never been able to explain the why behind how mortals save our sanity."

Uram had made the whole idea sound ridiculous . . . but he hadn't been revolted, while Titus'd had to fight his rising gorge. Sometimes, he wondered if that had been an early sign of Uram's madness, but then again, so many of the older angels thought little of discussing humans with such a lack of empathy.

Across from him, the headman frowned. "The goats were the first," he murmured to himself.

As Titus listened with forced patience, the older male went through the various animals in the village including domestic cats and dogs. "The *chickens*!" He smiled. "No oddities with our chickens. And also the cats.

"We've eaten some of the chickens since and are all unaffected, so I think they must've been kept safe by being in their coop. As for the cats, they're very fast and good at climbing, so they probably escaped being scratched by the rotting ones. It must also be said that cats will do as they will."

Throwing back his head, Titus laughed. "Cats are like women," he said in the aftermath of his mirth. "Unpredictable and as apt to hiss and claw as purr."

The headman cackled but Sharine's voice was frigid in his head. *I am astonished that Tanae has not murdered you in your sleep.*

Tanae is not a woman. She is a warrior.

Ah, all is clear now. Such sense you make. The tone of her voice declared him an imbecile.

Adding that to her list of infractions against an archangel, Titus returned to his conversation with the headman. "Did you notice any differences between the first attack by the reborn, and the ones that came after?"

"We've survived three nightmares, and each group of the rotting ones have been faster," the elder said without hesitation. "My son and the other young ones say they also seem to hunt more as a group. A pack."

He ran the long salt-and-pepper of his beard through his hand. "Many of us also believe their faces and bodies have changed as well, though it's hard to say for certain—I saw them only in fleeting glimpses as we fought them with fire."

The headman indicated the flaming torches Titus had seen from above. "It's why we religiously feed these flames—so they won't come near." Another hacking cough before he returned to the matter at hand. "The first rotting ones, they looked human but for the madness. The ones that came after . . . there was something twisted about their bodies and they walked in a way I find difficult to describe."

He ran his hand over his opposite forearm. "My skin is the deep brown of the richest soil, as is yours—if I may be so bold as to compare us even in this way. My wife's skin is darker yet, a gleaming ebony that has returned in our spoiled and loved third grandchild." A hint of a smile. "But you see we have people from the north in our village, and even Pieter who married our Sarra; he has white skin that burns before it alters its shade."

This time, the headman's cough had Titus nudging the other man's ale toward him. After taking a drink, and though his voice continued to rasp, the other man said, "So hear me when I say I know mortal hues. The skin of the rotting ones has darkened but not in any way that ordinary flesh might do so."

Chewing on his lower lip, his bushy eyebrows drawing

together, the headman stared unseeing at the table. "It has changed color in the way that a piece of fruit does when it rots from within, a greenish tinge below the skin, the darkness that spreads a sickly bruise."

"I understand exactly." Titus finished his ale, needing the taste to wash away the ugliness of what the headman was describing. "Is there anything else I should know?"

"I've told you everything I could think to tell, but if you will allow, my lord Archangel—"

"You can call me Archangel, or Archangel Titus. You don't need to add anything further." Such additions were nothing but affectations. Lady Sharine was a good and proper address, but every member of the Cadre already had a title. Archangel on its own was the most powerful title in the world.

Some, like Caliane, accepted Lady—or Lord—as an alternate title, but he'd never heard of anyone else in the Cadre using two titles in concert. Trust Charisemnon to have chosen yet another method to feed his vanity.

"Archangel Titus," the headman said solemnly. "If you will allow, I will ask a question."

"Ask—but the question must be a fast one." He put down his tankard. "I must soon be on my way—but I'll return to speak with you in the future, after we've dealt with the most significant problems at hand." Titus hoped the old man would make it to their next conversation, but he knew too well that mortal flames blinked out with a rapid fury that had burned him on more than one occasion.

There was a reason Titus tried not to become too close to mortals; he'd made mortal friends in his youth . . . and he mourned them to this day. Those who saw mortals as cattle had never danced close to their small, brilliant lights and been singed in the aftermath. It broke his heart to think of friends gone, gifts lost forever, dazzling minds silenced.

The headman took a deep breath, seemed to hold it before exhaling softly on his question. "How many of our daughters do you wish as a tithe?"

Rage was a thunder so violent in his veins that he was about to throw back his head and roar to the sky when a cool, crisp, and lovely voice spoke into his mind: *Don't terrify these people when you and your vaunted charm have made a bare inroad into their trust. It took incredible courage for him to ask that question. It's no insult on you but an insult on the one before you.*

Titus was so blindsided by the tone of her voice—*no one* spoke to him that way, not even his mother or sisters—that his rage morphed into red-hot insult. *You would do well to remember that I am an archangel, Sharine.*

I never forget, was the unflinching answer. *But as I have mentioned, I had a son with one. Strip off the outer trappings and he still has the same parts as any other man. Just. Like. You.*

We do not have the same parts, he said nonsensically, angered on a level so deep it rarely came to the fore. *Don't ever compare me to that*—He cut himself off, not sure what insult would be good enough. He didn't know all of what Aegaeon had done to Sharine; what he did know had him curling his lip. What honorable man *chose* to leave his child behind, chose to break a small and brave heart?

Titus, Titus! Look, I can fly good now!

Illium wouldn't remember meeting Titus as a child, but Titus remembered the small and fearless blue-winged boy who'd crossed mischievously from Aegaeon's Refuge territory into Titus's on a regular basis. He'd enjoyed the little one's grit and bravery, had thought Aegaeon a lucky man to have such a son.

"Archangel, I did not wish to anger you." The headman was a pasty brown from how his blood had rushed to his feet—quite a feat with skin as dark as theirs.

Titus refused to look at Sharine. "I'm not angry at you,"

he said, every muscle in his body locked to stone hardness. "I'm angry at that piss-stain upon the earth that you once called your archangel." He wasn't about to withhold his punches; it wasn't as if humankind didn't already know of the enmity between him and Charisemnon.

"I don't want your children or your women—any who wish to apply for a position in my citadel of their own free will are welcome to do so once your village no longer needs their assistance to survive." He crushed the metal of his tankard, barely noticing the damage. "I don't need or want young girls to warm my bed. I have plenty of women lining up to do the same."

Stop. Stop. Your modesty overwhelms.

Truly, she'd been sent to torment him. *It's not bravado or conceit when it's the truth.*

To the headman, he said, "Does that answer your question?"

The headman's eyes were wet and shining as he rose with Titus. Once up, he bowed so deeply that Titus was afraid he would tip right over. Instinct had him reaching out to catch the man's shoulder, say, "There's no need for that. We have shared ale. You have lived to be a graybeard and you have learned wisdom with it."

Though this man was but a fraction of Titus's age, human lives moved at a different speed, and so there were things the headman understood that Titus didn't and wouldn't for eons more.

It made him wonder what Sharine had experienced over her long immortal lifetime, the lessons she'd learned . . . the bruises she carried.

She came to stand at his side at that instant, an expression on her face that he couldn't quite comprehend. Since *not* asking her questions did nothing to keep her mild and content, he decided he might as well ask her to explain— and he would, once they were alone. Which they soon were, their good-byes short before they lifted off.

Titus let Sharine go first so that she wouldn't be buffeted by the draft created by his more powerful wings. "What?" he said once they were back on their flight path. "Have I grown a second head?"

"No," she said after a penetrating glance. "Let's just say I find myself surprised at your capacity for certain kinds of understanding."

As far as backhanded compliments went, it was one of the best ever inflicted on Titus; even Nala would be hard-pressed to better it, and his sister was renowned for her acerbic wit. Nala didn't talk much, but when she did, she made an impact. "How do you think I look after my territory? By being a reckless brute?"

"Such a course of action certainly seemed to have worked for Charisemnon."

Titus went to reply then shut his mouth. She was right. Charisemnon *had* ruled with brute power much of the time—but that hadn't been all of him.

"Much as I'd like for him to be remembered as a vicious idiot, he had a kind of cunning that I will never possess." A simple truth. "Charisemnon could manipulate his people in ways I find difficult to comprehend. Though he took their children, their daughters far too innocent and young to be in a man's bed, they *revered* him.

"Even in the headman's village, there will be some who think of him as the right kind of archangel, of me as too rough and unrefined in comparison to his sophistication. The horrors of war and the reborn have torn the veil from most eyes, but why did it take so long? Why, for such a long part of his reign, was he worshipped as a god?"

"Because they had no choice." Sharine's voice ran over him like water, silken and bitingly cold at once. "He was a being of devastating power—as you are a being of devastating power; they had no avenue of appeal. Either they lived under his rule and found a way to rationalize it—or they died, likely tortured and broken."

"That isn't true!" Titus raged. "They could've crossed the border to me."

"Leaving behind all they ever knew? Leaving behind their families? All the while with no way of knowing if you were any different?" Nothing cold or edgy in her tone this time, rather a poignant depth of knowledge. "To mortals, archangels are all one and the same. The Cadre is too far above mortal existence to truly understand them."

"You are all but an Ancient," Titus said, not sure why no one ever referred to her as such—perhaps it was the sense of bright freshness that clung to her. "You're no closer to mortals than I am."

"Before Lumia, I was even further away." Surprising words, soft and heavy. "Lost in the fragmented pathways of my mind."

Titus had so many questions, but he made no move to pursue that thread. No one became as she had unless it was a thing of terrible pain. He wouldn't rub that pain raw anew, no matter how she irritated him.

"Since moving to Lumia, however, and basing myself in the adjacent town," she continued, "I've come to see mortals not as a faceless mass but as individuals. I know that some are funny and sweet. Others are courageous.

"Still others have darkness in their hearts. And I know that outside Lumia, most mortals have never been in close contact with an angel. The idea of speaking to an archangel . . . It is beyond their comprehension."

Sharine knew that she was being hard on Titus; the truth was, she couldn't help it. It was simply that he reminded her so much of Aegaeon. Her former lover'd had the same confidence, the same swagger to him.

Though she was beginning to think that Titus had a far bigger heart. Big enough to rule this continent and bring it back from the brink of ruin. It was tempting to admire him for his clear moral lines and refusal to bask in his power, but Sharine wasn't about to fall prey to the urge.

Especially when she'd already found herself susceptible to his devastating smiles. No, the last thing Sharine needed was to begin to admire the Archangel of Africa. Big, brash, beautiful Titus would use any such admiration to walk all over her. Not because he was cruel, but because he was Titus.

19

*Avelina, your Titus challenged me to climb a
mountain—and the damned pup beat me! To assuage
my mortally bruised honor, I challenged him to climb
down in the dark. It is as well that he doesn't know
that terrain as well as I do, for otherwise, he would've
beaten me again, without remorse.*

*I thank you for trusting me with the gift of your
son. With each century that passes with him under my
command, he becomes less a stripling, and more a
man I consider a friend. It's a strange thing for one so
old as I to have a youthful friend, but I think I
would've considered him a friend no matter at which
point in life I met him.*

*Soon, the time will come when he leaves my court.
It is inevitable. He must learn more of the world,
learn more of himself. But always, I will hold a place
for him in my army.*

*Enjoy your sojourn with Euphenia. Tell the child
she owes me a concert.*

—*Letter from Archangel Alexander to
First General Avelina*

20

After flying for another ten minutes, Sharine said, "What do you have against Aegaeon?" She'd been startled by the depth of Titus's anger when she'd made the comparison between one archangel and the other.

Titus shot her a look darker than any she'd ever witnessed on his face. "I have sisters, do you know that?"

Sharine frowned. Perhaps she had known that once upon a time, but if so, she couldn't lay her mental fingers on the knowledge. "Are they older than you?" she asked instead of answering.

"The youngest was a thousand years old at the time of my birth. My oldest sister is now some eight thousand years old."

"Is it a mother you share or a father, or both?"

"Zuri and Nala are twins, thus share both parents. We, all five of us, are linked by our mother, Avelina. My sisters," he muttered, "are also bonded by their shared aggravating temperament."

"Your mother is very fertile." Sharine felt the stab of admiring envy, for such fertility was not often found in their kind.

"She also loves children and is brilliant at raising them to be strong, honorable angels—I'm quite sure I would have another sibling by now if the first general hadn't decided to go into Sleep a millennium after my birth. Truly, my mother would have to beat men off with a stick were she not so formidable they don't dare advance on her without permission."

His pride in his mother was open, as was his exasperated affection for his sisters. Again, her heart threatened to open for him, this man so blunt about his loves and his hates. With Titus, nothing was hidden, nothing was a subtle game. Despite all she'd told herself, he was nothing like Aegaeon but for the fact both were archangels.

That made Titus far more dangerous to her than she'd realized.

"My sisters are equally desired," he said, with a grimace only a brother could produce. "Aegaeon made a play for Charo, the scholar among us. Wickedly witty with her friends, but shy with others. He hurt her."

The potent simplicity of that statement hit hard. "Yes, he is that kind of man." One who seemed to have none of the empathy so evident in Sharine's son. "He hurt me, too."

"Is that why you were lost?" Titus asked, then made a grumbling sound. "All of angelkind says the Hummingbird is lost in her own world, but unfortunately for me, you seem to be quite present and aware in my world."

Her lips twitched, her amusement a surprise to herself. But his grumble was half-hearted at best . . . and that was a surprise. "I didn't fragment because he left me," she clarified, for the idea of Titus seeing her as fragile was unbearable. "I had a young son whom I loved with every part of myself. Illium was my reason for being."

"Then what?" Titus asked at his usual volume.

"Why do you feel you have any right to ask me that question?"

He shrugged. "How will I discover anything if I don't ask? It's not as if I'm holding your feet to the fire to force you to answer."

It was such a Titus thing to say that she felt laughter burst the seams of her being, such amused delight as she hadn't felt in a long, *long* time. She laughed with her son at times, but that was different, a moment between mother and son. This, laughing with Titus, it felt an adult thing that reinforced her feeling of wholeness.

He was staring at her when she caught her breath and glanced at him, his eyes stunned. "Doppelganger," he said at last, the boom of his voice a rasp. "It's the only explanation."

Laughing again, she wiped away her tears . . . and had to fight the urge to fly over and tug up his scowly lips into a smile. Such a childish impulse for an old immortal, but Sharine didn't feel old right then. Maybe it was because this blunt hammer of an archangel had given her the gift of laughter, and maybe it was because it was time, but she told him the truth.

"To understand why my mind fractured," she said, "you must understand my history." A single glance and she knew she had his full attention—though he continued to scan the landscape as they flew. "I loved a man named Raan at the very dawn of my existence. I was a decade past my majority and he thousands of years old when we fell in love."

Titus growled akin to one of the lions that roamed his lands. "He shouldn't have put his hands on you."

Anger was a whip in her voice when she set him straight. "Even with the gift of hindsight, I can tell you there was no coercion, no manipulation. Some souls are just meant to meet and to entwine."

A stubborn silence from Titus before he blew out a

breath. "I first became friends with Alexander when I was a pup of some two hundred. We are friends still, though he is an arrogant old man."

It took her a second. "You're speaking of Archangel Alexander?" Caliane called him "Alex" but theirs had always been a deep friendship quite apart from Sharine's own with Caliane.

When Titus gave a nod, she shook her head. "You astonish me, Titus." It was no lie; Alexander was an Ancient, would've *been* an Ancient during Titus's youth, and yet she could see why the archangel had formed a liking for the undoubtedly brash young warrior Titus had been.

"My apologies to your Raan," he said. "If you say he was a good man, he was a good man."

It shook her, how much that trust meant to her. Titus, she knew, didn't take honor lightly. Swallowing hard against the surge of emotion, she looked away from his handsome profile and carried on. "We had a joyous half a century together. Then Raan died."

Titus stopped flying, dipping a fraction in the sky before he pulled himself back up into a hover. "Battle?"

"No, I woke one morning and he was dead beside me." She could speak those words now and feel only a distant sadness; always, she would remember and love Raan, but she was no longer caught in the sticky tendrils exuded by the past.

Titus started to fly again, but he was silent for a good long while. She gave him time to digest the news, aware it was a big thing for an immortal to accept that death could come at them, silent and unseen. It didn't matter that Raan's and her parents' deaths were the last such ones she knew of in the eons of her existence—that the possibility existed at all was a horror story for angelkind.

"I don't know how to understand this," he said at last.

She liked him even better for his honesty. "It took me a long time, but, Titus, there is more. Do you wish to hear it?"

Now that she'd opened the door, she found she wanted to talk about it. Only one other person knew her full history, and Caliane was yet in *anshara*.

"Yes." Titus's response was firm. "I would hear it all."

"My parents went into Sleep when I was eighty-five years of—"

"WHAT?" It was a boom so loud that she half expected the sky to crack open. "Your parents left an infant on her own?!"

"I was hardly an infant." But she had been a scared child who'd spent her whole life trying to cling to parents who were never quite present. "But that isn't the story."

"I'm not sure my heart can take any more," he said, anger yet vibrant in his tone. "When your parents wake, make sure it's not in my vicinity. My fury would surely singe their flesh off their bones."

"My parents are dead," she said softly, this pain even more faded than the grief of Raan's death, for that good-bye she'd made as a child, never knowing if she would see them again. "I went to check on their place of Sleep when I was two centuries old, and I found their bodies just bones, their flesh dust."

Titus turned to look at her, his mind unable to comprehend the depth of her loss. Her radiant voice was quiet with sorrow, but the grief wasn't a sharp knife. No, it wouldn't be, not after so many millennia. "My heart would break should I go to check on my mother and find her gone."

To think of First General Avelina gone from this world in dusty silence . . . it was such a wrongness that he couldn't bear to imagine it. As soon as it was safe, he'd go visit his mother, make sure she was warm and whole . . . as Sharine's parents would never again be.

"My heart did break," she said, "but I think, not the same way as yours would." She angled her wings to take further advantage of the draft he was creating, and he could tell she was tiring. "My parents were old angels, and I knew from infancy that they'd one day leave me."

Titus simply couldn't imagine parents who'd abandon their vulnerable child, but then, Aegaeon had done the same. "Aegaeon's abandonment of your son? It reminded you of the loss of your parents?"

"No, the fracture lines were in a different place." A strand of hair that had escaped her tail kissed her cheekbone before flying back. "Death, you see, was my greatest fear. Specifically the quiet and unwitnessed deaths of those I loved."

Titus's skin grew cold with a rage so deep, it had no name. "He went to Sleep in your bed." So that when she woke, it would be to an unmoving, unresponsive angel. Her traumatized brain wouldn't have made sense of the single sign of life—a certain warmth of the skin.

To Sharine, Aegaeon would've appeared as the dead.

"His second and three others of his innermost court arrived the hour after dawn, to take him to his secret place of rest." Fury in every syllable. "I was whimpering in a corner by then, my fist thrust into my mouth to muffle my screams. My mind was gibbering that everyone I loved died. Over and over again in an endless loop, that was my only thought.

"After I first woke, I ran to check on Illium. In my screaming panic, I forgot that my baby boy was staying with his best friend that night, and when I saw his empty bed, I was convinced he was dead and someone had taken his corpse. In that fragment of time, I truly *believed* my child was dead."

No tremor in her voice as she finished the story. "The only mercy in it all was that Illium didn't have to see his mother break down and his father be carried out of his home by a solemn squadron in full regalia."

Titus's jaw worked, his hand fisted to bloodless tightness. "I've long known Aegaeon to be worthless, but now I know the depth of his cruelty." If the archangel's second knew to come for him, then Aegaeon had planned it. Most archangels slipped into Sleep without warning, and without assistance, so their place of rest would be secret; it was a measure of Aegaeon's cruelty that he'd chosen to allow at least four of his court to know of his place of rest in order to shatter Sharine.

"I've never known why he did it," Sharine said, and right then, she was magnificent in her cold anger. "If I ever see him again, I will ask him—if I can stop myself from first stabbing out his eyes."

Titus approved of her bloodthirsty need for vengeance.

"I think at times, that I should release the anger," she said, "that my vengeance should be to erase him from my thoughts."

"You can erase his face and his eyes instead," Titus muttered. "And release your anger in his flesh." It would still not be enough.

An unexpected burst of that astonishing laughter that was sunshine falling in a rain over him. He clenched his gut against the glory of it. If he'd thought her beautiful before . . . well, if the Hummingbird was beautiful, Sharine with her blade of a tongue and golden laughter was extraordinary.

Fighting the urge to touch her, this being beyond his reach, he said, "Am I to take it that you have no more feelings for the blue-green donkey?" He had to break the moment, break his entrancement. "If you are pining for him, admit it now so that I can smite you for bad taste."

"Smite me?" Sharine couldn't believe he was serious, but he sounded so very solemn. "Surely you have someone in your court who occasionally pops the bubble of your enormous ego?"

His response was a thunder of sound. Shifting, he flew away from her. She watched him go without concern, knowing he wouldn't leave her behind. Titus stuck to his promises.

When he returned after sulking a short five minutes, it was to say, "How did you fool angelkind into thinking you a soft, ethereal creature? Did you sit each night in your home and cackle over the game you were playing?"

It delighted her that despite all he knew of her now, he treated her exactly the same. No pity or even a hint of feeling sorry for her. Titus, it seemed, had come to see not the Hummingbird, but *Sharine*—and he wished to pick a fight with her. Sharine found she wasn't averse to crossing swords with the Archangel of Africa.

It was dangerously exhilarating.

"Just as I'm sure you must sit in your room at night and think up wooing words that have women dropping at your feet." She fluttered her lashes at him. "Please do try out your prepared charm on me. I promise to be a receptive audience."

"You've been sent by my sisters." A horrified stare. "They cannot torment me in person, and so they've sent you to torment me by proxy."

To think of Titus as a beleaguered younger brother astonished and intrigued her in equal measures. She had so many questions, but there was no time to ask them because below them came a movement jerky and unnatural that made her blood run ice cold. *"Titus."*

21

I see it," he responded, all irritation gone from his tone and his attention a blade.

Reaching to his back, he unsheathed his swords. She went to ask him why he didn't simply use his fire to scour the earth, but the answer was there in her question. The land had already been devastated by the burnings its people had to undertake in order to protect themselves. It'd take time for the soil to regenerate, for any poison from the reborn's decomposing bodies to dissipate.

Far better that Titus take down the slavering horde with the gleaming weapons in his hands than he create another scar in the earth.

Stay up here, he ordered as he began to drop from the sky. *You don't have the skills to avoid the creatures at close range.*

She didn't bristle; truth was truth. At least thirty of the reborn scrabbled under the late-afternoon light. The rotting beings were gathered around the long-limbed carcass of a giraffe they appeared to have brought down. *I'll remain aloft and out of reach.*

The reborn must've been desperate to resort to feeding on an animal. From the way they moved, however, while the animal flesh was keeping them functional, it wasn't truly revitalizing them—they didn't have the smooth motion of those who fed from humans. Wanting to help in a way that didn't make her a fatal distraction, she flew to where she could see the entire battle; this way, she could warn Titus if a creature was about to come at his back.

Power wreathed her hand, as if summoned by her fear for him—yes, he was an archangel, but there were a *lot* of reborn and they could do massive damage to his body, including tearing off his wings.

Curling her fingers, she held the power back with significant effort. She'd intervene only if it appeared that Titus needed the assistance . . . because while she had all this rich, old power, she had little experience with her aim. She couldn't afford to get it wrong with Titus down there, his big body surrounded by monsters.

Titus took out the first ring of reborn even as he landed *in* the remains of the carcass of the animal they'd brought down. It was as well that his boots were solid, came up to his calf, and were impenetrable to the blood and viscera in which he stood as he swept out his swords in a rapid-fire motion that cut off reborn heads so quickly that one hadn't yet fallen to the ground when another joined it.

His wings were his biggest vulnerability—this iteration of the rotting, voracious creatures had developed razor-sharp hooked claws. As a result, he had to keep lifting off when they got too close, then coming down again to lop off their heads.

Previously, reborn this hungry would've just kept coming, stupid machines driven by the urge to feed. The newer strains seemed to have gained a semblance of self-protective instinct—but from the emaciated state of their bodies, this nest was starving and thus too desperate to give up the fight, run.

Snarling, hissing, spitting putrid fluid, they kept on coming.

Behind you!

He twisted to eliminate the one about to go for his wing . . . and saw the creature was already falling, a blade in his eye. Grinning, he ripped out the blade and spun it back to Sharine, while stomping his boot over the reborn's chest. He preferred a clean beheading, but he had three others coming at him and crushing the heart to pulp stopped them in their tracks.

When he lifted off the next time, he took stock of remaining numbers. The creatures screeched and clawed up at him, their faces twisted into a caricature of life. Adrian, the very first reborn Lijuan had displayed to the rest of the Cadre, had been a man of glossy dark skin and rich brown eyes, and he'd possessed a mind. Mind enough to understand that his goddess had turned him into an abomination.

Titus could still remember how blood, scarlet and wet, had dripped down Lijuan's white skin after Adrian sank his fangs into her neck in a futile effort to end the nightmare, end his goddess. The reborn male's eyes had held infinite sorrow—and so deep a pain that it had scraped across Titus's bones.

Adrian had been the final truly intelligent reborn Titus had ever seen.

Unwilling to risk another defection, Lijuan had turned her reborn into stupid, mindless machines that wanted only to feed. It didn't matter if a person had been a scholar or a warrior before being infected, the infection that brought them back from the dead also erased all evidence of who they'd been in life.

For all Titus knew, some of these people had once been in his court. He'd lost many good people in the battle against Charisemnon and in the battles against the reborn that had followed. It was equally possible that they were so emaciated because they'd been buried a short time earlier; long enough for their flesh to begin to decompose, but "fresh" enough for the reborn to pass on their contagion.

The latter might explain the dirty, blood-dotted suit being sported by one of the reborn.

Whatever their story, Titus could have no mercy on them—and he knew none of his people would want to exist in such a form. Roaring, his dual swords a blur, he dropped. When he came up for air this time, sweat gleaming on his skin, it was to devastation. Decapitated bodies. Reborn cut in half. Some with all their limbs chopped off. His swords had become razors that sliced and ended.

To the right.

The reborn Sharine had pinpointed was using its chin to try and drag itself away. Two steps to close the distance between them, then Titus brought down a blade on the creature's neck. He took no satisfaction from the act; this hadn't been an honorable battle. These people hadn't had a choice. To him, this was simple mercy. *Do you see any others not yet properly decapitated?*

Sharine flew over the entire scene and hovered over several bodies before saying, "No." Landing not far from him, she held her wings scrupulously off the blood and gore seeping into the ground. "We'll have to burn the bodies."

Nodding, he wiped his swords on a clean patch of grass, then slid them home. "I'll take care of it." A single pyre would do far less damage to the soil than if he'd used his power to scour the entire area.

"It'll go faster if we both help." She picked up a severed arm. "Where do you want to build the bonfire? I'm assuming somewhere close to the main mass of bodies."

Titus blinked, but no, she was still standing there, radiant and ethereal . . . and with a rotting severed arm held by the wrist, while she bent to pick up a decapitated head.

"Yes, atop the animal carcass," he said, his instincts taking over; the longer they lingered, the higher the risk of attracting another nest, and the longer his people would have to fight the worst area of infestation without their archangel.

Sharine didn't complain even as her hands became slippery with putrid green-black reborn blood, her body flecked with more of the same. The two of them would stink of decaying flesh for the rest of the journey, but it couldn't be helped.

"Such cruelty," she murmured at one point, her eyes bruised.

Glancing over, he saw her picking up what appeared to be a small carving. And he understood. In those who'd come from the far north, such carvings were sometimes tucked into the pockets of the clothing worn by the dead, to act as guardians on the journey beyond death that mortals believed awaited.

Now those carefully and lovingly buried dead were being desecrated.

Jaw set, Titus carried on, even as he saw Sharine add the carving to the pile of bodies. It didn't take long to complete their task, the giraffe carcass at the bottom. After they'd gathered up some dry branches and leaves to act as kindling, he used a tiny fragment of his energy to start a flame. Then they watched, because he wouldn't leave this fire to burn and spread across the land.

The heat blasted their faces, sparks jumping out, but they stood firm with their slimy blackened hands and stinking clothes. That was when he noticed light coming from Sharine's palms. "I also wish I could blast them all into oblivion, but we must care for this land or it'll become a desert."

"What?" Following his gaze, Sharine stared down at one hand. Then, as he watched, the blood on her skin began to crystallize into dust and fall away.

Titus watched in fascination as she repeated the process with her other hand. "Useful." It wasn't a skill for which he'd give up his own abilities, but it would be a prized one in battle—something as simple as filth could demoralize an army.

Still staring at her own hands, as if she didn't understand what she had done, she said, "Why don't I know myself?" A vibration of anger.

"Do you want to see if you can repeat the process on someone else?" He thrust a hand in her direction—he was no stranger to the smells and liquids of battle but that didn't mean he enjoyed it.

Sharine seemed to snap out of wherever it was that she'd gone. "Yes, let me try." She took his hand in her clean ones.

Light glowed.

It felt . . . like a tickle across his palm, the gentlest power he'd ever sensed, yet it was paradoxically old and heady. He should've worried about what power lay dormant inside her, but as the blood and other fluids fell away into dust, he became aware of the softness of her hand, the gentle way she held him. As if he wasn't so powerful he could break her in half with his physical strength alone.

It was all he could do to stand still while she cleansed his other hand, too.

"Thank you." It came out stilted. "That'll make it easier to fly. Can you take the stains out of our clothes, too?"

As a distraction technique, it proved a marked success. "No," she said after trying multiple times. "At least the sun is hot enough to bake away the scent rather than causing the fluids to rot."

Shuddering at the idea, he decided on another option. After removing his sword harness, he released the wing slits of his tunic, then pulled it off over the top of his head and threw it into the flames.

* * *

Sharine sucked in a quiet breath, struck by the blunt force of Titus's masculinity. From the lack of differentiation in the hue of his skin, being shirtless was nothing new to the Archangel of Africa. His skin was smooth and silky-looking, his muscles flexing powerfully as he bunched up the filthy shirt and threw it into the flames.

The stunning sunlike golden marking on his chest—a marking that had emerged during the chaos of the Cascade—was a thing of beauty, potent yet oddly delicate in line and composition. It served to draw her eye back and back again to the raw beauty that was Titus.

Her mouth dried up.

Stunned and shocked by her visceral response, she forced herself to look away as he went to put his sword harness back on. It had been . . . a very, very long time since she'd felt the bite of physical attraction. She'd never been a woman of strong sexual appetites, more focused on looking for companionship and friendship and love. For an end to the loneliness that had haunted her since she was a child.

Her parents had left her long before they'd gone to Sleep.

It wasn't that she'd become celibate after Aegaeon. Some spark of the Sharine who'd flown with a battle army had remained in the Hummingbird and she'd fought against the fragmentation of her mind, tried to cling to the shreds of herself that remained. Part of that had included a foolish effort to find an anchor using her body.

Foolish, for she wasn't a woman for whom the physical had ever been a priority.

After finally realizing the futility of it, she hadn't missed being a sexual creature, as her life hadn't otherwise been devoid of touch. She'd had a son who'd hugged her often. Aodhan and Raphael, too, had been there for long periods. Her boys. Surrounding her with so much love and affection that she'd never even thought of the carnal, of the deeper needs of the body.

Today, however, her body had awakened with a vengeance, sexual need punching through her hard and brutal. For Titus, a man even more beautiful than Aegaeon. Though she still didn't understand the superlatives about his charm. Titus was too blunt a hammer.

A fact he demonstrated to good effect when he said, "Are you wearing anything under that tunic? If you are, I suggest getting rid of the tunic. Reborn fluids tend to be disgusting in the extreme even when they dry—they grow black mold."

Sharine hesitated; she *was* wearing a garment Tanicia had called a singlet. Soft and shaped to Sharine's body, the white item held her average-size breasts in place, the wing slits fastened with small enclosures. But never in her life had she worn anything so revealing as outerwear.

She shifted on her feet . . . and got a whiff of her own odor.

Stomach threatening to turn itself inside out, she reached back to undo the wing slits on her tunic, then pulled the garment over her head and threw it into the flames. "I liked that tunic," she muttered. "Now I only have one. My entire wardrobe in your stronghold is filled with dresses and gowns." She scowled at him, careful to keep her eyes strictly to his face.

His square-jawed and rough-edged and altogether-too-handsome face.

"Don't talk to me of gowns and clothing," he grumbled. "I'm a warrior, not your dresser."

"And how do your clothes appear, my lord Archangel? By magic?"

He threw back his head and roared to the sky, his shoulders bunched and his hands clenched as hard as his jaw. The sound was thunder that made the birds take flight from the trees and her own bones vibrate . . . but not in fear.

Holding her ground, her heart pounding, she met his gaze without flinching.

"I respect my people." His eyes flashed. "That means I leave them to their duties. My steward should be able to point you to the right person."

"Thank you for your kindness in sharing that information," she said, not sure why she was taking such pleasure in antagonizing him—never in all her existence had she behaved this way; it was oddly exhilarating. "I'm sure I wouldn't have figured that out for myself."

Titus stared at her, just stared at her. "Tell me the truth—have you taken up drinking some concoction that turns a sane woman into a shrew?" It was a solemn question and maybe that was why the meaning of it took a moment to penetrate.

She bared her teeth at him, feeling . . . free. For so many years, she'd been caged. Caged inside her parents' rules, then her own fears, then her broken mind. For the first time since she'd begun to store memories, she didn't—what was that statement she'd heard one of the young townswomen say?—yes, that was it: *she did not give a shit*. And it was *glorious*.

"Men who call strong women shrews," she said in a tone formed of sugar syrup and molasses, "are often men scared of a woman's strength."

"My mother," he enunciated with care, "was first general to an archangel. I was *born* with a respect for female strength."

"If you say so." She brushed imaginary dirt off her arms, then walked around to the other side of the bonfire. "I'll keep an eye on this side."

Through the curtain of flame, he was a big and powerful and infuriated man standing with his hands on his hips and his chest bare. His eyes pinned her to the spot as the fire began to die down—or they made the attempt in any case, his eyebrows drawn together in a glower.

Sharine smiled at him. She felt zero fear. All her life, she'd been afraid in one way or the other, but it was as if she'd gone through a fire of her own and come out reborn. On the other hand, the latter wasn't the best choice of word, especially with her skin hot from the heat of a fire built to turn the reborn to ash.

Shedding of the skin, remaking, resurrection, they were all just words. What mattered was that she was becoming someone new, a woman she'd always had the potential to be—an angel of whom her son could be proud . . . and an angel who could look herself in the mirror and smile.

22

*I'm fine, Tito. But thank you, little brother, for offering
to decapitate Aegaeon for me. I wouldn't give that
worm the satisfaction of beating my brother to a pulp.
You're a strong angel, but he is an Ancient and an
archangel. No, Aegaeon doesn't deserve the pain of
someone of your worth.*

*—Charo, daughter of First General Avelina, to Titus,
son of First General Avelina*

23

Titus knew he should keep his distance from Sharine as they flew on after the fire was dead. She was clearly in a mood. But he was so fascinated by the contradictions of her and so aware of the gift he'd been given to safeguard that he stayed within an easy distance.

Not that she looked anything like the mythical Humming-bird. She looked like the straight-talking and confident angel who'd embedded a blade in a reborn eye. Her pants had mostly escaped being splattered with gore, but they weren't pristine by any measure. But pants were far enough from the nose that you could mostly ignore the stench. Her boots, she'd managed to clean using the grass; he'd done the same.

He refused to focus on her form-fitting white top, though he'd seen many of his warriors fighting in far less. Not so many centuries earlier, the vast majority of them had fought with nothing but paint on their chests and fury in their hearts. It wasn't the lack of coverage that bothered him, but the lack of coverage on *Sharine*.

The great artist Titus had been sent by the Cadre wasn't meant to be a flesh-and-blood woman who had excellent aim with a blade, boasted breasts that plumped out slightly over the scooped neckline of her top and skin that glimmered with sweat. Neither was she supposed to have a curved-in waist and hips that flared just enough to have a man considering how they'd fit into his palms.

And it wasn't her body alone that was giving him trouble.

She'd pulled her hair back into a tail that caught the light with every shift in the wind, every angling of her wings. The silken black tipped with natural gold—a gold that glittered here and there elsewhere in the strands—was astonishingly beautiful. As beautiful as her wings. No one in the world looked like Sharine. But it wasn't a question of beauty, either. Many, many angels were strikingly beautiful, as were an equal number of vampires.

Plenty of women in his court could stand next to Sharine and not be deemed her lesser in beauty. Yet Sharine would shine regardless. She had in her a radiant light that drew others—the same rare light existed in her son. And Titus had a soft spot for young Illium. The youth was a little reckless at times, but Titus hadn't exactly been less so as a youth.

The most important thing was that as Titus had been loyal to Alexander, Illium was loyal to Raphael. He was also a warrior who fought with fierce intelligence, the reason why he was a squadron commander. And wherever he went, the blue-winged angel drew others, the flame inside him a bright, beautiful thing.

That flame had come from his mother. It certainly hadn't come from Aegaeon.

He growled deep in his chest, wanting to smash that hind end of an ass into paste, but sadly, his hands were tied on that score. Firstly, Charo would never forgive him for bringing up the pain of the babe she'd lost in the aftermath of Aegaeon's heartless rejection, and secondly, the world needed every archangel it could get.

It was the latter thought that reminded him of a question he'd intended to ask—or perhaps he just wanted an excuse to talk to Sharine. "Have you had any word from Suyin's court beyond the reports she herself has made to the Cadre?" The newest archangel in the world had been scrupulous in making those reports, conscious that everyone else needed to know how she was dealing with the devastation in her territory.

They'd all been honest in that way, and where possible, they assisted one another. Titus, for one, had used his Cascade-born ability to create a deep gorge between his territory and Alexander's so no one could cross over on foot. While Alexander was known as the Archangel of Persia, his territory actually began on the other side of the isthmus that had connected Africa to Asia until Titus shattered the link using his power.

The lack of a land bridge meant the two of them didn't have to worry about incursions from the other side, and could concern themselves with the dangers already present in their territory.

In time, their two peoples would find a way to traverse the divide, but for now, the only way to get from one side to the other was to fly or go by the sea. Neither of which the reborn could do—thankfully, the horror of Lijuan's black-eyed and dead angelic fighters had ended with her, her energy the only thing that had kept them functioning in a nightmare simulacrum of life.

The reborn infection couldn't take hold in angelic blood.

Streaks of green-black on stone, in the shape of dragging wings.

Gut cold at the memory of what he'd seen in Charisemnon's stronghold, Titus hoped he'd been wrong, that the pattern had been something other—perhaps two vampiric reborn crawling away together. Because if the sky, too, became a place of war against Lijuan's voracious "children" . . .

"I assume you're asking about Suyin because of Aodhan?"

"He's your son's great friend." The warrior-artist was also currently seconded to Suyin.

"He's also loyal to the archangel to whom he has been seconded," was the quelling reply. "Though it's only a temporary position, he treats it with all honor."

"I'd expect nothing less of one of Raphael's Seven." The pup who'd once been a stripling in Titus's army as Titus had been in Alexander's had done well to surround himself with such loyalty—and that extended to his consort.

A pang in his heart, powerful and deep.

Every so often, Titus looked at Elena and Raphael, as well as Elijah and Hannah, and wondered what it might be like to have a consort who'd walk with him through the ages of immortality. He'd never, however, come close to forging that deep a bond with any woman.

Some might say he was a true son of his mother's blood, that he'd never settle, and maybe that was so . . . but Phenie was also of Avelina's blood, and she'd been with her lover for two millennia and counting. Even Charo, gun-shy after Aegaeon, had settled into warm domesticity with not one but *three* men.

The first general would be immensely proud of her youngest daughter.

Sharine's rich tones broke into his pensive—and unsettling—thoughts. "But," she said, "Aodhan has spoken to me of his own feelings and overwhelming all else is a sense of grief.

"Lijuan has broken the heart of an ancient civilization. So many of China's treasures are gone, destroyed during the horror of the black fog that murdered. But the biggest lost treasure is the population. All those minds and hearts and their gifts and skills erased from existence."

Titus tried to imagine it, failed. "Even after the destruction of Beijing"—a destruction caused in the wake of the Cadre's effort to rein in Lijuan's lust for power—"I'm used to thinking of China as a place of deep history and culture, with a thriving populace."

"Last we talked," Sharine said, "Aodhan spoke of how eerie it is to fly over cities that should be bustling with enterprise and hope and yet sit silent, waiting for its people to come home. People who are long dead."

"Once, Lijuan was another angel." An angel with whom he'd never had a friendship, but an angel he'd respected. "A thousand years ago, I couldn't imagine her doing what she did. Is young Aodhan well?"

"He says he is, but the child feels deeply. I know it's difficult for him to see so much evidence of death over and over." A tone to her voice that he'd heard in his mother's more than once . . . and yet the maternal edge did nothing to dilute his response to her.

Sharine never spoke to him with that tone in her voice; she didn't see him as a child—and he'd have dared her to try if she'd given that indication. Titus was no one's child but the first general's.

"Aodhan is also far from his own people," Titus said, having heard enough of the angel to know that he wasn't a man who trusted many. "Is there anyone nearby with whom he can let down his guard?" It'd be impossible with Suyin right now—she needed Aodhan too much for him to ever be in any way vulnerable with her.

"Every warrior must put down his sword at times," Titus added. "Not even an archangel can go on day after day after day without respite." It was a lesson he'd learned at his mother's knee—the value of good comrades, friends, and family. His sisters drove him to lunacy, but it was to them that he went when he wished to just be their petted, harried, and beloved Tito for an hour or two.

"I've told him he must fly across to Caliane's territory to take a break," Sharine responded. "Even if he won't be with close friends, he'll be with warriors he knows from his ordinary life, and it'll be, as you say, a respite from the heavy duty that lies on his shoulders."

"I think Suyin feels the same weight." Her face had been thin and drawn during the last meeting of the Cadre. "But she can't leave her territory, even to gain a breath."

"I hope she's building a support structure around herself." Sharine's voice remained fierce and maternal. "Aodhan is too loyal to follow my advice and go to Caliane's lands for respite, but he can't stay forever—he's critical to Raphael's own tower."

"Has anyone asked him if he'd be amenable to a permanent transfer? Being second to an archangel is a position many covet."

A pause before Sharine said, "You must understand—for Aodhan, the Seven and Raphael are family, the bonds between them far beyond flesh and bone and blood. It is a thing elemental. Though he'll serve Archangel Suyin with all his heart, he'll always fly home in the end."

Sharine sighed. "Suyin, that poor child. It must be difficult for her to know who to trust, especially after being kept captive by Lijuan for so long. She can't trust *anyone* from the old court, for she has no way to know if the people with whom she speaks were involved in her captivity."

"Suyin isn't a child." She was older than Titus.

Laughter that fell like a sparkling rain against his senses. "You're all children to me."

He swore he saw a glint in her eye, was near-certain she was baiting him. Unbelievable of the Hummingbird . . . but not of Sharine.

Deciding to be the mature party in this conversation, he responded to her earlier comment. "As far as the Cadre has been able to confirm, everyone loyal to Lijuan died with her—Suyin doesn't have to fear sabotage from within." He curled his lip. "I truly can't see Lijuan leaving behind anyone, not when she wished to amass a force the size of a small nation."

Sharine rode a thermal for a while, her wings beginning to dip against the deep reds and oranges of the early-evening sky but not yet to the point where it was dangerous. Titus just watched her; she was lovely in flight, a graceful and jeweled creature akin to the bird whose name she carried.

Fire sparked on the gold in her hair.

He scowled at the timely reminder that this same angel could strip his skin off his bones with her tongue alone . . . but the reminder did nothing to soften the tightness in his body, the heat in his blood.

"I'd like to believe the same," she said upon returning to him, "but do you not think Lijuan might've left behind a small group, one tasked with retrieving her remains should she fall? They would've been told to put her in a safe place where she might regenerate."

"If she did, it was a foolish hope." Titus made no effort to hide his disgust; he'd lost all respect for Lijuan when she began to treat her people as expendable. "She is dead in a way that means she'll never again rise. But do not fear—I stay alert, as does Raphael."

He thought Neha, too, was paying sharp attention now that she'd risen from *anshara*, and Caliane would no doubt be the same. Titus missed Elijah's wise counsel and acute perception, but the Archangel of South America was yet healing, his consort by his side.

As for Alexander, he was physically fine, but Titus knew the Ancient too well not to understand that he was wounded within. It had to do with Zanaya, another archangel who might never again rise, her wounds had been so grievous. Not that Alexander would talk on the topic; Titus had tried to bring it up and been firmly rebuffed.

When it came to Lijuan, Alexander had come too late into the old Cadre to have the necessary knowledge of her court, but Titus knew Alexander would back him if Titus made a call on the point. The two of them might be friends, but they weren't always on the same page when it came to Cadre business—but on this subject, they were in full agreement. "We won't allow a viper to infiltrate Suyin's court."

"You're protective of her."

"She has ascended at a terrible time. Unlike the rest of us, she doesn't have a time of relative peace in which to grow into her strength." Titus'd had a good four centuries before Charisemnon began to show his ass over the border. "The only mercy in all of this is that with the entire world in chaos, she doesn't have to worry about territorial challenges."

Darkness had begun to touch the horizon in the distance, and now it spread over them, wingbeat by wingbeat, breath by breath. Until at last Sharine said, "I can't go any further without resting."

Titus was glad of the survival skills he'd gained from having four sisters; another man might not have held his tongue when he first noticed the dip in her wings. "I'll carry you." Keeping his eyes scrupulously off her chest, he held out his arms.

He half expected an argument, but she flew to hover just above him. "If you drop me," she muttered, "I will ferment reborn blood, then pour the resulting foul concoction over every inch of your sleeping quarters."

"Then I'll just sleep outside," he snapped, incensed by her lack of trust. "I'm an *archangel*, Sharine. I don't *drop* things."

"What's it like to be so arrogant?" she asked musingly. "Do you spend at least an hour a day imagining all the ways in which you are wonderful?"

"Do you wish to come or not? Or you can land and I'll pick you up on the way back." They both knew he wasn't going to make good on his threat—he wasn't about to leave her to the mercies of the reborn that crawled across the landscape. But a man had a limit.

Folding back her wings, she dropped—right into his arms.

Only once she'd looped one arm around his neck, her wings pressed tightly against her body to reduce drag, did he realize that this was going to make things extremely difficult. Because now, not only did he have the soft warmth of her pressed up against him, he could see down her neckline, to the rounded mounds of her breasts. If that wasn't enough, every part of her that was bare rubbed against his own bare skin.

The Hummingbird. The Hummingbird. The Hummingbird, he chanted silently. *This is not a woman. This is the Hummingbird. A great artist. A treasure of angelkind.*

"What do your myriad lovers think of being fleeting conveniences?"

24

A treasure of angelkind.

More like a jackhammer drilling into his brain.

"Why do you believe my lovers are fleeting conveniences?" he asked with a scowl, because holding her was like holding light and air; he'd have to ensure she ate properly whilst in his court or she'd waste away.

Only . . . how could a woman be so light and have such soft breasts and curving hips?

Hummingbird. Hummingbird. Not a woman with breasts and hips and nipples. THE HUMMINGBIRD. An artist. A treasure—

"Oh, come now, Titus." Her breath whispered warm and soft against his neck, her voice husky and her lush lips curved. "I may have been at a distant outpost of late, and I may have been quite insane prior to that, but I never lost my hearing. The revolving door to your sleeping quarters is well-known."

Titus didn't know which one of those statements to address first. In the end, he decided to go for the most unexpected one. "What do you care about the door to my sleeping chamber?" It came out rough and edgy, his cock growing hard in his pants.

He grit his teeth and thanked the skies that she couldn't see his arousal from her position in his arms. *Arousal!* He couldn't be aroused by the Hummingbird! It'd be like being aroused by a great work of art. You weren't supposed to *touch* such masterpieces.

The great work of art bared her teeth at him. "Oh, I'm not." She waved her free hand. "I just worry about the women you use and discard."

"That is enough!" he boomed, certain she was attempting to annoy him on purpose.

A wince. "I'm right here, my lord Archangel." A hand rubbing over her ear. "There's no need to try and blow out my eardrum."

Did nothing terrify her? "Are you certain you're not still insane?" In truth, he was sure that she'd never actually lost her sanity—she'd just lost herself for a period. "Baiting an archangel isn't considered good for one's health."

"It is possible," she said thoughtfully, tapping a finger on her lower lip. "But I find that I don't give a shit. Is that not a wonderful statement? Think about it. To care so little for a thing that you wouldn't even offer excrement for it!"

He was so agog at the vulgarity coming from her mouth that he stopped flying for a second. They both dropped. He recovered at once, but she dug her nails into his neck regardless. *"Concentrate."*

Titus's cock thickened even more, his skin hot, and his pulse rapid. "I've treated with respect each and every woman who has shared her body with me. I've never made promises of forever." That would've been a lie and Titus didn't lie. "Any woman who comes into my arms understands that I offer only pleasure and affection."

Uncharacteristically for the fascinatingly impertinent

woman he'd come to know, Sharine went silent. For so long that he began to fear he'd scared her to silence . . . and that chilled his blood. About to apologize for yelling at her, even though he'd been speaking at his usual tone, he was stopped by her saying, "Do you know what'll happen to Astaad's harem? I know they've been helping their people, but what'll happen to them in the longer term?"

He blinked. "Heartbroken though they are, they're not just helping on the ground—they've been acting as a kind of advisory board to Qin, assisting with the transition of power. Qin's asked Mele and the others to stay on, but if they don't wish to continue to advise him beyond the transition period, he's promised to pension them to lives away from the court."

"Do you think he'll keep his word?"

Titus hesitated. "Qin rarely speaks," he said at last, searching for the right words to describe the Ancient. "It's as if he has half a foot in this world, half in another." In that second world lived the mad, beautiful prophetess whom Qin loved so profoundly that for him to be in this world without her was pure pain.

"That he doesn't wish to be awake couldn't be more clear." Qin was a creature out of time and place, woken from the depths of the ocean by the pitiless Cascade and left stranded on the unforgiving sand. "But unlike Aegaeon's posturing, Qin is quietly going about doing his job as an archangel. So yes, I believe he'll keep his word."

He tightened his hold a fraction, so he could have more of Sharine's warmth against him. "Also, even if I'm wrong in my reading of him, Mele is too strong and too intelligent to take any deceit or force lying down. She'll find a way to protect herself and the other women of the harem."

"So she's a warrior? Good."

Titus frowned. Mele wasn't a warrior, not in the sense of sword and shield, but he couldn't argue with the characterization—from everything Titus's spymaster had managed to discover through her sources on the islands, Astaad's most beloved concubine was standing shield to the other ladies of the harem. Mele alone dealt directly with Qin, though she was but a vampire and he was an archangel.

"Yes," he said slowly. "Mele is a warrior who doesn't carry a sword."

Sharine searched his face. "I worried," she said, "because I saw what happened to Aegaeon's harem after he went to Sleep. A kind of bloody savagery as the women sought to find positions in the courts of other strong angels."

Titus curled his lip. "Aegaeon harps on about not wishing to be awake, but he's already begun to form a new harem, full of the type of women that he prefers. Vicious backbiting spiders who eat their own young." The words were barely out when he realized that he'd put his entire giant foot in his mouth.

Wanting to groan, he said, "I don't count you in that number."

The nails that dug into his neck this time were deliberate. "That's good, because I was never part of his harem." Ice-cold words. "He invited me to live in his court more than once, but I couldn't exist in that sphere. I couldn't survive there." The latter words were flat. "At the time, I was a soft creature, a crab without a shell. I preferred to live in the Refuge with my art and—later—with my son."

Titus had to fight the urge to crush her to him. "I think you don't have to worry about Mele and the others. They're a family, and they'll make the decision as a family."

"Do you believe Astaad will rise?" No more nails digging into his neck . . . and possibly a small caress of fingertips over skin to soothe the earlier bite. "Did not Lijuan suck out part of his life force?"

"As a small child," he said, soaring underneath a banner of brilliant stars, "I was told the legend of an archangel who was cut into a hundred pieces by his enemy then burned up with angelfire. But the enemy missed a fragment of his brain.

It was left in a rock crevice and there it stayed for many years. It was covered by snow and then by the grasses of the distant plateau where it lay among the rocks and it was pecked at by birds, but it didn't decay and it wasn't lost.

"Then, one day, a bird picked it up but lost it mid-journey, dropping the piece of brain matter into a massive gorge. There it lay in the dark shadows for hundreds of years as the archangel slowly rebuilt his body cell by cell, the action one of instinct, of the natural order. For all you need for an archangel to come back to life is a fragment of a healthy cell." That was also why he was sure that Lijuan would never return—*nothing* of her had remained.

"A most gruesome story." Sharine pressed her free hand to his chest. "Tell me the rest."

He grinned, delighted with the unpredictable woman in his arms. "Well, the archangel stayed silent even after his head grew, for his torso wasn't yet complete. He knew he remained vulnerable. So he lay there in silence for tens of years more—I'm told that once the brain and the head have regenerated, the rest of the body doesn't take as long.

"Still, because he had no sustenance except for the insects that flew into his mouth and the rainwater that fell on him, he regenerated far slower than is possible with more fuel to power the growth. Once he had arms, he dragged himself to a spot in the gorge that had a small stream, and in that stream lived such creatures as small frogs that he could catch and eat.

"He also ate the wildflowers on the stream's edge, and the moss that grew on the shadowed rocks that were his home. Even once he had his whole body, he remained weak, so he waited crouched in the dark crevices of the gorge and hunted any animal that came close. It's said that it took him another ten years to regain his strength to the point that he could fly out of the gorge. Once out, he hunted for bigger creatures until he was brimming with power."

He paused.

The Hummingbird slapped him lightly on the shoulder, a butterfly's sting. "Stop dragging this out, tell me the rest!"

He chuckled. "So, Sharine likes a good story."

"What Sharine likes is flaying infuriating men alive."

Grinning, he carried on. "Once he was full of power, the archangel didn't attempt to pull together his court. He knew who was loyal and who wasn't, and he knew they'd come to him. First, however, he had a task to complete. He stalked his enemy, and then, when the enemy was alone, he incapacitated him by chopping off his head."

"That seems a bit anticlimactic."

"Do you always interrupt your storytellers?" he asked, though he'd made a similar judgment as a child.

"Carry on, my lord storyteller. Please do carry on."

Despite her poor demeanor, he could feel the tension in her body and knew she was hanging on the edge, waiting for the next part of the story. "After chopping off his head, the archangel incinerated his enemy's body. Then, before he flew the head back to the same gorge where he'd lived all that time, he destroyed the mouth and jaw of his enemy.

"He hid the silent head deep in a shadowed corner, where no one would ever find it. He knew his enemy would regenerate his mouth but no one would hear him when he screamed. Then, for millennia, the archangel would fly back at regular intervals to destroy any part of his enemy's body that had regenerated.

"The enemy remained forever a head, sitting there oozing on the bloody stump of his neck, screaming into the void. It's said that he is there still. Insane beyond all understanding, a thing no longer sentient."

He lunged his head toward Sharine.

She screamed.

Titus burst out laughing, shaking so much with mirth that he was barely aware of her hand slapping his shoulder while she called him "a fiend." "I thought you were narrating a true story! Who came up with that hideous tale?"

"One of my sisters." Still chuckling, he found his gaze dropping to the sweet plumpness of her lips, had to consciously force it away before he gave in to temptation and broke about a thousand unwritten laws of angelkind. "I was perhaps five decades old." The midpoint between child and adult. "I spent the next five years searching every gorge I could find for the decapitated head of the insane archangel."

"Did you never wonder about the identity of the other one? The one torturing his nemesis for eternity?"

"I was fifty." A boy ready for mystery and adventure. "And it's a very good story. Charo has always had a great talent."

Sharine sat up in his arms, her inhale sharp. "Your sister is Charo of the Tales?" Her mouth fell open at his nod. "How did you spring from the same stock that produced such a glorious wordsmith?"

"I'm a gift," he shot back.

She parted her lips to reply, when her attention was caught by something else. Pointing down, she said, "Do you see that?"

"Yes." Another group of reborn, these ones moving in a crablike crawl, their heads hanging forward and their bodies hunched. "This area is uninhabited for many miles in all directions, and these reborn appear heavily lethargic from lack of food. I predict we'll find them in much the same place on our return."

"Yes," Sharine said, "you're right—it's more important that we unearth the strangeness I saw in that village." No amusement or bite in her voice now, simply a deep vein of sadness. "Why do we do this? Destroy that which we love?"

The golden filaments in her feathers glinted in the starlight. "Charisemnon loved this landscape as much as you do—he visited Lumia twice during my time there, and we watched the sunset together. We spoke of the animals and the sky and the colors of this land, and I would've staked my life on the fact that he was honest in his love."

"I don't doubt that." Titus's sorrow was more complicated, bled through with hate and disgust. "I, too, once sat beside him—it was long ago, soon after I became an archangel. We shared a tankard of ale, and we spoke of how lucky we were to have this land as our territory."

Then, Charisemnon had been content with his half of Africa, had welcomed Titus as his neighbor. "There are differences as you fly from the north to the south, but in the end, there's a feeling to this continent that you can't find in any other. It sings to my soul and it sang to his."

Titus could barely remember that Charisemnon. "But the thing is, he grew to love power more—or perhaps that hunger always existed in him. He chose power and vanity over his love for this land and for his people. In pursuit of that power, he poisoned our land of life and wonder, and he turned our people into prey. For that, I will never forgive him. Had he a grave, I would spit on it."

25

Sharine didn't disagree with Titus's judgment, harsh though it was.

The Archangel of Northern Africa that she'd gotten to know had been jaded and dissolute in a way that was difficult to explain. It was oft said that power corrupted, and archangels were the most powerful beings in the world— but archangels also had to deal with myriad problems to maintain a healthy territory, from keeping a firm hand on vampires, to—at the basest level—ensuring the population had work and didn't starve. That didn't even take lethal territorial politics into account.

An archangel couldn't simply sit pretty and "exist."

It was unlikely that Titus thought of himself as a crouching threat over the other members of the Cadre, but he was, as were they in turn. Power such as that of an archangel didn't sleep. It watched and so by default, the members of the Cadre watched each other. Friendships, love, logic might stop them from making constant war, but the threat of it loomed always.

Ennui shouldn't have ever been a realistic possibility for Charisemnon.

"Do you know what happened to him?" she asked. "I had little to do with him prior to my stint at Lumia."

"From what I've heard of his youth, he was always possessed of arrogance and the belief that he was better than others. However, many a young man believes so."

About to make a quip about Titus's own brash confidence, Sharine found herself remembering how he'd sat with the headman in the village, how he'd spoken to the elderly mortal with patience for his wisdom. Titus might believe strongly in himself but he didn't look down on others. It was a critical difference between the two archangels.

She had to stop trying to put him in the same box as Aegaeon or Charisemnon or their ilk just because she was discomforted by the fact he aroused urges in her she'd believed long dead and buried. Against her, his skin was like silk, his heat a delicious burn, and the vibration of his chest when he spoke an increasingly familiar pleasure.

"The tipping point," Titus said even as her cheeks glowed, "was Lijuan."

Another kind of heat blazed in her. "You can't simply blame another." It was lazy and absolved one party of responsibility in a circumstance that both'd had a chance to influence. "I say that as a woman who so long blamed Aegaeon for what I became. But *I*"—she slapped a hand over her chest—"made choices along the way."

Not the initial fracture. She hadn't been able to stop that. Her brain had gone into shock, her mind skittering. But she'd had moments of sanity at the start, moments where she wasn't lost, and to this day, she didn't know if she could've fought harder to come back. Had she surrendered? Had she chosen her prison?

"No." Titus cradled her closer, the action making her suck in a quick breath as her heart kicked. "What I mean is that it was akin to an explosive reaction such as my scientists create when they mix two inert substances together."

Sharine frowned. "You think they would've stayed rational instead of power-hungry monsters had they never met?"

"I can't speak for Lijuan, for she was already an angel of seven and a half millennia by my ascension, but I feel I knew Charisemnon well enough to say that he was a man who liked luxury and worked the utter minimum necessary. He wouldn't have thought to stir himself to such grandiose plans of war on his own."

Titus's neck and shoulder muscles moved strongly as he angled them into the wind so that they could ride it, his wings powerful above them. "One of my scholars once told me a tale of two mortal murderers and he used a term that seems to fit here: folie à deux."

A madness of two.

"I'm not sure I agree with you," Sharine said. "I've heard of Charisemnon's appetites—one such as him would always want a bigger thrill, more sensory fulfilment. But"—she pressed her fingers to Titus's lips when he would've interrupted her—"I do believe there's a grain of truth in your supposition. Charisemnon and Lijuan egged each other on, as children do on a playing field."

Titus didn't respond, his eyes locked with hers. Her pulse jolted, her cheeks burned. Jerking her fingers from the unexpectedly soft curve of his lips, she went to make some quip to diffuse the tension that locked both their muscles . . . only to realize they were nearly halfway to their destination.

It had taken Titus bare hours to cover a massive distance. She hadn't realized how fast he was flying, he'd done such a good job of protecting her from the wind. Sharine was in no mood to be protected from anything, but she couldn't fault him for the care he'd taken with her.

A curl of warmth in her stomach, an ache that was pure temptation; it had been a long time, whispered a deeply hungry part of her. Why not break her fast with such a lover?

Shrugging off the thought, for she had no intention of becoming another one of Titus's admiring legions, she said, "Do you need to rest?" Even an archangel couldn't go on indefinitely.

"At the dawn," he promised. "I have no desire to be covered in more reborn rot."

Sharine grimaced. "Agreed."

So it was that they flew on through the night hours. At some point, she fell asleep in his arms, and woke to find him sweeping down to a grassland. Skin hot, she sat up. "My apologies."

"Do not worry," he said as he landed. "You didn't snore."

Sharine would've snapped back a retort, but he was putting her on her feet and she groaned as she stretched out her body. Things creaked. Lovely. Titus, too, was stretching— and he was glorious under the soft gold of the dawn light. "Your tattoo," she found herself saying. "It appears almost alive in the light."

He scratched the ridged lines of his abdomen. "A trick of the light." Eyes narrowed, he was looking past her. "Damn."

Sharine followed his gaze, caught the darting movements. "Reborn."

The slide of swords leaving sheaths was the only warning she received before Titus took off. Sharine followed, her wings aching from having been collapsed in his arms for so long. But Titus had the situation well in control, and the reborn were soon dead. He used a small pulse of power to erase their bodies, then landed again.

"If you could, Lady Sharine." He pointed at the splatters of blood on his chest.

Sharine's hand was already coated in power. Stepping close, she began to get the blood and gore off him. Her focus only slipped when she was nearly done; she became darkly conscious of the heat and size of him, her stomach taut and her mouth dry. It was all she could do not to jerk back when the task was done.

Titus glanced down, his expression shuttered. "We should fly again."

"I know I'm slower, but it'd help my wings if I could spend at least an hour in the air on my own." Not being pressed up against him would be a bonus.

Nodding, Titus waited for her to take off first.

When she did eventually end up in his arms again, she had enough distance from that spike of need that she could be rational. Not lying to herself about the depth of the attraction didn't mean diving headfirst into a bad decision. She asked him of the political history between him and Charisemnon, listened intently.

Later, he asked her about her friendship with Caliane. Laughing, she told him stories of their long association, memories so strong they'd survived her lost years and more. And it struck her that she hadn't spoken for so many consecutive hours with another person . . . for a long time.

He murmured for her to sleep again at one point. "Your body needs it after your earlier long flight."

Discomfort at how good it felt being cradled in his arms made her want to argue, but she knew that was foolishness. Closing her eyes, she pressed her cheek against the steady drumbeat of his heart, and slept.

They flew on.

Night fell again, the stars shattered diamonds in the sky.

It was as the night was dawning into dark gray that she pointed to a smudge in the distance, darkness against darkness. "There it is, the place where I saw the mummified hand."

Titus didn't land in the center of the settlement as she'd done, but on the easternmost edge. "Dawn will come in the next two hours. I think it's better if we wait to examine your findings in the light of the sun."

Sharine had no wish to remain so long in this eerie, lifeless place, but she couldn't disagree with him. Nodding, she reached back to lightly manipulate one of her shoulders. Though Titus had carried her with care, being in the same position for so long had led again to a predictable stiffness.

"I intend to walk the village border," he said in what probably passed as a quiet tone to him, and that she found comforting.

Titus's voice was an outward manifestation of his honesty.

"A walk would also help ease your muscles."

She froze, unaware till then that he'd been watching her. It took conscious effort to keep her expression neutral and fall in step with his bigger, stronger form. Titus, in turn, maintained a scrupulous distance between them as they walked, not allowing his wing to brush against hers.

Both of them kept their eyes on their surroundings.

With the sky already graying at the edges, it was no longer pitch-black and so it was easy to see the signs of disturbance when they turned the corner—it was as if people had fought a desperate battle against an attacking force.

Titus crouched down to examine one particular set of prints. "I'll have to look at this more fully in the daylight."

"Wait." Bringing out the phone device, she pressed the symbol Illium had shown her would bring light. It shot a glow, bright and sharp, onto the tracks. Pleased with herself, she said, "You really should get one of these. It's quite clever—I can see why my boy loves it so."

Titus's response was muted, his focus elsewhere. "Could you move it so that the light falls on this point?" He indicated the relevant area with one hand.

Attention caught, she did as he'd asked. The beam of light hit a mess of dirt and grass that looked to have calcified around what might've been blood or other bodily fluids. "What do you see?" While Sharine could pinpoint the minute differences in a work of art that spoke the language of the artist's brushstrokes, she didn't know how to read the earth.

Titus brushed his fingers over the section. "It's difficult to tell after all this time, but I'm near certain these were made by wings dragging on the ground."

Sharine came closer, still saw only a bare glimmer of what was clear to him. "An angel who saw the reborn swarming the village and landed to help?"

"It's possible." His broad shoulders shifted as he angled himself to check another area. "The reborn could've ripped a young angel apart." Expression dark as he rose, he said, "You should preserve the energy of the device. We may need it to examine further such areas."

He was proven right. They stopped four more times during their slow walk, while the sky lightened from the east and the world became a kind of smudged gray that reminded her of fog in the mountains of the Refuge. She knew it would brighten until the sky turned a dazzling blue, the light so bright it hurt to look at, the heat intense enough to cut, but for now, the air remained cool, crisp.

"I thought I'd miss the cool summer green and icy winter white of the Refuge," she found herself saying. "But Lumia feels like home, as does this land."

"Perhaps it's because you're a different woman from the one who lived in the Refuge." She was still chewing over the perceptive statement when he said, "Why did you stay so long there? Why not move with Illium to New York?"

Sharine had asked herself that same question, had no real answer. "I told myself I stayed to keep vigil over Raan's grave, that I had to do it so people would remember him, my Raan."

A smile that held no joy. "But I'd long stopped such visits by the time I met Aegaeon, going only once a year on the anniversary of his death. Difficult as it is to accept, I think

I stayed because it was safe, with defined parameters. A cowardice on my part."

"You judge yourself harshly." Titus's dark eyes landed on her, the contact reverberating through her entire self. "Even a wounded boar will retreat to lick its wounds."

Before she could respond, he spotted more evidence of an angel having been present during the fighting. *During* because the imprint of dragging wings had been baked into the soil by the sun, along with the blood and other fluids. Then Sharine saw a hint of . . . "It's a feather," she whispered, pointing out the small discolored filaments stuck in the dried mud.

Spine stiff and voice grim, Titus said, "All of these imprints appear to have been made at the same time. They overlap and interlock with one another, as happens when we grapple in battle and our wings drop."

Titus rose again, his thighs taut against the fabric of his pants. "What I can't understand is why did the surviving villagers leave if you found evidence they managed to burn up the reborn?"

Wrenching her gaze away from his thighs, she said, "It's possible they were too few in number with too little food to survive here." Even as she said that, she found herself shaking her head. "But if that were the case, I would've thought they'd head toward Lumia. It's the closest settlement."

"They would've had to cross mountains," Titus pointed out. "Impossible if they had injured among their number."

Though dawn had come, bringing with it the first kiss of the sun, Sharine rubbed her hands up and down her arms. It had nothing to do with the temperature, however, her mind filled with agonizingly detailed renderings of the slaughter that'd taken place here. At times like these, being an artist was a curse.

"I hope that's it. I hope the survivors found safe harbor." She refused to even consider that their bleached bones might lie somewhere in the wild, far from safety.

"There's enough light." Titus looked up at the sky. "It's time to examine the site of the burning."

While she kept watch, Titus checked all the buildings they passed, found no one alive or dead.

"Do you think the pyre included the bodies of their dead?" she murmured as they walked closer to the shriveled, blackened remnants of the fire. "Not simply the infected ones, but those who fell in defense of the village." She'd seen no graves on their walk, no signs of disturbed earth as happened with a burial.

"I believe so, and I can't blame them for their choice." Titus's tone was grim. "Even if they had no knowledge of the fact the reborn can infect the recently dead, they're unlikely to have had the manpower to dig multiple graves, or the supplies with which to create more than one fire."

Sharine's throat ached for these people who'd been forced to make choices no one should ever be asked to make. "They had to know the danger they'd face out in the open," she said, thinking of the roaming packs of reborn, vicious and pitiless. "They must've been desperate indeed to head out."

"My guess is that they knew no one would be coming and, as you said, starving to death was a real possibility." Titus looked up. "From the charts we found in Charisemnon's court, this settlement isn't on any normal angelic flight path. No one would've seen a sign asking for help."

She touched the phone in her pocket. "Why did they not use modern devices?"

"We brought down the network across the entire continent during the battle." Titus's expression twisted. "It would've left them with no means of communication with the outside world. And so I was partially responsible for whatever happened here."

Sharine found herself touching her hand to his forearm, the warmth of him soaking into her skin. "This is the way of the world," she said simply. "When immortals fight, it's the weaker beings who pay the price. Yet you had to fight.

Had you not, chances are these people would've been just as dead, and the death wave would've continued unabated—you know your nemesis wouldn't have stopped."

Titus, his muscles rigid, didn't say anything. Dropping her hand, she carried on at his side . . . but his open distress at the deaths here caused a crack in the walls she'd put up around her innermost self. This man, this archangel, he kept surprising her with the depth of his heart.

"We're here." In front of the damaged wall through which she'd seen the bones.

Titus strode up to it. "Wait."

As she watched, he tore apart the wall with care not to damage the remains on the other side. Parts of the wall, almost burned through, crumbled into dust at his feet. She wondered why the flames hadn't engulfed the entire village. Perhaps it was that the bodies hadn't burned hot enough or the fire had somehow starved.

Enlarging the space with methodical concentration, Titus worked until he'd eliminated most of the wall and they were looking on at a makeshift crematorium. Piles of ash played witness to the intent of the fire. But the flames hadn't been hot enough and skulls rolled around on the floor, while long thighbones as well as smaller finger bones lay in the light falling through the new opening.

She pointed out what had brought them here, the elongated hand . . . which she now saw was attached to a body. No wonder she hadn't been able to see it during her first visit; the body was at the bottom of many others. Titus silently moved the other remains aside—with care, but at speed, to reveal the body at the bottom.

It hadn't burned up in the fire, simply been scorched in a way that meant it had mummified in the interim.

It had no head.

Her eyes widened but her horror had nothing to do with the decapitation. She'd just understood the import of the body's spinal structure. *"Titus."*

Titus went to crouch down, then seemed to decide against it. Sharine wouldn't want her wings dragging in all that death, either.

"That's an angelic back," he confirmed.

She forced herself closer. There was no avoiding the truth—under the skin, angelic bodies were built differently from mortals in ways both subtle and profound, because angels had wings and thus musculature not possessed by those who couldn't fly. This was especially so when it came to the back and chest areas.

Even though this angel's wings had been burned away, and no trace remained of any of the muscles or feathers that would've once overlaid the bones, that he was an angel was indisputable.

Her boots crunched on something.

Gut churning, she lifted her foot at once, and looked down. The bones on which she'd inadvertently stood were fine and long. Not mortal. "Wing bones." She shifted back so Titus could see. "An angel died here."

"No." His hand fisted at his side, his voice harsh and deep. "An angelic reborn died here."

26

Ice crackled its tendrils into Sharine's gut. "That's impossible. Angels aren't susceptible to this infection." Reborn could hurt them, but the creatures couldn't turn them. "Lijuan created the reborn as a twisted promise of immortality, did she not? Angels are already immortal and thus immune."

She wasn't sure she was correctly recalling her conversation with Raphael; it'd taken place while her mind was yet a kaleidoscope. But she *was* certain when it came to angelic immunity. "Angels don't get sick." It was a fact of nature, as immutable as the wind and the sky.

"Do you know of the Falling?" Titus folded his arms, his biceps flexing. "In Raphael's territory?"

Bile burned the back of her throat. "Yes. Charisemnon caused angels to fall from the sky."

"He was able to create something that affected angels—we never discovered what, but as he was given the gift of disease by the Cascade . . ."

Her heart pulsed in her mouth, the horror of what he was suggesting turning her mute. Angelkind had no way to recover from a devastating disease; its birth rate was far too low. A single infection could annihilate their entire people.

The rays of the rising sun cracked the sky above their heads right then, bathing the entire site in a terrible golden glow.

Titus found no other signs of an angel, though he and Sharine searched the entire village twice, looking under every rock and in every cupboard and external building. It was possible his scientists would discover more when they sifted through the impromptu funeral pyre, for he hadn't wished to trample through that and possibly destroy other fine wing bones, but for now he could confirm the presence of a single reborn angel.

"If the world is lucky," he said, knowing it wouldn't be so simple, "this angel will prove to be the one who crawled away from the court of my nemesis to die having infected no others."

The champagne hue of Sharine's eyes were haunted when her gaze met his. "Have you heard anything to suggest that other angels have fallen to this infection?"

"No, but I don't know this half of the territory as well as my own." He'd barely had a chance to catch his breath, much less do an intensive tour of his new territorial region. "It's possible the infected are hiding—we've seen that the new crop of reborn have a survival instinct. That instinct might be even stronger in reborn angels, if we assume the strength of our immune system means the infection doesn't progress as fast as it does in mortals and vampires."

Sucking in a breath, Sharine said, "An angel might know what he was becoming, know he shouldn't exist."

Horror churning in his gut, Titus rubbed his face. "For now, we'll inform my people using your phone, then head back home. If this angel was moving when you landed, it was nothing but a lingering spasm—he is very dead, and I need to return to eradicating the threat in the south. Especially if there's even a small chance we may have to deal with infected angels in the coming days or weeks."

"I can ask part of Lumia's guard complement to stand watch in the skies until your scientists land."

Titus considered that; he didn't wish to expose Lumia or its guard to risk, but he also couldn't chance this body being disturbed by the reborn or by animals. "Tell them to stay in the skies," he said to Sharine. "When they need to land to rest, they are to do so in open areas where reborn cannot sneak up on them. Lumia won't come to harm by this secondment?"

"It's not much farther than the sentries normally fly— even if anyone has covetous eyes on Lumia at this time of chaos, they'll notice no difference in its routine." After making the call to her second, she began to take pictures "just in case."

Leaving her to it as he was certain no danger lurked here, he decided to take a final look through the village on the slim chance that he might discover something more about the infected angel. It was on his last look into the general store that he trampled on something that crackled. It turned out to be an envelope.

Picking it up, he saw that it was covered in dust except for one corner that bore the partial imprint of his boot. Written on the front were the words: *For our lord Archangel Charisemnon.*

Titus gritted his teeth. Rather than opening the envelope, he took it with him to where Sharine had just finished photographing the scene of death. "The villagers appear to have left behind a note."

When she said, "Shall I read it out?" he held out the envelope. The missive within could contain no good news; all he could do to soften the blow was to listen to it in her rich tones complex with texture. "Is the language one you know?"

She checked. "Yes."

"'My lord Archangel,'" she began, after opening out the piece of white paper folded inside the envelope. "'We don't know if this missive will ever reach you, but we have hope. We are in a terrible state—we have lost so many of our young and strong and the monsters who roam the land destroyed our crops and killed our animals. We don't have enough food, nor the manpower to grow more before we run out of supplies.

"'After much thought and because we know not many angels fly this way, we've made the decision to trek to the next closest habitation in the hope we can find safe harbor. We carry with us information for you. However, we also leave it behind here, for there's a strong chance we won't make it. The tainted creatures with their craving for flesh appear more and more. We know that you, Archangel, are battling them and that takes priority.'"

Titus couldn't hold back a snarl at the trust, innocent and pure, that these people had shown in the traitorous waste of archangelic space named Charisemnon. Rather his boot had ground the archangel's face into dust than it had stepped on the envelope left behind in betrayed hope.

Sharine took a deep breath of her own before continuing. "'We wish to tell you that, today, we had to fight an angel who was sick with the taint. At first, when we saw wings in the sky, we were so grateful we fell to the earth in joy. We thought to send a message asking for supplies enough to get us through the worst of it. But then the angel landed and we saw that he wasn't right.

"'We didn't attack him. Please know that. We welcomed him as an honored guest, as we would do to any angel. Even though his teeth were sharpened at the edges, and his hands cold and wet, and a green rot was spreading under his skin.

We believed that he was sick because of a wound taken in battle, that he would soon fight it off.'"

"For that knowledge alone," Titus murmured, "Charisemnon would've executed them one and all." No mortal could ever see angelkind as vulnerable. "Should the Cadre become aware of this, the only choice will be death, or the erasure of their memories." The latter was a terrible thing, an intrusion and a violation, but Titus agreed with those who said it was better than wholesale slaughter.

Eyes shining with a wetness she didn't permit to fall, Sharine carried on. "'At first, the angel spoke to us and his voice was disturbing in its grating intensity. But that lasted only minutes. Then, snarling akin to a feral dog, he hauled one of the village women close and ripped off her head, bathing himself in her blood before tearing open her chest cavity to feed on the organs within.'"

Fingers trembling on the paper, Sharine lowered it for a moment. "I have heard of this type of behavior."

"Vampires who've given in to bloodlust act so; hunters often find them with their faces coated with blood, their minds drunk and bodies slack from the indulgence." He moved close enough so that his wing overlapped hers. She didn't step away or rebuke him for the intimacy. "I can read the rest of the letter."

"No. I'll finish it." Another long breath. "I do this for the scared, brave people who thought to leave this behind, to warn others." Exhaling, she read on. "'The angel acted drunk afterward, his actions uncoordinated, so we took the opportunity to defend ourselves.

"'Many of our strong were already dead by then, so we couldn't fight him with honor. We threw fuel on him and set him afire. We hope you will have mercy on us, my lord Archangel. We didn't wish to cause him pain or kill him without mercy, but we didn't have any other way to stop him.

"'Once he fell to the ground, we used a kitchen cleaver

to remove his skull from his spine; we believe that perhaps angels can recover from this, so we have left his head beside his body. That body, we placed with the others, both friend and foe, that lay decomposing around us. Then we lit a fire using what little fuel we had.'"

At least that explained why the fire hadn't burned its way through the village; it hadn't had enough fuel to begin with.

"'Fire was the only way we could think of to purify the blood of the tainted ones and farewell our own,'" Sharine read. "'We did a prayer for the lost, then began our preparations to leave.

"'We hope that you'll find us in the next village. It lies north-northwest in a straight line, a half day's hike for a young man or woman. For us, it'll take a day or more. We no longer have any working vehicles, and we have many wounded, children, and elderly. We thank you for fighting for us, and hope our letter helps you to save others from this horror. And if we don't make it, please send word of our passing to the two towns below, where many of us have family and friends who'll tell others that we are gone.'"

Sharine was crying now, her tears quiet and heartbreaking. "It's signed with what I assume is the name of this settlement. Below that is a description of the angel: tall, with white skin in the few areas where it wasn't green-black, black curls, and a marking on the left cheek that looked like a lightning bolt."

Titus hissed out a breath. "Skarde, a courtier of Charisemnon's—and a man rumored to be one of his best intelligence agents." The scar hadn't healed after a decade because it had originally been made by Charisemnon in a temper—the barest graze of archangelic fire.

Carefully folding the letter, Sharine placed it back in the envelope.

They stood in a moment of silence for the dead and the lost. When she looked up at him and said, "We'll go north-

northwest?" he didn't tell her that there was no hope. He nodded; it was beyond him to abandon people who'd thought of others in their most dire moment.

First, however, they made a second call to his scientists and scholars, giving them this further information. One of the scientists asked Titus to take a sample of any flesh they could find, as well as some bone as a contingency against a disaster that might make the body inaccessible.

He was still speaking on the phone when Sharine moved to fulfill the request. Taking off her backpack, she took out the packet in which she'd kept the energy bars she'd given the children; she used it to scoop up a small wing bone, then set her jaw and used her throwing blade to cut off a piece of mummified skin.

Dropping it into the packet with the bone, she sealed it before thrusting it to the bottom of her backpack, then pulled the backpack on. When she looked around for something with which to clean her blade, he took it from her and wiped it on his pants. One more stain made no difference.

Accepting the blade back as he finished talking to his people, she slid it away into its thigh sheath. Two minutes later, they took flight in grim silence, their eyes searching the land for bones.

A half day's walk wasn't so far by the wing even at low speed and the sun was not yet high in the sky when they reached a village that appeared alive, smoke coming from the chimneys and movement in the streets. Bones aplenty they'd seen on their journey here, but none had been human.

Their landing caused fear, chill and black, to ripple through the village, the people going down with their faces pressed to the earth, but Titus was ready for it this time. "Rise!" he ordered, and once they'd done so, he held up the letter. "I come from the village of Dojah. Did any of the survivors make it here?"

A thin girl with a worn face, her skin a light brown and her hair in braids against her skull, stepped forward. "My lord Archangel." Her voice shook. "Ten of us made it. Two died later, their injuries terrible. Of the remnants, there is one older than me but he battles a fever after our trek here, and isn't lucid. The others are all children, saved by the courageous actions of others, but wounded in their hearts."

"Do you know what's written in this letter?" he asked, striving to keep his voice gentle and knowing he'd failed when she flinched.

"N-no." A whispery response. "My grandmother is the one who wrote it, b-but she is now gone." Tears washed her cheeks.

Sharine moved to put her hand on the young woman's, murmuring to her until awe replaced the terror in her expression and she found her voice again. "I will tell you all that I know, Archangel Titus." That she addressed him as he preferred told him that Sharine had said something on the point.

I thank you, Sharine. He found it infuriating to deal with these people's blind terror even knowing it had nothing to do with him.

Sharine's lovely eyes met his. *One day, they will know you. Until then, you must be strong enough to bear their fear. I know you have the shoulders to carry this weight.*

It should've shaken him, how much her faith in him meant to him, but it settled on his bones as if it had always existed. "Come," he said to the young woman, "we three will speak under the tree in the distance."

Once there, separated from the others in the village by a stretch of trampled grassland, he asked her to tell him all she knew. Everything she said dovetailed with the letter. Including that, regardless of the "harsh grate" of his voice, the angel had spoken words intelligible and rational when he first landed.

"But his skin was like a bruise almost all over," she added, "and it was peeling away in places, shriveled in others. His fingers were hooked, his nails like claws, and it seemed as if his tongue was rotting green, his lips too plump and red."

When Titus asked who she'd told of the angel, her eyes got very big. "Our hosts," she whispered. "We didn't want them surprised if it happened here."

Titus's blood turned to black ice: the entire village knew of the diseased angel.

The people to whom they'd given safe haven had sentenced them all to death.

27

Sire, I thank you for allowing me to serve in your court for the past five hundred years. Though I leave now to explore other courts and lands, I will return often to challenge you to a climb—it's my duty to ensure you maintain your strength.

Watch over my mother. I know she is your first general and tougher than I'll ever be, but for me, she is my mother. But please never ever mention my request to her. She would strike me dead with her gaze, then revive me to sit me down and flay me alive with her words.

I will never forget all that you have taught me.

—Letter from Titus to Archangel Alexander

28

Sharine said nothing as they walked the young woman back to the village soon afterward. But once they were alone again, back at the tree, she touched her hand to Titus's, closing her fingers around his fisted one as his wings began to glow.

"There are only two choices," he ground out. "I steal a piece of their memory—or I end their lives." Distant sounds of children's voices raised in play added a painful coda to his words.

Having misty memories of her own from her lost years, Sharine had a very personal view into what it did to a person to not know their entire history; it was a hollow ache of helplessness and loss. "The decision is an awful one." She squeezed his hand, her heart breaking and her eyes hot. "It'll always be an awful one, but such choices maintain the balance of the world. Some knowledge dooms mortals to a life without freedom."

"Alexander told me a story once," Titus said, his voice

sounding thick. "Of a small mountain town in what is now Italy. The people there decided to rise up against the cruelty of their ruling angel—she, the angel, wiped out the entire populace, down to the smallest mewling babe."

Sharine's entire body went rigid. "Why? Children would've done her no harm." They were the most innocent of innocents; even Caliane, in her insanity, had not done direct harm to the smallest hearts.

"I asked the same." Opening out his fisted hand, Titus wove his fingers through hers and she clung to the rough warmth of him. "Alexander told me it was because she was cruel beyond all sense of reason. Then he said, 'I tell you this not to advocate for senseless mass slaughter, but to remind you that you must never permit rebellion to foment. Because in the end, it'll lead only to endless mortal graves.'"

He blew out a breath but his chest remained tight. "So I know what must be done. It just seems such a terrible thing to do to people who have already lost so much." Titus took in the village again, alive against the day's light. "The only mercy is they won't know what they've lost."

Titus was old enough to have learned how to erase memories with pinprick precision, and he could do it from a distance. Still, it took him several hours to erase all knowledge of the infected angel from the village.

"It's their courage," he said to Sharine afterward, a sadness in his bones. "The way these mortals fought and how they thought of others to the very end . . . It's a thing of honor, of bravery such as I would laud in any of my warriors. Yet I've stolen from them the memory of their own brave hearts in fighting off an angel who wanted only to butcher."

Sharine's pupils flared, dark against the sunshine of her irises. "But you know. You'll honor them in your memories— as I'll honor them in my art." Shifting her gaze on those determined words, she took in the village in the distance. "After it is permitted, I'll tell Jessamy, so she may write this chapter in the angelic histories. Their courage won't be forgotten."

He looked at the fine line of her profile, her skin shimmering with a slight golden hue that was ethereal—but she was very much real, very much a creature of flesh and blood, her skin warm and her grip firm. He didn't release her hand, even though he knew he shouldn't be so familiar with a treasure of angelkind. "You understand this can't be spoken of yet, even to angels?"

A nod that drew his attention to the way she wore her hair; she could've been a young warrior in his court just barely stepping out into the world. "It would spread terror among our own kind and could lead to needless massacres."

Slim shoulders rising as she inhaled. "There are some among us who'd think nothing of scouring an entire continent to bare earth in order to halt the spread of a possible infection." She brushed her wing against his. "There's been too much death already, Titus. We must find a way to stop this without drenching the earth in further blood."

Titus had no disagreement with her words. But he was an archangel. "I must inform the Cadre." It wasn't a matter of choice but of his duty to the office he held. "I'll take full responsibility for stopping the scourge. No one will argue with all else that's going on—they're all too busy battling their own fires." And when it came down to it, he was the final authority on this continent.

Titus contacted the Cadre as soon as he and Sharine returned to the citadel.

He could tell she was exhausted after the brutal speed of their return flight—even the fact he'd carried her couldn't ameliorate the impact. She'd curled into as small a ball as possible to reduce drag and now slowly stretched out her limbs under a cloud-heavy and dull afternoon, shaking life back into her wings, arms, and legs. "I want a bath more than anything."

So did Titus. But this had to be done first.

"Would you like to sit in on the meeting?" he found himself asking when he should've been ordering her to rest.

She stared at him for a moment. "Yes." Her expression was inscrutable.

"I need only to make a stop to put on my breastplate." Gold, it curved over his shoulders and bore the emblem of a sun in the center, lightning bolts of power arcing out from it.

But the breastplate wasn't a thing of vanity. Neither was it a warrior's armor in the strictest sense, for an archangel had no need for such—anything that took him down wouldn't be halted by a shield of metal. No, this was a symbol of power, and today, he needed the symbolism.

Sharine waited silently while he put it on, then gave a crisp nod. "Your face bears streaks of dirt and sweat, as do your arms. You look exactly what you are—an archangel fighting a battle."

Warmth spreading inside him, he led her first to his most senior technical specialist, and asked her to hand over her phone for a minute so the relevant photographs could be copied.

That done, they walked into a large room set up with screens that would connect him to the rest of the Cadre. "You'll have to stay out of sight of the cameras." He pointed out the devices that would broadcast his visage to the others. "You're not a consort and thus automatically entitled to attend."

"I understand," she said, but there was a scowl on her face. "Which one will show Aegaeon's face? I must prepare myself not to smash it to pieces."

Startled, he threw back his head and laughed, his chest expanding and light flooding his veins to push out the heaviness and darkness. "Alas, there's no specified order," he told her. "It simply depends on who responds when." He smiled at her. "You'll just have to be strong, Shari of the Throwing Knife."

Shari of the Throwing Knife.

His playful words, his smile, the tone of his voice, it all hit Sharine hard, it was so . . . real. With no hint that he was laying on his vaunted charm or chancing techniques of seduction. He was simply smiling at her, the two of them sharing a moment of humor. She hadn't been joking about Aegaeon, but Titus's smile had her lips tugging upward. "I'll grit my teeth and clench my jaw."

"Think only that he'd be most satisfied to see you lose control, and it'll be enough. I gather he is that kind of angel, yes?"

"Yes," she said and settled her yet-cramped wings. "I'll keep it together." Words she'd heard Tanicia use on one of her soldiers when that man was crying over a broken heart. Tanicia wasn't the gentlest of generals, but Sharine had been in sympathy with her on that occasion—for the soldier in question fell in love every Saturday and cried over a broken heart every Thursday, or so it seemed.

"Now I must do this." Smile fading, Titus turned to face the screens. He shifted his stance in the same movement. No longer was he the relaxed angel who'd hit her with that glorious smile; he stood with his feet apart, his arms loose and ready by his sides, and his wings held with precision control. His muscles carried a subtle tension.

A warrior angel at ease but ready to shift into an attack stance in seconds.

Exhaustion made it impossible for her to do anything similar. Saying to hell with pride, she slid down to sit on the floor.

Sharine?

I'm fine. I want to focus on the discussion, not my aching muscles.

Titus nodded. A moment later, the dark screens in front of him lit from within and began to show the image of a turning hourglass. He must've sent a mental command to the member of his staff in charge of this technology.

As she waited for the other archangels to respond, Sharine considered the fact that this was the first time she'd ever be in the presence of the entire ruling Cadre. She'd been a significant part of Aegaeon's life, yet he'd never bothered to do her the respect of introducing her to the other archangels.

By contrast, Astaad had introduced his Mele to everyone, and she'd often accompanied him to formal events. Even Sharine had met her, though she'd gone to few large gatherings in the past several hundred years; she still remembered Mele's stunning dark eyes, clear intelligence, and graceful way of speaking. But most of all, she remembered Astaad's quiet pride in having her by his side.

How foolish Sharine had been not to see through Aegaeon's motives. All she'd ever been to him was a shiny trophy. He'd never loved Sharine, had just wanted to own the Hummingbird. And she'd been so needy and wounded that she'd accepted the dregs of affection he threw her way.

That was on her.

You judge yourself harshly.

Even as the memory of Titus's words reverberated through her, the screen on the top left cleared to reveal Neha's face. From what Sharine could see of her torso, the Queen of India was dressed in warrior leathers of darkest green, and those leathers were dusty, as was her face. Her braided black hair bore the same patina of dust.

"My apologies for the slow response, Titus." Tight words. "I was in the field, helping Suyin clear out the nests of child victims Lijuan left behind."

A shudder rocked Sharine.

"I thought the children had already been given mercy," Titus boomed, his expression taut with rage. "You're saying there were more?"

Neha nodded, her brown eyes tired in a way Sharine had never seen in any archangel. "Either Lijuan was keeping them in reserve, or they didn't respond to her order when she gave it during the war. They've turned on each other in the interim. It is . . . a difficult scene."

Sharine couldn't imagine the horror of what the archangel was describing, the utter nightmare of having to execute children who'd been made monstrous without their consent or desire. Used as tools for an insane archangel. *There's no hope of a cure for these children?*

No. Titus's responding tone was somber. *There's no cure for any of it.*

"Suyin was dirty and bloody to the extent that she needs a moment to wash." One of Neha's beloved snakes twined its way up her arm, a living jewel of brilliant orange. "As she has no functioning communication center close to this border, she'll be entering the discussion from another room in my border stronghold."

Once more, the Archangel of India and the Archangel of China were working together, as they'd done often throughout history. But never in such a horrific circumstance.

Another screen cleared, this time to show Alexander's face, lines pressed into his cheek and the golden strands of his hair appearing finger-combed. It was the most natural Sharine had seen Alexander since . . . a time long, *long* ago.

A flicker of memory that had her fingers itching for a pencil—of a young and shirtless Alexander laughing with an equally young Caliane as they contemplated jumping into a waterfall. His hair had been damp already from the spray of water, droplets rolling down his chest, his limbs more slender than they were now. And his eyes had been . . . bright, untouched by life.

Was she so very old that she'd known Alexander as a youth?

Sharine had no answer to that, time having become an endless slipstream in her mind. But she knew the memory was true; a true memory had a taste, a textured reality to it. She'd ask Caliane about it when her friend rose from *anshara*.

"Titus, you'll have to excuse my appearance." Alexander's voice evidenced the grit of sleep. "I finally had to surrender and lay down."

As archangels needed even less sleep than ordinary angels, he had to have been on the verge of collapse.

The other screens cleared one after the other before Titus could reply, and none of the Cadre looked any better than the rest. Suyin's hair was sleekly wet, and damp spots marked the dust of her leathers—as if she'd dunked her head under a tap—while Raphael had streaks of what appeared to be grease on his face, and Qin just looked haggard.

Aegaeon was as bare-chested as Titus had been earlier, and on that chest was a silver swirl familiar to Sharine . . . below fresh claw marks. "One of the sick ones got me," he muttered while using a cloth to wipe away blood crusted around the edges, the blue-green of his hair matted and as wet as Suyin's. "Vicious animals."

"Do you feel any effect?" Titus asked, a new stiffness to his body.

"An itch, but it's already healing," Aegaeon said without concern.

The most powerful among angelkind were used to being unkillable except in very specific circumstances. Those circumstances always involved another archangel.

As she looked at him, this archangel with wings of deep green streaked with wild blue, Sharine felt both a deep rumble of anger and a crashing sense of relief. She saw him now, would always see him. Aegaeon would never again fool her, and with that realization went a fear she hadn't even realized she was carrying.

She was so glad he'd bequeathed nothing much more than a little of his coloring and a touch of his power to their son, so glad that he'd left the raising of Illium to her. Her boy would never be cruel, never purposefully cause others pain. Illium was more akin to Titus than he was to Aegaeon.

Neha was the one who first understood the import of Titus's words. "Does your question to Aegaeon have anything to do with why you've called an emergency meeting when none of us have time to spare?"

"Yes. I've discovered evidence of a reborn angel."

Silence.

It was Raphael who broke it. "You're certain?" The searing blue of his eyes was locked on Titus; today, he had no Elena beside him, his consort no doubt in the city helping to handle the chaos left behind by war.

Elena and Raphael were equals when it came to their relationship. One an archangel and one an angel barely born, yet it was true. The times that she'd seen them together, never had Sharine seen dominance and submission, an alpha and a beta. Together, they were simply two people who loved each other.

Her gaze went to Titus, this arrogant, beautiful, honorable archangel who valued her opinion enough to invite her to this meeting . . . and who hadn't thrown off her touch when she sought to offer comfort, had instead curled his fingers around hers and held on.

29

As certain as I can be without the results from my scientists," Titus said, then described the site, the burned-out body of the angel, and the evidence of the clawlike hand. "Lady Sharine was with me and she took photographs—they're being loaded onto the screens now."

"What was she doing there?" Aegaeon demanded, the golden hue of his skin stretched over bone as he raged. "I've been told she's extremely fragile, her mind fractured."

Even as Sharine's temper ignited, Titus proceeded to ignore him.

Temper morphing into humor, she had to clap a hand over her mouth to stifle the urge to laugh. If there was one thing Aegaeon couldn't stand, it was to be ignored.

Restrain yourself, Shari. A repressive order . . . given in an amused tone.

"Look with your own eyes," he said aloud after the photographs were all available. "None of us need scientific confirmation to know those are angelic wing bones."

More silence, though she could see Aegaeon's face growing hot from within. That flush of red at the very tops of his cheekbones, it was a dead giveaway to a rising temper. *Be careful, Titus,* she warned. *Aegaeon is about to blow.*

If you believe that I'm afeared of a temper tantrum from a doddering Ancient, you don't know me at all.

She almost snorted in laughter this time. If only Aegaeon could've heard himself being referred to as a doddering Ancient. On the other hand—*I'm of a similar vintage.* As so poignantly demonstrated by her earlier memory of Alexander and Caliane. She'd forgotten her age; she'd lived too long, had too many memories in her head. All she knew was that she was old, *had* been old for a long time.

You don't feel old.

Titus's response was a molten kiss. She didn't feel old, either; she'd felt strangely young ever since her new awakening. As if she'd been given a second chance to soar.

"I respect you, Titus," Alexander said, and in that patrician face, Sharine noted new lines of pain. "But I hope you're wrong. If this disease has crossed the immortal boundary, then we're fighting a battle we may never be able to win."

Raphael was quiet, but Sharine saw a certain distance in his eyes. She thought he must be thinking back to what the Legion had told him—the story of a disease that had bound itself permanently into the cells of angelkind, a toxin that lived in each and every one of them to this day.

"I hope I'm wrong, too." Titus ran a hand over his hair. "Unfortunately, from what we've discovered of what Charisemnon was up to behind the closed doors of his court, our hopes are unlikely to bear fruit."

He opened his wings, then snapped them shut. "I haven't shared everything of what we found in his court because we're all finding horrors. But this is relevant to our current discussion—Charisemnon was experimenting on people in his own court. Specifically on angels."

A hiss of sound from Alexander. "He dared cross that line?"

"He crossed it when he used his Cascade-born power to kill angels in my territory." Raphael's voice was brutal, no give in it at all. "I think we can all agree that he had no honor left in him. Neither did Lijuan."

Neha, who was at odds with Raphael for reasons Sharine hadn't yet remembered, said, "In this we agree." Hands on her hips, she looked at Titus. "Do you need assistance?"

"Yes." Suyin spoke for the first time, her voice haunted and haunting, and her uptilted eyes obsidian against skin as white as snow. "Neha is right—this threat supersedes all others. If you need us, we will come."

No one raised their voice in disagreement.

"Right now, I only have evidence of a single reborn angel," Titus said. "Should that change, I'll send out an alert, but for now you can do more good in your own territories." He shifted his attention to Alexander. "Our borders are the closest. I would speak to you after this meeting is over."

Alexander gave a curt nod.

"As we are all here—all seven of us," Neha said with a twist of her mouth, "is there any other business to discuss?"

Qin, an archangel with eyes that echoed the beauty of an aurora, and wings the shade of a smudged sunrise, whites segueing to soft pink, parted his lips. "It appears that despite Astaad's best efforts—and I cast no aspersions on his honor or courage, for he fought valiantly—he didn't manage to eliminate the poisonous insects from his territory."

His territory.

It was telling that Qin hadn't yet claimed ownership of the Pacific Isles. Most archangels wouldn't have hesitated, even if it was a temporary posting. *He really isn't part of our world, is he?* There was something preternatural about Qin, a kind of haunted grace to him.

He has no choice but to be, Titus responded with rough frankness. *The Cadre is running with seven right now, one of them a brand-new archangel. My spies in the Pacific say Qin has worked tirelessly since taking up Astaad's mantle.*

Sharine thought it was because Qin just wanted to go back to Sleep. The faster he cleaned up the mess left behind by war, the faster he could retreat. Now, the silken ebony of his hair shone like jet, his cheekbones sharp slices against his skin as he continued to speak.

"It takes multiple bites to kill a vampire, but mortals are more susceptible." Pain, such pain in him. "I have no choice. After evacuating the uninfected onto a quarantine ship, I will have to sterilize three affected islands."

"You mean a burning with archangelic fire?" Aegaeon's brash tones—but his next words were of an archangel. "Such will turn the islands into a wasteland for a long period. You're certain it's the only possible option?"

That was the thing with Aegaeon, part of what had first enchanted her. He was a good archangel, one who took his responsibilities seriously. But that honor hadn't stretched to a blue-winged little boy who'd idolized him.

No matter how long she lived, Sharine would *never* forgive him for that. He'd broken her mischievous, laughing boy's heart, and for what? Because he couldn't be bothered to stay awake just a few more decades? Decades were nothing in the span of an Ancient's life, mere drops in an ocean.

It was Raphael who'd taught Illium how to lift a sword, Raphael who'd given her little boy the life lessons that should've been imparted by his father, Raphael who'd hugged Illium with ferocious pride when he won all the winged races in the Refuge.

Raphael had been the best big brother any child could wish.

Yet Aegaeon had the gall to be angered that Illium refused to shift his allegiance to Aegaeon? It was Elena who'd told Sharine that Aegaeon had tried to recruit Illium to his new court and been soundly rejected—Raphael's consort had done a terrible job of hiding her delighted satisfaction and Sharine was in charity with her.

Illium knew the value of his loyalty and he knew Aegaeon deserved none of it.

"I hope for another solution." Qin's voice was like water, lovely and sinuous. "Astaad's scientists work on to discover a less violent remedy."

"That is troubling news." Neha sighed. "I'd hoped . . ." She shook her head. "We cannot hope. We must deal with the reality."

Alexander spoke into the resulting quiet. "Suyin, how is your territory?"

"Painfully quiet," was the answer from the woman who was one of the greatest architects in all of angelkind, the dot of a beauty spot below the far edge of her left eye bringing attention to the resolute sorrow in those eyes.

"I intend to allow huge areas of the landscape to go wild for the foreseeable future. There won't be enough people to maintain the fields, towns, and cities for many generations. The numbers are catastrophic." She pressed her lips tight. "I'll have to rebuild as if I were an archangel given a territory no one else had ever ruled—except that I must do so in the shadow of Lijuan's horrors."

At any other time, Titus said, his voice resonant in Sharine's mind, *such words would've left Suyin ripe for a takeover attempt from another member of the Cadre. Now, no one knows what surprises Lijuan left behind.*

Sharine could see the reason behind the reserve: China had been Lijuan's to rule for millennia, the landscape itself imprinted with her mark. *Is Neha the only one of the Cadre helping her?*

She helps at the border but doesn't land inside China itself. Raphael, however, spent a full week with Suyin before he came to Africa—and Caliane will be by her side as soon as she rises. We won't allow Suyin to drown before she finds her wings; we can't afford to lose any one of the Cadre.

"Any resurgence of the poison Lijuan left behind?" Aegaeon's tone had Sharine rolling her eyes.

Condescending ass, Titus said into her mind at the same
time. *Suyin is an archangel, not a child to be patted over
the head.*

In this, Titus, we are in absolute agreement.

"No." Suyin's response was firm. "Whatever it is she did
with the fatal black fog, it died with her." Obsidian eyes
landing on Titus. "I think you have the most difficult task.
If your enemy created a way to ensure the sickness thrived
in angels . . ."

The meeting concluded soon afterward, leaving Titus
and Alexander alone. The two spoke of precautions to
make sure no threat could fly over the border. They'd just
decided on a small squadron of winged fighters whose job
it'd be to control the area when Sharine remembered something Illium had told her.

Titus, she said on their mental wavelength. *I apologize
for the interruption, but my son told me of eyes in the sky.
Do you have those?*

"Alexander!" A thunder of sound, the vibration comforting. "What about satellites?"

Alexander frowned. "I'll ask my grandson if the eyes in
the sky can watch that closely. It's not something about
which I have too much knowledge, young pup."

Listening to his answer, Sharine found herself thinking
that it wasn't good to stay ignorant of the new ways. Her
son adored this world, was constantly telling her of its technologies and inventions. She would learn everything he
wished to teach her, she decided, live in the here and now
and not the past.

"We'll speak again, Grandfather," Titus said with a grin.

Making a rude gesture on the other side, Alexander said,
"Careful, Titus, or I'll send the twins to visit."

"I'm not afraid of my sisters," Titus said staunchly. "But
please do keep them on your side of the border, I beg of

you. Already, they send me three letters a week, full of much advice." The affection in his tone belied his words.

After Alexander signed off with a laugh, Titus waited for the screen to close out before turning to her. "I thank you, Sharine. That was a very good suggestion and may save us from losing a squadron from the front lines," he said before reaching up to rub at the lines on his forehead, his shoulders lower than usual.

It stunned her to see such vulnerability in the big and brash Archangel of Africa. Even more so because it was a thing of deep trust for him to allow her to see him this way.

"You need sleep," she found herself saying, overcome by an unexpected wave of tenderness. "You flew an incredible distance in a short period of time, and didn't eat the entire voyage, either. It's not good to push yourself to the extreme and then collapse."

He glared at her, hands on his hips. "I'm not a toddler, to be sent to bed."

"Fall on your face, then," she muttered, as she got to her feet. "I, for one, am going to bathe then rest." Though she had every intention of expanding her physical limits as she grew in strength and endurance, it wouldn't happen overnight. Rest was a necessity.

Pulling open the door, she stepped out—but she was still near enough to hear Titus mutter a single word under his breath: *"Women."*

Her eyes narrowed, but she resisted the temptation to head back in there—tired as she was, he might well win a verbal battle. Red-haired Tanae came around the corner just as the door was closing behind her. "My lady." The curt bow of a warrior. "Is the sire within?"

"Yes. And the meeting has concluded."

Another short but respectful bow before Tanae walked past and through the door, her competence and confidence unmistakable.

Not sure she'd ever understand Titus, and annoyed she

was even interested in trying, Sharine returned to her room to do exactly as she'd described to the stubborn archangel who refused to believe he had any vulnerabilities.

First she removed her grimy clothes, then she washed the dirt, dust, and traces of reborn—a shudder—out of her hair. That done, she scrubbed herself down until her skin was flushed with heat and so clean that it all but squeaked. Her eyes were already closing by the time she managed to wrap a towel around her hair, but she made herself stay awake long enough to set an alarm on the old-fashioned clock on the bedstand.

She fell into bed swathed in towels and woke to the shrill bell what felt like a heartbeat later. Groaning, she looked outside and saw that while the sun had begun to set, she had time yet to prepare herself for the horrors that would come with the hours of night.

When she unwrapped the towel from around her hair, it was to discover that the strands were still damp. Brushing it out, she opened the wardrobe in an attempt to find something to wear. But nothing had altered since she'd last looked within. She found herself faced with gown after gown, floaty and pretty.

They weren't items she'd have eschewed in another time or place, but such clothing wasn't conducive to dealing with reborn—and if nothing else, Sharine planned to fly guard over the ground fighters and use her ability to stop reborn from attacking from the back. Wars *could* be fought in gowns, but these airy things would fly up and engulf her head while displaying her body to the masses.

Making a low sound in her throat, she grabbed a gown at random and threw it on the bed. Perhaps she could borrow more suitable clothing before night fell and the fight against the reborn began in earnest once more. Pulling on a robe for now, she decided to eat something before she dressed. She'd noticed a small jug and a covered platter of food in the living area when she'd first returned to her room.

The jug was still there but the platter had been changed, with the earlier food hopefully utilized by others. All of that was peripheral, however; what caught her eye was the pile of neatly folded clothing that sat on the settee in front of the low table that held the food and drink.

She walked over on curious feet to pick up the first item.

It fell open to reveal a sleeveless tunic in dark green with black embroidery around the rounded collar as well as on the hems. Modest slits at the sides meant the tunic would fit easily over her hips. While clean, it was obviously used, but she didn't care in the least.

Smile wide, she picked up the next item. It was another tunic, this one with three-quarter sleeves—the shade was a mauve that probably wouldn't suit her complexion, but she didn't care about that, either. This was about practicality and being an asset rather than a liability.

The pants in the pile were a prosaic black and brown respectively. She hugged them close, not too proud to accept gifts given. Even if it was Titus who must've arranged those gifts.

Scowling, she nonetheless took the clothing back into her bedroom and found fresh underwear. At least she'd packed extra there. Deciding to wear the black pants with the dark green top, she left her hair down so that it would dry more easily, but pulled a hair tie around her wrist for later use.

The woman who looked back at her from the mirror was fresh-faced, no artifice or age to her. "Foolishness," she said with a laugh and walked out onto the balcony that flowed off her bedroom.

Activity buzzed in the courtyard and in the skies, Titus's people using the final hour of light to prepare for the night. She searched the courtyard . . . and realized she was looking for one particular warrior with wide shoulders, skin of ebony, and a smile that knocked the breath out of her.

30

Sire, I write to you from the home of my eldest. You and I, we have spoken our good-byes, but I wouldn't go without this final message: It is my time to Sleep, but my children will forever be your allies. Call them if you ever have need, and they will come.

Until soon, sire.

—Letter from First General Avelina to Archangel Alexander

31

Flushing as she realized she was looking for Titus, Sharine nonetheless didn't step back inside. She needed to speak to Tanae or a senior vampiric commander, find out how best to assist.

That was when her eye caught on the wings of an angel who'd just landed, his feathers brown but for small splashes of a familiar wild blue. She looked at the sky again; she had time. Taking out her phone, she pressed the number that would link her to Illium.

It rang multiple times before he picked up. "I've been hefting debris," he said, his voice a touch breathless, and his sweat-damp hair pushed off his face. "Galen says I've become soft, but I'd like to see him lift the wall I just did."

Sharine smiled, well used to the byplay between Tanae's son and her own. She had the faint idea that it was the weapons-master who'd given her son the nickname of Bluebell. "Galen's in New York?" She knew he was based in Raphael's Refuge territory.

"Raphael's recalled all of us but for Aodhan." He looked to the right. "Barbarian! My mother asks after you—though I don't know why!"

Pale green eyes set in a square-jawed face entered the frame; Galen's dark red hair hung shaggy and thick around his features. "Lady Sharine," he said with a smile, "it's good to see you." He frowned before she could answer and then was gone in a sudden flurry of gray-and-white wings.

"An angel lost his grip on a big piece of wreckage," Illium said, his gaze upward. "Galen has it."

"Your city is grievously wounded." Sharine had glimpsed a little of it when Illium moved the phone.

"Yes." A bleak confirmation. "We're finding that some of the areas Raphael had to scorch are reading as poisonous— it looks like there was something special about the insects Lijuan loosed in that direction, and their poison burned itself into the soil."

The sheer scale of Lijuan's and Charisemnon's power-hungry evil continued to shock her. "Is there a solution?"

"Our scientists are working on it," he said. "But for now, the entire area's under quarantine. We're also having to constantly monitor the situation to make sure that nothing from that sector is seeping into the groundwater or into the river. Even dead, Her Batshitness continues to haunt us."

She had no idea what "Batshitness" meant but, from context, guessed it must refer to Lijuan. Listening as he filled her in on his other news, she noticed one omission. "Are you still feuding with Aodhan?" It would not do. "You know now that life isn't guaranteed, even for an immortal. Don't be so stubborn."

"*I'm* not the stubborn one." He sounded so like the little boy she'd propped on her hip as a babe that she smiled.

"I'm quite aware Aodhan is your equal in stubbornness." Her memories from her lost years continued to be problematic, but she remembered sitting and painting with Aodhan for hours at a time when Aodhan had been swathed in broken darkness. Even in the fog, she'd known that the small, quiet, loyal boy she loved was hurting and she'd gone to him.

"But regardless of his mood," she said to Illium, "he's in a very dangerous situation—and he's far from home and those he loves most. Tell me you're looking out for him."

"Of course I am," Illium muttered. "I even sent him a package from home, full of his favorite things—including a horror movie Elena says he loves. But will he thank me? Hmph. He's probably sharing everything with Suyin."

Sharine frowned, unused to hearing such a lack of generosity in her son's voice. "Do you not like her?"

An intense silence, followed by, "It has nothing to do with her." Another quiet, so taut it hurt. "Mother—"

Her hand clenched on the phone as he broke off; she wanted to go to her knees and beg for him to confide in her. Beg for him to tell her what strained his voice and hurt his soul. All those years when she'd been lost, he'd been forced to rely on others and then to rely only on himself. She wanted him to know that she was here now and that she'd never again let him down.

"You can say anything to me." Her voice came out rough, husky. "I won't be shocked or dismayed. I will love you to the end of time."

"He has always been my best friend," Illium said at last, something in his voice that she couldn't read and the aged gold of his eyes looking to some distant point. "I waited so long for him to emerge from his self-imposed exile, but now that he's done so, he spreads his wings and leaves me behind."

Placing one hand on the wall outside her suite, Sharine staggered under the unknowing blow Illium had just struck. Did Aodhan understand that Illium had lost not one but *both* of the most important people in his life to their own demons?

Her eyes stung, her mind cascading with images of two

small boys who'd been as thick as thieves, one taking the blame for the other no matter what the situation, no matter what the other had done. "I know my son," she said when she could speak again, glad that Illium was distracted enough not to notice the pause. "He isn't small-hearted, and he wouldn't begrudge his friend finding happiness, so tell me what it is that truly pains you."

A shuddering breath, the wind his only reply for long moments. "I look back and I wonder if he hadn't suffered such terrible harm whether he'd still be my friend. I wonder if he only stayed my friend *because* he was so badly damaged in the aftermath—" Voice ragged, he broke off again for several seconds.

When he came back, his voice was so small it caused her physical pain, and he wouldn't look at her. "I wonder if the man I've always thought of as my best friend considers me nothing but a weight tying him to a past he's attempting to forget."

Her heart broke for her son, who loved so fiercely. "It took but a single word of your need to have him flying from the Refuge to meet you in Lumia," she reminded him. "He didn't have to do that."

"That's just it, Mother." Illium looked up, his eyes fierce and hot; she could tell he was clenching his entire body, as he had a habit of doing in tense situations. "Aodhan is loyal and he pays his debts and I'm certain he believes he has a debt to me—because I waited so long, because I never gave up on him.

"I don't want a friendship based on obligation." Angry, hurt words, his face flushed. "If he wants to cut the bond between us, I wish he'd simply tell me instead of putting distance between us."

She felt lost. So many pieces of time were missing or blurred from her head. She remembered holding Aodhan in the years he'd locked himself in the shadowed dark of his home, away from the sunlight that turned him into a shooting star against the sky. She remembered rocking him for hours, and telling him he would conquer this, that he would sparkle again, but no matter how hard she tried, she couldn't remember what it was that had hurt him so badly that he'd turned away even from Illium.

But one thing she knew: "The Aodhan I met in Lumia is no one's fool. Don't do him the disservice of believing you know him better than he knows himself—I think, for the first time in an eternity, he knows himself." In this, she and Aodhan were mirrors of one another.

"What if he decides that the man he's becoming wants nothing to do with me?" Raw, the words bled Illium's pain.

"Then you'll let him go," she said quietly, her hand fisted against her chest and her gaze locked with his. "Freedom and love are entwined. And you, my blue-winged boy, you love more deeply than anyone I've ever known."

She almost heard the hardness of his swallow. She wished she could be there to wrap him up in her arms and in her wings, as she remembered doing for Aodhan. All wide shoulders and a height that eclipsed hers, he'd been so quiet, so stiff, but he hadn't rebuffed her.

Crooning gentle words, she'd cradled him close, and led him to where he could lie with his head in her lap and his body partially under her wing. So much pain contained in that big, strong body, his own wings limp and his face expressionless. Memory upon memory of doing that for the sparkling boy who'd gone deathly silent.

"Until then," she said, "love him with all your strength. Aodhan may one day shatter your heart, but at this critical time when he's spreading his wings, he needs the support of a friend who's never once let him down." Anguish twisted through her to give such advice, but she knew her boy would never forgive himself if his friend needed him and he wasn't there.

Another flash of memory, this one bound with fog. A grown Illium's shoulders slumped and his wings as limp as

Aodhan's had become. "I tried so hard, Mother," he sobbed, "but I couldn't find him. For so long, I couldn't find him. Now that we have . . ." A shudder so violent it seemed to rattle his bones. "I don't know if he'll ever come back to us. I don't know if he'll ever heal from what was done to him."

"My beautiful boy," she said on the wave of memory, "you've never loved with boundaries. Don't begin now. Don't alter who you are because you're afraid that you'll lose what you love."

"I wish I could be a child again, when your kisses used to make every pain better."

"I'll come see you after my sojourn in Titus's territory is over, and Lumia is running well once more." She would hold him then, because no child was ever too old for his mother's love.

"Mother."

"Yes?"

"I'm glad you're awake again. I've missed you."

She stood there, heart aching after ending the call, but she wasn't yet done. She had more than one boy to check up on.

"Eh-ma." Aodhan's astonished voice as he spoke the affectionate term by which he'd always addressed Sharine. "You're on the phone!"

"Yes," she said, smiling at hearing him alive and well. "I've joined this new age." Catching the sound of wind, she said, "You're in the air?" That explained why he'd answered with his voice alone, rather than so she could talk to him face-to-face.

"Night patrol," he told her. "There's such silence in this landscape, but I feel an itch at the back of my neck, the sense that Lijuan has left us one more surprise."

Sharine straightened; Aodhan had always been intuitive. "Listen to your instincts."

"I will," he promised. "I didn't initially wish to be left in charge of the stronghold while Archangel Suyin went to the border, but now I'm glad of it."

"Do you have backup?" China's forces had been decimated, and with the country apparently devoid of reborn but for the children at the border, they hadn't been allocated many relief troops.

"A skeleton squadron. But Lady Caliane's prime squadron is on alert to assist should it become necessary." A sweep of wind that indicated a turn. "How are you, *Eh-ma*?"

"Surviving Titus."

A laugh that had gone silent for too long, followed by words more hesitant. "Have you spoken to Illium?"

"Just now. He is well." She considered how much to say, decided not to interfere, for they were grown now. But she could give advice—such was the maternal prerogative. "I get the impression you two are still at odds."

A deep sound she'd never before heard Aodhan make. It was more in Titus's wheelhouse. "He's the most stubborn person I know."

Her lips curved, her heart hurting less. That wasn't the sound of a man attempting to disengage from a friendship. "I seem to remember you swearing up and down and sideways that you'd stolen the cookies, even as the real culprit sat there with crumbs all over his face."

Sudden, dazzling laughter. "You know too many of my secrets." He said nothing more on the point, and she let it go—she had to be neutral territory, so either one of them could speak to her without worry of their words going any further.

Instead, she asked about how he was faring so far from home, and listened to all he had to tell. Afterward, she stood there on the balcony and worried. If Lijuan *had* left behind a final terrible gift, Aodhan was in the epicenter of it. But unlike when he'd been a child, she couldn't pull him back from a dangerous edge.

"Have you fed?" A booming question from down in the courtyard.

Hand slamming to her heart, she glanced over the edge

of the balcony to see a shirtless Titus standing there with his hands on his hips, his head tilted back to look up at her. He appeared suspiciously well-rested, and if the grin on his face was anything to go by, his good humor was restored. She didn't know why she found that so attractive.

"Shari! I'm waiting!"

"And I'm in a position to drop something on your head!"

Throwing back his head, he laughed. His next words were in her mind, his voice resonant and beautiful. *I'm going to eat. Will you join me, or will you throw knives with your tongue?*

As she watched, he flew up and to the right of her own balcony. He was beautiful in motion and she flushed when he landed and almost caught her staring. "Sharine?"

"I'm coming."

Since his rooms were right next to hers and he'd left his door open, she walked in without knocking. She didn't know what she'd expected of his private quarters, but this entrance section was warm in its embrace, decorated with a huge earthen-colored rug and equally large and comfortable seating.

Nothing had sharp edges except for the weapons he'd mounted on the walls. All were unique, from different times and places. He also had art on those walls, leaning toward paintings that spoke of the vibrant heart of this land. She was drawn to one in particular—ink on textile done in the same tones of earth and sunset that dominated this part of his quarters.

"The art appreciation can wait." Titus stood in the wide doorway to the balcony, his arms crossed and his lips curved. "Come, Shari, the food will get cold."

A single glance and she was in danger of a hot flush. Standing there like that, with the light from the courtyard backlighting his body and his skin aglow with health beneath the sleeveless dark brown tunic he'd thrown on, he was the embodiment of fantasies she'd had as a young girl—when she'd still believed in the foolishness of passionate attraction and lived for the thrill of a rapidly beating heart.

In front of her, his expression turned intimate . . . welcoming, and she knew he wouldn't reject her should she decide to cross the room and rise up on her toes to touch her mouth to his, her hands flush against the muscled ridges of his chest.

Even as her blood turned to honey, she knew it wasn't just physical, what had taken root between them. The days they'd spent together on the journey to the settlement and back, the hours they'd spent speaking to one another, it had altered their relationship on a fundamental level.

"There's always time for art appreciation," she said, but walked toward him—she had to always stay conscious of her propensity to hide inside art. Art was safe. Art didn't demand. Art didn't look at you in a way that made embers smolder in your stomach. And art didn't hurt you in the way people hurt you. "But I am hungry."

Titus angled his body so she could pass, and though the doorway was wide and he made no attempt to hinder her, she felt buffeted by the wall of strength and heat that was his body. Spine stiff, she took care that her wings didn't brush him as she walked out.

If she had to be attracted to a man, why did it have to be someone so big and brash and beautiful? It wasn't any longer about comparing him to Aegaeon. The two might have surface similarities, but she wasn't foolish—she'd seen the heart of Titus now and that heart was bigger than Aegaeon's would ever be.

No, it was because of Titus, who he was—this man would leave a mark on her life if she let him in, and Sharine already had far too many scars within. She had to decide if it was worth chancing another for a fleeting slice of pleasure.

I've never made promises of forever. Any woman who

comes into my arms understands that I offer only pleasure and affection.

Sharine didn't want forever, wasn't sure she'd ever again be in a place where she could trust enough to offer her heart. On the flip side, however, she also wasn't sure she was built for quick dalliances.

How do you know? asked the part of her that had been getting more and more mouthy of late. *It's not as if you've ever tried it. Take a risk, dance with Titus. You're tough enough now to pick up the pieces—if there are any pieces to pick up in the first place.*

You're not who you once were, Sharine. Take the risk.

32

When Titus pulled out her chair for her, she was startled to see a scowl mar his smile. Had he picked up on her discomfort and uncertainty? She'd hope she was a better guest than that—but Titus, she was learning, had more sensitivity than the majority of the world realized; never would she forget his internal struggle as he readied himself to wipe the villagers' minds.

"I see we are to starve." The table was piled with dishes upon dishes, all of them steaming and aromatic, but that wasn't why she made the comment—she found she didn't like it when Titus went quiet, and as he seemed unable to resist responding to sarcasm or dry words on her part, she'd use it to break his mood.

"I told you, I'm hungry—and I have a cook who signed on to feed an archangel's court but is now managing troop meals. The man can't help himself," he grumbled and picked up a dish. "Try this. You'll like it."

Wondering if his mood resulted from hunger, she took a

spoonful. When he stared at the tiny amount on her plate, she rolled her eyes. "I want to taste all the dishes and I won't be able to do that if I stuff myself on the first one."

Not appearing convinced in the least, he nonetheless began to dish out his own portion while she tried her spoonful. It bloomed an array of fresh and bright flavors on her tongue. Moaning deep in her throat, she glanced up. "I'm not saying you were right, but maybe I should've taken more."

A dazzling smile shattering the scowl, he handed over the bowl . . . even as her breath caught. He was *beautiful*, with a warmth to him that drew her like a moth to a flame. And while he might flit from woman to woman, he was honest in his attentions. He didn't lie and make false promises.

Any mark he left wouldn't be one scored by cruelty.

"You're thinking too hard." Another aromatic spoonful placed on her plate. "Eat. You gave away your food during our journey, and you'll be in the skies again as soon as darkness falls."

Her stomach chose that moment to growl.

When Titus laughed, the sound a booming wave of joy, she found herself joining in, sparks of delight in her bloodstream. It had been so long since she'd laughed with such open happiness, but being with Titus . . . yes, he made her feel good. He might infuriate and aggravate her, but he never made her feel lesser or unimportant.

They ate in friendly harmony for the next fifteen minutes, passing each other dishes, and having a little of that, a lot of that, until their stomachs were sated to the point that conversation was possible. "You slept?" she asked, as he refilled his plate.

She could tell he hadn't eaten properly for too long—she could see it in the sharpness of his cheekbones, the subtle leanness of his torso. It could happen that way with the incredibly powerful—a sudden physical shift when they burned too hot.

And Titus would be running at this pace for some time to come.

Picking up a dish he'd particularly enjoyed, she held it out. She'd never again wait on any man, but she was a woman who took care of her people, and she wouldn't permit Aegaeon to steal that part of her nature—especially given that Titus would feed her to the brim if she permitted it.

Creases forming in his cheeks and light in his eyes, Titus accepted the dish. "*Asante*, Shari."

She had no trouble recognizing the language. "You're welcome."

"I did sleep and you were right, I feel much better for it." A scowl. "Don't say 'I told you so.' I get quite enough of that from my sisters."

"Why have I not heard more about your sisters?" It was true she didn't pay much attention to casual gossip, but surely she should've heard of the family of an archangel.

"Probably because they're so much older." He took a long drink of ale. "I suppose those who don't know us believe that, with such a difference in age, we mustn't be close." A grin. "As if the first general would permit anything but full cohesion in her personal family squadron."

Her lips curved. "You're very proud of your mother."

"Yes." He put a choice bit of meat on her plate. "I'm also happy she's currently Sleeping. A man needs a break from mothering every few millennia. Of course, with my sisters taking up the cause, I'm not so sure I'm better off."

Fascinated, she waited for him to go on.

"One thing is certain—under no circumstance will I let my mother join my army when she wakes, though she is a brilliant general who is feted by others," he added, brow dark. "She'd probably tell me all my strategies were wrong, and also ask me why I wasn't wearing a shirt."

Sharine wanted to laugh, but wasn't about to break the moment.

"Alexander is ready to take her back with open arms any time she wakes—and once there, she'll no doubt slay half his court with her magnetic presence." A huge grin, the sun slamming into her with brilliant force. "I inherited my charm from her. We both must beat off suitors with a stick."

Sharine narrowed her eyes. "Once again, I'm blinded by your modesty."

Her dry comment just made his grin deepen . . . and her stomach drop. Because oh, he was unrepentant and bright and he *loved*. That was one of the most attractive things about Titus. He might mutter about his sisters and mother, but that he loved them was a candle flame in his heart she could almost see.

"My father was so spent by his time with my mother that he has been Sleeping since I was seven hundred years old." A chuckle. "Before he went to Sleep, he told me she'd worn him out and it was glorious. Now he must recover."

Her lips twitched, he was being so consciously wicked.

Eyes sparkling at her, he leaned forward. "She stayed with him some seventy-five years. She fell with child five decades into it."

Shadows in her heart, memories of another little boy with parents who hadn't been bound throughout his child-hood. "Did you grow up with your mother?"

"My mother, my father, my sisters, their loves, the entire damn lot of them." He groaned. "My father bought a home right next to my mother, and so we were a family even after they were no longer lovers." More love in his voice, open and proud. "He's a warrior, too, and between them, they taught me how to wield a sword before I could fly."

The shadows burned away under the searing warmth of his voice. "Surely, with such a mother, more of your sib-lings must be warriors."

"Our mother always told us to be true to our nature, to be honest in the path we chose to walk." Again, such love and respect in every word. "Zuri and Nala are squadron commanders in Alexander's army. You know of Charo. Phenie is a musician."

"*Oh!*" She gasped. "Phenie? Your sister is Phenie?" One of the most celebrated harpists in all of angelkind. "Goodness, Titus, talent runs strong and fierce in your family."

"Do you know how much harp music I had to listen to growing up?" His groan vibrated in her bones. "Every time she babysat me, it was harp, harp, harp. Phenie says she was attempting to soothe the feral beast that was her little brother, constantly jumping on the furniture and flying from the chandeliers, and diving off balconies."

Laughter spilled from her as he reached for the tankard of ale at his elbow and, head tilted slightly back, drank it down in long, hard swallows.

His throat moved, the tendons strong against his skin.

Toes curling and stomach tight, she picked up her own tankard and took a drink. It was potent, burning fire into her guts. But she liked that, liked that it cleared her mind and brought her back to her senses. Until by the time Titus put his tankard down and wiped the back of his hand over his mouth, she had herself under control.

Yet her voice came out husky when she said, "I think I would very much like to meet your sisters."

Titus knew all four would love her. Not the distant and admired Hummingbird, but Sharine, as she was now. Brilliant with life and energy and with a subtle but undeniable sensuality of which she seemed unaware, but he'd very definitely noticed. The way she ran her fingers over different-textured surfaces from velvet to wood, the way she drew in scents, her eyes fluttering half-shut as she lost herself to the sensation, and the way she sometimes watched him as if she'd like to take a bite out of him.

Titus wasn't unwilling in the least. He'd like her artist's fingers to trace his body and learn his textures, grew hard at the thought of her drawing in then luxuriating in the scent of him, and as for the bite? He'd cup her lower curves and lift her up so she could take that bite directly from his mouth.

The woman was an inferno in a bottle.

No one looking at her would ever guess that she was millennia older than Titus.

His gut clenched again, his shoulders locking. He'd forgotten the age difference as they ate together, only now recalling the long life she'd lived. Far longer than his own. Such things didn't matter among angels after a few millennia of existence, but for all intents and purposes, Sharine was an Ancient.

A beloved and revered Ancient.

Who'd made him itch to stroke the slope of her back as she passed him in the doorway, and whose laughter rippled over him like stroking hands. His cock had reacted to that same laughter, and to the light in her eyes as she listened to his tales of family with open interest.

She . . . compelled him.

Titus tensed. He was a man with strong carnal appetites, but he had those appetites under strict control. While he loved his mother, he'd seen her lead men around by the cock since he was a child—Titus had no desire to become akin to those lustbound men. No woman with whom he'd ever dallied had come close to wielding such control over him.

Picking up a grape from the platter on the table, Sharine parted her lips to put it inside, and his entire body hummed with need. He was half of a mind to sweep his arm out to smash all the food to the floor, then lift her up and sit her down on the table so he could feast on her instead.

Teeth gritted, he pushed back his chair and stood. "I must return to the patrol. It's possible we may be able to spot and eliminate entire burrows of reborn while they're resting."

Sharine shot him a penetrating look. "Have you heard from your scientists about the reborn angel?"

"Nothing conclusive yet." Stretching out his wings, he

said, "If you don't wish to work on your art, you're welcome to use my library." He was well aware he was lighting the wick of her temper, and yet, despite the danger she presented to him, he couldn't stop. Crossing swords with Sharine was far too tempting.

Dagger eyes, exactly as he'd planned. "Is it safe to visit Charisemnon's court?"

Snapping back his wings, he stared at his most uncooperative guest. "Why would you wish to go there?" He'd assumed she'd want to go out with a squadron—and they could use her abilities in the field.

"Not now—in the light hours," she clarified. "I want to hunt through Charisemnon's court for anything that might've been missed—notes about his experiments, other information."

On her feet, she put one hand on the back of her chair. "You and your people went in as warriors, to clear enemy territory of dangers. You weren't looking for notes or information on an angelic disease—and I'm not unskilled at hunting for information."

Everything inside him rebelled at sending her to that place.

Seeking time to think, he turned to where he'd left his breastplate and other armor. He pulled it on today, complete with the shoulder, wrist, and back guards.

His fighters were tired, his people equally so. Sometimes, a symbol mattered. Sliding his swords into crisscrossing sheaths on his back, he came to a decision.

"If you're looking for information on the disease," he said, "it'll most likely be at his border stronghold—he holed up there for some time prior to the war." His mouth twisted. "I thought he was being a good ally, readying himself for the battle we all knew would come."

"Yes, he would've kept his notes close by." She searched Titus's face. "That you didn't immediately assume dishonor says much about you, Titus."

Waving aside her words, he said, "We don't know what ugliness pollutes the air of Charisemnon's border stronghold."

"If it's enough to kill an angel of my age," she said with equanimity, "then the world is indeed in trouble and it'd be better if we knew now."

Titus didn't want to agree with her, but she was right. He gave a curt nod.

But when dawn broke after a night of brutal work against shrieking, vicious reborn, he said, "If you wait until I've finished with the stragglers, I'll accompany you."

Sweaty and dirty and tired above the field of battle, a small woman with a giant spirit, she compressed her lips. "Will I cause a security problem by going as soon as I clean up? Do you need me in the field in the hours to come?"

He could lie to her and she wouldn't know any different, but Titus was no liar. "No, I'm sending most of the squadrons and ground teams back home to rest and recharge."

"What of Charisemnon's court?" she asked. "I don't wish to cut into your people's precious rest time by needing to take a security detail."

Again, he didn't lie. "The stronghold is safe, with a permanent guard squadron." He'd always intended to more fully investigate his enemy's base. "It is, however, apt to be disgusting. We hauled away the bodies and blasted water over the main floors, but had no time for a deeper clean."

"I'm not afraid of a little mess."

No, she wasn't, he thought, recalling how she'd helped pile the reborn carcasses for the bonfire. "I'll assign you a fighter from the guard squadron on the off-chance we missed anything."

Titus's people had swept the stronghold top to bottom, but there was no point in taking chances . . . especially with Sharine, this angel who was causing a reaction in him for which he very much wasn't ready. "I wouldn't have angel-kind after my head because I didn't take care of the Hummingbird while she was in my keeping."

"I'm not a relic to be hidden away." Streaks of color on her cheeks that made her glow. "Neither do I belong to anyone but myself. I am not in anyone's *keeping*." Fire in her eyes, oh such brilliant fire.

It scalded him. And it made him hunger to burn himself in it.

He wanted to grip her chin, initiate the beginnings of a kiss. She'd probably stab him with her blade for daring. Because this woman, she wasn't angelkind's fragile treasure. She was Sharine, who'd bickered with him as they flew, and who'd offered him seconds of the dishes she'd noticed he liked best. A woman who was even now hovering toe-to-toe with him, her head tilted back to meet his gaze as he looked down.

He didn't remember moving, didn't remember her moving, but heat steamed the air between them. It was madness, but still he dipped his head and took her lips in a kiss that devoured. His hand was cupping the silken skin of her cheek before he knew it, and he well felt the shock of her own hand gripping his biceps; her nails bit into his flesh in a warning that she wasn't happy.

But she didn't end the kiss even when he hauled her closer and stroked one hand down to cup the lower curves of her body, his other arm locked around her upper back and his rigid cock pushing into her stomach. His head was smoke, filled with intoxication, his breathing jagged. And he *craved*. More and more and still more.

33

When she tore away her mouth and put air between them, they stared at one another, their chests heaving.

"No," she said very firmly.

Mind hazed in a way it hadn't been since he was a youth just discovering women, Titus didn't react. Then the word finally penetrated and he took an automatic "step" back in the air; unlike some angels who burned with power, he didn't believe that it was his right to take any woman he wanted.

He'd been raised by five very strong women, all of whom he respected to the core and all of whom would come after him with unsheathed blades if he disrespected any other woman in such a way. His mother would wake from her Sleep out of sheer disgust.

No, Titus didn't force women. Ever.

However, there was no rule against making sure he had it right. "No for today?" he asked, because if so, she was right in stopping this—it wasn't the time or place. He'd probably already shocked half his troops into a coma by manhandling her with such familiarity. "Or no forever?" It made his stomach tighten to ask the latter and the raw need of it terrified him, and yet he asked.

She'd dug her way under his skin, a burr he couldn't dislodge . . . and didn't want to reject. Surely, if he believed in such things, he'd say she'd done sorcery on him. But he didn't believe in such things, and so he knew that this was something altogether different: a combustion between two opposing forces who'd somehow proven to be passionately compatible.

Her breathing, he was gratified to see, remained as unsteady as his when she said, "No for today." Even as his lips began to curve, she brushed dust off her tunic and pants. "I have no desire to tie myself to any man—and you wish to remain free of entanglements also, yes?"

He blinked, disconcerted in a way that made no sense. "Yes," he said, because of course it was so. "I'm not looking for a consort, but for a lover."

"Then we'll speak further when the time is not so inopportune." Calm words, but her breathing remained uneven.

Titus knew she was right. But he took a moment to cross to her and raise his palm to her cheek—telegraphing his intent so she could pull back if she wished.

She didn't.

Cradling the softness of skin he wanted to kiss inch by inch, he looked into eyes enigmatic and old and young at once and said, "It will be a fire between us, Shari." Not a gentle one, either. "I wait to be burned."

She reached up with the confidence of a woman who knew herself and gripped the arch of his wing, stroking down firmly. Erotic pleasure rocked his entire body, his blood molten. "Then we burn," she whispered and dropped her hand. "Stay safe from the darkness, Titus. We have unfinished business, you and I."

Her touch was a brand on his feathers and he half

expected to see the marks of her possession when she broke contact, streaks of glittering champagne that laid claim to an archangel. "Your escort is on her way from Charisemnon's stronghold." Then, though worry for her gnawed in his gut, he left without further words.

Sharine watched Titus's powerful body cut through the dawn sky, her heartbeat thunder and her skin hot. The gold of his armor turned him into a piece of the sun, the embodiment of archangelic strength. She felt a hushed quiet fall around her as his people looked on, drawn by that golden fire.

All the while, she had to fight the urge to press her fingers to her throbbing mouth. Never had she shared such a kiss. The embers smoldering inside her had burst into flame the instant his mouth touched her own, wrapping them both in wings of fire.

She'd wanted to run her hands over his muscled flesh, press her lips to the heated silk of his body, explore him with a carnal physicality that felt natural, right. As if there was nothing she could demand that he wouldn't give . . . and nothing she wouldn't give to assuage his hunger in turn.

Making herself turn away from the force of nature that was the Archangel of Africa, she flew back to the citadel at the highest speed she could manage. She'd just eaten a quick meal after bathing as rapidly and dressing in clean clothes when she heard the susurration of wings on her balcony.

Exiting her room, she found a slender female warrior standing in wait, her hair a deep black halo around her head, her wings a cool peach shade intermingled with threads of russet, and her skin the gold-flushed brown of a pigment Sharine had hand-mixed for her current work in progress.

The warrior's eyes were the same brown, and acutely sharp. Lush lips provided a soft counterpoint. She was extraordinarily beautiful.

"Lady." A deep bow. "I am Kiama. The sire has appointed me to escort you to the Northern border stronghold."

"I thank you," Sharine said, reaching for Titus's mind.

When he indicated he heard her, she said, *Does Kiama have the seniority to know for what I search?*

She commands the border garrison, and has my full confidence and trust. His tone was resonant but distant, his attention clearly elsewhere. She withdrew at once, loath to distract him if he was dealing with one of the reborn.

Returning her attention to the young woman—though youth was a relative term when you were as old as Sharine—she said, "I go to Charisemnon's court to search his laboratories and anywhere else he might've hidden information. We have evidence that he was working on an infection that could fatally injure angels."

Kiama's pupils flared, a burst of night against the intense and lovely brown. "I understand. Do we fly now?"

"Yes. Will we need supplies?"

"My squadron is stationed at the stronghold garrison—it's fully stocked."

With that, the two of them took off into the sky.

The journey wasn't long. Given their enduring enmity, the two archangels appeared to have built their most heavily fortified fortresses across the border from each other—you couldn't see one from the other, and neither was on the border itself, but it was a swift journey for winged beings.

As a result—and despite her long night—Sharine was in no way on the edge of exhaustion when they landed in the courtyard of Charisemnon's former stronghold. Unlike with Titus's citadel, this fortress, while sprawling, had no city around it. It sat in magnificent isolation in the green of the landscape.

Nature had begun its slow creep across the stone structure even in the short time since it had been abandoned. Vines spread across the roof and hung down from the eaves, and she could see that a bird had made its nest in the alcove formed by a turret window. Give it a little more time and this symbol of immortal power would be absorbed back into the landscape as if it had never existed.

Dried leaves crunched underfoot as they crossed the courtyard, and she spotted the slinking bodies of cats prowling about. From their sleek healthiness, either they were being fed—or they were making a feast of the vermin that soon infested any abandoned place.

Kiama had already arranged for one of her people to come in behind them and stand guard outside in the courtyard, just in case they needed quick assistance. "Is this a permanent post for you?" Sharine asked her, curious why Titus would sideline a warrior with such watchful eyes.

Yes, she had a faint limp, and it was obvious she'd lost weight recently, but that meant nothing to a trained fighter. Limp or not, Kiama still moved with deadly grace, and was no doubt a dervish in battle.

"No, we do one-week stretches. My squadron will then go back to fight alongside the sire while another squadron takes the chance to rest. Truly, Lady Sharine, I would've defied the sire himself had he tried to bury me at this post." She indicated her leg. "As it is, a week will be just enough to recover from my injury—one of the reborn almost took off my leg."

Sharine understood warrior pride well enough not to offer to help when Kiama went to the heavy metal doors of the stronghold. Even here, in this battle stronghold, the door wasn't just practical—it was carved with scenes of battle, with Charisemnon in full glory. Dust fell off those carvings in a musty shower, the metal groaning as Kiama began to flip the levers to gain them access.

A curious cat, black as night, wandered over to watch as Kiama lifted the final lever. The door seemed to shake and sigh, more dust falling to coat Kiama's hair.

Proof enough that no one had been here since Titus's people shuttered it. It hadn't been a long period of time in immortal terms, but this environment was unforgiving. And nature was no gentle mistress.

Kiama pushed open the left door, the painful screech of the heavy metal making the tiny hairs on Sharine's arms quiver in warning.

The cat hissed and stalked off.

"Well," she said, "should the reborn wish to make a dramatic entrance, now would be the time."

Kiama, sword already in hand, spoke stiffly. "If you do not mind my impertinence, my lady, it's too soon for such humor."

Abashed, Sharine apologized at once, then admitted the truth. "I'm speaking out of turn because I feel a visceral fear though there is no need of it."

Expression tight, Kiama nodded. "I helped clear this stronghold of any and all threats and I feel the same. Evil has seeped into the walls of this place. Darkness lives here."

Such a simple, powerful statement that rang with emotion. "You saw some of it?" she asked gently.

"I was part of Charisemnon's court two hundred years ago." Turning her head, she spat on the external cobblestones. "It was a loyalty of my family, to serve the same archangel. My mother and my father both stayed loyal to Charisemnon even as they saw him changing and becoming something far different from the archangel to whom they'd first pledged their swords."

"I wish you'd speak freely," Sharine said when Kiama abruptly flattened her lips and stopped talking. "I've been lost from the world for many years and my knowledge of such things is limited. I will never use what you say to slander you to your family or to others."

A careful look, the warrior weighing her up. Sharine liked Titus even more so for having another such self-assured woman in his forces. She also felt a sense of deep pride when Kiama nodded, accepting Sharine's word . . . accepting that she had honor.

"Charisemnon was always a man who liked power, liked beauty," the young commander said, "but things began to twist inside him at some point. He started to cross lines that shouldn't be crossed—especially by an archangel who has power over the lives of all who look to him."

The two of them stepped inside, Kiama's eyes alert even as she continued her story. "I couldn't stand it and refused to follow orders if those orders were to take young women from their homes, or to enforce punishment for the lack of a tithe from the poor. I fought with my mother and father over it—and in the end I left. It was that or end up executed."

Moving to the left, Kiama touched her fingers to a switch that filled the entrance hall with a soft light that added to the daylight coming through the windows. From beyond the open doors came a whisper of wings at the same moment, the warrior from Kiama's squadron arriving to stand guard.

"My parents died in defense of him, that creature of filth and degradation," Kiama said in a voice cold and hard. "I will hate him to the end of my days for stealing what time I had left with those I loved most."

As a woman who'd been betrayed and who held her own anger close, Sharine understood. But as a mother, she was torn. That same maternal instinct compelled her to speak. "I know that should something like that ever happen to me, I wouldn't want my son to live his life nurturing hate in his heart. Hate poisons, as much as a lust for power or envy."

Commander Kiama looked at her, eyes flashing. "With every respect, my lady, my emotions are my own."

Sharine smiled. "Yes, child. But I'm a mother—I'm afraid we can't help trying to make things better."

Kiama looked at her for a long moment before surrendering to a slight upward tug of her lips. "Even when we were on opposing sides of the line, my mother would send me messages ordering me to make sure that I was looking after any injuries, and that I was eating well."

Sharine laughed, but left it at that. The other woman's hate and anger were new yet, the wound fresh. It'd take her time to come to terms with the loss, and to make a decision about how she wanted to live her life. She did, however, have one other thing to say. "I hope you'll allow me one more moment."

When Kiama gave a small nod, she said, "Hate can be a poison, but turn it into an anger that fires you from within, and it becomes a strength." She exhaled. "My anger has become my resolve." It wasn't about being revenged on Aegaeon any longer; she looked back and saw him as unworthy of such attention, of any further space in her head. This anger drove her to be the best she could be—for herself and for her son.

She took a step forward on that thought, into the court of an archangel who had chosen power above all else. He'd been willing to sacrifice not only those of his own kind, but mortals and vampires, too. No one had been safe from his ambition. And for what? To rule at the side of the Archangel of Death? Had he not understood that sooner or later, Lijuan would have no more use for him?

This first section of the stronghold proved relatively clean—a bit of dust, some cobwebs, but the tiles that lined the entranceway as well as the hangings on the walls weren't marred by dirt or blood.

She ran her fingers over the intricate knotwork of one hanging and wondered at the lives of those who'd spent so long creating what was unquestionably a masterpiece. She recognized this work as coming from the region near Lumia; it was done only by mortals, the tradition so ingrained no immortal tried to change it.

That mortals made such hangings was part of why they were so prized. It was a thing of time and of devotion. This large a piece would've been the work of a lifetime for multiple artisans. For those artisans in turn, it would've been a thing of great generational pride that their work hung in the hall of an archangel's court.

She walked on, under the wide curving roof, plenty of room for multiple angels to pass, and found herself at the lip of a sunken area that seemed to be a place designed for feasts and other large gatherings. Similar to the first level of Titus's home, it was a massive space, with a soaring emptiness all the way up to the ceiling. But where Titus's gathering area was square and all on one level, this was round with three steps leading down into it.

Ledges had been built into the walls, wide enough for several angels to use as a seat. Here, in this celebratory area that seemed far too baroque and richly decorated for a border stronghold, was where she found the first signs of chaos. Chairs overturned, carpets missing, smears on the walls.

"We washed those walls." Kiama pointed at the stains. "But there's no way to get rid of the stains without getting to work with steel brushes, and we had more looming problems. We just hauled out anything that was encrusted, threw out any carpets or hangings that were filthy with bodily fluids or ale or who knows what else. The sire incinerated all that with his power, and we left the rest for later."

"The chances that it *was* blood or other fluids of life that stained the walls?" If so, that blood couldn't all have been left by mortal hands. Some stains were too high up. Vampires were capable of climbing smooth walls, but she saw no telltale marks on these walls.

That left angels.

34

Kiama's forehead furrowed as she looked up at the stains. "I can't say. Whatever it was on the walls was very dry by the time we came here—it could've been anything, even food that had been thrown at the wall and left to rot." She made a face. "Archangel Charisemnon was fastidious about cleanliness when I left his court, but I don't know if he held to such things by the time of battle."

Sharine continued on through the space, taking in the artwork—paintings, rugs, sculptures, and more—much of which had survived the violence that appeared to have taken place here. Most of it was local to the territory and it made her wonder if this was the public hall.

Not many archangels allowed their populace open access to them, considering it a waste of time and resources, but Farah had mentioned that Charisemnon opened his doors on a regular basis. "Did Charisemnon continue his tradition of open houses while here at the border?"

"Until the very eve of battle." Kiama curled her lip. "According to Ozias, the sire's spymaster, it was more an exercise in vanity than a matter of allowing his people magnanimous access."

As Charisemnon wouldn't have done anything private in such a communal space, Sharine didn't linger.

After exiting the public hall through doors at the back, she found herself with multiple options. Across from her was an archway that led to another courtyard open to the sky, beyond which lay another ornate building. To the left and right flowed staircases. "What would you recommend?" she asked her escort.

"Across the courtyard, then inside," Kiama said at once. "Ozias's spies confirmed that to be the archangel's private area. From what we've been able to gather from those of his court that survived, he became increasingly paranoid about allowing anyone but his most trusted people inside in the months leading up to war. It's also where we found the bodies."

Abdomen tight, Sharine stepped out into the courtyard littered with dry leaves. When she looked up out of habit, she felt her heart catch at the searing beauty above. The sky was clear but for gossamer clouds of decoration. It filled her heart with hope; this beauty would exist no matter what they did or didn't do on this earth.

"Why was he not content with this?" Kiama gestured at the sky, and at the stronghold silent and abandoned around them. "Why did he always want more? They call Titus the warrior archangel but in all my time in his court, he never picked the fight—always the aggression came from this side."

With those words, Kiama stepped forward to cross the courtyard. "I'll go first, Lady Sharine."

Sharine didn't argue. The other woman was the expert here—and Sharine had the power to back her up should danger come out of the darkness. But all that emerged from within the next building was a musty odor that had an undertone of rot.

Kiama coughed into the curve of her elbow to clear her throat. "Unfortunately," she said afterward, "the only way to maintain security with our limited numbers was to shut things up after the basic clean."

"I don't like what I smell below the decay." Sharine forced herself to take a deep breath in an effort to work out what it was that made her neck prickle and long-forgotten memories struggle to rise to the surface.

She'd scented something like this before.

Pinprick flashes of memory. The clash of swords. Wings crumpled and falling. Fangs in a pale face. Mortal bodies frozen in fear. "A mortal, caught in the crossfire of an archangelic battle—his leg was amputated. He became sick with gangrene." Vivid memories now, of the crawl of green on his leg, the putrid odor. "Sickness, it is the taint of sickness that colors the air."

"Why were you with the mortal?" Kiama asked without altering her intense focus on their surroundings.

"I—" Sharine frowned, followed back the thread. "I was a war artist . . . and I thought it was important to make note not just of immortal losses, but also of the other costs of war." She shook her head. "I was naïve, I think, to believe most immortals would care for a dying mortal."

Yet Sharine was glad to have done it, her fingers curling in as she remembered holding the feverish man's hand so he wouldn't be alone as he slipped away into the finality of death. Going where Raan and her parents had already gone. A place from which there were no return travelers.

"Here, this is where we found the dead." Kiama stopped at an archway framed in a glittering array of semiprecious gemstones that shimmered and flashed in the sunlight coming from the high windows at either end of the entrance hall.

Beyond it stood a set of heavy double doors.

"There are no functioning windows inside," the warrior informed her, "but this switch will bring light." She flicked it with her elbow before using her body to shove open one of the doors.

Sharine could swear she heard a soft *pop* of sound, a seal breaking.

Chest tight, she walked inside to discover another large gathering area, but the chaos here was magnitudes worse. No rugs softened their footsteps and the walls were almost equally as bare. Scorch marks covered the floor.

When she looked up at where windows should be, she found only boarded-up squares of darkness.

"Boards were in place when we came in," Kiama said before she could ask the question. "Those bloody marks on there, too."

Sharine felt a chill in her blood. "An attempt at freedom?"

"Bound to fail. Windows have pretty but strong iron-work on the outside." The warrior's lovely eyes held cold reason when they met Sharine's. "Thanks to Ozias, we know the ironwork was an addition, done some months before battle."

Charisemnon, Sharine realized, had been building a prison in preparation for his plans to experiment on his own people; this had never been a quick decision. Turning on that chilling realization, her intent to examine the wall behind her, she found herself facing a sprawling painting of a small region in a land now called Mali. It was a place she'd visited an eon ago, Raan by her side.

Shock, a sudden jolt of memory.

She'd been so young and full of hope, happy and in love, and the painting was a riot of joyful yellows, oranges, even hints of pink. It depicted the sun rising over a field in which farmers worked and animals grazed, while two angels stood talking with an elderly human woman.

A simple scene really . . . but one of those angels was

Raan, and so this was a piece of her history. The other one was the angel who'd hosted them. A fellow artist, she'd taken them to the nearby mortal settlement to show Raan the origin of a specific cloth dye.

Too full of excitement and happiness to stay still, Sharine had left them to their talking and climbed a nearby hill. It was when she'd looked back down that she'd seen this snapshot of golden-hued life. "I remember being struck by the perfection and harmony of this scene."

Her fingers wanted to trace the lines of Raan's face, even though he was recognizable only by the colors of his wings. *Thank you,* she wanted to say. *Thank you for teaching me that love can be gentle and kind.* Had he lived, the young woman she'd been might've one day flown from his arms, but she would've done so with love in her heart.

"It's an extraordinary work, Lady Sharine." A touch of unexpected awe in Kiama's voice. "The sire was so angry when he saw it here; he said Charisemnon had no right to display a work of such beauty and heart in a place he'd turned into a death chamber. The only mercy is that it escaped unscathed from the carnage."

Sharine looked, could see no signs of staining, or of physical deterioration.

"The sire—we all—wanted to fly it right back to the citadel," Kiama added, "but we couldn't take anything out of this room. The risk was too great."

"It was the only possible decision," Sharine said, warmth in her heart for the arrogant and blunt archangel who had kissed her with such passionate hunger, and who she already knew would leave a memory she'd never forget. "Charisemnon must've had the painting a long time."

She smiled; nothing could dull her joy in the memories associated with this work. "Raan, the first man I ever loved, asked if he could gift the piece to the friend who hosted us for the visit that inspired it.

"Though I loved this painting, I loved him more." And so she'd given it to him, to gift to his friend. "She wasn't a very powerful angel and she now Sleeps, so I can't ask her to confirm, but I would assume Charisemnon saw it at some point and liked it enough that she gifted it to her sire."

"Does it cause you pain to see your work in such a place?"

"No. Perhaps there was one here who needed hope and beauty in the darkest time. If so, I'm glad that they could look up and see the sunrise."

"I should've guessed that would be your answer—no one who doesn't possess a heart could paint with such glory." She hesitated before blurting out, "One day, I hope to be able to purchase one of your pieces." It was a thing of sweetness how this honed warrior admitted her dream, with a stifled excitement that had her lifting a little on her toes.

Sharine had lived a long and creative lifetime, but she tended to gravitate toward large canvases such as this one. Some were even bigger, covering entire walls. Her current project—a secret hidden in a light-filled warehouse Tanicia had organized for her on the edges of Lumia—was an image of Raphael, Elena, and their Seven with the gleaming skyscrapers of their city.

She intended to make it a gift to the archangel with eyes of devastating blue, this son of hers that she hadn't borne. But the scale of it meant it'd take her years to complete. That tended to hold true for the majority of her work. The intricate piece that currently hung in Lumia had taken her a full half century.

Such was why, though she'd had a steady output for much of her lifetime, her pieces were beyond the reach of ordinary angels. It didn't help that the passage of time and natural disasters had damaged any number. By the time she completed one piece, two more may have been lost or destroyed or just become brittle and fragile due to age.

"I'll make sure you have one of mine," she said to Kiama. "I ask for payment in the form of you sitting for me."

"My lady—" A sucked-in breath. "I didn't mean to—"

Sharine squeezed her forearm. "Hush, child. Not only do you have a face and a presence that make me itch to sketch you, I like you and I give my art to those I like." She'd gifted Raphael a piece on his ascension to the Cadre, and as for Illium and Aodhan, she'd done countless studies of them throughout their childhood, several of which they'd "stolen" with her laughing permission.

She was wealthy, she supposed. Money had never really been the reason she created, but, thanks to Raan, she had a powerful financial support structure that meant she'd never have to seek a patron. That support structure took the form of two old angels who'd withdrawn from life except for what they did for her—not only did they husband her finances with fierce protectiveness, they acted as the conduit through which others might acquire her work.

Sharine had come to realize that they'd stayed awake so very long because she was broken and they were too loyal to Raan to abandon her. She'd decided to go to them as soon as she could, thank them with all her heart, and tell them they could lay down to rest without worry. She was no longer lost; they had more than honored their friend's memory.

Sharine knew herself well enough to accept that she'd never be the right person to manage her finances or the sale of her art, but she knew how to get good people. All she'd have to do was mention it to Raphael and he'd send five scrupulous and talented candidates to her door.

Kiama yet had a stunned look on her face as they continued on, but she pointed out the spots where they'd found the bodies, her stance always that of a warrior on alert. "The dead included mortals, vampires, and angels," she said first of all. "From the smell and the extent of the decomposition, they'd been dead for some days before we found them. But the decomposition was . . ."

The other woman frowned, lines carved into her forehead. "There is a way that flesh rots," she said at last. "The flies come to lay their eggs, then the maggots are born. There is a progression." She looked around the room again, her eyes intense. "Here, things were just . . . wrong. When touched, it felt as if the flesh had liquefied from within, the decomposition going from the inside out."

A hard swallow. "I made the mistake of prodding one of the bodies with my sword—I wasn't doing it to be cruel, but because I thought I saw movement and wanted to ensure I wasn't setting myself up to be attacked by a reborn.

"I was careful not to push hard but the skin erupted as if it was so taut all it needed was the barest nudge, and liquid flowed out of the body. A greenish slime that got on my boots and caused such a pungent odor that we had to evacuate the room for an hour."

The soldier's breathing had turned unsteady. "Before we evacuated, I and the warrior-scholar standing next to me both saw insects swimming in the slime. That was the movement that had caught my eye—a massive nest of insects *within* the body." Hand on her stomach, she shuddered.

Sharine couldn't blame her. Her own skin was crawling.

"We were lucky that the sire was with us. He used his angelfire to cremate the body and reduce the insects to dust." She indicated one of the scorch marks Sharine had noticed. "I don't want to know what those insects would've done had they been able to burrow into the body of one of our own."

"Did anyone take samples for further study?"

A hard shake of the head. "It all happened too quickly. We were terrified of the possibility of the insects getting out. We already have a plague of reborn, don't need anything more. And the insects were *moving.*"

Sharine couldn't imagine the horror, knew she'd have made the same call. "Was he the only one so infested?"

"We didn't attempt to find out. Given the risk of containment failure, the sire made the decision to incinerate all the bodies in situ—he did the same with all the furniture."

That explained the large burned patches on the floor.

"It was the safest possible option. If the contagion had been contained in this room, we didn't wish to let it out." A sad look at the painting. "The sire couldn't bring himself to destroy it, but I don't think it'll ever be permitted out of this place."

"All things come to an end, child." And she'd been given an unexpected chance to say good-bye. Poignant sadness entwined with a sense of thankfulness as she turned away to glance up at the walls again; Kiama's words had triggered another awareness in her mind. "There are seals around the boarded-up windows."

35

You see it." The warrior's voice was grim. "A vampire member of the entry team—Sarouk is his name—took images of this entire place on a phone. Our scientists looked at the images. They say the window boards are constructed in such a way as to create an airtight seal."

Around them, the air pulsed with hidden knowledge.

"The door is the same," Kiama said. "Our entry team did some damage to it as we had to force it open, but that's now been repaired."

Ah, there was the answer to the *pop* of sound she'd heard on their entry. "Was this the room where Charisemnon did his experiments?"

Kiama shook her head. "We believe it was more of a holding chamber, a gallery where he could watch the progress of the disease." She pointed to several dark circles in the walls and ceiling. "Cameras. He might've preferred to live like the kings of old, but Archangel Charisemnon knew the value of technology."

This, Sharine wouldn't have expected. The Charisemnon she'd met had been scathing about the modern world and its conveniences. Just another example of his hypocrisy and lies.

"We worried about Sarouk and our other vampire warriors," Kiama said. "It was possible there might've been something in the air that could've infected them, but nobody has shown any effects. We had no reason to worry about angelic infection then." A glance at Sharine. "Are airborne contagions a viable risk?"

"Given that Charisemnon chose to use insects to carry disease, and experimented with making the reborn even more virulent," Sharine said, "I don't believe he possessed the ability to launch an airborne attack. At least not a fatal one."

She hadn't forgotten the Falling—but there, the deaths had resulted from angels falling into the streets in the path of traffic, and other such accidents. Whatever Charisemnon had done had only pushed them into unconsciousness, not death—and she'd heard Illium say that Charisemnon had suffered terrible consequences as a result.

From what she knew of Charisemnon and what she'd learned of late, she didn't believe he would've taken the risk of becoming so debilitated a second time around. Especially since his goal had been to kill Titus—for only an archangel could kill another archangel. Hence the insects, and his use of Lijuan's reborn as a poisonous base on which to build.

"Was Charisemnon showing signs of disease when he fought Titus?" she asked, to be certain.

Kiama's face was a picture of disgust. "I was never close to him, but the sire has said his breath smelled of decay, as if he was rotting from within."

"But he was able to fight?"

"Yes." Kiama's jaw worked as she lifted a finger to her

cheek. "He managed to harm the sire, shatter his arm, damage part of his face."

A burn inside Sharine's blood at the thought of Titus being injured by someone so unworthy. "Then I don't believe he'd been working on an airborne disease—I'm told he was bedridden and covered with sores after the Falling. And that was to create mere moments of unconsciousness; an airborne disease might well have ended him."

Kiama's expression altered to watchful scrutiny. "You have better sources than many spymasters I think."

What she had was an archangel who treated her with the same respect he gave his mother, and a son, as well as a protégé who knew their liege begrudged her no information. She also had Caliane. Her friend, too, told Sharine anything she wished to know, for Sharine had held faith with Caliane longer than these young ones could imagine. "I'm old, child, and I value my loves and friendships."

Perhaps one day, this young and angry warrior, too, would call Sharine friend, but for now, the divide of years stood between them. How very strange when Kiama was likely not that much younger than Titus. There was no distance with Titus, no sense of a chasm formed by age.

Now, Kiama gave a slow nod. "I hope you are right in your supposition of Archangel Charisemnon's capabilities, Lady Sharine. Else we are all doomed." She stepped to an area to the left. "The dead vampire here, he looked as if he'd been attacking himself. Biting at his own arms, chunks of flesh missing."

Shifting on her heel, she pointed in another direction. "Another one was completely naked and had rolled herself up into a ball under the table. It was as if each was part of a different experiment, but why then they'd be thrown in here together, we can't answer except that perhaps Archangel Charisemnon was forced to rush at the end."

"What of evidence that an angel might've been infected?" she asked, remembering what Titus had told the Cadre.

"If you'll follow me." Kiama showed her to a door on the other side, made sure it shut behind them, then led her down the wide hallway to the left.

Stopping at the first door, she opened it to reveal a large empty room. "The furniture within had been badly damaged and the lock was warped. It was as if someone or something had broken out. The sire found a trail of . . . I'm not sure how to describe it."

After a long moment's thought, she said, "It wasn't blood, but there was blood mixed in with what appeared to be liquefied decomposing flesh. It had a greenish edge, and we thought the streaks on the stone of this hallway could've been from wings dragging on the ground, especially after we found a feather petrified in the substance. And these"—pointing at gouges in the floor—"appear to be claw marks."

She then indicated a spot on the wall only a few inches from the ground. "We also discovered smeared handprints at this level made in the same liquid, as if the individual was dragging themselves along the ground. Later we found multiple bodies beyond the walls of the stronghold, including several dead angels, so we hoped that whoever or whatever had escaped was dead."

A single angel, Sharine thought, could've easily slipped out in the time between Charisemnon's departure with the majority of his forces, and the arrival of Titus's. Especially if that angel was heading outward, past the cities, to more rural areas. Even more so if that angel had experience with remaining unseen.

The latter wasn't always a skill possessed by courtiers, who were all about flash and show. But given Kiama's story about her parents, Charisemnon's court hadn't been filled only with the useless. Titus had also identified the reborn angel as Skarde, a man rumored to be a skilled intelligence agent.

Skarde had been betrayed by his hunger for flesh, but if the angel who'd escaped this room had been someone other than Skarde, but of the same ilk . . . Well, a spy with a functioning mind could hide for a long time in the expansive landscape of Africa.

Shoving that fear aside, she said, "Did you find anything that looks like a laboratory?" She wasn't truly expecting such a place—whatever it was that Charisemnon had done, it'd come from him, from the same thing that made him an archangel.

He'd birthed poisons in his blood.

"No," Kiama confirmed. "But I can show you to his personal quarters."

Those quarters proved opulent and overtly sensual to an extent far beyond her personal tastes, with too much red and gold, too much texture, just generally too much, but that didn't stop the rooms from being surprisingly beautiful. But no . . . it *wasn't* a surprise.

Sharine frowned, paging back through the book of memory. Michaela had long been called the muse of artists, but Charisemnon had been known for being a patron of the arts. "Once, long, long ago," she murmured almost to herself, "Charisemnon offered me a palace in his lands where I could live and work. No strings except that he wished to be known as having the Hummingbird as a guest in his lands."

She'd forgotten that until this very instant when she stood on a thick velvety rug of black with a design picked out in ruby red. "I hadn't been to this land for far too long, so came to see if I wished to accept the offer and we met for a private dinner. He was a different man then." The person he'd been before he decided to join Lijuan on a path to death and pain and murder.

"I can't imagine you sitting across from him," Kiama said, her voice taut with a thrumming anger. "My mind simply refuses."

Sharine hoped this warrior would one day find peace, but it wouldn't be today, in the space of her enemy. "Did you and the rest of Titus's people do an intensive search of this part of the stronghold?"

Shaking her head, Kiama said, "We didn't think it necessary. We were looking only for living creatures—of any size—rather than documents or notes."

The pages of her memory book continued to flip. Charisemnon had sent her a letter with his invitation. "You have a beautiful hand," she'd said to him when they met.

He'd smiled at her, a handsome man with silken hair the shade of mahogany and skin of dark gold, his lips lush and perfect in their shape. "Words and ink, they hold our history even as we grow old and the memories become lost in the tangles of our mind."

Such a man would keep records.

With that in mind, she left Kiama to keep watch, then began to methodically search each and every place where an archangel sure of his privacy would hoard important documents. She didn't think he'd have thought to hide them—first of all, he'd been confident in his power, and secondly, he'd had no reason to hide anything from the people in his court.

They'd seen what he could do and had chosen to stay with him.

Books lined the walls of the large study beyond the bedroom and living areas. A lot of knowledge; you'd have thought some of it would've given him pause as he began his association with Lijuan and with death, but, in the end, people chose their identity, and Charisemnon had chosen a life of darkness.

A metal ladder was built into the frame of the bookshelves on both the left and the right of the room. They proved to move smoothly along the rails when she tested them.

She'd check each and every one of the books on the

shelves if necessary, but first, she went to Charisemnon's desk. In the top drawer was a leather-bound notebook. Something about it struck her as familiar and she looked over to the shelves—to realize that this room held the history of Charisemnon, the memory journals he'd kept year after year, decade after decade, century after century.

She was holding the most recent one.

Aware that she was standing in a treasure trove—angelic historians would clamor to be allowed access to this room—she took care with the journal as she sat down in Charisemnon's ornate chair. Placing the book in front of her, she opened it.

The words made no sense.

She tried again, working her way through all the languages she knew. She was about to give up and ask Kiama if Titus had a linguist on staff, when Raan's voice whispered into her mind.

My little bird, your talent for art strips mine. I can't wait to see you fly.

Raan's favored language had been so lyrical, so lovely, born on the banks of the Nile among an enclave of angels who'd made it their home for centuries. His friend in this land had spoken the same tongue. Charisemnon hadn't been of an age to have lived in the enclave, but perhaps he'd learned it from a parent or grandparent.

Sharine knew nothing about his parentage, and she didn't care at this instant.

Raan's enclave had faded from existence long ago, the language rarely spoken, but Sharine had learned it from her lover and it remained inside her. That it took her a while to turn those rusty gears was inevitable.

Yes, little bird. You have the skill and the heart for this.

He'd been such a good man, her Raan, one who'd always been gentle and kind with her.

Yes—and paternal.

She winced at the unsheathed words from another part

of her psyche. But it was true; their relationship had hardly been one of equals. But it had been a relationship that made her happy in that time and place, and it deserved to be honored for that. *Raan* deserved to be honored for that.

Consciously shaking away the errant thoughts to focus on the here and now, she looked down at the journal. She'd opened it to a point some months before the beginning of hostilities.

They think I'm a fool, that I will tie my loyalty to the weak rather than ally with the strongest one of us all.

I'm not the fool here.

Lijuan will emerge the victor in the war to come. There's no question on that point—she has evolved far beyond the rest of the Cadre, and she is right when she says we are immortals and capable of far more than is permitted by the current power structure.

Why should there be a Cadre of Ten? Why can there not be a Cadre of Two if those two archangels are the most powerful in the world? There's no point in sharing power with the more feeble among us. The others, the ones who survive the war, will serve the Cadre of Two. That is as it always should've been.

The last line was underlined twice, a blunt insight into Charisemnon's mind. It did confuse her a touch because she'd believed that he wasn't an archangel much driven to stir himself. He enjoyed a life of ease and comfort, and yet now he spoke of absolute dominion.

What had changed?

Settling in, she went back to the beginning of the journal and began to read, for in the genesis of Charisemnon's change of heart might be the information she needed about a disease that could end angels forever.

36

Archangel Titus, I write to you on the faith of your long friendship with my father. Before he went into Sleep, he reminded me that yours was a bond that remained unbroken across millennia. Now, I bow my head and ask if that friendship might extend to the mentoring of my son?

Xander is not yet at his majority, but he shows signs of becoming a warrior like his grandfather. It would be a great honor if you would consider taking him under your wing.

—Letter from Rohan, son of Archangel Alexander, to Archangel Titus

37

Rohan! I saw you running around naked while you were a babe, giggling manically all the while! I've broken bread with you. Why are you writing me such a formal letter?

Send your boy. I'll care for Alexander's grandchild as if he were my own flesh and blood.

—Letter from Archangel Titus to Rohan, son of Archangel Alexander

38

Titus wiped the sweat from his brow and looked down at the pile of beheaded bodies below. He and his people had followed a straggler who'd led them to a massive nest of reborn, but what worried him was that the nest had existed in the first place. "These reborn came from somewhere." There was a settlement out there that no longer had any living citizens . . . children included.

It broke his heart to execute the smallest reborn, though he knew they weren't alive in any true sense of the word. They were shambling abominations of life, without reason or thought. They'd never grow any older, would never under-stand speech or love or tenderness or anything but their voracious hunger for flesh.

To allow them to exist was equal to murdering the chil-dren who'd yet escaped the scourge. For even in the darkest hour, angels, vampires, and humans, they all hesitated when it came to harming a child, and in that hesitation could fall an entire town or city or territory.

"I've dispatched scouts." His second's voice was grim, the pale green of his eyes on the carnage. "Did you notice how fresh these ones were?" When Tzadiq, his shoulders broad and his body as big as Titus's, landed beside the pile, Titus followed suit. "Look at their bodies, the lack of rot."

Tzadiq was right; beneath the greenish tinge that began at the moment of transition, these reborn boasted pink and brown and black hues of flesh ordinary among living people. Some of their wounds bled as much red as green-black.

He and his squadrons could keep killing wave after wave of reborn but if the creatures were multiplying this rapidly, he'd lose half the people in his territory before they were done. Yet what other way was there?

"How are we on overall troop numbers?"

"We haven't taken any losses today, but our people are exhausted." Tzadiq's tone was brutally honest. "We're going to start making more and more mistakes in the coming days."

Titus had known that, but it was still hard to hear it laid out so clearly. As he considered all possible options on how to rest his troops, his eye fell on the crossbow bolt embedded in the eye of a reborn creature, the reborn's head long separated from its body. On the shaft of the bolt was a symbol—a small gold G in a circle.

"How bad is the Guild's situation?" The African complement of the Hunters Guild, those mortals born—or trained—to hunt rogue vampires, had sided with Titus and fought with his army. As a result, they'd also taken heavy losses.

"Not as bad as we first expected." Dirt streaked Tzadiq's pale skin and clean-shaven head, but it wasn't as bad as it could've been—at least he'd mostly escaped being covered with reborn fluids. "They're at seventy percent capacity, and of those, twenty percent are badly wounded and still recovering."

That meant that—aside from a small number running

things at the top—fifty percent of the Guild was currently fighting the reborn on the ground while Titus's angels fought from the air. It struck him that the hunters, all of whom were trained in tracking techniques and used to working alone, were a resource he could use far more wisely.

"Clean up here," he told his second, for the majority of reborn had scuttled into their holes under the bright light of day. "I need to speak to Njal."

"He's at Guild HQ today," Tzadiq said.

"One day, you'll have to tell me how you know everything that happens in Narja."

"Tentacles, sire." Dry words, his expression without apparent humor. "I have tentacles in every nook and cranny and blood den."

Titus slapped his second on the shoulder—Tzadiq was one of the few people who could not only take his full strength, but who could give it back in equal measure. There was a reason they'd been sparring partners for centuries. "Your archangel thanks you for your diligence."

That was when Tzadiq's face cracked a smile and so did Titus's. Because before sire and second, they were friends and had been for over a millennium and a half. Titus had known Tzadiq before his second met Tanae, before the two had a son. Titus didn't understand the relationship Tzadiq and Tanae had with each other, and with their warrior offspring, but as his second and his troop trainer, they were faultless in their dedication.

Leaving Tzadiq to his task, Titus made his way to Guild HQ, which was near the edge of Narja, and thus closer to him at this moment than his own citadel. Situated in an old stone fortress, it had a flat roof that allowed for an easy landing. The head of the Guild, the tight black curls of his hair buzzed close to his skull and his beard equally neat and precise, was there waiting to meet him, some scout having no doubt sighted his approach and guessed his destination.

"Archangel Titus." He bowed, a tall and slender man dressed in worn brown fighting leathers with a sword strapped to one thigh and a heavy knife on the other—but despite the bow, there was no sense of obsequiousness to him.

The bow Njal used was one Titus might receive from one of his generals.

Some might say the mortal was being presumptuous in acting as if he had so high a status, but hunters chose strong people for their leaders, and Titus appreciated them for it. He could speak to Njal as a warrior and know his bluntness would be reciprocated.

"Is there a problem?" the other man asked after rising from his bow, the golden brown of his eyes piercing against the blue-black hue of his skin.

"No." Titus laid out what he wished for the hunters to do. "Your hunters are an asset I wouldn't lose. Tell me if this is a risk too great."

"You don't want them to attack the reborn, just to track and pinpoint nests so that angels can strike from the air to eliminate entire nests in one blow?"

Titus nodded. "Should they come across lone reborn, they can feel free to eliminate the reborn—as long as such contact doesn't present a danger to their own lives. At present, I'm less in need of ground fighters, and more in need of information." Not many archangels would speak to a Guild Hunter with such openness, but Njal had fought beside Titus on the battlefield, resolute and tireless.

Titus knew that despite his attempts to stay distant from mortal friendships, Njal was a man he'd miss when the hunter passed from this world. "I need to use my resources more strategically." Else, the reborn would keep feeding on the people of his land, decimating it.

"We've been reacting for too long—driven by our lack of numbers and the way the reborn continue to spawn." Cut down one and two seemed to take their place. "But again, there's no point in doing this if I end up losing a large number of highly trained fighters."

"It'd be no more dangerous than going after a bloodlust-driven vampire," Njal replied in his calm, thoughtful way. "I won't send out the newer, less experienced hunters, but I have a strong complement of experienced hunters, even after the losses of the war."

Pain carved deep lines into Njal's skin, his serenity breaking into shards under the weight of it. "I'll send them out in various directions, with the majority going south, but a dedicated group heading north."

"Excellent. We can't leave stragglers in the north to continue to breed—but instruct the ones going north not to engage even with lone reborn. It's possible Charisemnon created a new strain limited to that region and we don't know all the possible dangers. They're to report any unusual sightings directly to me."

A small lie, because he couldn't tell even Njal about angelic reborn; some secrets were too deadly for any mortal. If a hunter ran across an infected angel, then Titus would work out a solution. Of all the mortals in the world, Guild Hunters were the most used to keeping secrets.

Njal grimaced. "Another new strain. If only Archangel Charisemnon had used his power to create cures instead of diseases." He put one hand on the hilt of his sword. "I'll make certain my hunters know their value is in the information they send back, not in taking physical action."

"Good man." Titus clapped the other man on the shoulder, careful of his strength. Njal was far stronger than his slender frame might lead an opponent to believe, his muscles ropey under the flawless night of his skin, but he was still human to Titus's archangel.

"If your northern hunters run across other mortals, ask them to be polite and share that I've tasked them to assist in hunting reborn," Titus added. "It'll help spread calm on that side of the border. Charisemnon left his people in fear of me."

A piercing look out of eyes that reminded Titus of a lion's. "All archangels create fear in mortals. I've fought at your side, Archangel, but should your wings begin to glow, I'd sure as hell know terror."

"Yes, but some fear is healthy—and some fear is crippling." Titus didn't wish for a cowed, quivering populace. He wished for one that respected his rule while continuing to grow and thrive.

"Understood," Njal said. "I'll make sure they know that, on this task, they're also ambassadors of your reign."

Taking off after a nod, Titus was aware of the Guild leader already turning on his heel to head inside, and knew Njal would dispatch the first teams within the hour. The man led the Guild partially because he was so ordered and practical. It was also why Tzadiq and Njal had been known to have a drink or three on occasion.

If Titus would miss Njal when he was gone, Tzadiq would deeply mourn him.

"Why do you maintain this friendship when you know it'll cause you nothing but pain in the end?" Titus had asked before he, too, began to know Njal as more than the leader of the Guild.

Square-jawed face not prone to heavy emotions, Tzadiq had quietly said, "The same reason my son's mate plants flowers even though their death is inevitable. Njal's heart, his mind, they're no less valuable for existing only for a moment in time."

Titus had thought that way as a youth, but the pain upon pain of losing mortal friends had jaded that part of him. This war, however, had shattered the jaded distance, and though he remained wary, it'd become impossible not to see mortals as individuals once more.

Sire. The mental touch was strong, for Tanae had one of the biggest mental voices in his court.

Tanae, I'm in the air heading toward the citadel. Though he had the intention to keep going past it. *Do you need me to land?*

No—but I have good news. Her mental voice held a jubilant tone that had him worried for her; she was a brilliant trainer, but jubilation wasn't in her wheelhouse. *Seven relief squadrons have just flown over the border, courtesy of Archangel Alexander. They've quashed the vampire uprising on their side and thus have the capacity to assist us.*

Titus was caught between a burst of joy and a frown; much as the assistance was needed and would help him rest his troops, protocol was for Alexander to speak to him directly about it first. And why had his people just let those squadrons pass instead of halting them at the bord—*Oh, dear unseen Ancestors.*

He rubbed his face. *Who is commanding the squadrons?*

Zuri and Nala are in joint command. Xander is part of one of the squadrons.

His sisters—and Alexander's treasured grandson, both such clear indicators of friendship that it was no wonder they'd been waved across the border. Of course, Alexander was also probably having a good laugh at sending the twins to haunt him. He scowled. *How distant are they?*

They can arrive within three days if you wish, but Zuri has asked if you want them to clear reborn as they move; they're well provisioned to do so.

He found himself smiling at the thought of his sister's fierce countenance and equally fierce love, despite the sure aggravation to come. *Yes. The north has an infestation— smaller than ours, but deadly all the same. But tell her to send three squadrons forward so we can use them to rest our own troops on this side.*

Understood.

As Tanae dropped off, Titus allowed himself a deep breath and exhale. Seven extra elite squadrons—because his sisters would command nothing less—could well turn the tide in their favor.

Almost to his citadel by now, the sunshine liquid gold around him, he reached for another mind. *Are you still at that bastard's stronghold?*

Yes, said a voice as strong as Tanae's, though of a different timbre and resonance.

Titus overflew his citadel, kept on going.

In a dark mood by the time he landed in the inner courtyard of Charisemnon's stronghold, he first greeted the outside guard, then stripped off his dirty armor and dunked his head under an external water pipe hidden in one corner. Any place that expected warriors to fly in and out on a regular basis had such areas.

He also used the water to wash off sweat from the top half of his body, as well as any reborn fluid that had gotten in under his armor. His pants were a lost cause, but he washed off his boots, too. Leaving his armor piled neatly to one side, to collect later, he contacted Kiama to find out Sharine's exact location.

It took him less than two minutes to make his way to her. The rays of the noon sun fell on her hair as she sat at a large desk, her wings flowing gracefully on either side of the chair back. She looked ethereal, a creature out of some other world.

Then she lifted her head and raised an eyebrow. "Are you attempting to smite me with your glare?"

Striding into the room, sure she'd sucked in a breath a moment before she spoke, he put his hands on his hips so she could more fully admire him. When she didn't fall over at the sight of his masculine beauty, he scowled and looked around at all the bound volumes. "What, did my enemy write of his great exploits and heroic deeds?"

He hated that she looked so at ease here, in a place where he would rarely venture—he had a huge library in his citadel, but it was for his scholars and those others of his staff interested in scholarly pursuits. Titus knew he was intelligent, but he'd never been at home in the world of books and learning.

"You did know him well." Sharine's tone was dry. "Because yes, this is his history."

Astonished, he took a second look around the room, noting the rows upon rows upon rows of volumes. In the end, his innate fairness had him giving a grudging nod of acknowledgment. "Charisemnon was a boil on the hind leg of a rabid feral pig, but he had determination, a certain kind of grit if he managed to keep this up for his entire lifetime." He couldn't help adding, "Pathetic that he then decided to spend his strength of will on manufacturing diseases."

"I think I found something." Whispers of sound, her wings settling, as she rose.

He turned and watched her walk toward him, a small woman made of light, but with a spine that was a steel rod. This woman wouldn't bend except by her own will and she very definitely would not break. She stopped so close to him that their wings almost touched, and held out a journal opened at a specific section.

Wrenching his gaze away from the softness of her skin, and his attention from the heat of her body so dangerously near to his own, he looked down at the neat handwriting in the book. It looked familiar in a vague kind of way. "What's the language?" He could speak a great many of them, but he had more knowledge of the spoken version than he did of their written forms.

"Oh, I apologize, Titus—I've been so deep into it for hours that I forgot it's a highly specific tongue, spoken by those who grew up in an enclave on the Nile."

Titus thought back, then spoke a line. "Is that it?"

An appreciative look on her face as she nodded. "Where did you learn it?"

He rolled his eyes at her. Her responding glare was very satisfying. Now she knew what he felt like. "That festering sore of an archangel was my enemy," he said. "*Of course* I learned all the languages in which he might give orders in the field."

He'd asked a warrior-scholar to track down an angel friendly to Titus who knew that obscure tongue, then he'd studied with that angel until he knew the language inside out. He'd also hired his teacher to decode any documents his spies picked up in the same language—Titus *could* read the language, but he was far slower at it than an expert.

"Sarcasm does not become you, my Lord Titus."

He knew she'd used that address just to irritate him, so he said, "I am but your servant, my Lady Hummingbird."

The two of them glared at one another, but below the aggravation was a fire that had the pulse in her throat skittering, and his cock beginning to harden. He and Sharine, they'd battle in bed together, too . . . and it'd be even more satisfying than this small battle.

He lifted his hand to run his fingers along the fine line of her jaw.

39

A cough from the doorway had him turning to face Kiama. Hands held crisply behind her back, she was looking anywhere but at the two of them as she said, "Sire, if you don't need me, I'll leave to take up my duties at the garrison—one of my people just went down with a wing injury."

"Reborn?"

She nodded. "He spotted a lone one crawling away into the shadows of a tree, dropped to take it out—but a second one jumped out at him from a hiding spot. He wasn't scratched or bitten, but his wing muscles need a day to heal."

Titus nodded his permission to her request and told her to take along the angel who stood guard in the courtyard. He was here to watch over Sharine now. After Kiama's departure, he turned to find Sharine looking down at the book again. Her long tail of hair had slipped to one side to reveal the slender line of her neck and the gentle slope of her shoulders.

No one looking at her would believe that she was made of titanium and had a temper hot enough to set the sky aflame. And still he tempted that temper by bending to press a kiss to the spot where her neck flowed into her back.

She shivered. *"Titus."* No anger after all, and her eyes held an otherworldly glow when their gazes met.

Outside of a Cascade, only one thing was supposed to glow among angelkind—an archangel's wings when he was about to release his deadly power. Yet her eyes held a light that wasn't from the sun. He accepted that. She was Sharine, and Sharine made her own rules.

Today, she rose on her toes and he bent, and they met in between in a kiss that had him groaning, his hands gripping her hips. When he lifted her up, she wrapped her arms around his neck and met him lick for lick, taste for taste, her chest pressed to the damp plane of his. Heart booming and air no longer necessary, he crushed her close and kissed her like a man starving.

Her breasts were the perfect size for her body and they had nipples that pressed at him through her tunic until he wanted to tear off the tunic and suck hard, make them wet and slick. Shifting his hands to her lower curves, he bounced her up and she wrapped her legs around his waist.

Groaning, he turned to sit her down on the desk . . . and reality hit.

"Not here," he said, breaking the kiss, his breath rough and his chest rising and falling in a ragged rhythm. "Not in the home of my enemy."

Sharine ran her hand over his jaw, the touch unexpectedly tender. "Agreed," she said, then leaned in to kiss him one more time.

He didn't want to release her when she began to unfold her legs, but he forced his grip to ease, though he kept his hands on her so she slid down his body. A smile was his reward, and he was gratified to see that her breathing was as jagged as his. Damp patches marred the light purple of her tunic.

"You make me feel young and reckless, Titus," she said, and touched her lips to his chest before pulling away.

The spot where she'd kissed, it ached deep inside.

His response flat-out terrified him and he was man enough to admit it.

"What have you found?" he asked, his voice coming out rough with the weight of the emotions he didn't want to feel.

"Let me read out Charisemnon's own words—you tell me what you think it says." She held up her hand when he would've spoken, his eyebrows lowered. "Stop glowering— I'm not testing you in some fashion." Razored words that should've killed his arousal dead.

His cock hardened even further; clearly his body wasn't interested in being rational. "Then what's this about?"

Lips plump and pink from the passion of their kiss, she said, "I'm simply unsure if my emotions toward what Charisemnon did have colored my interpretation."

"If you searched the world for the least objective person on the subject of Charisemnon, you'd find me," Titus pointed out, hands on his hips. "He is lower than a cockroach in my estimation. At least a cockroach knows no better."

"Just try," she said on a huff of breath. "You're a highly intelligent man. Think with the strategic part of your brain that you utilize in the battlefield."

Preening a little—though he wasn't about to show it— he folded his arms and jerked up his chin. "Read, then, and I'll see what I hear."

Her reading voice was lyrical and lovely and he had to fight to pay attention to her words.

"'I am racing to a great success in building a master-work out of Lijuan's gift and my own,'" she read, "'such success as has not been seen among my kind for eons upon eons. Lijuan says that she has reason to believe there was another as great as me at the dawn of our existence, that she has scrolls in her keeping that hint at the reason behind vampires and why the toxin lives in us. If she is right, that first architect of disease was indeed terrible and strong.'"

Moving around the room because standing still wasn't his natural state, Titus snorted. "Of course he worships the worst of us."

Ignoring his interruption, Sharine carried on. "'But I will be better than that unknown angel. They are *forgotten*. No one will forget me for I will do the one thing he could not. He infected angels, but he wasn't in control. I will be in control. I will decide who lives and who dies. My legacy will be of power so deadly that no one will stand against me. Not even Lijuan. Should she try, well, I have my weapons.'"

Throwing back his head, Titus laughed long and hard, his amusement profoundly real. "There is never any honor among evildoers. They would've eaten each other had they survived the war." The image gave him great pleasure. "Is there more? Or has he finished patting himself on the back?"

"There's more, but what do you hear in that part?" Closing the book, Sharine turned so that she was looking at him as he walked along the other side of the room. Her wings were brilliant splashes of color in this otherwise staid space, as if a butterfly had flown in from the outside.

"If the story the Legion told Raphael is true, then the archangel who created the toxin infected us all." An act so terrible that it existed in their cells to this day. "So what could Charisemnon do that the other hadn't already done?"

Sharine didn't interrupt, letting him pace as he worked the options through in his mind. There was only one answer. "He's talking about being able to infect and save people at will." Blood hot, he met Sharine's gaze. "The ass is talking about an antidote."

"Yes, I had the same thought." Putting the journal on the desk, she picked up another one bound in identical leather.

"This is the previous journal. I decided to read it after completing the most recent one—I had a feeling he'd been planning this for far longer than we realized, perhaps far longer than even Lijuan was aware."

"I've long thought that he must've had a backup plan that included a place to hole up and recover should the battle be going against him." But Titus hadn't given him that opportunity. "You think he's hidden the antidote in his secret place?"

"Nothing I've read says he had the antidote, only that it was in progress." She flipped to a section in the journal. "But here, look."

She walked to him again, and in her excitement, didn't stop fast enough. Their wings overlapped once more, her arm brushing his chest as she held out the journal. An odd feeling bloomed inside him at the realization that she was comfortable enough with him to stand so close to him.

A kiss in passion was one thing, an act done while they were both fully rational quite another. Because when it came down to it, he was an archangel and there was nothing she could do should he decide to harm her.

"There, do you see?"

Jerking his gaze to what she was indicating on the page, he went to remind her he couldn't fluently read Charisemnon's native tongue. But it wasn't words this time. It was a diagram. A location. But the map had been sketched without markers or compass headings, done by someone who knew the location and thus had no need of such instructions.

Taking the journal from her, he ran a finger over the slope that had been sketched across two pages. Stars dotted the sky, but those stars didn't appear to be in any kind of real-world order. A river or a stream ran in the distance before disappearing without warning—either it went underground at that point, or Charisemnon hadn't bothered to fully sketch it because it was of no interest to him.

What was most curious, however, was that within the hill was a residence. Charisemnon had drawn it like a dollhouse, with the front removed.

Either this was just an abandoned plan, or he'd built an entire stronghold under a mountain.

Right under Titus's nose.

He rubbed his jaw. "I must speak to my spymaster. Let me see if she's within reach."

Sire, came the immediate response, *I'm at the garrison. I came to speak to Tarik before I begin my sleep period.*

Join us in the inner courtyard, Titus said. *You can return to your foster brother soon.* The two orphaned warriors had grown up together in Titus's court and their bond was as tight today as the day they'd been born.

Turning to look down at Sharine's uptilted face, he wanted to rub his thumb over her lips, steal another moment that had nothing to do with reborn or death. Curling his fingers into his palm instead, he told her what was happening. Sharine kept the relevant journal in hand as the two of them walked down to the inner courtyard.

"This place should be protected," she said. "I know what you think of Charisemnon, but this repository of knowledge will be worth a great deal to our people."

"Who knows what poison he dripped on those pages," Titus muttered, "but I bow to your greater knowledge of such things." He wasn't so vengeful toward Charisemnon that he'd deprive angelkind of its rightful history. "I'll tell our historians and librarians of its existence after things aren't so dangerous. Else they might attempt to fly here now and I don't need noncombatants taking up time or resources."

A glance up, a raised eyebrow.

He rolled his eyes again, delighted at the effect it had on her. "In case you had failed to notice, you can fire energy bolts. You're not a noncombatant."

Sharine was quiet—unusually so—until he couldn't stand it. "What are you plotting now?" he asked in open suspicion.

Her eyelashes flickered. "I was just thinking that you have many more facets than I first realized." An almost prim statement, one he wasn't sure quite how to take.

But they'd reached the courtyard, and his spymaster was landing in front of them. An angel of six feet one with striking bones, Ozias didn't look like she could fly anywhere unseen or unwatched. However, this woman with skin of darkest brown and wildly curly black hair, her eyes only a slightly paler hue, had the ability to blend in anywhere. Especially since she often wore colors in the brown-black range and used makeup to soften her dramatic bone structure.

People didn't notice her. Didn't see her.

Her wings were like a falcon's, all streaks of brown and black, with snaps of white. It was as if she'd been born to blend in, but that was a clever illusion. In battle, all the soldiers under Ozias's command looked to her and found her every single time.

"Ozias," he said, "this is Lady Sharine." The introduction was more so his spymaster knew how to address Sharine than because Ozias wasn't already conscious of her identity. "Sharine, my spymaster, Ozias."

Ozias bent at the waist in the most respectful of bows. "My lady. It is an honor to meet you."

"I think you are like Jason and must've often been in Lumia, a phantom unseen," Sharine said, a laugh in her voice.

He saw the flicker in Ozias's eyes as Sharine spoke, understood her stunned beat of silence. Sharine's voice was a thing of beauty, luxuriant with elements it was impossible to describe, but that brushed over the skin like a caress. Titus was coming to think that it was a gift of sorts, as with his ability to cause quakes.

Because it wasn't only archangels the Cascade had

altered . . . and Sharine had lived through more than one Cascade.

"You have caught me," Ozias said, her voice having turned a touch husky. "But to spy on you from a distance is one thing, and to meet you in person quite another."

Sharine held out the journal. "Here is what we wished you to see."

Taking the journal with careful hands, Ozias examined the diagram with care.

When Titus asked her whether or not she'd seen or heard anything that might indicate the construction of such a hidden new stronghold, she shook her head. "I would've put it in my reports, sire." No edge to her tone; she had been by his side for hundreds of years, knew his question was no judgment.

"I never saw anything to indicate such construction, and neither did any of my people." Ozias wasn't one to show much emotion, but now she frowned. "But it'd be the height of arrogance for me to say it couldn't be done. Even Jason, who I deeply respect, was unable to find the location where Lijuan Slept before her rising and I know he hunted with intense focus."

Jason was Raphael's spymaster and considered one of the best in the world. Titus would try to steal him except that it'd be a useless effort because Jason was blood-loyal. Also, despite her admiration of Jason, his own spymaster wouldn't forgive him for at least seven decades. Ozias held her grudges tight.

"But," he pointed out, "you have a far stronger network in Charisemnon's territory then Jason did in China." It was a matter of simple logistics—Titus was right across the border from his enemy; Ozias had double agents who'd lived so long in the north they were considered locals. "Is it even possible that you could've heard nothing at all about a project this big?"

She looked down for a second, the sunlight picking up

the hidden red tones in the black of her hair. Slowly, she nodded. "You're right, sire. I should've heard *something*, and that I didn't makes me believe that either the diagram is of a historical residence—or it was constructed in one of the few locations where such a large enterprise could take place without anyone talking out of turn. It won't be here."

"Agreed." Not only had they searched the entire stronghold compound, Ozias had too many spies in this court. A massive stronghold couldn't run without all kinds of people, including low kitchen staff and cleaners. Charisemnon hadn't been great about ensuring that his courtiers knew to treat those workers well. As a result, they'd been the easiest for Titus's spymaster to turn.

"His far northern stronghold," Ozias said, "two hours east of Lumia, is much smaller. I could never get a source within that stronghold, and we had to be content with stealth flyovers or things glimpsed from a distance. We've only done a cursory check there, to ensure nothing dangerous lies within."

Looking up, eyes distant in thought, she added, "The only other possible location where an underground structure could've been built on the quiet is right on the border."

Titus stared at one of his best people. "Have you had enough sleep, Ozias?" he asked in genuine concern.

A rare smile from a woman who'd once drunk him under the table on a lethal brew created by Charo of all people. Not that Titus had become drunk; the archangelic system was too strong for that. But he'd had to give up on the fiery burn of the stuff going down.

"I'm not losing my mind, sire," she said. "I'm aware that was one of the most heavily watched and guarded areas while Charisemnon was alive."

"Then how do you believe something of such significance could've been built without Titus's knowledge?" Sharine's brow was creased.

Titus wanted to take a finger and rub those marks away,

yet at the same time, he accepted that Sharine had earned her marks, her scars. She would never be a woman he could leave safe and protected inside his citadel . . . and that was assuming she even agreed to stay with him.

Stay with him.

The thought hit him like a kick to the gut from a stone boot.

40

Titus was still reeling from the unforeseen blow when Ozias began to speak.

"Because of the constant battles that took place at the border—the vast majority of them initiated by Charisemnon," his spymaster said, "the buildings of the border garrison suffered relentless damage. All it would've taken was for Charisemnon to deliberately hit one of his own buildings by apparent accident. No one would've paid too much attention to any resulting construction, it was such a common sight."

Wrenching his mind back to the present by literally shoving his other thoughts aside until he had the time to process them without panic, Titus considered Ozias's theory with care. He was loath to credit his enemy with anything, but Charisemnon had never been a fool. "If he did this, it was an act of subtle genius." The words pained him. "You had spies at the border yet you heard nothing of it."

"That's exactly it, sire." Ozias shook her head. "No one

would've thought to bother me with news of more construction. Even an underground structure isn't unusual on the border—we have our own bunkers." That last piece of information was directed at Sharine.

"Such cunning," Sharine murmured, her wing brushing Titus's . . . because he'd shifted closer.

Titus folded his arms. "If your supposition is correct, Ozias, I can't believe that dog's shat of an archangel fooled me."

"You speak for me, too, sire." Ozias had a strange look on her face—a mixture of pained admiration and horrible embarrassment, but she recovered valiantly. "If I were Archangel Charisemnon, I wouldn't have kept the construction a secret.

"I would've even allowed the resulting building to be used for various border garrison purposes, then slowly shifted people out, except perhaps for a trusted few. Done gently enough, no one would think anything of it."

"Especially," Titus said, "if the building atop the underground structure was damaged again and never properly rebuilt."

Ozias nodded. "Charisemnon could've told his people to abandon that oft-hit area and put their energies into constructing a building away from such a dangerous location."

Titus clenched his jaw, a nerve jumping along his jawline. "It aggravates me intensely that you're most likely right."

"I'm afraid you cannot be as aggravated as I am. It's a brilliant strategy. I'm angry that I didn't think of something similar myself. We could've tunneled to attack the other side for one."

Titus shook his head. "That would've only worked once or twice before they began to do the same in retaliation and we ended up back where we began." He put his hands on his hips. "Go back to your foster brother."

His spymaster stared at him, unblinking. "Sire, you

know full well I'm incapable of returning to my brother without first discovering if our theory is correct."

Sharine's laughter was gentle, a sound that pleased the ear and had Ozias turning to look at her in a way that was . . . Not intrigued. More than that. Fascinated and with an edge of wonder. Because this was the Hummingbird and Titus realized that most people had never seen her so alive, so vibrant, with no fog in her.

If she'd been lovely and ethereal before, she was now dazzling in her brightness, a small and brilliant sun. "That's something my son would say," she said to Ozias. "I can just imagine Illium standing where you are now, his hands on his hips and his wings twitching with impatience."

Ozias, some thousand years older than Illium, smiled again and it was deeper, more real, revealing the beauty she turned to dull invisibility with such skill. "I tried to recruit your son once," she said.

"I know he'd never leave Raphael." Sharine shot Titus and his spymaster both a dark look. "And I believed that you were friends with Raphael."

Titus chuckled. "It's a game." A most satisfying one. "Every so often, one of us makes an offer to a member of the other's court that should be irresistible—but it's a point of pride with us that none of our high-level people have ever taken up those offers."

Even as Sharine shook her head, lips fighting a smile, he added, "For those who are younger, such movement can be beneficial. I teach them to be warriors and they return highly trained to Raphael when he makes a counteroffer. The pup, in turn, teaches my people how to thrive in a world that is constantly changing, and they return home with knowledge that stops my court from slipping into the dark ages."

The two of them were quite content with this silent and never acknowledged exchange. As Titus and Alexander were content with their far more open and always friendly game of one-upmanship. Though neither one of them had had the chance to challenge each other to a daring escapade since Alexander's waking.

"Now, we fly," he said. "Let us discover if we're attributing too much intelligence to my enemy, or if he did indeed get one over on me."

"Wait, I must leave this journal in the study." Sharine turned on her heel to run quickly inside, her wings a shock of color in this dreary place.

Ozias looked at him once she was gone, the brown of her eyes unusually soft. "Lady Sharine isn't who I believed her to be . . . but she remains a treasure, a star captured in a small frame."

Scowl heavy, Titus folded his arms. "Are you telling me to leave her be?" He had every certainty that Ozias had noted exactly how close he'd stood to Sharine, seen the brush of their wings, spotted the faint dampness of her tunic, and put it together with Titus's yet-drying hair and the damp patches on his pants.

No smile, her expression deadpan. "On the contrary, sire. I'm saying we should steal her for ourselves so we can conspire to protect her from those who'd attempt her harm."

Grinning, Titus slapped his spymaster on the shoulder, careful to modulate his strength. Ozias was strong, but she wasn't Tzadiq. Yet even as Ozias permitted a rare grin to light up her face, he knew full well Sharine didn't wish to be protected. If he did it, it'd have to be by stealth. Not exactly Titus's strongest skill.

His scowl returned along with Sharine.

She raised an eyebrow at him, but asked no questions as the three of them lifted off. The journey didn't take long, though Titus had to hold back so the other two could keep up. His spymaster contacted him mind to mind as they were about to reach this side of the former border.

Lady Sharine is far faster than I would've predicted.

She's maintaining my top speed and she doesn't appear tired.

Titus knew she'd tire on a longer run at this speed, for she hadn't yet built up the necessary endurance, but his spymaster was right about her pace. He'd always assumed young Illium was as fast as he was because he had an archangel for a father, but the clue to the actual truth had always been in front of their faces.

The tiny, jeweled hummingbird could move at incredible speeds relative to its size—even faster than an archangel. A small fact he'd picked up at some point in his life and that had stuck. Yet he'd never made the connection with the delicate and lovely treasure of angelkind.

Landing, Titus folded back his wings, looking to Sharine as she landed together with Ozias. "How did you get your nickname?" he asked, to confirm his theory. "The Hummingbird?"

"Why are you asking me that question now?" She lifted her hands, palms out, but answered anyway. "Raan used to say I flew like a hummingbird. Here and there and everywhere, so quick I was a streak of color in the sky." She opened out her wings then folded them back in with neat precision.

"I'm not as fast as I once was," she said with a grimace. "Unquestionably due to a lack of practice on my part. But I can feel the muscles beginning to wake up and I won't permit them to atrophy again."

I feel very stupid today. Ozias's mental tone was morose.

The entire world joins you in this, Titus assured his spymaster, even as he stamped down a ridiculous burst of heated green fire in his gut. Being jealous of a man long dead would make him an imbecile of the highest order, and he was already feeling the lash of being fooled by his enemy.

"So," he said aloud, taking in the abandoned garrison buildings. "We need to look for a section that's either collapsed and has been left that way for what looks like some time, or one that is new—in case Charisemnon decided to hide the truth by building and rebuilding."

The three of them took off again, heading to scan different parts of the garrison. Titus went high into the sky, so he could see every part of it; at the same time he tried to remember the battles fought. Charisemnon had never attacked the troops on the field of battle except when Titus was also present.

In that, at least, he'd held to the unwritten rules of the constant battles between them. One archangel wouldn't seek to decimate the forces of the other. There was no point in "winning" a skirmish if it meant crushing angels who had no hope of saving themselves from an archangel.

Odd that Charisemnon had honored that bright line when he'd crossed so many others, but as with any creature thousands of years old, he'd been created of layers upon layers. The same man who'd written all those journals that captured millennia of his history and that of his territory had also created insects that crawled under mortal or vampire skin and murdered.

He saw a number of cracks in the earth from his vantage point, evidence of his Cascade-born power. One was looking to turn into a small gorge. Spotting a likely location—a building on the outer edge that appeared to have taken severe damage and that had been left untouched for so long that plants had begun to crawl over it, grasses growing in the nooks and crannies—he flew down to examine it with more care.

It wouldn't work were Charisemnon unable to access the underground facility, and this pile of debris was just that. No way to get inside to whatever lay beyond. The two buildings on either side of it, however, stood whole but for some minor damage. *Hmm . . .*

Cobwebs kissed his face as he went to enter the building on the right; he heard wings come down behind him at the same time as he brushed the webs away. "Wait outside," he ordered Sharine. "I'm not sure of the structural safety of this building." What appeared minor damage from the outside could have a significant impact on the inside.

"Then why are you going in?" A sharp question. "It could as easily fall on top of your stubborn head."

He turned to look over his shoulder, wondering if he should be insulted, but no, genuine concern marked her features, her lips flattened and her eyes dark. Deep inside him, an unknown thing twisted. No one had worried about him in such a way for an eternity. Not even his mother or sisters, all of whom often referred to him as the baby of the family.

"I'm one of the Cadre," he reminded her with a gentleness that came from the same unknown thing inside him. "A building falling on me will do no damage that my body can't repair in a matter of minutes." It would take her far longer.

"Just be careful," she said after a pause. "I don't feel like spending hours digging you out of the rubble if you get stuck." Though the words sounded harsh, she reached over to close her hand over his. "Don't take any unnecessary risks."

It felt natural to dip his head and kiss those worried lips. "I won't."

Releasing her hand with a squeeze, he walked into the dusty building, the floor of which was coated with flakes of debris from the ceiling, and made his way to the steps he could see on the left-hand side. Those steps led down into what appeared to be a large storage area, but he soon discovered another set of steps beyond that.

Heading down those after turning on lights that flickered but still worked, he found himself in a space filled with neat piles of boxes. A thick layer of dust coated the tops—far thicker than could be explained by the lack of movement here since the war.

He opened one, found weapons.

Titus's cargo master would've long since shifted these unused boxes to open up space. Unless, of course, Titus told him that the weapons needed to be kept in place in preparation for a specific action of which his archangel would inform him when it was time. No one would then touch it.

A curious warrior who opened a box would find weapons—nothing unusual in a battlefield. What was unusual was the door concealed behind a set of boxes at the very back. He only spotted it because he'd cracked the earth under Charisemnon's infantry. The land had shifted . . . and the wall had moved to reveal the lines of what would've otherwise been a hidden door.

Invisible. Unseen.

Something smashed above, the building shaking around him. He was considering his next step when he heard footsteps, light and swift, coming down the steps. "I told you to stay upstairs!"

He couldn't bear it if those wings of indigo and gold were broken, that small body crushed. Not because she was the Hummingbird, a treasure of angelkind, but because she was Sharine, who worried about him and who had a quick wit and who he was finding he could talk to without ever getting bored.

"The building is falling down around you." She walked over to him, unrepentant . . . as the translucent champagne of her eyes scanned him for injury. "And, as your lordship pointed out, you are part of the Cadre. I'm sure you can protect me should anything happen." Then she reached out and took his hand, tugged. "Come."

He realized she'd come to drag him to safety.

Astonishment turned him to stone.

Not simply because, physically, she couldn't drag him anywhere, much less up two flights of stairs. No, because she'd been worried enough about his safety that she'd disregarded the danger to her own. It was foolishness, but it opened a vein inside him, one so profound that he wove his fingers through her own and said, "I've found a hidden door."

Widening eyes, before her gaze followed his. When he tugged at her hand, she came with him. Only to protest when he put his arm around her shoulders, tucking her close to his body.

"If I'm to protect you from a falling building," he grumbled, "you must be tight to me." His bones could take far greater damage, and he'd also wrap his wings around her, protecting her own.

"You're making sense. It's aggravating." With those grumpy words that made him want to smile, she slipped an arm around his back, pressed a hand against his bare skin.

The contact burned . . . and was a strange kind of comfort.

With her at risk, he walked to the doorway without delay. "Stay close," he ordered, then released her so he could use both hands to pull at the exposed edge of the door. It creaked, its mechanism stuck or warped as a result of the quake.

A shower of dust as he finally wrenched the door off its hinges and put it aside. Sharine coughed and waved her hand in front of her face, the dust swirling in the doorway making it difficult to see beyond until it settled.

"The smell," she said on another cough. "Decay and neglect and a wetter, more fetid odor."

"Yes, as if something died within."

Using the back of his hand to wipe the dust off his own face, Titus told Ozias to stay above. *Warn us if you see any sign of movement in the cracks caused by my power.* He was certain the earlier shake had resulted from such movement.

Sire.

And, to satisfy your curiosity so you don't expire from the frustration—you were correct. This building connects to the building hidden beneath the rubble next door. With that, he stepped into the hidden underground bunker, Sharine by his side, their wings rubbing against each other, they were so close.

It was pitch-dark beyond what little light fell into the space from the doorway, and the first warning he had that they weren't alone was a scrabbling sound as *something* rushed toward him on a rattle of chains.

41

Punching out his hand with warrior precision, he wrapped his fingers around the throat of what he expected was a reborn. Nails clawed at him as Sharine wreathed her hand with her power. Dim light suffused the room . . . to reveal a reborn such as he'd never seen. Her wings had been clipped so she couldn't fly, her eyes were reddened, her flesh holding a greenish tinge.

Yet she wasn't rotting, was alive in some bizarre sense.

His anger at Charisemnon's malevolent actions a storm, he went to tear off her head out of instinct when Sharine put a hand on his forearm. "No, Titus, don't!"

He stopped mid-motion, even as the reborn scrambled weakly at his arm, its strength fading at rapid speed. "The creature is a danger, and it's also cruel to allow it to exist in such a state." No angel would ever choose this life.

"*Look.*" That single word was full of horror, her gaze not on the reborn's face, but lower.

To the creature's swelling belly.

His stomach revolted so badly that he almost threw up, as might a young soldier faced with the viscera of battle for the first time. "I'll do it quickly," he promised Sharine. "I won't extend its torture." Such a thing as this was beyond evil. "Women who are with child when attacked don't survive and rise as reborn—I've never seen such."

But she put her hand in his and squeezed. "Don't you understand, Titus?" Her body trembled. "I think she's carrying the cure."

He stared at her, then at the weak creature in his grasp. There was little flesh on its body—not a surprise if it had been trapped in this room since Charisemnon's death; it would've had only the food the other archangel had left behind for it. That food was apt to be flesh . . . and while the reborn had become smarter, they were nowhere close to smart enough to know to hoard food against a shortage. Their instinct was to gorge.

"Find another light source," he said to Sharine; he focused on the practical action because the horror would otherwise overwhelm him. "There must be something brighter here if this was Charisemnon's workspace."

It didn't take her long, the room soon drenched in a clinically white light. The space that stretched out in front of them was massive, but it was also open enough that he could see at a glance that it contained no other reborn.

A filthy mattress and a pile of blankets lay in one corner, along with iron restraints that had come off the slightly cracked wall. He looked down, saw the chains dragging from the creature's ankles. Though it turned his stomach, he carried the now unmoving reborn to that bed—even the chains didn't add much to her weight.

She'd fouled part of the mattress, but he found a comparatively clean patch on which to place her.

"This must've held food." Sharine pointed to several now broken containers near the mattress. "Oh, sweet mercy."

Following her gaze, he saw a mound of small bones.

Muscles bunching, he looked again at the starving reborn. "When I moved the earth, it must've cracked the joints enough for rats to get in."

"She did what she had to do to survive," Sharine said, her face taut with sorrow.

"It's not a she, Sharine. *She* died when Charisemnon and Lijuan did this to her." Sharine had to understand that, or she'd hesitate against a reborn at the wrong time, and end up torn apart. "This is a creature created by a monstrous evil."

A shuddering breath, but Sharine nodded.

Sire, the cracks in the earth are moving and heading your way.

Titus felt the first whisper of a rumble under his feet even as Ozias's warning hit his mind. That this structure was still standing told him it was solid and built to be resilient, but they couldn't rely on that—not after all the damage caused by earlier quakes. "Gather any documents you see," he told Sharine. "I'll do the same—this creature's body is limp. We don't have to fear an attack."

It was Titus who found the still functional cold storage room. Rows upon rows of bodies lined the walls, all of them angelic females. Clipped wings were standard . . . and someone had slit open the stomachs of several. Small twisted forms with no faces and with skin a rotting green were stacked in another corner.

He shut the door when he heard Sharine coming closer. "You don't wish to see what lies within," he said, holding tight to the door handle to stop her from even attempting to open it. "Trust me on this. As a mother, you don't want to see that."

She looked at him for a long moment before inclining her head. "I trust your judgment." In her hands were several thick notebooks. "Can you get a box from the external room?"

He made her come with him, not wanting the building

to come down on top of her while he was away. After returning with the box, they quickly filled it with all of Charisemnon's notes that they could find, then Sharine hefted it up in arms that trembled, but held. He, in turn, wrapped the reborn angel in multiple blankets so that no one would know it was an angel he held, then followed Sharine out of the bunker.

He'd send an excavation team here once the shakes had stopped and it was safe, but for now, this would have to be enough.

Ozias took the box from Sharine the instant they stepped out, her eyes narrowed as she observed Titus's burden. But she didn't ask any questions, her faith in Titus overwhelming her shock. "Back to Charisemnon's border court?"

Titus nodded. He wasn't about to carry this infection into his own court.

"Wait," Sharine said. "May I have that?" She was pointing at the water flask his spymaster had strapped to one side of her thigh.

When Ozias, her hands full of the box, nodded, Sharine reached for it. Opening the flask . . . she began to pour the cool, clear water over Titus's wounds. He could tell the scratches were already healing, and he felt no sense of sickness, but he let her do what she needed—with the blood washed away, she'd be able to see the healing edges for herself.

"It's itching," he murmured, his gaze on her downbent head, and his heart . . . soft. "You know what that means."

A sharp, tight nod. "Good." Closing the lid on the empty flask, she held on to it as the three of them took off.

She flew right next to him while Ozias went a little ahead, and they spoke as they flew. "She looks to be either at term or very near it."

"You must advise me on this. Do we need a midwife?" He couldn't believe he was asking such a thing, not when what was growing inside this dead creature brought to shambling life was apt to be a thing of horror. "Or can I open her womb after ending her life, and retrieve whatever germinates within?"

Sharine's face went white, her bones sharp against her skin as she looked at the reborn angel in his arms.

"Think of your people," he said gently. "Would any one of them wish to be in this state? Would they want for you to prolong their torture?" That was when he felt a movement against his chest, where the reborn angel's stomach was pressed.

A rippling spasm.

He'd never been in such close contact with a woman about to have a child, and the ripple felt too big and strong, but he was old enough to know what was happening. "The decision's been made—she's having contractions."

"I can act as midwife." It wouldn't be the first time Sharine had delivered a child; with age came many experiences, and she remembered acting as an emergency midwife to another angel well enough to do this. "It's probably for the best if we don't bring anyone else into it. We don't know what either mother or . . . child, if it is a child, carry in their blood and other bodily fluids."

For better or worse, Sharine and Titus had both already been exposed. Ozias hadn't come in actual contact with the victim, nor had she spent time in an enclosed space with her. Sharine, in contrast, had scratched her hand while inside that room. Nothing but a minor scrape that was already all but healed, but still, a significant exposure.

She went to say something to Titus on that point, but went silent when her gaze fell on him. He was staring at the reborn angel in his arms, a twisted pain in his features.

"I recognize her from my last visit to the Refuge," he said roughly. "Two hundred years old at the most. Barely out of training."

So young. Sharine's heart broke. A child this young shouldn't be with child herself; it was beyond rare for such a young angel to fall pregnant. She'd also most likely have parents who were yet awake. Their world would shatter at this terrible loss.

She and Titus exchanged no further words the rest of the journey to Charisemnon's stronghold. After landing directly in the inner courtyard, Titus ordered Ozias to stand guard, then carried the reborn to the closest bed. It happened to be a feminine room, dressed with soft fabrics and delicate embellishments.

Sharine was glad of the softness of the coverlet on which Titus placed the dying woman. No doubt they could revive her with a meal of flesh, but such an act would dishonor not only who this woman had once been, but the concept of life itself. Titus was right to say no angel would choose this existence.

Sharine tugged the blankets free, so the reborn was no longer bound up in them.

When Titus tore strips from one of those blankets, she wanted to protest that the reborn no longer needed to be tied up, that the creature was too weak—but she knew that was her heart speaking. Whoever this being had once been, that being was gone. Charisemnon had stolen a dignified death from her, turning her into this abomination of life, and now she couldn't be trusted.

But she stepped in when Titus would've tied her ankles to the bed. "I'm in no danger from her feet. And it's better if she has control of her lower body."

Titus nodded. "I'll be here should she somehow break her bonds."

The reborn woman screamed then, a thin shriek of sound that raised every hair on Sharine's body, it was so inhuman. Still, careful to keep her hand away from the woman's snapping teeth, she stroked her hand over her hair. This child was dead, its torment close to over, but at this instant it was a creature caught in a trap it could never escape; Sharine would do it what kindness she could.

Oddly the stroking seemed to calm her, and when Sharine said, "Push!" she screamed but obeyed. The few shreds of clothing that still clung to her frame were no impediment to the birth. So Sharine kept giving the order—the contractions were coming one on top of the other now, in a rhythm that wasn't that of a healthy angel.

No angel's stomach had ever bulged and rolled this way. No angel's body had gushed a greenish black fluid. And no angel's eyes had been devoid of white, the sclera a sea of crimson.

Another scream, the reborn angel's eyes locked with Sharine's. For a moment, Sharine saw sanity within those eyes, saw a knowledge of horror, and she heard the whispered words, "Give me mercy. *Please.*" Then the woman snapped her teeth before screaming again and bearing down as she thrashed in her bonds.

Shifting lower down the bed, Sharine pushed up her sleeves and got ready to grab whatever it was that was about to come out, but Titus nudged her gently aside. "You don't know if what'll emerge will do so biting and clawing."

She shuddered, her imagination conjuring up a nightmare. "Did you hear her?" Grief thickened her voice. "She asked for mercy." Sharine couldn't imagine the pain of this woman—to know that she was a diseased and dying creature, but being unable to do anything to stop it.

A curt nod. "She shouldn't be conscious in any way. Once they rise, the reborn of this iteration—even the most cunning—have no sense of reason and no language. It confirms what we were told about the first angelic reborn."

Grabbing a throw from the settee by the windows, she passed it to Titus. "So you can protect your arms at least a little." After he took it, she went back to the head of the bed. Though the reborn woman's eyes were now crazed red with no sign of sentience, her mouth bared as she sought to bite, Sharine stroked her hair and murmured gentle words that she hoped would make this a little easier.

The screaming suddenly reached a pitch that was pain in the ears, glass shattering. The reborn angel's body erupted in a gush of dark, *dark* green-black fluid as she gave birth to whatever it was that Charisemnon had planted in her. Sharine only glanced over long enough to see that Titus was safe. Her attention was on the woman, whose breathing had altered dramatically, her chest rattling.

And though she knew there was a chance of being clawed, Sharine slid one hand into the reborn angel's. A weak grip around her own, her eyes holding Sharine's for a profound moment of purest peace . . . then she gave one last breath and went still in a way only of the dead. The reborn did not pass in this way, but this woman had never been an ordinary reborn.

A single droplet of green-black rolled from her eye and down her cheek.

Tears burning her throat, Sharine gently closed the woman's eyelids. By some mercy, they stayed that way. When she turned to Titus, it was to see him staring down at what he held cradled in the throw in his arms.

"Titus?" Breath lodged in her throat, she stepped over.

Her stomach churned—all she could see at first was putrid black-green. But then she saw the waving fisted hands with perfect tiny fingers, the mouth that was gasping for air in a face that Titus must've wiped clean, and felt an even colder horror run through her blood. Her words came out a whisper. "It's a baby."

"Check her fingers." Titus's voice was crushed stone. "See if she has claws."

Gently wiping one fist clean using an edge of the throw, she unfurled those delicate baby fingers with care. Then she examined the babe's feet. "Nothing. She has the same soft nails as any other infant."

Shifting on her feet, she walked quickly into the suite's bathing chamber and found what appeared to be an unused towel set hanging on a railing. Dampening the soft hand towel with warm water, she went back into the room and began to gently wipe down the child.

But it wasn't enough; the slime was everywhere and it stuck. "Bring her into the bathing room." Going ahead, she found a pitcher sitting to the side of the bathtub. It must've been for bathers to pour water over themselves—or perhaps for a body servant to do so.

She filled the pitcher with warm water, then made Titus get rid of the soiled throw and hold the child in the sink while she poured the water over the strangely quiet infant's skin, washing it until it was clean all over its front. Unlike most babies this young, its eyes appeared to be able to focus and the baby watched her with eyes of a strangely familiar hue.

Deep gold with slivers of brown.

The last time she'd seen such eyes, they'd been set into a strikingly handsome male face, his lips lush and his hair a silken mahogany.

The face of an archangel.

42

I must use my own seed.
That is the key. That has always been the key.

—*From the journals of Archangel Charisemnon*

43

Wondering if Titus had noticed the infant's eyes yet, if he'd realized the import, she said, "Turn the little one over."

Titus said nothing, but his big hands were careful as he turned the baby so that her back was exposed; Titus made sure to support the child's head. It took only a splash of water to clear away enough of the slime to reveal wings. The translucent and soft wings of an angelic child, with no deformity or malformation. She took care as she cleaned all of the slime off those wings, then the rest of the child's body.

The babe's skin was a dark gold that echoed her father's. It had been impossible to see the original hue of her mother's skin under the reborn rot, but it had probably been similar to Charisemnon's for the child to so closely echo the shade.

Only once the child had no trace of slime on its tiny body did she pick up the biggest towel and spread it out on the counter so Titus could place the child on it. With the still eerily silent little one lying on her back, she began to wipe down her skin. She kept her touch gentle, patting the water from her skin rather than rubbing. "See if you can find some powder. It'll help her skin after all it's been through."

Titus hesitated.

"She can't do anything to me, Titus. She doesn't have any teeth, far less any claws."

He left at last.

In the interim, Sharine picked up and rocked the child in her arms. "What are you, little one?"

The baby hiccupped . . . then, throwing back her head, *wailed*. Wailed as if she was being beaten, as if the world had done her the greatest insult.

"At least she has a strong voice," Titus said in an approving tone as he walked in with several canisters of powder in hand. "I didn't know which was the right one."

"Hush, my sweet," Sharine murmured, rocking the child—to no avail. Her face turned red under the gold of her skin, her sobs jerky in between the wails.

"Hah, she is stubborn. Give her to me."

Placing the baby's tiny body against his shoulder, Titus patted her back with firm motions that didn't rub or otherwise abrade her fragile wings. A slew of hiccups before the wailing trailed off. "See?" Titus beamed proudly. "It's not difficult."

Sharine felt her lips twitch. He'd be insufferable if not for the sheer adorableness of this picture. And she couldn't blame the babe for snuggling against him. Were Sharine in the mood to snuggle into any man, Titus's broad shoulder would be at the top of the list. "I see you've done this before."

"Many children call my court home."

Once the child's eyes had closed, her little form in a snuffling sleep, Titus laid her down on the towel again and Sharine put the powder on her. She massaged those little limbs as she did so, in the same way another mother had shown her to do with Illium when he'd been a babe.

The child was still fast asleep by the time she finished, and Sharine gathered her up in a soft new towel in lieu of a blanket before carrying her out. She knew the child couldn't understand anything she might see, but she made sure to keep the little one's face turned away from her mother's already decaying body.

The reborn angel had melted in the time they'd been in the bathroom. Greenish fluid leaked from her every pore, and right then, her fingers degloved to bone, her flesh plopping to the floor.

"I wish you peace, child," Sharine said before she walked out of the room.

Titus followed, pulling the door shut behind them. "I'll leave the body instead of incinerating it." No smile now, his features grim. "I need to call our scientists so they can begin the tests."

"You'll have to tell the Cadre about her, won't you?" Sharine said, her arms protective around the child. "You know they'll consider her a threat."

"She could mean death for every angelic child," Titus said gently. "But we will give her a chance. I'll ask my scientists to test her blood against the infection and see if she carries within her a cure . . . or if she is a sweet-faced carrier, designed to slip under our guard."

Sharine didn't resist when he plucked the child from her arms. Holding the tiny body in one arm, he sighed. "She's his child."

So he'd noticed the eyes after all. "Yes. Does that make a difference?"

A lopsided smile. "Only that that ass's behind managed one last trick." Leaning in, he pressed a kiss to the baby's forehead. "She is but a babe dreaming innocent dreams, and if she's no threat, then I'll raise her as I would any other orphaned child in my territory. I'll also tell her of her mother's brave heart, she who fought to stay alive so her child would live."

When he raised his free arm, she went into his embrace, this man warm and strong and with a heart capable of incredible kindness. And she tried not to think of what would happen if the tests showed the child to be a carrier, the unknowing bringer of a devastating disease.

Two days later and Titus could tell that Sharine didn't want anyone taking blood from the child, but she clenched her jaw and gritted her teeth and watched eagle-eyed until the deed was done.

The babe's sobs soon turned into sniffles after Titus picked her up and patted her back, her little body snuggled against his shoulder. "You are a courageous one." It was true—the child cried as would any child, but she also recovered quickly, her hands fisted as if in a stubborn refusal to surrender.

He knew he shouldn't become attached to her, that he might yet have to execute her—and he knew damn well it'd destroy him to do so even if he hadn't bonded with her. But he couldn't suppress his feelings of affection. She was so tiny and so helpless. Some would say that made her the perfect weapon to annihilate the world.

"Is there any word?" Sharine asked, sweat dampening the hair at her temples and flecks of unknown substances on her tunic—she'd just come in from doing a shift watching over a ground team. "Does she carry the virus?"

"My scientists are having difficulty understanding what they see in her cells—hence the need to take more samples and confirm their findings." He'd been blunt that they were to be careful with the blood they harvested, to not spend it too quickly. It was a baby, after all, from whose body they were drawing the samples.

The only reason he'd permitted it at all was because he had to give the Cadre a reason to allow this child to live. No one could *force* him to execute anyone in his territory— but were she the bearer of a plague, he wouldn't have a choice. "Sometimes, being an archangel isn't a gift," he gritted out.

Sharine touched her hand to his upper arm, then reached up to stroke the baby's back. "I don't envy you, Titus. But I know that whatever you do, you'll do with honor. This child will have the best possible chance with you as her champion."

He dropped a kiss on the baby's downy head and hoped he could uphold Sharine's faith.

While the scientists worked, dressed in protective gear such as normally only used by mortals, the baby continued to live in the nursery inside Charisemnon's court. Were she a carrier, to take her anywhere else risked spreading a disease. So Titus and Ozias had brought in everything the baby might need.

Sharine watched the child for multiple shifts, with Ozias volunteering to take the risk of infection and stepping in so they had another person in the rotation who could be with the infant without protective gear.

"No child should spend her first days in the world without the comfort of touch," Titus's spymaster had said firmly. "I know enough about babysitting after surviving all the children that have been raised in your court, sire, that I'm unlikely to kill the infant by accident."

Needless to say, Ozias was a most unusual babysitter.

The one mercy was that Sharine had found confirmation in Charisemnon's journal that the infection set in early and visibly, so the three of them only had a stand-down period of two hours after contact with the infant. After that, they were safe to return to the fight, sure they wouldn't inadvertently carry the infection to Titus's troops and staff.

On the evening of the fifth day since the child's birth, Titus came by with dinner for Sharine and found the child asleep in her crib. As they ate, seated side by side on a sofa,

Sharine asked for an update on the reborn situation; her last external shift had been twenty-four hours earlier, when she'd single-handedly saved three ground teams from being overwhelmed by a hidden nest.

Day by day, hour by hour, she was becoming ever more comfortable in her power and better able to direct it. Titus had the strong feeling they'd still only seen the tip of the iceberg—Sharine had plenty more surprises up her sleeve.

His people were over the shock of the Hummingbird not being at all what they'd expected, and were now well on the way to total adoration. Tough, loyal, and newly hard-of-heart Kiama often tracked her down for conversation, Titus's harried cook somehow had the time to make a "little some-thing" for her each day, and one of his lead vampiric com-manders had threatened mutiny if Titus didn't manage to hold on to her.

"I said nothing when you scared away the others," India had said with a flash of fangs, "but, sire, I'll surely rebel if you lose Lady Sharine."

Tall and heavily built Amadou, a fellow senior com-mander, had nodded in solemn agreement.

Even Tanae had been moved to say, "I like her." From his troop-trainer, that was praise unbounded.

"The extermination effort is continuing to pick up speed now that the hunters are out pinpointing nests." Which was partly why he wanted to talk to her. "We've now gone so far out from our initial starting point that it makes no sense for me to fly back each morning, then fly forward again. I'll be staying in the field for some time."

"Do you need me to watch the babe full-time?"

"No, you're too necessary in the field." Sharine's reserves were deep, her bolts of power of violent intensity. It had become clear over the time she'd been with them that she was stronger than Tzadiq—and Titus's second was in the top tier of non-archangelic fighters.

"Do you think she knows she could've been a general?"

Tzadiq had said to him the last time all three of them had been in the field at once, the pale green of his eyes following Sharine in the night sky as she protected the vampiric troops with precision fury. "People follow her, she has the martial power, and the quick-thinking intelligence."

"I'll ask her," Titus had said, "but can you imagine a world without Sharine's art?"

Tzadiq had paused to wipe off his gore-encrusted sword. "You're right, sire. We have enough generals. We have only one Hummingbird."

Today, however, Titus was forced to ask her to be the general and not the artist. "I need you to fly northward with Ozias's squadron and two ground teams, clearing any reborn nests as you go. You'll meet Alexander's troops at some point, and the group of you can do a final comprehensive sweep of the north to make sure it's clear."

He didn't want to send her away from him, but it was the best possible use of resources. Nala and Zuri also had the ability to fire energy bolts in their arsenal—adding Sharine's firepower would make the team unstoppable against the numbers of reborn in the north. "Once the north is clear, I don't have to worry about reinfection from that side."

He paused, scowled. "Remember—don't listen to anything my sisters say about me."

A twitch of her lips, but her gaze was solemn. "What'll happen to the babe with all three of us gone?"

"It appears she has charmed one of the scientists." No surprise that—the babe smiled in her sleep and cried but rarely. "Asiah is more than willing and happy to watch the child without protective gear. The little one will be safe and tended while we are gone."

"Asiah . . . yes, she's the only one of the scientists I'd trust with her," Sharine muttered. "She treats her like a baby rather than a science experiment." Glancing at Titus, she put one hand on his thigh.

The muscle jumped, went rigid, his entire body focused on the heat of her. *"Sharine."*

"Take care of yourself, Titus." It came out an order. "Simply because you're an archangel doesn't mean you can go forever without a rest." Then she leaned in and kissed him, and his abdominal muscles clenched, his pulse staccato.

Breaking the kiss before he could reach for her, she rose. "I'll see you when our task is done."

Titus had never ached as he watched a woman walk away from him, but he was one big bruise an hour later when Sharine took off into the early-evening sky with Ozias's elite squadron. The ground teams had departed ahead of them.

Pressing a fisted hand to his heart, he watched her until she was invisible in the sky, then took off to join the southern squadrons. It took everything he had not to turn north, in her wake, but he was an archangel. His first duty was to his people and his territory. That didn't mean he didn't glance over his shoulder one more time, hoping to see wings of indigo and gold in the sky.

Sharine felt a wrench inside her as she flew away from Titus, and she wasn't certain she liked it. At the same time, she couldn't help from looking for his big, solid form in the courtyard. He was wearing his breastplate and other upper-body armor, his hands on his hips, and his wings held with exquisite control against his spine—and she was pretty sure he was scowling.

For some reason, that made her want to smile.

But then her squadron gained height and she could no longer pick him out in the land far below. The ache inside her becoming a knot heavy and hard, she angled her wings north and away from the archangel who'd come into her life at a time when she wanted no man in it in the romantic sense.

She'd thought before that Titus would leave a mark.

Now she knew that mark would be deep and painful and would hurt for a long, long time to come. But still she'd take the risk. No longer was she the Sharine who'd grown up scared and afraid, a child who'd tried to cling to her parents by being always good; the Sharine she was today shot fire from her hands, she made mistakes and learned from them . . . and she took risks.

Even when it involved a man as dangerous to her as Titus.

Ozias sounded the first alert two hours later—because they were pacing the ground troops, they hadn't covered as much distance as an angel otherwise might, but this wasn't about speed; it was about ensuring they unearthed every single reborn in the landscape.

"Guild Hunter marked that hill as the site of a small nest!" the squadron commander said in a tone that'd carry to all the airborne troops. "Obren, do a high flyover, report any movement. It's after dark so they may have gone hunting and we'll have to track them."

Looking down, Sharine saw the ground vehicles setting up a perimeter, vampiric and mortal warriors stepping out with weapons ready. The ground commander, a grim-eyed vampire named Amadou, was at the forefront. The ground teams called themselves the "cleaners"—their task was to eliminate any reborn that got through the angelic barrage.

Thus far, they'd seen no new signs of an angelic reborn—though Titus had briefed all his senior people that it was a possibility—so angels remained less at risk from reborn than vampires or mortals. It made sense for them to be the first line of defense. And for Sharine to do everything in her power to ensure the reborn didn't get a chance to harm any of the team.

"Commander." Obren was back. "Definite movement at the mouth of the nest."

Ozias raised a hand, dropped it in a hard sweep downward.

Acting as per their plan, Sharine blasted a hole in the hill, reborn scrambled out, and the angels took off their heads. The ground crew didn't have to fire a single shot.

The second nest, however, proved to be a—

"Fuck, this is a fucking clusterfuck!"

Sharine had no idea which one of the vampires below had yelled that and even less knowledge of what it meant, but it sounded right. The Guild Hunter who'd pinpointed this site had been correct to say it was a big nest, but what the hunter hadn't realized was that it was a maze of interconnected nests.

Some of which were *behind* the ground troops.

The creatures swarmed the ground troops while the angelic fighters were caught in furious battle against a massive knot of reborn in the center. Sharine was the only one still high enough in the air to see what was happening, how the reborn were spilling out of burrows everywhere and heading to attack the ground teams.

She thought quickly. *Ozias! Get your squadron in the air and out to assist the ground teams. I'll take care of the central core of reborn.*

Ozias would've been in her rights to question Sharine; after all, Sharine was no battle strategist, but the spymaster's squadron lifted off near instantaneously after Sharine made the request. They stayed low as they flew in all directions to help the ground teams.

The creatures in the middle screeched and began to run after them.

Sharine set her jaw and began blasting out her power in pinpoint strikes—she'd gotten much better at it since her first strike what felt like a lifetime ago and it didn't take her long to create an effective moat around the reborn. The creatures fell into the hollow she'd created, and immediately began to try to climb out.

But her action had given the ground teams enough backup that they were able to move in and use their weapons to pick off the creatures. Sharine stayed high, and when she saw an angel fly too low and a reborn grab their wing to pull them down, she slammed a bolt into the reborn that evaporated its frame.

Peace be with you, she thought, for all these creatures had once been someone's child, with dreams and hopes that would never now come to fruition.

The angel who'd gone down dusted himself off and waved to her in thanks.

And the battle continued.

44

Titus fought himself to near exhaustion in the days that followed, going further and further from Sharine. In desperation, he asked Tzadiq to get him a phone device, and he began to learn to use it so that he could see her face when they spoke.

His second said nothing to the request, but his eyes did plenty of talking.

Titus cared little; he wasn't a man to hide his emotions even if he knew the future held rejection and a terrible hurt. Sharine had been crystal clear that she didn't wish to be tied to any man.

Titus couldn't blame her for her stance.

His heart twisted, the pain more difficult to bear than any battle wound he'd ever taken. She'd flown inside him, had Sharine, and the idea of not having her there always . . . it was brutal.

"Some would say it serves you right," Tanae said with a distinct lack of sympathy in her tone when she came upon him muttering imprecations at the phone device when it wouldn't do as he ordered. "To fall so hard for a lover who doesn't see you as the sun in her sky."

Titus glared at her. "Gloating doesn't become you, Tanae."

"I said 'some,' sire." Her gaze grew distant, his troop trainer focused on a secret inner landscape. "I'm happy for you, that you've finally come to know the depth and passion of your own heart and the intensity with which it can feel."

She glanced down at the ground, her flaming hair in a braid. "I've kept my heart confined for centuries upon centuries, my fears old enemies, and now I have a son who is my pride—but to whom I can barely speak. When I do, I say all the wrong things and I see him move even further from me."

Stunned speechless by this unforeseen and startling show of emotion, Titus watched Tanae in silence as she carried on past him. She'd never been particularly maternal with her son, but this was the first evidence he'd ever seen that the distance between them was a wound that bled.

Perhaps, after the world had settled into some semblance of sanity, he'd speak to Galen, see if his former protégé wished to fly home for a visit. Or would that simply lead to more pain for both parties? Fact was that Tanae could be a hard mother—Titus had thought that even when Galen was a babe, hungry for his mother's approval.

He knew the gentle and pampered flitterbies—a particular group of orphans raised in his court—had tried to baby the boy, but Galen had been stubborn and resolute even then. That didn't mean the boy's brave heart hadn't bruised each time Tanae withheld her approval. Tzadiq had done his best, but he was more warrior than father. Titus had spent more time with the boy than either parent, but even an archangel's approbation couldn't erase the hurt caused by a mother or father.

He sighed; he could appreciate Tanae and Tzadiq as warriors while disagreeing with their parenting strategy. Titus had been raised with discipline tempered by overwhelming love, and that was his template for how he dealt with children. To withhold affection from a child . . . no, he couldn't agree with it.

He'd ask Sharine her opinion on the matter when he got this blasted device working and they spoke. At least he'd worked out how to send a message.

His fingers felt too big and fat on the sleek screen of the device, but he missed Sharine too much not to persevere. He wrote: *I broke the original device by hitting too hard at the screen.*

Her response was pure astonishment that he was even attempting to use a phone.

When he did finally succeed with the device, and asked her about Tanae and Galen, she was silent in thought for long moments. "I made awful mistakes as a mother," she said, her eyes dark with sorrow, "but the one thing I did right was love Illium fiercely when he was a boy.

"I think Tanae has a much harder road to walk—her son is weapons-master to an archangel, and settled with a woman he adores. He's no boy with a soft heart . . . but she remains his mother. If she truly wishes to build that bridge, she must be willing to forget pride and accept that he could choose to reject her outright. He has that right."

Expression pensive, she added, "Talk to her, Titus. If she opened up to you, it's as close to a cry for help as she might ever make."

Titus had no expertise in such things, but he trusted Sharine's, so the next time they broke from battle at dawn, he found Tanae and as they cleaned their weapons side by side, he said, "If you die, there ends the chance to speak to Galen—and to make any apologies you wish to make."

Tanae grew stiff . . . but didn't move away.

The next day, she said, "I don't know what to say to him. I get it wrong every time—I'm harsh and mean when I want to be otherwise."

Out of his depth, Titus asked her if she'd speak to Sharine. "She's a mother, too, and she understands what it is to make mistakes as a parent."

Three days later, Tanae said yes, and Titus passed the baton. He knew his skills and he knew Sharine's.

Together, they made one hell of a team.

It felt good to have her at his side in such a way, to have her strength aligned to and augmenting his own. He could only hope he did half as much for her. Because for the first time in his existence, Titus knew he needed a woman—but he was rawly conscious that the need might not be reciprocated.

He felt like a pup, waiting for her every call or message.

Then one day she sent a message that sheared ice through his veins.

Titus, we've found another infected angel.

Sharine should've expected this. The first infected angel had gone north for a reason—from all they'd been able to divine from their conversation with the survivor, the angel had retained a limited sense of reason until the final break from sanity. It was safe to assume he'd been more rational at the start.

As he'd been part of Charisemnon's inner court, he'd also have known the battle was taking place in the other direction. While the border was no longer a political fact, the north remained safer if you wished to hide. Until now, Titus's people had focused on the more badly overrun southern side of the continent.

It was Ozias who'd found this infected angel, her sharp eyes spotting the primary wing feathers of an angel lying outside a small cabin in the middle of nowhere. In angelkind, primary feathers didn't shed in the same regular fashion as other feathers. For the majority of angels, it took a long time for a damaged primary feather to grow back, and the feathers on the ground were each the same shade of charcoal gray. They belonged to a single angel. For one of their kind to have lost that many . . .

"I'm going to check if we have a wounded angel," Ozias had said, the sun a glow against the left side of her face, her features exposed because she'd braided her hair at the sides before pulling the rest of her curls into a tight bun. "Everyone else, stay up here."

Sharine had disagreed. "Ozias," she'd said softly, "there's another possibility."

The spymaster's pupils had dilated before she gave a small nod. "Lady, I'd be grateful for your assistance."

The two of them had landed together, but Ozias had insisted on going first. Inside the cabin was an angel; he lay on a cot pushed against one wall of the small and sparsely furnished space. The cot was narrow and obviously not built for an angelic body, but the angel who lay within it was beyond caring about that. He was flushed, his body hot with fever, and his eyes unseeing.

Under the brown of his skin crawled patches of green-black.

Sharine thought back to how the surviving villager had described the angel who'd attacked their settlement: *His skin was like a bruise almost all over and it was peeling away in places, shriveled in others. His fingers were hooked, his nails like claws, and it seemed as if his tongue was rotting green, his lips too plump and red.*

The angel on the cot looked relatively healthy in comparison, if the word could be used in this context—as if the infection hadn't advanced as deep. Despite that, he showed no awareness of their presence, one of his arms hanging limply over this side of the cot. One wing was the same, the other crushed under his back.

When Sharine looked around the cabin, she spotted something that had her last meal threatening to rise from her stomach. "Unless I'm very wrong, that was his food source."

Ozias crouched by the pile of bones and used her sword to nudge out the skull. "Mortal." A pause, a closer look at the teeth. "No, vampire." Voice cold, she said, "From the state of the bones, they've been here a number of days." She got to her feet. "There's no flesh or marrow."

"A lack of food might explain his current state." No normal reborn would appear as healthy after being deprived of food for days, but that was the thing that had become clear since their first discovery—infected angels might not be reborn at all. "Charisemnon's journal states that his goal was to create an infection that didn't need death as a starting point."

Sharine had read the relevant journals over and over in an effort to discover the tiniest bit of data, and it had struck her that for an antidote or cure to work, the individual had to be alive in the first place—Lijuan had been the strongest of them all and even she hadn't been able to bring the dead back to true life.

Add to that the information that Charisemnon's "gift" had been disease, and it became even more probable that he hadn't been capable of creating reborn on his own. *All* the initial stock of reborn had been birthed by Lijuan. "Our only indication that he might've succeeded is the pregnant angel."

Titus's medics, healers, and scientists were united on that one point: life, actual *life*, couldn't come from one of the dead. Disregarding all philosophical discussion on the point, the internal organs of the reborn started to undergo a metamorphosis at the very moment of "resurrection"—a number of the more intrepid healers, including Sira, the leader of the entire team, had flown with the fighting squadrons and had studied enough "fresh" reborn to be sure of their conclusion.

The metamorphosis included the total desiccation of certain internal organs—including the womb. No reborn who'd existed longer than twenty-four hours could carry a child. Neither could a reborn sire one, as those organs also desiccated into nothing. The latter discovery had apparently caused a shudder to run through the ranks of all those who possessed said organs.

"You think he might be alive?" Ozias, Sharine had learned, was as adept as any spymaster in concealing her emotions—but now she compressed her lips and swallowed. "I'll check his blood. Did Sira's healers not theorize it might remain red until the infection took a strong hold?"

"Yes." Sharine shifted to take position near the angel's head. "Should he rise in an attack, I'll bring him down with my power." Sharine had an artist's soul, violence not in her usual lexicon, but she'd come to accept that violence was the only answer in the current situation—the reborn would never listen to reason, never agree to live in peace side by side.

And whatever the connection between Lijuan's reborn and Charisemnon's disease, the victims of both shared a single overriding desire: to feed on living flesh. Sira's team was of the opinion that Charisemnon had used the blood of the reborn as a base to synthesize or "birth" his disease. Sharine was apt to agree with them.

"Ready, my lady?"

At Sharine's nod, Ozias slid away her sword and took out a knife. Using the razored edge, she made a tiny cut at the tip of one of the angel's fingers. The angel didn't recoil, though his chest continued to rise and fall, his eyes to blink. What emerged from the miniscule cut was a fluid of viscous green streaked with black.

The smell was putrid and overpowering.

The spymaster staggered back. "I've smelled that stench before," Ozias choked out. "It's of a body decaying in the grave."

Sharine thought back to the infant's mother; had she had such an ugly odor to her? She couldn't remember, her entire being had been so focused on giving the poor child peace in her final moments. "We must consult Sira."

If this angel *was* alive—not reborn, simply badly infected with Charisemnon's disease—then he could prove critical to those studying the infant and thus, to the infant's life. "They may be able to use him to test if the babe's blood holds a cure."

Ozias sucked in a breath, then choked all over again. "Let's talk outside."

Once there, they both took huge gulps of the bitingly clean air and decided to call Titus. He was the archangel of this territory; the final decision had to be his. Sharine's heart clenched at seeing his worried face on the small screen.

"Your opinion aligns with Ozias's?" he asked after Ozias laid out all they knew.

A tightening of her abdomen, his words threatening to knock the air out of her and not for the first time. This man, he wasn't afraid of strength, wasn't afraid of using that strength to ensure the best outcomes for his territory—and for his people. "Yes," she said. "He may be the key to understanding the babe."

"I'll dispatch Sira and their team." His attention arrowed in on Sharine as Ozias went to speak to the three angels she'd be leaving behind to watch over the infected angel. "Your skin has become more golden, your bones sharper."

"I'm becoming stronger the more I fly." She wasn't losing weight but adding lean muscle to her body. "How goes it in the south?"

"Day by day," he said with warrior practicality . . . then touched his fingers to the screen, as if he would touch her.

She found herself responding in kind.

Titus ended the call with no good-bye, a little quirk of his that made her wonder in ways that weren't good for her heart. Yes, Titus would leave a mark on her.

"Lady Sharine!" Ozias called from where she'd been briefing the angels who were to stand guard. "It's time to fly!"

Sliding away the phone, Sharine rose into the sky.

As they fought on through the days that followed, she remained on edge, but they discovered no other signs of infected angels—until the commander of a large city to the northeast reported the appearance of mauled mortal and vampire bodies in a particular dark corner of her city.

Though the general angelic populace knew nothing of the infection, the commander said, "I've heard rumors that my sire was involved in terrible experimentation. If true, it's possible one of his subjects escaped." She swallowed. "I know little more—I'm a city commander, wasn't part of the inner court.

"I've sent people to hunt the perpetrator," she added, "but with protecting the city from the reborn threat, it's been a low priority." Exhaustion carved lines into the cream of her skin, her golden hair a feathered cap. "I'd more than welcome any assistance you can provide."

Prior to this meeting, Ozias had briefed Sharine on the commander. "Eryna isn't evil—she's akin to Kiama's parents: stupidly loyal." No harshness in her voice, the words a simple truth. "As a city commander, she's one of the best."

Sharine felt a deep sense of compassion for those like Eryna, who'd been let down by the person they trusted above all others. Hadn't she been much the same with Aegaeon? So needy and broken that she'd clung to the familiar even when it turned hurtful.

"Alexander has dispatched a number of relief squadrons," Ozias said, and Eryna's face visibly brightened, her spine no longer rigid. "In the meantime, it's best if you maintain your border watch while we see what predator roams your streets."

Eryna inclined her head. "A sound plan." Then, for the first time, she met Sharine's gaze with the blue of her own. "Lady Hummingbird, when you paint this war, will you make those of us who flew with Charisemnon into shadows? Into monsters?"

So much pain in the questions, a savagery of regret. "I think, child, you carry the shadows within. I have no need to create them with paint."

Expression twisting, Eryna bowed from the waist before departing to resume her duties.

"Regret has a taste, does it not?" Sharine murmured to Ozias. "Like ozone in the air but a far heavier and darker thing."

"She made a choice." No mercy in the spymaster's tone. "All of Charisemnon's people made a choice, but the ones like Eryna? They had the power to defect and stand against him. Instead, they helped Charisemnon with his ugly quest— even if it was only by doing nothing. I can accept Eryna isn't evil without ever forgiving her for her choice."

Sharine could say nothing to that. Ozias was right.

Some choices echoed through time.

"How do we hunt the perpetrator of the maulings?"

"Lady Sharine, I am a spymaster," was the quelling response.

Even with Ozias's skills and underground contacts, it took them two days to track down the murderer. An infected angel, as they'd feared. One who was beyond saving. Her entire body was a rotting green-black that was nothing natural, her claws hooked. But even had the physical deterioration not been so bad, her mind was gone. She was crazed.

Her lack of reason was part of how Ozias had tracked her down—she'd become careless and devoid of cunning, wanting only to feed, only to gorge. Dropping her current victim's body to the alley floor, she came at Ozias with claws outstretched, her mouth coated with blood.

The spymaster was at the wrong angle to behead her without sustaining at least a small injury, and Sharine wasn't about to risk her to infection as a result of those claws or teeth.

A pinprick bolt of power, and she obliterated the angel's chest.

Crumpling in the alleyway in slow motion, the infected angel looked to Sharine and there was no peace in her eyes, nothing but fury and the manic need to devour. Then she was gone, one more victim of an archangel's greed and vanity.

45

Titus was covered in reborn filth and exhausted from a night of fighting when his phone rang. He didn't wish to speak to Sharine in such a state, but neither was he about to miss her call.

But when he answered, it wasn't her face that filled the screen. Two identical ones had taken her place; the interlopers had skin of deep brown and hazel eyes slanted sharply over equally dramatic cheekbones, their hair in matching sleek black tails. Most of the world couldn't tell them apart.

Titus wasn't one of those people.

"Zuri, Nala, I see you couldn't help poking your nose into my business," he grumbled, but his heart expanded to see them alive and well.

"Oh, Tito"—Zuri blew him a kiss—"you know you missed us."

Nala, the quieter of the two, just smiled, and it was the roguish smile of the sister who'd snuck him out of the Refuge so they could go track a bunch of tiger cubs. Zuri, meanwhile, had taught him to ride a wild stallion. Creatures with wings didn't usually ride such beasts, but his sisters had never much cared for the ordinary way of things.

"What have you done with Sharine?" he asked, wondering what she'd made of the twins.

"We asked with much politeness if we could use her phone to speak to our brother—since *you* now have a phone." A gleeful Zuri held up another phone. "I've put your number in mine and Nala's phones, too. Now we don't have to write you letters!"

Titus half groaned, half laughed, while the twins grinned. "The reborn cleanup?"

"Close to done on this side. Your beautiful and dangerous spymaster agrees with me."

Lowering his brows, Titus pointed at Zuri. "*Do not* seduce Ozias." His sister had inherited their mother's ability to turn lovers into slaves. "I don't wish to deal with a spymaster with a broken heart."

Nala spoke for the first time. "I don't know, Tito. I think your Ozias might crush Zuri here under her boot, and Zuri will be grateful for it."

As Zuri shot her twin a glare, Titus found himself laughing. It was good to see his sisters, good to speak with them, good to hear their banter. "Is the boy with you?"

"Xander is gazing in awe at Lady Sharine." Zuri waggled her eyebrows. "Careful, baby brother, or young Xander might steal your lady."

Of course his sisters had already worked out that Sharine was special to him. "Sharine will shred any man who dares lay a hand on her without permission. She can't be stolen." No, his Shari would decide to whom she'd give herself . . . and if she decided to give him nothing but a fleeting moment of eternity, he'd take it.

Not that Titus was going to give up on fighting for forever. He wasn't a man who surrendered at the first hurdle. The choice, however, would be hers. Always. "Report," he said.

The words Zuri spoke now were of a commander in an archangel's forces. She gave him numbers of nests cleared, updates on the situation in the outlying regions, and a rundown on the wounded among their squadrons. "The reborn infestation in the north was nothing in comparison to what we've heard of the south," she finished. "A week at the most to deal with the final nests, and we should be in Narja."

"Rest there, then fly on to me," he said. "Much work remains to be done in the lower half of the southern part of the continent."

"I've been an astonishingly brilliant ambassador for you, little brother," Zuri added after the formal report. "Half the continent is now in love with me." Buffing her nails on the leather of her jerkin, she beamed. "The other half are panting after our enigmatic Nala."

He couldn't help his bark of laughter; he did love his sisters.

After a touch more family chatter, including updates on Charo and Phenie, the twins passed the phone to Sharine. As always, the sight of her knocked all the air out of his lungs even as sunshine flooded his bloodstream.

Sharine had become his sun, the star around which he revolved.

The realization still terrified him on a daily basis, but Titus was no lily-livered coward. "I hope my sisters aren't driving you too mad?"

"Truly, they're wonderful." A smile so deep he could almost touch it. "They do adore you, you know. Such praise I've heard of your exploits, Titus. If I didn't know you, I'd think you a god among men."

He scowled. "I *am* a god among men." But he had something far more important on his mind. "Zuri tells me that another week or so and you'll be back in Narja."

Sharine inclined her head. "It'll ease your heart to know that this side of the continent breathes easier. They've found hope in the heavy presence of angelic squadrons, as well as the methodical cleanup of reborn nests."

"Good." Titus wanted his people to be able to live without fear. "I must continue to fight in the south for weeks to come." Gut clenched, he said, "Will you be able to stay?"

"No, I must return to Lumia." No smile now, the remnants of play eclipsed by harsh reality. "All is well there at present, but the world is fragile and Lumia is a symbol. Angelkind needs to see that everything remains stable in that small pocket of civilization."

Titus had known her answer before he asked; he understood the responsibility she carried on her slender shoulders. "Then I will come to you." A rough promise. "After this is done, I'll come to you and we'll dance in that fire."

Her eyes glowed from within.

As it was, fate changed their plans six days later.

The team in charge of discovering the secrets held in the body of Charisemnon's child contacted Titus with the news that they'd solved the enigma of her blood. Aware he could no longer justify leaving the Cadre in the dark, he flew back home at speed and arrived at sunset to find the northern squadrons settling in.

Sharine was in her suite, preparing to leave for Lumia on the dawn.

Taking her hand, the gauntlet around his wrist and lower forearm catching the fading light, he ran the pad of his thumb over her skin. "Sira called you?" Titus had instructed the healer to share all knowledge of the child with Sharine.

Fingers sliding between his, their hands entwined, she said, "Yes. I went down to the isolation ward after my arrival and had a face-to-face chat, was able to view the results. Have you had a chance yet?"

"Yes, it was my first stop." Titus wanted badly to close the door to her suite, shut out the world, and just drink in

Sharine, but he wasn't Charisemnon, to wallow in his own desires when the fate of the world hung in the balance. "I must call a meeting of the Cadre."

A fleeting brush of her fingers on his jaw, then they were moving.

Sharine went once more to take a position in a corner of the meeting room, out of sight of the cameras, but he shook his head. "Stand with me. You are my witness to all that has gone before." No one would dare call him a liar, but given the utter depravity of what he planned to share, there was no reason not to add another voice to his own. It might stop the inevitable wave of disbelieving questions.

In truth, it was all an excuse; he wanted Sharine beside him.

It took several minutes for the entire Cadre to respond. Each and every one of them had faces worn with exhaustion, though Aegaeon's grew fiery with new energy the instant he laid eyes on Sharine. "Lady mine," he began.

"You may address me as Lady Sharine," was the icy interjection from Titus's side.

He tried not to look smug.

"Caliane, my friend," Sharine said with unhidden warmth while Aegaeon was yet gaping at her, "it's good to see you."

Eyes of intense, pure blue smiled. "Sharine."

Since Caliane was the last one to join the meeting, Titus decided to begin without further delay. "Our friend Charisemnon left us another gift."

As they listened, their faces growing angrier and more tense word by word, he told them of the pregnant infected angel—and of the child she'd borne. "The babe is of Charisemnon's line and she's typical of an angelic child in every way," he said before the more hotheaded among the Cadre could explode at the fact he'd permitted her to live. "A perfect little girl."

Caliane wrapped her arms around her body, her skin

suddenly seeming thin over her bones. "She's a carrier? Did the mother's infection spread to her child?"

"No. The babe is a miracle." A treasure undeserving of Charisemnon. "Her blood holds the cure to the angelic infection."

A roar of questions.

Titus gave as many answers as he could, with Sharine answering an equal number.

"Yes, I was with the squadron that discovered the living infected angel," she said after Titus told the Cadre of that angel. "He is the test subject for the cure, and he's showing visible signs of improvement. Titus and I stand witness to that."

Titus nodded. "The man no longer appears as if his skin is in the process of rotting. He'll need much more time before he is himself, but the scientists tell me they've run laboratory experiments to test the cure against samples of his infected blood. The cure defeats the infection every single time."

"Yes," Sharine said, smoothly picking up the narrative. "Once cleansed of infection, the tested blood has proven immune to any attempts to reintroduce the sickness to it."

He could see the members of the Cadre—all but Raphael—assessing and reassessing her as she spoke, but the only one in whose reaction he was interested was Aegaeon. The horse's ass kept attempting to capture her attention.

She was having none of it.

Oh, she answered Aegaeon's questions, but she gave him nothing more. The blue-green-haired donkey finally got the message and stopped shoving himself to the forefront—but Titus knew this wasn't the end of it. Sharine was . . . radiant in her full power, and the piece of steaming shat was realizing too late what he'd thrown away.

Today, however, was about an innocent babe.

"We can't begin this new era by killing a child." It was

Caliane who spoke. Caliane, who'd already admitted that the massacre she'd once orchestrated made her less than an impartial party in such discussions.

Neha, too, nodded. "I've had to kill far too many children in the recent past. It is enough." Her face was haggard, exhaustion heavy on her shoulders. "We must allow this child to live—while maintaining a careful watch and running regular tests to ensure Charisemnon didn't hide within her, another plague."

Titus had already considered that the infant might be both a treasure and a weapon. "I propose that we keep her in Charisemnon's border court for the time being. As young as she is, so long as she has attention and care, she won't miss the lack of other children." Angelic children grew at a glacial pace in mortal terms; Sira's team would have plenty of time to unearth all the answers.

"Does she have a name?" Caliane's quiet voice. "Every child should have a name."

"Zawadi." All this time, in a foolish attempt to maintain distance, he hadn't given the child a name, but he'd always known what it would be—and his Shari agreed. Her second name would be Asmaerah, the name of the courageous woman who had been her mother.

"A gift," Alexander murmured. "I hope you prove right to name her thus, my friend."

"You don't have the capacity to raise her." Hands on his hips, Aegaeon filled the screen with himself. "Not with the world as it is."

True words—just brayed by a self-important peacock.

"One of my people has already bonded to the child and is willing to take the position."

"She is young and full of hope," Sharine added. "Most importantly, little Zawadi is happy with her. Titus and I will oversee her care regardless—in saving her life, we took responsibility for that life."

"When can your scientists send the cure to the rest of us?" Alexander shoved a hand through his hair, the strands overlong in a way Titus had not before seen.

The Ancient hadn't been the same since he'd carried Zanaya's wasted body to her place of Sleep. It made Titus believe that Zanaya was to Alexander what Sharine had become to Titus. If so, he could well imagine his friend's anguish.

"Yes." Aegaeon, butting in again. "It's possible the infection did cross the border."

"Within the week," Titus said. "It's a priority for the team on the task."

Dropping her arms, Caliane spread out wings edged with a glow. "Then we're done here—unless any of you have an argument with the decision?" When no one raised an objection, she said, "The Cadre has spoken."

The archangels began to sign off. Raphael did so with a smile for Sharine that reached his eyes. For a second, Titus was sure he saw a glitter of light in the Cascade mark on Raphael's temple, but no, the mark was as dark as it had been since the end of the war.

"I'll call once you're at Lumia," the pup said to Sharine, "and we can speak longer."

"You need rest, Raphael." Maternal chiding. "I can see you haven't been eating or sleeping as you should."

That Raphael simply took the chiding told Titus there was much he didn't know about the relationship between Sharine and the youngest member of the Cadre. So much life she'd lived, so many loves she nurtured in her heart.

"I'll recover." Raphael's smile formed creases in his cheeks. "So will my city. Elena has voluntarily promised to organize a block party when New York shines once again."

"I await my invitation!" Titus boomed; he'd had a grand time at the last one. But this time, he'd either dance in the streets with Sharine . . . or he'd stay home, a brokenhearted mess of a man.

The image should've made him back off, run. It was the one thing he'd never wanted—to be so reliant on a woman's favor. But not only did he stay in place, he gloried in the lush caress of her voice as she farewelled Raphael. "My love to you both. Tell Elena I wear her gift each and every day."

"I know my consort will be glad to hear it." Raphael signed off.

When Titus saw Aegaeon hovering in wait, he sent his technician a mental command to "accidentally" cut the connection. At last, he was alone with the woman who'd ruined him for all others.

He had no fucking idea what he'd do if it all went wrong.

Turning to her, he held out a hand. "I'm filthy now, but after I bathe, will you spend the night in my arms?" The next hours would be the last free ones he'd have for weeks— perhaps months—to come. "I must rest before I fly back to my troops. I wouldn't do it without you."

A slender but strong hand sliding into his, eyes of champagne light dazzling in their penetrating beauty. "Yes."

But she didn't pull away at the door to his suite, to wait for him while he bathed. No, she followed him inside, then very deliberately locked the door. He'd landed on her balcony when he flew home, so his balcony doors were already shut.

Heart thunder and breath tight, he stood motionless as she moved toward him.

When she dropped her hands to his left gauntlet, he held it up and allowed her to unclasp it. She put it aside on a nearby table, then returned to unclasp the right gauntlet. He had to go down on one knee so she could remove the shoulder guards, and though he'd never knelt before any other lover, it didn't feel wrong to kneel for her.

This, what lived between them, it was no game of power.

It was a thing deep and true and terrifying.

Rising again after the shoulder guards were gone, he spread out his wings so she could unclasp the intricate mechanisms of the back guard and breastplate, then lifted off both and put them on the table beside the other pieces. His next action was to strip off his black undershirt. His boots and socks, he'd already abandoned on her balcony, they were so encrusted with gore.

It left him dressed only in battered pants of dark brown.

Taking his hand, Sharine led him to the bath that Yash had already prepared—his steward, when not out in the field, was a stickler about doing certain tasks himself. It was a huge tub, as befit an archangel and a man of his size. Steam rose from the surface, the water a milky aqua-blue as a result of the natural minerals of the springs from which it was fed.

He looked down at the filth of himself and grimaced. "I need to wash off first." Not a man in any way uncomfortable with his body, he went to strip off his pants so he could step under the large showerhead to the right when a sudden heat burned his cheeks. "Do you . . . ?"

Husky laughter. "Did I not tell you archangels have the same parts as any man?"

He was about to scowl at her when she put her hands to the bottom of her tunic and pulled it off over her head. He almost swallowed his tongue. Sharine wasn't wearing a singlet today.

Holding his gaze, she pushed down her pants and the little scrap of lace and silk she'd been wearing beneath.

Titus was finding it difficult to breathe, and when she said, "Hurry," he thought his rib cage would crack in two.

Almost tripping over himself in his haste to strip off his pants, he looked up just in time to see her undo the tie on her hair. A river of gold-tipped black tumbled down her back, almost reaching the curve of her ass.

He hitched on the last word. It seemed a highly inappropriate way to think of the Hummingbird.

But this wasn't the Hummingbird. This was Sharine, who stepped under the falling water and gave him a look sultry and impatient. He joined her, his hand already on her very fine ass. Turning, she picked up the simple washcloth he preferred over the fripperies his staff occasionally attempted to foist on him, and soaped it up.

Then, as he threw back his head under the cleansing cascade of water, she ran the washcloth over every inch of him she could reach, wiping away the blood and gore and the stain of death. He'd been hard since the moment she entered his suite but his erection was a rigid length of iron by the time she was done.

Closing soapy fingers around it, she stroked.

He gripped her wrist. "Enough torture for now, Shari."

Laughter full of primal delight and a kiss so reckless that he gripped her hips and hitched her up. She immediately wrapped her legs around his waist. Pressing her back against the simple black tile of his bathing chamber, her wings a dazzle of color, he reached down between her legs to pleasure her . . . only to find her slick in a way that had nothing to do with water.

A groan tore out of him as he broke the kiss to look down, watch his fingers move on her, in her. She clenched around his finger, her hands tight on his head when he bent to suck one dark pink nipple into his mouth.

He could feast on her for days, months, years . . . forever.

Shoving aside the need in his heart and all that it implied, he worked another finger into her. She wrenched up his head. "Enough." Chest heaving, she kissed him again, all tongue and demand. "I would have you now, Titus."

He could no more deny her than he could suddenly become a quiet man. Moving backward and out of the water, he sat down on the wide ledge of his bath, with her seated on him, and then he let Sharine take him. He, a warrior archangel who'd never allowed anyone to have him, allowed her whatever it was she wished. She was incredibly tight and at one point, he gripped her at the waist to slow her descent.

"No pain, Shari." It came out ragged, the pulsing heat of

her clenching on the top half of his cock scrambling his mind. "I'll never cause you pain."

"I'm just"—a breath—"a little"—another breath—"out of practice." Pushing away his hands, she put her own on his shoulders and sank home with a soft cry that almost made him lose his seed then and there.

Muscles quivering—*he, Titus, quivering*—he held motionless as a hunting lion as she adjusted to his length and girth. Her core spasmed around him. It tore a primal and aggressive sound out of him, but Sharine didn't scare. She slid her hands up his chest as she leaned in to kiss the center of his Cascade tattoo.

He swore the gold of it pulsed.

"You're perfection in how you're built," she said to him. "But more, you have a courage and a heart that beguile me."

He wanted to preen at the caress of words, but he had his teeth clenched in an effort to find a small measure of control. Cupping her ass, he squeezed, then slid his hands up to cup her breasts, play with her nipples. The champagne of her eyes grew cloudy, her body starting to move on his.

Bending his mouth to her throat, he covered one taut breast with his palm at the same time. His breath was hot against her skin as he said, "I want to devour you in a million ways." Lick and suck and taste and *keep*. "I want to make it impossible for you to ever forget Titus, Archangel of Africa." Raw words spoken so roughly she couldn't have understood them.

"Titus, Titus, Titus." Hot little breaths against him, her body moving out of rhythm.

Sweat rolled down his temples, his control ragged and prone to fracturing. Wrapping her up in his arms and in his wings, he took her mouth in a rampantly possessive kiss as she pressed her palms to his chest and pulsed so hard around him that it was the final straw.

One hand on her sweet lower curves, he thrust into her in a rhythm that she reciprocated with a fury, no delicacy or ethereal distance to her. Perspiration dotted her skin, and sexual fire burned in her eyes. She was earthy and *real* and beautiful beyond compare. When she sighed his name again as her pleasure overcame her in waves that rocked her entire body, he broke into a thousand pieces that only she could put back together.

Titus, Archangel of Africa, had given his heart to Sharine, once the Hummingbird.

46

Sharine looked at the letter in her hand. Once again, it was Trace who'd handed it to her and, once again, the envelope was of expensive and heavy paper. But this bore the seal not of the Cadre, but of Aegaeon.

She stared out at the horizon, toward the south, as she did every evening at sunset. It'd been two weeks since she'd last spoken to Titus; he and his troops had hit a massive cluster of reborn who were no longer obeying the day and night divide—they'd been fighting nonstop for the past fourteen days.

It had been even longer since she'd parted from him in the sky above the thriving heart of Narja. Months of distance. She knew she'd made the right decision in coming to Lumia, as even among angelkind, symbols mattered. It was why Titus wore his armor and why New York's Archangel Tower was the first structure to be repaired in the city. Right now, Sharine wasn't just the guardian of their artistic histories and glories, she was the embodiment of angelic survival.

"No matter how awful the world," Archangel Neha had said to her only a week earlier, "all of us can look toward Lumia and know that we as a people are capable of creating things lovely and extraordinary. I do believe it'll break us all should Lumia fall."

Be that as it may, Sharine strained against the urge to race to Titus's side, her bighearted archangel who'd loved her with such raw passion their one night together. He'd left an imprint not just on her body but on her heart. She knew worrying about him was foolishness, that an archangel couldn't be so easily harmed.

Yet she watched the skies.

Because those skies would shatter should Titus fall. She knew that as she knew the sun rose in the east and set in the west.

As for the far less honorable archangel who'd sent her a letter . . .

Breaking the seal, she removed the folded piece of paper within.

My dearest lady, I know you are angry with me, and you have every reason to nurture such anger, but I hope you'll do me the honor of accepting a visit fourteen days hence.

I aim to arrive by the evening hour, so that we may enjoy a meal together and reminisce. It has been too long, and I find myself lost often in thoughts of our life together—and of our son, so headstrong and brave.

Till then.

Sharine snorted.

"Is this a bad time, Lady Sharine?"

She glanced up at Trace's smooth tone, the vampire having returned through the door via which he'd only recently left. "Did you know that egotistical arrogance has a scent?" She lifted up the page she held. "This letter reeks of it should you wish a sniff."

"I'll take your word for it," said the scamp, his eyes dancing. "I came to convey an invitation—the Lumia squadron would be honored if you'd dine with them this eve."

"Of course." Sharine enjoyed speaking with her warriors, and tonight was a special one, for tomorrow, three of her warriors would rotate out and head home, to be replaced by three others.

It was the second of an archangel who'd quietly made the request that three of his senior warriors could do with a respite, and she'd as quietly made a personal request of all three. The warriors had agreed because she was the Hummingbird, and now they'd have time to heal their hearts while they watched over Lumia.

She'd never again be the angel of old, but she'd decided not to leave the Hummingbird totally in the past. She'd done a lot of good and all of angelkind trusted her.

A rare and unique gift that shouldn't be squandered.

"I leave you to the scent of arrogance, my lady." A bow so suave it was poetry.

Smiling, she returned her attention to the letter. It was just like Aegaeon to pretend to be asking permission, but to actually be dictating terms. Her immediate response was to carrier back a cool rejection, but then she paused, thought about it. The past was past, yes, but one question haunted her to this day.

So she'd take this chance to ask it.

She'd face the man who was, to her, the embodiment of cruelty. "Come, Aegaeon. I think it's time this was done."

It was as she was returning inside to ready herself for the dinner with her squadron that her phone rang. Illium's face filled the screen. "My son," she said, her heart ablaze with piercing love. "You surprise me."

"Ha! *I'm* not the one dispensing surprises." Suspicious eyes. "A little bird told me that you and Titus . . ." He blew out a breath, the arches of his healing wings shifting against a background that told her he was in his Tower suite. "Is it true?"

Sharine smiled at the streaks of color on his cheekbones. "Would it shock you if it was?"

Eyes of beaten gold connecting with hers, the blush forgotten. "I like Titus, but I don't want you hurt."

Still protecting her, her beautiful child who'd had to look after his mother for far too long. "I'm living now, Illium," she said, gentle because he'd earned such gentleness even when he trod where most children would never be permitted. "I won't hide, not even from pain. I'll never again choose to hide when I can spread my wings and breathe the air and yes, make mistakes and grow."

Her son took in her face. "You're truly different," he said at last, a faint smile edging his lips. "Do you remember how I once insisted you paint me blue from head to toe and you did?"

"Oh." Her hand flew to her mouth. "You were so very small! How do you remember?"

A shrug that reminded her of the boy he'd been. "I was so excited to be blue." Smile segueing into a grin, he said, "Does Titus know who you are when you're you?"

Bubbles of laughter in her bloodstream. "Oh, yes, I've concealed nothing from him. He considers me stubborn and aggravating in the extreme."

A burst of laughter from Illium that made her join in, it was so wildly infectious. When they both calmed down, he said, "I think I'm going to mind my own business now, and not think too hard about what you might be up to with Titus."

She bit back her smile. "Such is wise indeed, else you might have nightmares."

"Mother." His tone was stern, but when she asked him

about his life, he answered in good humor, and they ended the conversation with words of love from a mother to her son, and a son to his mother.

Then, of course, she had to call Aodhan, too, to ensure he was well. He'd heard rumors of a possible liaison between her and Titus, and had the same reason to ask her about it. "I wouldn't have you in pain, *Eh-ma*." Emotion-filled words, his eyes shards of blue and green shattering outward from a black pupil.

Truly, she thought after the conversation ended, she was blessed to have known two such hearts from childhood.

Darkness lay heavy on the horizon now. She knew the worst of it was about to begin for Titus and his people; her stomach clenched as it did every night at this hour, a visceral fear thick in her blood. "Stay safe, Titus. Fly home to me."

Titus had been battling the reborn for months.

So he could hardly believe it when the day came that he found himself standing at the southern tip of his territory, after a blazing wave of battle that laid waste to reborn nest after reborn nest. The Guild Hunters had come through again and again, and though Titus knew that he and his troops hadn't wiped out the scourge, it was now a matter of isolated nests, and of hunting down lone reborn who'd managed to evade the hunt.

The rotting and infectious creatures were no longer a plague over his land. His people could once more farm their lands, build their homes, live lives free of constant fear.

The first thing he did—after allowing himself a roar of victory echoed by his troops—was gather together all senior field commanders, loop in Tzadiq from Narja, and nut out a plan for eliminating those reborn who'd slipped through the net. Tzadiq took on the duty of creating specialist squadrons who'd work with equally specialist vampiric and Guild Hunter teams.

The other members of the Guild would return to their normal duties because sadly, Africa wasn't proof from idiot vampires.

The rest of Titus's forces would turn their minds to assisting people who'd been scraping by with far too little. With the northern half of the continent declared clear much earlier, Tzadiq had already repurposed the standing force of multiple cities to outward areas, their task to assist farmers to rebuild, put up heavy-duty fences, and take other such necessary protections against any lingering reborn.

"Charisemnon's commanders stared at me as if I was talking gibberish when I gave that order," Tzadiq had told him when they'd spoken at the time. "The idea of sullying their hands with anything but battle glory seemed to be beyond them."

Titus had snorted; he felt no surprise that Charisemnon's troops knew nothing of what it was to be part of a functioning ecosystem. "How do they believe the cities will be fed if the farms go fallow? No other territory is in a much better position, so we can't rely on imported food."

While vampires could survive on blood, angels needed to eat. And Titus would be damned if he permitted food to be redirected to angels rather than mortals. The latter starved far quicker than those of his kind. "Charisemnon's angels know immortals won't be head of the queue for any food supplies?"

"I did point that out, and light dawned for half of them—but with the rest, I showed them the rapid pace of rebuilding in New York. A shot of Raphael lifting a wall into place seemed to rip the blinkers from their eyes."

Titus hadn't been the least angered that his second had used the image of another archangel to inspire the commanders. New York had been devastated in the war, archangelic fire taking out huge areas of the city. If a sense of competition was what it took to kick their lard asses into gear, he'd use it.

"Commander Eryna," Tzadiq had added, "she's proved one of the best. The regions under her command are back up and running, with the first fast-growing crops ready to harvest.

"I've also been impressed with one of the junior vampire commanders—Khan's on the ground in one of the cities worst-hit by reborn in the north, and he's managed to organize mortal and immortal teams into efficient cleanup and rebuild crews. He's doing more work than the angelic commander, but I've left the angel in place for now for continuity."

Titus made a note of the names, but he knew he could rely on Tzadiq to build him a list of those commanders who could be trusted to work without constant supervision; such angels and vampires were priceless. As for the others, he'd be demoting them as soon as things began to equalize.

Titus had no room in his territory for those who rose up the ranks by standing on the hard work of others.

With the planning meeting over, he stood on the rocks above the crashing water that broke against the tip of his territory and felt a fierce pride in every man, woman, and child who'd fought with such defiant courage to get them to this state. His pride in the Cadre was no less intense.

In this devastating time, they'd forgotten politics and vanity and acted as one.

Neha, exhausted and heartsick, had shipped his fighters massive cases of a wine made only in India. *I hope this gives your troops a little joy,* she'd written in her elegant hand.

It had, and he wouldn't forget that.

Elijah's second had shipped equally large cases of dark chocolate, a beloved export of Eli's territory. Rather than using it as an indulgence, Tzadiq had utilized the chocolate as high-energy food to tide over those settlements that were down to the bare bones, their cupboards empty and their fields unplowed.

Qin, distant in the Pacific, had worked with Raphael and with Eli's people to ensure that part of the globe didn't crumble and shatter. Caliane had thrown her weight and power behind Suyin and Neha. As for Alexander and Raphael, both the old man and the pup would always have Titus's friendship and love.

Even that donkey Aegaeon had sent multiple squadrons to Africa to assist in the final two weeks of reborn cleanup. Titus's lip curled. He despised the other archangel as a man and would do so for eternity, but he had to admit Aegaeon did his duty as an archangel.

Titus's own territory had been the worst hit postwar, and the rest of the Cadre expected nothing from him but that he stop the reborn advance, but Africa had gone much further. Every single territory now had access to the cure. Titus's healers and scholars and makers of such things had worked day and night to accelerate the pace of production. As for the angel discovered by Ozias and Sharine, he'd regained his senses . . . and his memories of eating living flesh.

Physically yet weak, his biggest trouble at this point was his mind. He tended to vomit at the sight of solid food, so the healers had him on liquids. Nothing that might remind him of tearing off hunks of his victim's flesh.

"It's psychological, not physiological," Sira had confirmed. "He's cured, but as to whether he will ever heal . . . that I can't predict."

It was a nightmare to imagine what angelkind would've looked like had the infection spread widely before they discovered the cure. Charisemnon could've brought their entire people to their knees, horror their breath.

But Charisemnon was defeated, his legacy of evil extinguished.

It's done, he messaged Sharine. *The rest of the hard work begins.*

Archangels, one and all, were worn down to the bone, and while Elijah's consort had shared the good news that his healing had progressed to the point where he'd soon wake, they still had no idea when or if Astaad and Michaela would return.

To date, Titus hadn't had any real problem with vampires giving in to bloodlust; everyone had been so afraid of the reborn that they hadn't had the energy to do anything but fight. Other territories hadn't been so lucky.

Which was why, despite his need to see Sharine, touch her, hear her voice, he set a slow and steady pace on his flight back to his citadel. He wanted to be sure he was seen, his power noted. Landing in multiple locations, he was frank about the fact that vampires who forced him to divert resources because of bloodlust or simple stupidity would all be given the same sentence: death.

"Make it known," he told the leader of a large vampire kiss. "I have no patience and even less inclination to tell the Guild Hunters to return rogue vampires to their masters for punishment. Field executions have been authorized across the board." If a hunter balked, one of Titus's commanders would do the task. "This is the only warning you'll get."

The vampire in front of him, a mostly useless type who'd cowered behind the safe walls of his residence during the past months, went deathly pale, then bowed. "Sire, I'll spread the word."

Certain it would travel with wildfire speed across the continent, Titus continued on. On reaching his citadel, he bathed properly for the first time in what felt like an eon, then dressed in dark brown pants that hugged his thighs— for Sharine did like his thighs—and a crisp white tunic with a standing collar and no sleeves. Gold embroidery curled around the collar and on the bottom edges of the tunic.

His eye fell on the small velvet box that sat on the table beside his bed.

Tzadiq had come through for him on the highly specific item Titus had asked him to procure. Removing it from the box, he slipped it into a pocket in his pants with care, then pulled on his sword harness. Thrusting his swords into place on his back not long afterward, he looked at himself in the mirror and nodded. He looked what he was: a warrior in mind to court and win his lady.

Titus didn't even think of failure. That way lay a paralyzing anguish.

His first step, however, was to find his second.

"It's good to see you, sire." Tzadiq clasped forearms with him, the two of them coming into the back-slapping embrace of warriors.

"I thank you, Tzadiq." He didn't need to spell out why—Tzadiq had run the territory while Titus was in the field; it had been a sacrifice to remove him from battle, and he knew Tzadiq had chafed at being in the citadel, but his second also understood the reason why.

There was no point in winning the war if the territory collapsed in the interim.

"Is there anything I should know?" Tzadiq had kept him up to date with daily briefings until Titus began the journey home.

"A number of updates." After quickly going through the list, Tzadiq ran his eyes over Titus. "I see you're going courting."

"She is a rare treasure. But I'm a rare man. I will win her." It was a hope rather than a certainty; for the first time in his existence, he knew this was a private battle he could lose and lose hard.

"I wish you well, sire. Lady Sharine would be a most glorious consort."

It was a dream potent and piercing.

"Focus on wooing her first," he ordered himself as he left the citadel. "Until she can't be without you." After all, he already dreamed of her every night, only to wake with an aching sense of loss.

It took him longer than usual to fly to Lumia, as he stopped multiple times on this side of the continent, too—

including at the village where he'd shared mead with the headman in what felt akin to another lifetime.

A lifetime in which he hadn't yet understood who Sharine was to him. Such seemed an impossibility now, she was so embedded in every part of him.

"Archangel!" The headman was alive and well, his eyes sparkling and his legs planted on the soil of a freshly turned plot. Hands pressed atop the handle of a spade, he beamed at Titus. "You kept your promise." A wetter shine in his eyes and no hint of a cough in his voice. "Our village didn't starve and now we begin to grow again."

These small wins, Titus knew, were the fertile soil in which would grow the loyalty of this entire new section of his territory. When he flew on, it was with the knowledge that he'd continue to face pockets of sullen dislike for years to come, but he was an immortal.

Time was on his side.

He stopped to wash himself and his clothes the next morn, and they dried as he flew; he crossed the border into Lumia at sunset, the scouts acknowledging his presence while staying out of his way. He knew they'd warn Sharine of his arrival—he might be the archangel of this territory, but he wasn't Archangel of Lumia. Lumia was its own small civilization, one that belonged to all angelkind, and functioned under the auspices of the Cadre as a group.

Unfortunately, it also meant no one gave him early warning that *another* archangel was about to land in Lumia. From the steep rate of Aegaeon's descent, the blue-green donkey had flown high above the cloud layer as he crossed the border into Titus's land on his way to Lumia. High enough that no one could accuse him of breaching Titus's territory.

His destination was Lumia, his target Sharine.

Titus's hands curled into heavy fists, his wings beginning to glow.

47

Titus. A voice layered in silks and built of music, from a woman who stood on a distant rooftop, her gown a floating creation that reminded him of starlight. *I see you.*

Her unhidden happiness punctured the bubble of his fury. *Shari. Your wings glow against the falling night.* But he couldn't simply admire and charm her as he'd planned, not with the blue-green irritation on the horizon. *What is the donkey doing here?*

If you mean Aegaeon, he wishes a conversation. She didn't turn to look up at the plummeting form of the archangel who'd once been her lover. *Don't murder him. I'll deal with this myself.*

Titus's spine felt as if it would snap; to not act as her shield went against every part of his nature. *Shari!* It came out a mental boom when he'd been aiming for calm and considerate.

This battle is mine, Titus. His metaphorical blood is mine. Pure tempered steel.

His Shari was a warrior, he reminded himself. Not the kind of warrior to whom he'd long been used, but a warrior nonetheless. And Aegaeon's hide was hers to take. But another thing was also true: *I won't be able to help myself if I'm there on the roof with him.*

I know. His posturing will lead to bloodshed. She spread out her wings in a dazzling display that he knew was a caress. *Land elsewhere while I do this—but you can listen in.*

About to argue before she added that last, he snapped his mouth shut just as she reversed their mental link so he could hear what was going on in her conversation. *Extraordinary.* It'd taken him a chunk of his reign as an archangel before he'd worked out that technique.

Sharine was never going to stop surprising him.

She had within her knives far more lethal than Aegaeon realized.

Smiling with a sudden grim anticipation, he shifted course to land on a nearby mountaintop scattered with rocks and the odd hardy grass. He was *not* in the mood for people. He was also fast enough to intercede should Aegaeon forget himself and dare lay a hand on Titus's Sharine.

The silken blue-green of Aegaeon's hair was showcased to perfection against the falling edge of the day, his eyes equally brilliant against the gold of his skin. He'd put on silver upper-body armor that hid the silver swirl on his chest, but that armor was more decoration than protection.

Silver bands clasped his biceps, and on one wrist—

Sharine fought back a scowl. Had she thought of it, she'd have expected the sight of the thick heavy bracelet to be a kick to the stomach, but all she felt was a wave of irritation. Metalwork wasn't her forte, but she'd spent an entire month working on the piece because she'd been so enamored of her—then—new love.

If she could go back in time . . . No, she wouldn't slap

herself. She'd be kind to the woman who'd never had a chance to heal from the first mental fracture before the second widened it to a dangerous fragility.

She'd been a hurt creature who'd thought the best of people. That didn't make her weak. Because from that same inner empathy came her art. It existed in her to this day— what didn't were the thinly papered-over cracks that had made her susceptible to Aegaeon's surface charm.

"Sharine." Aegaeon smiled, folding back wings of an intense dark green streaked with a wild blue that reminded her of Illium.

Their son, mischievous and loving, whom Aegaeon had abandoned.

"I assume you're the reason Titus altered course?" His smile now cut grooves into his cheeks. "It's good you made it clear to him that this is a private dinner—it'll be a delight to speak and eat in quiet intimacy."

When he went to reach for her, she said, "I can throw bolts of power now," in a pleasant tone of voice. "Shall I separate your hand from your wrist?"

A snort of booming male laughter along the mental link from Titus.

Shh. I must concentrate, she chided even as the warmth of his laughter filled her blood. Quiet intimacy indeed! Aegaeon truly thought he could slip in sly insults about Titus and she'd permit it? *Fool.*

Aegaeon's eyes narrowed before he dropped his hand and lowered his head in a slight bow. "I'm too eager, my love—I know I must earn your regard again. I can take nothing for granted."

Sharine had no trouble seeing the truth he hid behind the pretty words. For whatever reason, Aegaeon had decided he wanted back the toys he'd thrown away as worthless. He wanted his son, who'd grown into a man any father would be proud to have by his side, and he wanted Sharine. Why?

For the simple reason that she was now desired by another?

Then he said, "You are astonishing." Eyes as deep and evocative as the ocean held her own, the color so vibrant she could nearly hear the waves rolling to shore. "When I saw you on the screen, I fell all over again."

I'm about to throw up.

Ignoring Titus's sarcastic commentary, though it did make part of her want to laugh, she said, "I'm much the same as when you left."

"No. You're . . . awake and vibrant and dazzling in a way I can't describe." Opening out his arms, he stretched. "It's been a long journey for me. Will you not offer me mead and bread?"

"No."

Dark clouds thundered across his handsome features, all square-jawed and powerful, but then he gave a rueful tilt of the head. "You're so angry with me, my pet."

"No, I'm not." Anger, she'd come to understand, tied her to him, and she'd much rather be free, the memory of him a venomous insect crushed under her heel. "But I do have a question."

Forehead furrowed, Aegaeon said, "You wish to know why I went into Sleep as I did." Shoving a hand through the thick fall of his hair, he swallowed hard. "Truly, my love, I raged at myself all my years of Sleep. You were the only one of whom I dreamed."

His expression was torn and ragged, his shoulders taut. "I loved you too much," he ground out. "Until it frightened me to the bone. So I chose the cruelest possible way to push you away." Rough words, his face shredded with emotion. "It makes me a coward, but I hope, in time, you'll find a way to forgive me and see the insanity of love that drove my actions."

Sharine stared at Aegaeon. "That's it? That's the best

excuse you could come up with for being such a colossal ass?"

Aegaeon's jaw fell open. "My pet, what has gotten into you?"

"Tell me the truth." A flat demand. "Why did you do it? Why did you seek to re-create the two most horrific moments of my existence? *Why?*"

He stared at her as if she'd grown a second head. "I'm not lying. I am Aegaeon! I don't *lie!*"

No, he simply used and threw away people when he was done. *Do you think he actually believes what he's saying to me?* She had to ask for an outside opinion, she was so flummoxed by this strange turn of events.

Titus's answer wasn't the disgust she'd expected. Instead, after a long pause, he said, *I think, Shari, some part of you did scare him, for you are a woman with a rare light within. I don't believe Aegaeon can love anyone but himself, not in truth, but there was something about you that made him want to be other than he was . . . and instead of taking that risk, he chose cowardice and cruelty.*

Sharine heard an unmasked depth of feeling in Titus's words, but she also heard a painful clarity. "What was the trigger?" she asked Aegaeon with conscious gentleness, not to be kind, but because she needed him to stop blustering and give her an answer.

His jaw worked before he turned away and strode to the end of the roof then back. "I began to think what it would be like to have another child and soon I started to want it," he admitted. "Where before, I could imagine siring that child on any one of my harem, then I saw only you."

All artifice and vanity stripped from his face, he bunched his hands, flexed them open. Once. Twice. "Our son was a delight, courageous and wild and curious, because of you. You were the reason for my joy."

Sharine believed him. He'd orchestrated an act of inexplicable cruelty because he'd been running from his own emotions. "Yes," she said at last, her voice soft. "You were a coward."

He flinched, as if she'd landed a physical blow, and she knew that to Aegaeon, her words were more vicious and wounding than any cut from a blade. But she wasn't done. "I feel no anger toward you any longer," she said, "but neither do I feel any sense of love or affection or even interest."

Her world was now far bigger than he would ever be; she'd outgrown Aegaeon for all that he was an Ancient. There was an incredible sense of finality in that knowledge.

"*But*," she added before he could respond, "if you do anything to hurt our son, I will find a way to end you." Absolute calm in her words because they were the truth. "I know archangels can only be killed by other archangels, but should I come after you, I won't meet you face-to-face in battle.

"I'll be cunning and stealthy in my vengeance, and I'll find you when you believe yourself safe. Then I'll cut off your head and put that head in a dark cavern where no one can hear you scream, and I'll come back every so often to chop off any parts that have regenerated."

Titus's stifled laughter inside her head was nothing in comparison to the naked horror on Aegaeon's face.

"You are yet mad," he whispered. "I thought you were recovered, but . . ."

Sharine smiled.

One of the most powerful beings in the world took a step back from her.

"I'm quite sane," she said in the same gentle tone filled with serene resolve. "I also have the respect of people from members of the Cadre to the most junior servant in your court. My threat isn't an empty one. Cross me, and you'll spend eternity screaming into the void."

Aegaeon's face flushed, his wings beginning to glow. "I can end you here and now."

Shari, I'm flying to you.

"Yes." Sharine looked at Aegaeon without fear, knowing she had to end this soon—she had no desire to embroil Titus in another battle. "If you wish to be an outcast shunned by our people for all eternity." She was no longer the needy woman who'd fallen for his blandishments; she knew her own worth and she understood that kindness reverberated through time.

"This isn't about violence or power, Aegaeon." This time her smile held an edge of sadness. "It's about two people who once could've been something, but will never again have that chance."

A shifting in his expression, a hint of the man she'd seen at times during their relationship. The man who'd played for hours with their little boy and who'd looked at her with eyes full of wonder. "So, this is to be my penance. To see you glow and know I will never again be in your orbit."

Then, to her absolute astonishment, he bent at the waist in a bow an archangel gave no one. It swayed nothing in her, but she accepted that the gesture was one with meaning.

"Good-bye, Sharine."

"Good-bye, Aegaeon."

I want to drive my fist into his face, came a deep male voice in her head.

He'll enjoy it, Sharine said. *It'll reignite his belief that I foster lingering emotions for him, causing you to act out in jealousy.* She watched Aegaeon's wings disappear into the night-dark sky. *Don't give him the satisfaction.*

An ominous silence.

Sharine said nothing further. Titus had to make this decision for himself. When he landed on the roof a good hour later, she was ready to strip off his skin with her tongue. She'd *handled* the situation, and in a way that she knew would bite at Aegaeon for eons to come.

Rejection and disinterest were two things her former lover couldn't take.

First, she looked Titus up and down. He appeared none the worse for wear. Folding her arms, she tapped her foot. "What did you do?"

He put his hands on his hips. "Nothing. I only followed the donkey at a distance to ensure he was indeed departing the territory." A definite hint of sulkiness twined with real anger. "I will punch him one day, be assured of it, for he'll show his ass again." Dark eyes landing on her. "But today was your victory. I wouldn't assault a man when he was already bleeding so grievously."

How had she once thought him without charm? There it was, packaged in a scowl and all the more potent for being so rough and honest.

Walking across to him, she "fixed" the collar of his shirt, wanting only to be close to the vivid heat of his body.

When he said, "Fly with me," she spread her wings.

48

The vise around Titus's chest grew ever more agonizingly tight as they flew. He'd already taken out his gift; it now burned a hole in his palm. Leading them away from the village and past Lumia's scouts, he flew toward skies that were private and dark but for the starlight.

This, what he was about to do, it needed no audience.

If she would break his heart, he'd rather bear the blow in private. It had nothing to do with pride and everything to do with pain—he knew he wouldn't be able to hide it, not at the first feeling. His people were already battered and bruised. They didn't need to see their archangel's devastation.

When he landed, it was in an area uninhabited by either mortals or immortals, long golden grasses brushing against his calves and the landscape a rolling emptiness on all sides, all the way to a lake in the far distance that was a patch of cool dark. Sharine landed a few meters distant, where the grass was shorter and less apt to catch on her dress. He walked to her through the golden strands, to this extraordinary woman who'd caught him in a net she hadn't thrown.

He was caught just the same.

When he lifted his hand to cup her cheek, she leaned into it, but her eyes, lovely and penetrating, didn't break from his.

"I've missed you," he said, the words rough. "You've made a hole in my heart and it causes me pain when you aren't there to fill it."

"It'll pass." Husky words. "Has it not always before?"

"No." He knew that to the bottom of his soul. "I've never had a hole inside me. It's permanent and it aches."

"What of all the butterflies in the world? What of all the other lovers you could have?"

The answer was breathtakingly easy. "They won't be you." He'd been approached more than once in the time since they'd been apart, both by warriors and by civilians, all with a smile and with affection.

He'd had no desire to dance with any of them.

The hole in his heart was in a very particular shape and it could be filled by only one person. "I find myself turning to tell you clever thoughts, but you aren't there. I wake wishing to kiss you, and sometimes, I even wake wanting to hear you flaying me to shreds with your tongue."

No laughter, and none of the biting wit with which she'd so successfully destroyed Aegaeon. A champagne gaze that gave nothing away. "Do you ask me to be your lover for more than the now?"

Shaking his head, Titus dropped his hand from her cheek to go down on one knee among the grasses. His heart pounded, his mouth ran dry, and his sense of being exactly where he wished to be was so resonant that it felt as if he was bound to the universe itself.

"No, Shari," he said. "Though I'll be your lover any day you wish, what I ask is for you to be my consort." He opened out his hand, in which lay a fine golden chain, at the end of which hung a pendant made of amber in the shape of a hummingbird soaring in flight.

. . . Be my consort.

Sharine's mind emptied of all thought, Titus the center of her universe. He was extraordinary, her Titus, strong and loyal and with a heart so huge it encompassed his entire territory.

He was also honest to a fault.

And he'd just asked her to be his consort.

She sank into the grass in front of him. *"Titus."* Cupping his face, she kissed him with all the passion—and yes, love—in her heart. She'd fallen for this brash, blunt hammer of an archangel despite all her plans to the contrary, and she wouldn't lie to herself about that, either.

Wrapping her in his arms, he crushed her close, devouring her mouth. Breathless in the aftermath, she nevertheless shook her head when he beamed a smile that engulfed her in its love, and went to put the necklace around her neck.

"Shari, you can't kiss a man so, then reject him." Open anguish.

"It's no rejection." She touched her hand to his jaw, unable to bear to wound the huge heart that loved her. "I'll wear your amber so the world knows my heart is taken."

The vise around Titus's chest began to ease its grip at last. "Do you love me? Tell me, then."

A glow in eyes that shouldn't glow, their beauty incandescent. "I love you, Titus, Archangel of Africa." In her voice were tones he'd never before heard, layers of love that wrapped around him with primal sensual intimacy.

"Don't ever use that voice with anyone else," he grumbled, "or you'll break my heart, and I'll break them."

Laughter, as sensual and as addicting. "I'll always protect your heart, for it's mine now." A slender hand pressed to that very organ, her voice unbending on her next words. "You, too, will wear my amber—a single piece, embedded into your breastplate."

Titus puffed out his chest, his hands on her hips, and a smile curving his lips. "You can embed within it as many pieces of amber as you like." He'd never budge in his devotion to her.

Running the back of her hand over his jaw, she said, "I'm not ready to be your consort." A finger pressed to his lips. "Consorts must be aware of politics, must undertake certain duties. I can't, not only because I watch over Lumia, but because I've barely awakened. I can't be your consort before I'm complete in myself as Sharine."

"Shari, if you grow any more radiant, I shall burn up in your light." He pressed his forehead to her own. "But if you need a millennium or three to be ready to stand officially at my side, so be it."

As long as she wore his amber.

As long as she made him wear hers.

"I'm telling you now, so you can't accuse me of falsehoods later," he said, because he'd never lie to her, "but I'll treat you as I would my consort, and though you don't take the title, the world will know who you are to me." He couldn't hide it; he wasn't built that way.

Sharine searched his face. "Will it not cause you hurt if angelkind questions why I don't take the title of Consort?"

"No. All I care about is your love." His pride in being loved by her was a thing so huge, it could withstand endless raised eyebrows and pointed questions. "As long as you're my Shari, and I'm your Titus, I'll be an archangel who struts about like a cock in the roost."

Joyous laughter from his love, her kiss soft and wet and deep.

Groaning, he allowed her to pull him down over her, so that he lay braced above her as she lay on the grasses.

"I accept your intentions," she said in that voice private and for him alone. "I don't know when or if I'll ever be ready to be your consort, and I'll push back firmly against anyone's attempt to make me fill that role, but I'll always be your Shari."

Titus's heart boomed, loud as thunder.

When he went to put the necklace on this time, she lifted her head to make it easier for him. The hummingbird settled perfectly in the hollow of her throat. Smug and happy, he lifted the pendant to press a kiss to that hollow.

Hand on his neck, she murmured, "You do know the amber in your breastplate is going to be in the shape of a hummingbird, don't you?"

He groaned, but it was half-hearted at best, his delight too obvious to hide. Her dancing eyes said she knew that well. Pushing at his chest until he'd moved aside, she rose to her feet and reached up to the shoulder clasps of her gown.

A second later, it fell to her feet in a pool of starlight, her body nude under the moonlight but for the gossamer fabric that covered her mound. Stepping out of her slippers, she held his eyes as she removed the final barrier between his gaze and her body.

Then she stretched, a small goddess with gentle curves and hair that tumbled a golden black rain down her back, her eyes aglow in a way that said she was a rare and powerful creature. He wasn't aware of getting up, wasn't aware of stripping. But his skin burned against hers when he clasped her hips and bent his head to kiss her throat.

Shivering, she slid her arms around his neck. "Dance with me, Titus."

He covered her in his glamour even as he vaulted them both to the sky, glamour a gift of archangels. It made them private, unseen by any other eyes as they tangled limbs and wings, kissing and touching and claiming. He'd said they'd burn together, and they did, but there was also a luminous joy to it all, happiness so profound that it was melded into his bones.

Sharine's wings shimmered with angel dust of pale gold that coated his skin, entered his mouth. He dusted her in turn, until she glittered against the moon and the stars, the glow of her eyes echoed by the faint glow emanating from her wings. Titus gripped the arch of one wing, stroked with intimate possessiveness.

She repeated the caress on him.

And they danced.

The Archangel of Africa and an angel so unique that she couldn't be classified as anyone but herself: Sharine, Guardian of Lumia, and Hummingbird in flight.

Bodies locked together against the velvet night, they fell and fell . . . into the cold waters of the lake that would ripple azure blue in daylight. Aware of her strength now, he hadn't shielded them from the water, and it was a shock of cold against the heat of their bodies, but they tumbled deeper and still deeper until the pleasure became sunlight exploding through their veins.

Titus surfaced together with her, and she was a sylph who pushed her hair off her face and smiled at him. Titus fell all over again.

Epilogue

Dearest Caliane,

The phone device is most excellent and I become more enamored with it each hour that passes, but Charisemnon's journals show me that there is value in taking the time to follow the old ways, too. So today, I write you this letter that I'll send by courier to wherever you intend to be in the coming days.

I know you continue to assist young Suyin, and Neha, too.

I think, dear friend, you're right in what you said to me when we last spoke—the Archangel of India is tired beyond bearing. Her heart is shattered. So much so that Titus tells me even her twin has laid down her arms; she refuses to fight a Neha who will not, or cannot, fight back.

Neha does her duty, that much we all see, but I think when the world is once more sane, we'll lose her to Sleep. I can't blame her, or any of her people, who make that choice. The horrors unleashed on their border should never have existed and will be a blot on our history forever more.

At least the last of the victimized children have been discovered and given mercy.

I know you, too, bear many more bruises on your heart as a result of this same evil. I understand it has awoken old pain. I'm here for you in the daylight hours and in the deepest night. Do not ever hesitate to come here, or to make contact. Please, my friend, don't let the bruises fester and turn into sores.

You know I'll hold your words close, repeating them to no other.

The news from Africa is much the same as when we spoke. We discover the odd reborn now and then, but the people are much better situated to fight them, and north and south both know they can call on their archangel's troops. No more infected angels have surfaced, but the cure team continues to manufacture and store more doses in the hope they will never be needed.

I'm certain we stopped Charisemnon's evil here, before it could begin to spread, but that's no reason to be complacent. You'll want to know of Zawadi—the babe is happy and beloved of her foster mother. I see her often, as does Titus. The little one has more likelihood of being spoiled rotten than to lack anything in life, but even knowing this, I'll continue to enjoy spoiling her.

Her history is dark enough. Let her future be full of light.

You asked me how it went with Titus. My friend, I've never known such contentment and joy. It lives in me each moment of each day. I miss him desperately while he's in Narja or at another one of his citadels, and he's open in allowing me to see that his heart breaks each time he leaves me.

Yet his pride in me, in what I've achieved in Lumia . . . I don't need anyone's approval, not anymore, but there is much to be said for a lover who boasts about me to anyone within earshot. Here, I'll boast about him in turn, for Titus is extraordinary in his ability to love. Such a heart he has, Caliane.

His love is a joy I never expected, and it's a gift as great as my son.

Illium has begun to call him Stepfather when they speak, and Titus threatens to pluck his new-grown feathers for the cheek every single time. Then Illium laughs and my being overflows with delight, that these two people whose names are written on my heart like one another, too. My boy is young yet, but Titus says he's becoming a power.

You know how I feel. I worry about him. I'll always worry about him.

Our familial world has tilted the right way after being too long imbalanced. Illium no longer has to watch over me. At last, I watch over him.

Oh, how could I forget to tell you about the visit from Titus's sisters! All four of them descended on Lumia some days past, and now I understand why he has such a voice, and such blunt ways. It's a survival mechanism. I'm happy to report that I, too, survived the storm that is Phenie, Charo, Nala, and Zuri.

I laughed with them, but my laughter has faded in the past day, with the news from Suyin. I can't help but agree when she calls it the nexus of darkness. Stay safe, my friend, and look after Aodhan. I carry your names on my heart, too. As I can't stop you from

*flying to help Suyin, I can't stop Aodhan from being
an angel loyal and courageous, nor would I try.*

*But I will hope. And I'll worry until I hear from
you both.*

With all my love,

Sharine

ABOUT GOLLANCZ

Gollancz is the oldest SF publishing imprint in the world. Since being founded in 1927 Gollancz has continued to publish a focused selection of bestselling and award-winning authors. The front-list includes **Ben Aaronovitch**, **Joe Abercrombie**, **Charlaine Harris**, **Joanne Harris**, **Joe Hill**, **Alastair Reynolds**, **Patrick Rothfuss**, **Nalini Singh** and **Brandon Sanderson**.

As one of the largest Science Fiction and Fantasy imprints in the UK it is no surprise we have one of the most extensive backlists in the world. Find high-quality SF on Gateway written by such authors as **Philip K. Dick**, **Ursula Le Guin**, **Connie Willis**, **Sir Arthur C. Clarke**, **Pat Cadigan**, **Michael Moorcock** and **George R.R. Martin**.

We also have a strand of publishing in translation, which includes French, Polish and Russian authors. Gollancz is home to more award-winning authors than any other imprint, with names including **Aliette de Bodard**, **M. John Harrison**, **Paul McAuley**, **Sarah Pinborough**, **Pierre Pevel**, **Justina Robson** and many more.

The SF Gateway
More than 3,000 classic, rare and previously out-of-print SF novels at your fingertips.
www.sfgateway.com

The Gollancz Blog
Bringing you news from our worlds to yours. Stories, interviews, articles and exclusive extracts just for you!
www.gollancz.co.uk

GOLLANCZ
LONDON